GARDEN OF LAMENTATIONS

ALSO BY DEBORAH CROMBIE

To Dwell in Darkness

The Sound of Broken Glass

No Mark Upon Her

Necessary as Blood

Where Memories Lie

Water Like a Stone

In a Dark House

Now May You Weep

And Justice There Is None

A Finer End

Kissed a Sad Goodbye

Dreaming of the Bones

Mourn Not Your Dead

Leave the Grave Green

All Shall Be Well

A Share in Death

Garden of Lamentations

DEBORAH CROMBIE

WM

WILLIAM MORROW
An Imprint of HarperCollins*Publishers*

GARDEN OF LAMENTATIONS. Copyright © 2017 by Deborah Crombie. All rights reserved. Printed in the United States of America. No part of this book may be used or reproduced in any manner whatsoever without written permission except in the case of brief quotations embodied in critical articles and reviews. For information, address HarperCollins Publishers, 195 Broadway, New York, NY 10007.

HarperCollins books may be purchased for educational, business, or sales promotional use. For information, please email the Special Markets Department at SPsales@harpercollins.com.

FIRST EDITION

Title page image by Deliverance/Shutterstock, Inc.

Library of Congress Cataloging-in-Publication Data has been applied for.

ISBN 978-0-06-227163-1 (hardcover)
ISBN 978-0-06-266208-8 (international edition)

17 18 19 20 21　LSC　10 9 8 7 6 5 4 3 2 1

For Wren

ACKNOWLEDGMENTS

This book would not exist without a veritable tribe of friends who have given me insight, ideas, and heaps of moral support. In the UK: Kate Charles, Barb Jungr, Kerry Smith, Abi Grant, Steve Ul-lathorne, and especially Karin Salvalaggio, tireless companion in my search to find the perfect pub.

Huge thanks to my friends who have read this book in various stages and offered invaluable advice: Gigi Norwood, Kate Charles, Marcia Talley, Theresa Badylak, and especially Diane Hale, who stuck with me from the very first scene and who often knows my characters better than I do.

Special thanks to Caroline Todd, who inspires me with her energy and enthusiasm, and who constantly encourages me to WRITE FASTER.

My fellow Jungle Red Writers have been with me every step of the way, and I am daily grateful for your friendship and our online community: Rhys Bowen, Lucy Burdette, Hallie Ephron, Susan Elia MacNeal, Hank Phillippi Ryan, and Julia Spencer-Fleming. Reds rock!

Marian Gracis and Edward and Thomas Miller were kind enough to lend me their names.

Illustrator Laura Maestro has once again provided a brilliant endpaper map which brings the book and its characters charmingly to life.

Thanks, as always, to my agent, Nancy Yost, for her patience (and for the puppy photo encouragement!).

And, of course, many, many thanks to the brilliant team at William Morrow: Carrie Feron, Tavia Kowalchuk, Danielle Bartlett, Lynn Grady, Liate Stelik, and many more.

On the home front, hugs, kisses, and much gratitude to Rick Wilson, Kayti and Michael Gage, and my darling granddaughter, Wren.

GARDEN OF LAMENTATIONS

CHAPTER ONE

She stood at the bus stop, shuffling her feet. It had been twelve minutes, and still no bus. You'd think on bloody Kensington High Street on a Friday night, you could get a freaking bus. This sucked.

Not to mention the creepy guy in the hoodie and earpods who kept glancing at her when he thought she wasn't looking. She felt too exposed in her white, filmy spring dress, and she hadn't even brought a cardigan to throw over her shoulders. What had she been thinking, wearing the damned thing? Well, she knew what she'd been thinking. It was a gorgeous night, unseasonably warm, and she'd thought things would turn out differently.

Deliberately, she turned her back on hoodie and checked her mobile. No text. No missed call. It seemed she'd been wrong.

And still no bus. Hoodie edged a little closer.

That did it. She'd walk round the corner into Kensington Church Street and catch the 52—that way she wouldn't have to change at

Notting Hill Gate. But it meant going back past the piano bar and she didn't want to see *them*.

She hurried, looking back once to make sure hoodie hadn't followed. When she passed the club, music came thumping through the open first-floor windows. She ducked her head, as if that would make her invisible. When she'd stormed out, she'd half hoped someone would follow, but now she didn't want to talk to any of them. Not tonight. Maybe not ever.

And Hugo, she was finished with him for good, she really was. Just thinking about last night made her flush with shame. Feeling guilty about wanting to break things off, she'd slept with him again. And then, tonight, she'd found out what else he'd been up to. Jesus. Wanker.

Her sandals slapped on the pavement as she cut across the open forecourt of St. Mary Abbott's church. It seemed dark and deserted with the flower stall closed, and she was glad to round the corner and climb the hill to the 52 stop.

The bus came trundling round the corner, squeaking and sighing to a stop, and she climbed on with relief. She sat downstairs—no way she was attempting the spiral stairs in the full-skirted dress. Settling into the seat, she looked away from her reflection in the glass, but not before she'd seen the dark hair curving against her cheek and the bare line of her neck. She shivered.

Back at the club, she'd taken one sip of the nasty drink the bartender had made her, then left it on some stranger's table. Now she wished she'd held her nose and got it down. At least it might have made her sleep.

When the bus rattled to a stop at Elgin Crescent, she got out and walked the rest of the way. The gardens were dark, the streets quiet. The house, when she reached it, was dark, too, except for a faint glow from the lamp in the basement kitchen.

Taking her key from her bag, she paused for a moment on the step, suddenly reluctant to go in. She wished she had someone to talk to. Her mum, maybe, who would give her sensible advice. But her mum was miles away, and she couldn't ask for her help. She'd promised not to tell anyone what she'd learned, and it was a promise she was bound to keep.

She'd been an idiot with Hugo. She could see that. She could also see that it didn't matter in the long run. He was trivial, never more than a diversion, and her life would go on very much the same without him.

It was the other thing that was going to have consequences she hadn't foreseen. Consequences that were going to change her life, one way or the other, whatever happened.

Jean Armitage never set an alarm clock. She had awakened at 5 A.M. every morning of her adult life, winter or summer, rain or shine. She took great pride in this. To her mind, people who weren't ready to meet the day were lacking in fortitude.

When her husband, Harold, had been alive, she'd slipped carefully from the bed, tiptoeing to the bathroom to dress so as not to disturb him. A banker, he'd thought it uncivilized to rise before six.

Now, she enjoyed the freedom of switching on the bedside lamp, of dressing as she pleased, of making the bed with boarding-school neatness before going downstairs. On this Saturday morning in May, she fluffed the pillows and gave the flower-patterned duvet cover a final, satisfied pat. Crossing to the window, she pulled open the curtains and stood for a moment, looking down into the communal garden. The sky was a clear, pale rose and the first rays of the sun were just gilding the tops of the trees.

Her pleasure was marred, however, by the sight of the half-finished extension jutting into the garden proper from the back of her neighbor's house. Jean frowned and gave a tsk of disapproval. Just because the people had suffered a loss didn't give them an excuse to encroach on community land. She'd complained to the Council, as had some of the other residents on the garden, but so far nothing had been done. Well, she'd never been one to back down from a challenge.

A few minutes later, armed with coffee, she let herself through the iron gate that separated her small private patio from the communal garden proper. In fine weather, she liked to stroll the path that wound round the garden's perimeter, sipping her coffee and taking stock. The perfectly raked pea gravel crunched under her feet and she caught the heady scent of the blooming Cecile Brunner roses. Clive Glenn, the hired gardener, had surpassed himself this year. The hedges were immaculately clipped, the trees were in full leaf, and the late-spring flowers were bursting in full glory. Cornwall Gardens had never looked more beautiful, and she had no doubt it was the finest garden in Notting Hill.

Jean tugged her cardigan a bit more firmly over her shoulders as she walked. A slight chill lingered in the air, but the day promised to be warm and sunny. Perhaps it would give her a good chance to canvas some of the other residents for support.

She'd begun to formulate a plan when something caught her eye. Frowning, she stopped, gazing at the brilliant green swath of lawn that meandered through the garden's center. The vista was marred by something white bundled under a plane tree in the heavily wooded area she thought of as the grove. Those bloody builders working on the extension, she thought, allowing herself a silent curse word, leaving rubbish where it could blow about.

Or had there been a burglary? she wondered, her heart quickening a little with alarm. Whatever the object was, it lay in the grass not far from the garden shed, and there had recently been a rash of break-ins in London's communal garden sheds.

Any burglars would be long gone, she chided herself, leaving the path and setting off across the dew-damp grass with renewed purpose. But she slowed as she drew nearer. What had looked like a large white bundle of plastic or paper had begun to resolve itself into what looked disturbingly like a human shape. It was, Jean realized with a start, a woman. A young woman in a white dress, stretched out beneath the great branches of a plane tree.

She lay on her back, her face turned slightly away, but as Jean drew nearer she recognized her profile and the dark shoulder-length hair. It was the nanny from across the garden.

Incensed, Jean Armitage drew a breath, ready to scold as she charged forward with renewed purpose. What sort of a prank was this? Young people did anything these days. Sleeping in a private garden after a night on the town, she guessed. Such behavior was not to be tolerated in Cornwall Gardens, not among civilized people. She would have a thing or two to say to the girl's employer when she'd got the young laggard up and about.

Suddenly, the sun climbed over the tips of the treetops, the light painting the green grass and the white dress with rippling, shifting dapples.

Jean stopped, her shoes squeaking on the wet grass. The heavy scent of the roses seemed suddenly cloying. Instinctively she put a hand to her breast. There was something not quite natural about the girl's position. And she was still, so still. A sparrow swooped down, almost brushing the girl's dark hair, and yet she did not stir.

Any reprimand died unformed on Jean's breath. She moved a step closer, then, slowly, another. And saw that the girl was not sleeping at all.

"You're up early for a Saturday," Gemma said as she padded into the kitchen barefoot, still in her dressing gown. "I thought I heard you."

Kincaid turned from the coffeemaker. He'd taken a quick shower, then thrown on jeans and yesterday's slightly wrinkled shirt. "I tried not to wake you." The machine hissed as coffee began to drip into the carafe.

His wife slid into a chair at the kitchen table, smothering a yawn as she pulled back her tumbled copper hair and anchored it with a scrunchie. "That smells heavenly," she said, taking a deep sniff as the aroma reached her.

"Want some?" Kincaid lifted her favorite mug from the shelf beside the cooker. It was festooned with garish pink roses, some of which cascaded over the chipped rim, but Toby had bought it for her at the market with his pocket money, so it would never be thrown in the bin.

"Of course." She watched him as he added a dash of milk to her cup. "But I thought we were having a lie-in. It is Saturday."

"So it is." He handed Gemma her coffee, summoning a smile, and poured his. But he was too restless to sit. Standing with his back to the cooker, he went on, "But I couldn't sleep. This damned case is giving me nightmares."

"I thought it was all sewn up. Open and shut." She was eyeing him warily now.

He shrugged, aiming for nonchalance. "I just want to have one more look over the file before it goes to the prosecutors. What if I missed something?" It had been a simple enough case. A coke dealer in Camden, found shot in his flat.

"You promised to take the kids and the dogs to the park," said Gemma, sounding unconvinced. As if to make her point, Geordie padded in, tail wagging, and plopped down at Gemma's feet.

"I know. I'm sorry. I won't be long." That earned him a disbelieving look. "No one will be in on a Saturday morning without an active case," Kincaid added. "I just need—" He stopped.

He couldn't tell her what he needed. He couldn't say that he meant to force himself to look at the crime scene photos—or that he hoped that if he could do that, he might stop dreaming of another crime scene, and of the man he had called a friend, dead, with a gun in his hand.

Turning, he set his cup in the sink, sloshing coffee over his fingers. He wiped his hand with the good tea towel, then went to kiss Gemma's cheek.

But she didn't turn her face up to him. "What is wrong with you?" she asked, her voice sharp. "What am I supposed to tell the kids?"

Kincaid's hands shook with a sudden rush of anger. "Whatever you like. Since when do I have to apologize for doing my job?"

He walked out of the kitchen without giving her a chance to answer. As he left the house, the front door banged behind him with a sound like a gunshot.

"Don't let the kittens out." Gemma looked up as the patio French doors opened, wiping a grimy gardening glove across her brow. She'd thought it was Toby or Charlotte, and at seven and three— and a half, as Charlotte regularly reminded her—they were easy game for tiny feline escape artists. But it was Kit, with Captain Jack, their black-and-white kitten, draped over his shoulder.

"Um, need some help?" he asked tentatively, surveying the spilled bag of potting soil and the empty plastic containers littering their small flagstone patio. Beyond, the shady spots in their Notting Hill communal garden begged for lemonade and lawn chairs. The fine morning had turned hot as noon approached, and Gemma could feel her dirt-stained nose going pink with sunburn.

"You've done more than your share today already." She sat back with a sigh, wondering if it had been her knee she'd heard pop.

This gardening lark was not half what it was cracked up to be. The begonia she'd just put carefully in a pot had a broken and bedraggled stem, and her back hurt.

Kit shrugged, keeping firm fingers on the scruff of the kitten's neck. But he had looked after the younger children while they all paid a visit to Rassells, the garden center on Earl's Court Road. Thank goodness, too, or Toby would undoubtedly have wreaked havoc among the roses and rhododendrons.

Her enthusiasm for her project was waning. Having grown up above a high street bakery in north London, gardening didn't come naturally to her.

"Has Dad rung?" Kit's tone seemed deliberately neutral. Gemma couldn't tell if he was upset by Kincaid's failure to give the kids their promised outing to Hyde Park.

"No," Gemma said, suppressing a sigh, "not yet." She'd regretted her irritation with Kincaid as soon as he'd slammed out the door. She'd stood, frowning, watching him from the kitchen window as he got into his old green Astra and drove away.

They'd never criticized each other for the long hours they spent on the job. Both detectives, it was one of the things that had made their relationship work. But this—this wasn't the job. It was something else, and it worried her. He hadn't been the same since the day in March when they'd heard Ryan Marsh had died.

Gemma had tried to talk to Kincaid about it, but he'd merely given her a blank stare and changed the subject. They'd always been able to discuss things, first as partners on the job, then as lovers, and, eventually, spouses. She wasn't sure how to deal with the wall he'd thrown up between them lately.

Shifting the squirming kitten to his other shoulder, Kit glanced at his watch. "It's just that I've a history exam to study for, and I promised some mates from school I'd meet them at Starbucks this afternoon." He disentangled sharp little claws from his shirt and Jack gave a meow of protest. "Oh," Kit added as he turned back towards the house, "you do remember that Toby has ballet in half an hour, and Charlotte is supposed to go to MacKenzie's?"

Gemma glanced down at her dirty hands, her jeans and sweaty T-shirt, and said, "Bugger."

Kincaid looked from the interior glass window of his office in Holborn Police Station into the CID room, momentarily empty in the lunchtime lull. Staff had been in and out during the morning, but his team were all off for the weekend, pending any new cases, and for a Saturday the Borough of Camden seemed relatively calm.

He'd edited his report on the Camden shooting a half dozen times, changing a word here and a word there, only too well aware he was wasting time. The prints of the crime scene photos lay at the bottom of the file folder, untouched. What kind of a cop was he, unable to look at a gunshot wound?

His mobile lay on the too-tidy surface of his desk. Reaching out, he touched it, then adjusted its alignment with the blotter by a millimeter before drawing his hand back. He knew he should call Gemma, but the longer he put it off the harder it got. What would he say?

Maybe he would just pick up flowers on the way home. Clichéd, yes, but perhaps a bouquet and a "sorry" would suffice.

And the kids? He grimaced. He couldn't bear the thought of Charlotte's disappointment. Disgusted with himself, he stood and slipped his mobile into his pocket. It was time he behaved like a proper father. And a proper husband. Maybe he could still keep his promise to the kids.

He'd grabbed his jacket from the clothes hook and closed his office door behind him when Detective Chief Superintendent Thomas Faith came striding into the CID room. Tall and thin, with fair hair going gray and a clipped mustache, his governor wore even his Saturday civvies like a uniform.

"Duncan," said Faith, "glad I caught you. The desk sergeant said you were here."

"Just going, sir." Kincaid wished he'd made his escape a moment sooner.

But Faith didn't look like a man with an urgent mission. "Good work on the case," he said. "The DAC will be pleased."

The deputy assistant commissioner, Crime, had been taking all the murder investigation teams to task on their clear-up rates recently. Kincaid understood the politics and the numbers crunching, but he also knew that too much emphasis on targets encouraged sloppy policing. And now, with the things that had happened—

Faith interrupted his thoughts. "Tell your team a job well done. And I'll be sure to mention it to your former governor when I see him."

"Sir?" Kincaid looked at him, puzzled. His former boss, Detective Chief Superintendent Denis Childs, had taken personal leave from Scotland Yard in February, after requesting Kincaid's transfer to the Borough of Camden's murder investigation team at Holborn Police Station in central London. And not only had Childs offered Kincaid no explanation for his decision, he hadn't answered any of Kincaid's subsequent attempts to communicate.

"Oh, I assumed you knew." Faith looked as surprised as Kincaid felt. "Chief Superintendent Childs is back on the job."

Gemma had managed to change into a cream-colored summer blouse, but had to make do with dusting off the knees of her jeans and splashing her flushed face with cold water.

If she'd had her wits about her, she'd have walked both children to their destinations, but now, pressed for time, she bundled them into her little Ford Escort. The car had been sitting in the sun and the seat was hot enough to sear the backs of her thighs.

Their friend MacKenzie Williams lived just up the road, in a house with a deep blue door, tucked away behind a high garden wall. Roses bloomed all round it, and it looked more like a fairy-tale cottage than the typical Victorian Notting Hill villa. As Gemma pulled up, MacKenzie and Oliver came to the gate to meet them.

"Stay in the car," Gemma warned Toby as she unbuckled Charlotte from her child seat.

"But I want to see Bouncer," protested Toby. Bouncer was the gray tabby kitten they had given to the Williamses, one of the four Kit and Toby had rescued from the shed in their communal garden back in March.

"Toby, do you want to dance or not?" Gemma asked as Charlotte climbed from her seat and jumped to the pavement with a resounding smack.

"Ye-es," Toby said after a moment's silence, subsiding into his seat.

Charlotte tugged on Gemma's hand. "Mummy, can I go?"

"Of course, lovey. You mind MacKenzie, now." Gemma gave her daughter a kiss, then a farewell pat on the bottom as Charlotte ran to join Oliver at the gate.

MacKenzie ruffled Charlotte's cloud of caramel-colored hair. Then, nodding towards the car, she said softly, "Is that a changeling you have there? Where is the Boy of a Thousand Arguments?"

Gemma grinned and rolled her eyes. "There are miracles, apparently. Thanks to you."

It was MacKenzie who was responsible for Toby's newfound interest in ballet. Her son, Oliver, was Charlotte's best friend at school. MacKenzie had taken Charlotte and Toby to visit Oliver's tots' ballet class. Charlotte had been unimpressed, although she'd fancied a tutu. Toby, however, had been absolutely smitten. A trip to the Royal Ballet with MacKenzie had cemented his determination to do what he'd seen on the stage. But when Gemma had begun to explore lessons, she'd been horrified both by the lack of nearby classes for boys and by the cost of the general classes that were available.

"Take him to the Tabernacle," MacKenzie had suggested when Gemma discussed it with her.

"The Tabernacle has ballet?" Gemma asked, surprised. The round redbrick building on Powis Square had a long history in Notting Hill, first as a church, then as a counterculture mecca, and now as a community center and the headquarters of the Notting Hill Carnival. It had a garden, a full service café, an art gallery—and, apparently, dance classes.

"There's a ballet school during the week," MacKenzie had told her. "And Portobello Dance on Saturdays. Portobello Dance is first-rate training, there are lots of boys in the classes, and it's very reasonable."

MacKenzie had, as usual, been right. There were two other boys in his class, and the instructor was male, a celebrated professional dancer and choreographer.

Now, as Gemma hunted for a place to park on Powis Square, Toby began to fidget. "I don't want to be late. Mr. Charles will say something."

Toby, who had never minded being scolded, took any correction from the gentle-voiced teacher seriously.

"All right," said Gemma, pulling up in front of the center's wrought-iron gates. "You go on in. Don't forget your bag." She watched until Toby had disappeared into the building, then went to find a spot for the car.

Once parked, she walked back to Powis Square and into the Tabernacle's bustling front garden. Outdoor tables were filled with people eating or just enjoying the sun. Children played, safe within the gated space, and several dogs tethered to tables watched the activity with interest.

The round center part of the building reminded her of the oast houses she'd seen in Kent, but with a taller square tower tacked on either side. The building should have been awkward, but it somehow managed charm instead. The orangey-red brick glowed in the bright sun, the color a pleasing contrast to the leafy green of the garden's trees.

Gemma was tempted to find a spot to sit in the sun. Thirst won, however, and she went in, eyes adjusting to the dimness of the interior. After a moment's deliberation, she bought a fresh-squeezed lemonade from the café counter at the back. Sipping her drink with a sigh of pleasure, she climbed slowly up the right-hand staircase, taking in the photos of Notting Hill celebrities that adorned the walls.

The ballet studio was at the back on the first floor, behind the theater. Parents were not allowed inside during classes, but she thought she might peek through the glass insets in the doors that separated the studio from the upper vestibule. She hadn't become accustomed to seeing Toby in his white T-shirt and black leggings, his small face set in concentration, and it made her heart contract a bit with wonder. How could her unruly child seem suddenly so serious and focused? Not that she was complaining, she thought, smiling as she pushed through the doors into the vestibule.

When she'd come to previous classes she'd seen a few other parents waiting, but today the space was empty except for a boy. He was, she guessed, nine or ten. He wore the requisite white T-shirt and black leggings, but his calves were covered with ratty, unraveling leg warmers, and his white ballet shoes were dirty and scuffed. His ash brown hair brushed his collar and there was a dusting of freckles across his slightly snub nose.

In the silence that followed the click of the closing door, Gemma heard him counting under his breath. He was practicing positions, steadying himself with outstretched fingertips touching the top of a wooden chair—an impromptu barre. She recognized some of the basic positions Toby was learning, but this boy did them with a grace and precision that spoke of years of practice.

Stepping away from the chair, he muttered, "One, two, three, turn," then pushed up with one foot and began a series of pirouettes that made Gemma's eyes widen in admiration. He stopped, facing Gemma, but began to spin again without acknowledging her.

He reached ten before he lost his balance, put his extended foot down, and said distinctly, "Shit." Now he did look at her, warily.

"Oh, too bad," said Gemma, ignoring the swearing. "I must have distracted you. Have another go."

After a moment, he nodded, then lifted into another series of pirouettes. This time he reached twelve. His breathing, Gemma noticed, was even and relaxed.

"Don't you get dizzy?" she asked, as he moved effortlessly into a stretch.

He shook his head, then pushed his light brown hair off his forehead. "Not since I was little. You find something to look at. I use the sticker on the door."

Gemma glanced at the blue oval FIRE DOOR sticker behind her, then looked back at the boy. "You've been dancing a long time, then."

"Since I was three."

Toby was getting a late start, she thought. The muffled thump of piano music came from the studio, and through the glass door panel she caught a glimpse of Toby's blond head bobbing. "My son's just starting. He's seven."

"He might still be okay," said the boy, with the careless condescension of the professional for the amateur.

"Are you waiting for a class?" Gemma asked.

He nodded. "Not the next one, but the one after—the advanced class. But I do lessons during the week in Finsbury Park."

"You dance six days a week?" Gemma had slightly horrified visions of what it would mean for their family if Toby ever became that serious. "I should think you'd want your Saturdays to do things with your mates."

Shrugging, he said, "Mr. Charles is brilliant at choreography. And I can come by myself."

"You don't go to Finsbury Park on your own?"

His friendly expression disappeared in a scowl. "My mum doesn't think I'm old enough."

"Well, mums can be like that," Gemma suggested gingerly. "How old are you? Eleven?" she added, guessing at the upper end of the scale.

"Almost." His wide mouth relaxed again. "My mum wants me to try out for the Royal Ballet School when I'm eleven. That's why I have to practice." As if reminded, he stepped back to the chair. Touching it with one hand again for balance, he raised the opposite leg to his ear in a position Gemma would have thought anatomically impossible.

Mr. Charles's voice came clearly from the studio. "Good, good. Now, again." The piano thumped a little more vigorously.

"I should let you get on with it, then," Gemma said. She suspected she'd exhausted the boy's conversational patience, and it was too small a space for two people to ignore each other. "I'll just go downstairs. Good luck with your audition. I'll bet you'll be terrific."

A quick smile lit his freckled face. "Thanks."

She gave him a small wave as she turned to the door and let herself out. Perhaps she'd sit in the garden, after all, and finish her lemonade while she waited for Toby's class to finish.

Gemma opened the doors leading to the garden and cannoned into someone coming the other way. In the instant of shocked apologies, she realized she'd just bumped into MacKenzie Williams. "MacKenzie, are you okay?" she asked, patting her friend's arm.

Then she felt a stab of alarm. "MacKenzie, what are you doing here?" she said sharply. "Where's Charlotte? Is she all right?"

"Gemma. I forgot you were here." MacKenzie frowned at her. "No, no, the kids are fine. I've left them with Bill. But—" She shook her head, words deserting her.

"What is it?" Gemma put an arm round MacKenzie's shoulders and gently steered her out of the traffic path. Her friend was trembling. "Here. Sit," she added, guiding MacKenzie to an empty table in the shade. Realizing she still held her half-drunk lemonade, she handed MacKenzie the cup. "Drink this." When MacKenzie had taken a few obedient sips, Gemma sat beside her and said firmly, "Now. Tell me what's happened."

"It's— It's the most dreadful thing. It's Reagan," MacKenzie said on a gulp. Her skin looked parchment pale against the mass of her dark curly hair. "You won't have met her. She models for us," she went on, "and minds Oliver sometimes." MacKenzie and her husband, Bill, ran a very successful online and catalog clothing company called Ollie. "But she"—MacKenzie took a breath— "Reagan lives with a family in Cornwall Gardens. She's nanny to their son."

"Okay." Gemma nodded encouragingly.

MacKenzie gripped the plastic lemonade cup with both hands. "Gemma, she's dead. Reagan's dead. They found her under a tree in Cornwall Gardens this morning. But Jess—the boy she looks after—doesn't know. His mum sent me to look for him."

"Okay," Gemma said again. "That's terrible. But, MacKenzie, why are you *here?*"

"Oh." MacKenzie looked surprised that Gemma hadn't understood. "Because he's a dancer. Jess is a dancer. That's how I knew this was a good place for boys. Jess has class here every Saturday."

CHAPTER TWO

Until a few months ago, New Scotland Yard had felt like home to Kincaid. Now, as he entered the great glass tower just off Victoria Street, he felt like an intruder. The faces of the ground-floor security officers were unfamiliar, and they checked his identification with no flicker of acknowledgment.

Once buzzed through, he took the lift to the floor that housed Detective Chief Superintendent Childs's office. He'd driven straight to the Yard from Holborn, hoping to catch Childs working on a Saturday. It was his former boss, after all, who had set him that example.

As long as Kincaid had worked with Denis Childs, he couldn't say he'd ever known him well. But up until the previous autumn Childs had had his respect, and his trust. Kincaid might even have called him a friend.

They had been on good enough terms that Childs had recommended Kincaid and Gemma as long-term tenants for his sister's Notting Hill house.

Then, the previous autumn, Childs had personally assigned Kincaid to a high-profile case involving the death of a police officer in Henley-on-Thames. Kincaid had disagreed with his superior's actions—he had, in fact, held Childs responsible for the unnecessary deaths of two people, one of them a senior Met officer, the other the officer's entirely innocent wife.

That had been his last case before taking family leave to care for their daughter, Charlotte. When he'd returned to the Yard in February, he'd found his office cleared out and a reassignment letter waiting on his desk. Kincaid was told his boss had taken an extended personal leave.

Denis Childs had never struck Kincaid as vengeful. So why had Childs removed him from his command and cut off all communication? And where had he been for three months?

The lift dinged as he reached Childs's floor. As the doors opened, he took a breath and moved his shoulders, trying to ease the tension across his shoulder blades. The corridor was empty, although he felt the ever-present hum of activity in the building. Voices came from behind half-closed doors, phones rang, but no one emerged.

Although he'd avoided his own former office, the sight of the chief superintendent's office brought an ache of familiarity. As did the sight of Childs's personal assistant, Marjorie, working at her desk in the anteroom.

Her pleasant face lit in a smile as she looked up and saw him. "Detective Superintendent, whatever are you doing here?" Marjorie had always made him feel he was one of her favorites—but then he suspected she gave all the officers the same impression.

"How are the family?" he asked, eyeing the proliferation of photos on Marjorie's desktop.

"My daughter's expecting her first." Marjorie beamed. "I'm just finishing up some things here as she's due any day and I expect to take a few days off."

"So you should. Congratulations," he said, and meant it. Then he nodded towards the closed door to Childs's inner sanctum. "I thought I might catch his highness in on a Saturday, as well." The reference was a joke that Kincaid and Marjorie had shared, but now her face fell.

"Oh, no. I'm sorry, Mr. Kincaid, he's not."

Kincaid was not entirely certain that he believed her. Her eyes had flicked towards the closed door. Marjorie was cheerful, friendly, and very efficient, but guile was not her strong suit. "No overtime?" he asked. "Old habits, you know," he added with a smile, hoping to put Marjorie at her ease again.

"Oh, no, he's been good as gold," she said, as if eager to be back on safe territory. "I told him he'd answer to me, otherwise."

Kincaid propped a hip on the corner of Marjorie's large desk. "I've just heard he was back. How is he?"

"Oh, brilliant, Mr. Kincaid. You won't believe how well he's—" She stopped suddenly and flushed. After an awkward moment, she said, "I'll leave him a note saying you popped by, shall I? That way he'll be sure to see it if he does come in over the weekend."

Kincaid knew when he had been dismissed, and he could hardly storm the door. "Thanks," he said, standing and forcing a smile. "Best wishes to your daughter. And give the chief superintendent my best."

With a cheery wave to Marjorie, he turned and walked towards the lift.

When the lift doors had hissed shut behind him, he said, very loudly, "The bastard."

Kincaid felt eyes on the back of his neck all the way across the main lobby. He told himself that it was daft, that no one had any interest in him, but he couldn't shake it. The uneasiness that had begun with the Henley case and his subsequent reassignment had turned into something more the night Ryan Marsh died.

Of course, he'd always known there was corruption within the ranks of the Met. Kincaid had seen enough of human nature—and of officers seduced into minor and major transgressions—to know it was inevitable. But, until Henley, he'd never imagined it would affect him personally.

Just how deep did it go, the rot? And was Denis Childs part of it?

He was waiting in the queue to exit the Yard car park when his mobile beeped with a text. Gemma, he thought as he fished the phone out of his jacket pocket, and he'd better have an apology at the ready. He felt a renewed stab of guilt over the missed expedition to the park.

But a glance at the phone screen showed an unfamiliar number. And the text said simply, "The Duke. Roger St. 8 P.M."

The afternoon found Gemma unexpectedly on her own in the house. Duncan had taken the two younger children and the dogs, not to Hyde Park as originally promised, but just down Ladbroke Road to Holland Park. Now, Gemma wondered if Duncan's efficient marshaling of the children had less to do with pleasing them and more with not wanting to talk to her. He'd come in, kissed her, and apologized for snapping at her that morning, but he hadn't met her eyes. At least the commotion of getting the children ready for their outing had kept her from worrying over MacKenzie and the boy she'd met at the ballet class.

The pair had left the Tabernacle a few minutes after Gemma had spoken to MacKenzie, Jess looking mulishly furious, Mac-Kenzie distressed. Gemma hadn't intruded, but now she wondered how the girl had died, and how ten-year-old Jess would take the news. And she was a little surprised at how much she'd hated seeing MacKenzie so shocked and upset.

Searching for a distraction, she sat down at her dusty piano and tried a tentative chord. The sound seemed unexpectedly loud in the quiet house, but she felt herself relaxing as the reverberation died away. Encouraged, she began to play, haltingly, working the stiffness from her fingers. After a while she thought only of the progression of notes, and without the dogs to bark, it took her a moment to recognize the chime of the doorbell.

Pushing back the piano bench, she hurried to the door and opened it. MacKenzie stood on the porch, looking unusually di-sheveled. "I hope you don't mind," she said. "I thought I'd stop in before I went home."

"Of course," Gemma said, giving her friend a quick hug as she ushered her in. "Are you okay?"

"Yes. No." MacKenzie's voice shook. "I don't know. I just couldn't go home and face having to explain about Reagan to Oliver."

"Come in the kitchen and I'll make us a pot of tea."

MacKenzie followed her obediently, but as Gemma reached for the kettle, she said, "Um, anything stronger on offer?"

"That bad?" Gemma turned to study her. MacKenzie wore one of her trademark Ollie printed skirts and a crisp white blouse, but she looked thoroughly wilted. Her dark, curly hair was pulled into a haphazard ponytail, and her lips looked bloodless.

Still, even in the worst of circumstances, MacKenzie Williams was stunning. MacKenzie had a model's poise combined with the confidence of a born entrepreneur, and the money and the social status of the Notting Hill elite. But Gemma quickly discovered that there was no artifice to MacKenzie—she was as down to earth and as kind as anyone Gemma had ever met.

MacKenzie nodded. "Awful."

"We'd better fortify you, then." Gemma retrieved a bottle of Pinot Grigio from the fridge and gave two wineglasses a quick swipe with a tea towel. "It's stuffy in here," she said when she had poured wine for them both. "Let's go out on the patio."

"Where is everyone?" MacKenzie asked as Gemma led her through the sitting room. "I've never seen the house so quiet."

"Duncan's taken the little ones and the dogs to the park. Not that you'd know it from the mess," Gemma added, navigating through the litter of toys on the floor. "Kit's at Starbucks with his mates. Supposedly studying."

MacKenzie managed a smile. "Texting and watching videos on their phones, more likely." She stopped to stroke the small furry bundle on the sofa back. The bundle moved, resolving itself into two kittens, black-and-white Jack and tortoiseshell-and-white Rose. They stretched and yawned, showing tiny needle-sharp teeth, then Jack gave MacKenzie's finger an experimental nibble. "Ow." She jerked her hand back. "Little bugger."

"He is that," Gemma said, laughing.

"At least you have two. They can keep each other entertained. Bouncer is climbing up my legs. Even when I'm not wearing trousers."

Gemma was glad to hear MacKenzie's voice sounding steadier.

The patio was still in the sun, but the air had cooled a bit from midafternoon and it felt pleasant. "It looks lovely," MacKenzie said as they sat, and Gemma felt gratified to have her flower-potting efforts appreciated.

"I'm not much at gardening. But I thought with the fine weather, we should be enjoying . . ." She stopped, seeing MacKenzie's expression.

MacKenzie waved a hand at her to go on and took a gulp of her wine. "Of course you should," she said when the wine had gone down. It's just . . . I can't help thinking . . ."

"Would you rather go in?"

"No. Don't mind me. I can't go avoiding gardens just because of where they found her."

"Cornwall Gardens, you said?" Gemma thought for a moment, trying to place it.

"Just north of Blenheim Crescent—"

"Up against Kensington Park Road," Gemma finished. "I know where it is." It was one of a string of communal gardens strung jewel-like through this part of Notting Hill, much like the one stretching before them in the afternoon light. Other than the two of them on the small gated patio, the space was deserted. "You'd think," she said, wanting to ease MacKenzie's tension, "that people would use these gardens more, as coveted as they are. Our children play in the communal area, but we hardly see anyone else, even out of term time."

"The adults work all day, and the children are in boarding school or scheduled activities." The disapproval in MacKenzie's voice was clear. The Williamses were an anomaly in their social circle. They'd managed to build a successful business that included their child, and family remained their top priority.

"I have one in a scheduled activity now," Gemma reminded her, teasing a little.

"Oh, that's different." MacKenzie waved her now half-empty wineglass, sloshing it. "Toby wants to do it. Most of these kids are shuttled from one activity to another because their parents can't be bothered to spend time with them."

Glad she'd had the forethought to bring the bottle, Gemma topped up MacKenzie's glass. "What about Jess, then? He obviously does ballet because he wants to. I've never seen a more motivated child."

MacKenzie looked surprised. "You know Jess?"

Earlier, Gemma had merely said that she thought she'd seen him outside the ballet class. "I interrupted his practicing. We chatted a bit."

"I would never have described Jess as chatty," MacKenzie said, raising her eyebrows.

"He's remarkably gifted, isn't he?"

"Yes. But he can be a bit surly with it. Not out of meanness, but because he's so . . . driven." MacKenzie gazed at her glass, her eyes filling. "And now . . . no child that age should have to deal with such a thing." Glancing up at Gemma, she added, "This sounds absurd, but I've never known anyone who died before. I mean someone young. It just seems so . . . so wrong . . ."

"Yes. Of course it does. Tell me about Reagan," she said, gently. "How did you come to know her?"

MacKenzie's neck was long and slender—it was one of the things that made her photograph well—and Gemma saw the muscles in her throat move as she swallowed. "It was Nita. Jess's mum. Bill used to play racquetball with Jess's dad, Chris, before he and Nita divorced. I saw Nita in Kitchen and Pantry one day, and Reagan was with her."

At the corner of Elgin Crescent and Kensington Park Road, the café was a well-established Notting Hill gathering spot, especially for yummy mummies, as the area's trendy, well-off mothers were called. It was, in fact, where Duncan and Charlotte had met Mac-Kenzie and Oliver.

"I had Oliver with me," MacKenzie said, "and she was so good with him. So I wondered if she might look after him occasionally, if she had any time free from Jess."

Gemma had not figured out why a ten-year-old required a full-time nanny, but she didn't interrupt.

"But I didn't want to poach on Nita's territory—she can be a bit touchy—so I asked her first and she said it was fine. After that Reagan began coming for an hour or two a couple of mornings a week, when Jess was at school. Watching her with Oliver, I started thinking that she might be a real find for the catalog. She wasn't turn-your-head pretty, you know? But there was something about her—a . . . a sort of . . . freshness."

When MacKenzie paused, Gemma refilled her glass once more, then topped up her own. The moisture on the bottle felt cool under her fingers, and a breeze lifted the hair on the back of her neck. She shivered, suddenly chilled, but MacKenzie, intent on her thoughts, didn't see it.

"She has—had—the most marvelous skin. It seemed to glow. And there was always a sort of sparkle to her . . ." MacKenzie faltered, shaking her head. "We were supposed to do a shoot this afternoon, after you picked up Charlotte. That's how I found out what had"—her voice failed and she swallowed again—"had happened. I kept trying to call her this morning. When I didn't hear back from her I called Nita, and she—she said . . ."

"You said Reagan was found under a tree. Tell me exactly

what happened." Gemma heard a dog bark, and distant voices. There were people now in the dappled shade at the far end of the garden.

"I only know what Nita told me. One of Nita's neighbors was out walking in the garden just after sunup," said MacKenzie. "She found her—Reagan—and called the police. Nita didn't know anything had happened. She had a yoga class. When she got home, she checked on Jess, but he and Reagan were both gone. She thought Reagan had taken him somewhere, maybe to K and P for breakfast. Then she saw all the commotion in the garden, but before she could ask what had happened, the police came to her door. The neighbor had recognized Reagan, but Nita had to identify her bod—" MacKenzie stopped and drained her glass, but shook her head when Gemma offered her the bit left in the bottle.

"That must have been awful," Gemma said. "Was Reagan"— she'd started to say assaulted but tried for something a little gentler—"hurt?"

"Not that Nita could see. She was wearing the dress she'd gone out in last night."

Gemma frowned. "The garden is gated, right?"

"Yes. There's only the one entrance other than through the residences."

"Nita didn't see her come home last night?"

"No. She said she took a sleeping pill. She does sometimes, when she has to get up early."

"What about Jess? Did he see her when she came in last night?"

"Nita said he went to bed early."

"Hmm." If Jess's mum had been asleep and Reagan had been out, Gemma thought it highly unlikely that an unsupervised ten-year-old had gone willingly to sleep. She thought over her conversation with the boy earlier in the day. He hadn't seemed as if he had anything other than dancing on his mind, and she hadn't sensed any guile in his manner. But if his mum had been looking frantically for him since she'd learned of Reagan's death, where had he been before he came to the ballet studio? "What about this morning?" she asked. "Where was Jess?"

"I don't know," answered MacKenzie. "He refused to say."

In the end, Kincaid told Gemma part of the truth.

That was what the lawyers always advised their clients—tell the truth as far as possible.

He'd worried over what to do all through his outing to the park with the children, and then through dinner, glancing surreptitiously at the anonymous text when no one was looking. He'd caught Gemma watching him as he pushed his food around on his plate, but she hadn't said anything in front of the children.

At seven o'clock sharp he carried his plate to the sink and told the children to go play in the sitting room.

"You only want to get rid of us when you want to have a conversation," said Kit. "But it means I don't have to do the washing up. I'll be in my room." A moment later his footsteps clattered on the stairs.

"What—" Gemma began, when they had the kitchen to themselves, but he interrupted her.

"I'm sorry, love, but I've got to go out for a bit."

"Now?" She frowned. "Is it work?"

"I'm not sure." That, at least, was honest. "I got a text this afternoon from an unfamiliar number." He took his phone from his pocket and showed her the text.

Gemma had risen and begun clearing the table, but she stopped, crockery in her arms, and studied the phone. "The Duke? You're not seriously thinking of going?"

"Well, I thought I would just see—"

"You have no idea who this is from?" She looked up at him, the frown deepening. "And where the hell is Roger Street?"

He had, in fact, replied, "Who is this?" to the text, but hadn't been surprised when he didn't get an answer. "It's in Holborn. Not far from the station."

"Someone from work, then?"

"It's possible," he said cautiously. He wasn't going to mention going to the Yard, or the fact that the text had come in just as soon as he'd left Denis Childs's office. Had someone seen him there?

"Have you been to this pub?" asked Gemma, putting the plates in the sink with a clunk and picking up a dishcloth.

"Never heard of it until today. Most of us go to the pubs round Lamb's Conduit Street. The Lamb, or the Rugby."

"It has to be someone who has your number."

Trust Gemma to be logical. "True. Probably someone from work playing a prank, but I won't know unless I go." He thought he sounded believably casual, but Gemma gave him a thoughtful look over her shoulder. She'd been drinking wine with MacKenzie Williams when he came in, and now she looked flushed and slightly pink with sunburn.

"If I didn't know you better," she said with a half smile, "I'd think you were looking for an excuse to spend Saturday night drinking pints with the blokes."

Just then Toby shouted from the sitting room, "Begone, thy evil scum!" There was a squeal, and Charlotte began to wail.

Gemma rolled her eyes. "Can't say that I'd blame you." Handing him the dishcloth, she left the room and came back a moment later with Charlotte, tear-streaked and sniffling, on her hip. "I've sent Toby to his room. That's your cue, I think. Go while the going's good. But take the tube, not the car. And I expect to hear all about it when you get home."

Permission granted, Kincaid thought, and he didn't know whether he should feel relieved or worried.

He'd had to wait for the train from Holland Park to Holborn. The delay had made him pushed to reach the pub by eight o'clock, and when he turned into Theobald's Road, the darkening sky to the east made it seem even later.

As he reached the police station he stopped and checked the map on his phone. The Duke in Roger Street was certainly near enough to the station, but it was several streets to the east and not easily accessible. It was a good brisk walk and he was puffing a bit by the time he reached the pub. He stopped to catch his breath and survey his surroundings.

Lamps flickered on in the nearby buildings. Much of this little part of Holborn was Georgian, but the triangular-fronted pub before him was the apex of a terraced art deco block of flats.

Kincaid whistled. The mansion block was a hidden gem, indeed, and the pub's steel-framed art deco windows glowed cheerily. But in spite of its welcoming facade, the pub had no Saturday evening spillover onto the pavement and Kincaid wondered if he had indeed come to the right place. Perhaps it was someone from work playing a joke after all, and they'd got him out of the house for nothing. Out of the house—

Shit. Gemma and the kids. Panic welled up in his gut and for an instant he saw it, the image from his dreams, the ruined head, and blood seeping into the carpeting. Swallowing against the sudden nausea, he told himself not to be stupid.

Gemma and the kids were fine. Lifting his shaking hand to the door, he pushed it open.

His first impression was of pink. Not just pink, but the sort of mauve pink of Victorian parlors—or Victorian brothels. The walls might have been splashed with a liberal coating of Pepto-Bismol. The unexpected Victorian effect was heightened by the potted palms tucked into every available corner—there were even two on the bar itself. The place was tiny, but mirrors hung all round the walls made it appear larger. The tables and booths were filled, but the only patrons standing were at the curved wooden bar itself. The pub was a true local, then, Kincaid guessed, and perhaps a secret happily kept.

He stayed just inside the door, scanning faces. At first he thought there was no one familiar. Then he swung back, staring at the man sitting alone in the farthest booth, the one tucked away by the back door. Gone was the familiar bulk, and the once-sallow skin looked rosy in the light reflected from the pink walls. But Kincaid would have known the dark hair and the slightly slanted eyes, black as jet, anywhere.

Denis Childs raised a glass to him in greeting.

CHAPTER THREE

"What the hell are you playing at?" Kincaid said when he reached the table. He stared at Childs, his breath coming a little too fast. "And what the hell happened to you?" he added before he could stop himself.

It wasn't that Childs looked bad. Although his color was not quite as pink as it had seemed from across the room, he appeared remarkably healthy. The man actually had cheekbones, for God's sake, and the hand resting on the tabletop was no longer pudgy, but large-knuckled and bony.

"Why don't you have a beer?" Childs gestured to the filled pint on Kincaid's side of the table. "I understand it's quite good here. And you might consider sitting," he added, his voice still smooth as treacle.

A glance round the room told Kincaid that the other patrons were staring at him. He slid into the booth, landing a little heavily on the hard bench, but he didn't take up the pint. "You seemed quite sure I'd come," he said, with a gesture at the beer.

"I thought it worth the gamble."

"Why here?"

"It's not far from where I live."

"In Holborn?" Kincaid was shocked to realize he'd had no idea where Childs lived—he'd always assumed it was somewhere in the suburbs.

"A bit to the east," Childs said. "Clerkenwell, actually. We bought the house years ago, when people thought we were daft to take on a Georgian house in central London."

A canny decision, Kincaid thought—but then the man had always been canny. He rested his hand absently on the pint.

"Go on. It's not poisoned," Childs said, raising his glass and lifting a mocking eyebrow.

Kincaid hesitated, then touched the pint to Childs's glass and sipped. The beer was good, creamy and malty with just the right hint of bitter. "Thanks. You're not drinking beer?"

"Tonic. No beer for me these days, alas." Childs waved a hand at himself, as if encompassing his changed appearance. "I'm a new man. Quite literally. Or at least part of me is. I had a liver transplant."

Kincaid stared. "What? But when? No one said—"

"I had it done in Singapore. That's why I was away. And I'd asked that it not be broadcast."

"But—" Kincaid was still trying to digest this.

Childs sipped his tonic, then set his glass on the table and steepled his hands together—a gesture that Kincaid knew well. "One reason I went to Singapore," he said, "is that, as you know, my sister is there. She gave me part of her liver. And"—he forestalled another question with a shake of his head—"we could have done that here, yes, but even with a donor, it can take years to get the procedure scheduled. I didn't have years."

"You knew," Kincaid said, thinking of Childs's increasingly sallow skin over the past few years. Of course. He'd been jaundiced. And he had been losing weight for at least a year before his sudden leave. "The slimming. I thought it was for your health."

"It was for my health," Childs agreed, "although perhaps not in the usual sense. Excess weight complicates any surgery and recovery."

"But you didn't—I mean—" Kincaid stopped. He'd never seen Childs drink much, but then he was discovering how little he actually knew about his former boss.

"If you're trying to find a delicate way of asking if I was an alcoholic, the answer is no." There was the hint of amusement in Childs's voice. "I contracted hepatitis when I was a very green detective. It was only in the last couple of years that the extent of the damage became apparent."

Taking another swallow from his pint, Kincaid mulled over Childs's revelations. It explained his absence, all right, but not the things that had turned Kincaid's life upside down. "You knew you were taking leave," he said. It came out as an accusation. "Why didn't you tell me you meant to transfer me?"

"Ah. I knew we'd get to that." Childs sounded resigned. "I didn't tell you because it was better if they thought I'd cut you loose."

"What are you talking about?" Kincaid set his pint down, all ease gone. "Who're 'they'?"

"Better you don't know. There are people who don't like me, Duncan." The set of Childs's mouth was grim. "There was more than one reason I didn't have the transplant here. I'd have been forced to wait until I was too ill to work, and there are those who would have been more than happy for an excuse to push me into early retirement.

"And with me gone, even temporarily, I thought some of that . . . ill will . . . might rub off on you. I've known Tom Faith at Holborn for a long time. He's a good copper."

"You're implying some aren't? At the Yard?" Kincaid's stomach had tightened into a hard knot.

"Those are just the sort of questions you don't need to be asking, Detective Superintendent." There was no warmth now in Childs's dark eyes.

"So you arranged my transfer for my own good?" Kincaid's voice rose. "What about Gemma's? Were you behind that, too?" Belatedly, he realized that people were staring at him again.

Childs gave him a look he couldn't quite read. Then he leaned across the booth, so that his gaze met Kincaid's directly. "Drink up, laddie," he said softly. "Go home to your wife. Mind your children. Do your job, and keep your nose out of things."

Childs sat back and finished the dregs of his tonic. Then he slid out of the booth with surprising grace for a big man. He stood for a moment, as if hesitating, then, with a last nod at Kincaid, made his way out of the bar.

What more could he have said? Denis Childs hunched his shoulders as he walked into the unpleasant east wind. It was late in the year for an east wind—what was the old saying? An east wind blows no good? That would certainly be true tonight, he thought, tugging the lapels of his jacket together with a fist against his chest. The jacket's tails flapped behind him like crow's wings. He hadn't had the time or the inclination to have many things altered, and his clothes hung loose as a scarecrow's.

He had long experience with parceling out the truth, but tonight had been more difficult than he'd expected. No—he should at least be honest with himself—the difficulty hadn't been unexpected. But it had been more difficult, even, than he had anticipated.

Of all the officers he had worked with in his career, Duncan Kincaid was his favorite. And the one in whom he saw the most of himself, both the good and the bad. Kincaid, who couldn't leave well alone. Kincaid, who with all his charm and polish, had to say things he shouldn't. Kincaid, who had yet to learn to balance the narrow line between what was right and what was expedient.

As if he had, thought Childs, with a rueful grimace. The wind picked up another notch and, ducking his head, for a moment he missed the weight he had shed. He felt insubstantial, powerless. Perhaps he should have taken that medical retirement. Perhaps he should have let the decay in the Met spread unchecked—his attempts to stem it felt as feeble as a gnat swatting at a tiger. But the tiger stank, and the rot within it was spreading like the bloom on a corpse.

He reached the entrance to the churchyard of St. James Clerkenwell. The graves held no fear for him. He'd grown up a server, and the rituals of the church made him comfortable, even if he no longer believed them. The path through the churchyard was a regular shortcut on the walks he'd begun months before for exercise, and the site—originally the medieval nunnery of St. Mary—was certainly well-steeped in prayer. He smiled a little at the pun, but his thoughts circled back to Kincaid. Had he alleviated the man's peril, or merely increased it?

It had been folly, he thought, if he were to be totally honest, his little confessional. He guessed he had merely dangled a tasty scrap of meat under a dog's nose. He'd been weak, unable to resist the temptation to salvage his character before a man whose opinion he valued.

The gate banged behind him as he entered the churchyard proper, then clanged again as the wind grabbed it. It was calmer under the tall trees in the churchyard itself, but a few remaining dead leaves and scraps of paper rustled along the ground, caught in an eddy.

What could he do, then, to repair the damage?

He'd been practicing damage abatement for a long time. Perhaps it was time he bit the tiger in the arse. The thought made him laugh out loud, but the sound suddenly seemed strangled, even to his ears. He chided himself for a ninny and hurried on, his eyes now on the churchyard's far gate.

The blow when it came was from behind, realized only in the moment of impact. Then the root-twisted earth rose up to meet him, and blackness descended.

CHAPTER FOUR

The Thames lay wide and flat above Putney Bridge, gleaming like molten glass in the early morning light.

It was a deceptive calm, however, which Doug Cullen knew very well. The tide was coming in, and the current running beneath the river's smooth surface was strong enough to pull under the careless or the unwary. Or to snatch a single sculler unlucky enough to capsize, and he was rusty, to say the least.

He stroked a little to the left, aiming the feather of a boat up-river, towards Hammersmith, and squinted into the sun. He'd forgotten his sunglasses, essential gear for a rower. On his right, the boathouse flags were beginning to flutter and snap—the wind was rising. But for now, the advantage of the current allowed him to work the kinks out of shoulders and knees without too much strain. The ankle was another matter.

His doctor had warned him that he might not be ready to row, but after months of enforced inactivity, he'd been determined to give it a try. He'd bought the house in Lacy Road, just a few streets south of the river, because he wanted to take up rowing again, and he was damned if he was going to let the stupid broken ankle keep him from doing it. He'd joined a club and bought the sleek little single scull. It was only now he was beginning to admit that he was woefully out of shape and that the ankle might still not be up to snuff.

The end of the shingle slid by him, then Beverly Brook. Putney Bridge was receding, the red buses looking like toys as they trundled across it. The creak of the oarlocks and the faint splash of the blades as they dipped in the water took on a rhythm that seemed as natural as breathing. Doug's confidence began to rise. He could bloody well do this. Damn the naysayers.

He was glad his friend Melody Talbot hadn't come to help with the garden. She'd been promising to help him sort out his little patch of earth since he'd moved into the Lacy Road house in February. Melody, as clueless as he, had spent hours perusing gardening sites and drawing up a plan. Today was the day they had meant to dig the beds for the flower borders.

But when he'd rung her, she'd sounded sleepy and confused. "Oh, Doug, I'm so sorry," she mumbled. "I forgot. Let me get dressed. I'll come right over."

"Don't bother," he'd snapped, offended. "I'm taking the boat out." He'd disconnected before she could protest, then turned his mobile off so he wouldn't be tempted to answer if she rang back.

Now he was regretting his temper. She hadn't sounded well. There had been something not quite right about Melody lately, and he realized that it had been several weeks since he'd actually seen her. This wasn't the first time she'd canceled an engagement, pleading work or tiredness.

Doug could have blamed her lapses on her recent relationship with the guitarist Andy Monahan, but Andy was touring in Europe. No, whatever was wrong with Melody, he didn't think it was that.

But who was he to even hazard a guess? He, who'd prided himself on his tidy life—his progress in the job, his relationship with his boss, his decision to buy a house—had apparently got it all wrong. He'd been transferred out of a position he loved, second to Detective Superintendent Duncan Kincaid, then Kincaid had not only moved away from the Yard, but seemed to be shunning him.

And now was Melody avoiding him, too?

Suddenly, Putney Bridge seemed very far away. His bad ankle twinged on the next stroke, and glancing round, he found he could see Harrods Book Depository on the south bank of the river. He'd rowed farther than he'd meant. Easing the little scull round in a wide circle, he began to stroke back downriver. But he was fighting the current now, and the rising breeze cut across his bow and kicked up the surface of the water. The pain in his ankle quickly grew worse than a twinge, but there was no choice but to keep rowing unless he wanted to be carried upriver until the tide turned.

Doug gritted his teeth and plowed on. Damn and blast Melody Talbot. If he was crippled by the time he got to shore, it would be her bloody fault.

"You wash, I'll dry," Kincaid said, pulling the tea towel from the bar on the front of the cooker. He knew it was the easier job—as did Gemma, from the look she gave him—but he liked it. It was a visible result, and he liked visible results. They were an antidote to the frustrations of the job.

They had finished their Sunday-morning family breakfast and

the kitchen still smelled of bacon and fried eggy bread. The younger children were playing in the hall. Checking on them, he'd found Toby lowering the kittens from the stairwell in a basket, and Charlotte looking on, entranced. When the kittens reached ground level, none the worse for their adventure, Kincaid had dutifully scolded Toby while trying not to laugh.

"I think Kit's been reading Jules Verne to Toby," he said as Gemma handed him her Clarice Cliff teapot, brought out for the occasion of Sunday breakfast. He took it gingerly. When visitors told Gemma it was too valuable to use, her usual practical reply was, "Why have it, then?" But he knew that if he broke it, he would not be readily forgiven.

The look she gave him said she was not amused by Toby's antics, or by him. He couldn't blame her for being cross. Last night, he'd stayed at the pub long after Denis left, finishing the pint Denis had bought him, then drinking another, trying to make sense of what Denis had told him. And trying to decide exactly what to tell Gemma.

As he sipped his beer, he'd watched the patrons in the tiny pub, guessing at their jobs and personalities and relationships. How long, he'd wondered, since he'd been anywhere alone? Other than driving or riding the tube, he was with either his family or his team at work all day, every day, and he suddenly realized how much he needed that small window of time on his own to let his mind unwind.

He'd roused himself to finish his pint and nod goodnight to the barman.

The tube service was slow, however, and when he finally reached the house he found Gemma and the children asleep.

Now, however, his reckoning had come.

"So," she said, handing him the dripping plate with a little more force than necessary, "tell me about your mysterious meeting. Who was it?"

Try as he might, he hadn't been able to figure out any way to ease into this. "Denis," he said, rubbing vigorously at a smudge on the plate. "It was Denis."

Gemma just glanced at him, then dunked another dish. "Bollocks. The children could come up with something better."

"No one could invent Denis." He kept his tone light, but this time she really looked at him, the forgotten dish dripping suds on the floor.

"That's daft," she said, but with less certainty. "Our Denis?"

"None other."

"But—" She shook her head. "He's back? Where the hell has he been all this time? And why on earth didn't he just ring you?"

"He's been in Singapore. He had a liver transplant."

"He had what?" Gemma abandoned the washing up, leaning back against the sink so that she could look at him directly. "You really are having me on. This isn't funny."

"Who would joke about a liver transplant?" Kincaid shuddered involuntarily. "And you wouldn't doubt it if you saw him. The man's positively glowing. Thin as a rail, too. Well, thin for Denis, anyway," he amended.

"But—I don't see—why didn't he tell anyone? And why Singapore?"

Kincaid gave her an edited version of the story Denis had told him last night, leaving out the bit about Denis being afraid he'd be turfed out of his job if anyone discovered how ill he was.

When he'd finished, she looked a little less skeptical, but said, "Why didn't he tell you?"

"Maybe he thought I'd refuse to see him."

"With good reason. Did he offer you your job back?"

"No."

"Did he at least say why he transferred you?"

Kincaid almost answered, *Because he thought I'd be safe with Faith,* but caught himself. "Because he thought I needed a change, and that I'd get on well with Chief Superintendent Faith."

Frowning, Gemma took the teapot from the draining board and set it carefully on the shelf by the cooker, then turned back to him. "It's Henley, isn't it? He's punishing you because you questioned his judgment over Angus Craig."

He shook his head. "No, it's—" Kincaid stopped. He might have said the same before last night. Shrugging, he said, "Maybe. But I suspect Denis has had more important things to worry a—"

Gemma's mobile rang, making them both jump. "Oh, blast," she muttered, interrupting him. "Sorry." Digging the phone from under the accumulated pile of Sunday newspapers, she glanced at the screen, then answered with a neutral, "Hi," that gave him no clue as to the caller's identity.

He was just as glad of the distraction. God knew what sort of admissions he'd have waffled himself into if he'd kept talking.

Mobile held to her ear, Gemma nodded several times, then said, "Right. Right. Of course. No, we've had breakfast—brunch, really." She glanced at him, then at the kitchen clock. "Let me see what I can do. I'll ring you back."

"Who was that?" he asked when she'd rung off.

"MacKenzie. She needs a favor."

Melody looked like hell. Her dark hair was matted, and the blue eye that peered blearily back at her as she squinted at the mirror was bloodshot. Her cheek was creased and stamped with the imprint of the patterned sofa cushion. Not a pretty sight. God, how had she done that again, gone flat out on the sofa for an entire night? Turning away from the mirror with a grimace, she switched the shower on full force.

When Doug had rung, Melody had started awake, finding herself almost nose to nose with a carton of congealed Indian takeaway teetering on the edge of the coffee table. Beside the carton stood an empty bottle of wine, a cheap Italian red. Had she really drunk it all? Surely she hadn't . . . But when she ran her tongue around her teeth, they felt as fuzzy as her head.

The last thing she remembered was watching grainy YouTube videos of Andy and Poppy playing in a club in Munich, trying to stay awake in case Andy called. It was difficult to find a time to have a proper conversation, with him playing late nights and sleeping during the day. By the time he finished evening gigs, it was usually well after midnight London time. He'd be wired and wanting to chat, and she'd be half dead from exhaustion. So she'd been particularly looking forward to Saturday night, when she could afford to stay up, but he hadn't rung.

Probably just as well, she thought now, considering the empty wine bottle. Had she been mad to think this relationship would work? The buttoned-down cop and the suddenly famous rock guitarist? When she met Andy Monahan, he'd been doing session work and playing in a mediocre band, barely paying his bills. Then his manager had paired him up with twenty-year-old Poppy Jones, a vicar's daughter from Twyford with an amazing voice and virtuoso chops on the bass guitar. The duo had made a breakout video and were now touring Europe, getting more notice with every date they played.

Melody couldn't see where she fit into any of this, and certainly nothing she had to say about her days on the job could compete with Andy's tales of life on the road.

The bathroom was filling with steam from the shower, obscuring her reflection as she glanced once more in the mirror. She closed her eyes, glad to shut out even her foggy image. The truth was, she couldn't compete with Poppy. And the thought of losing Andy made her hurt in a way she didn't even want to contemplate.

Well, if there was nothing she could do about Andy, she could at least try to make things right with Doug. She rubbed the steam from the mirror, looked herself in the eye, and said, "Bloody buck up, Melody Talbot."

After a quick shower, Melody had rubbed her hair dry with a towel, then pulled on jeans and a leaf green T-shirt that was, she thought, appropriate for gardening. She left her flat in Notting Hill without breakfast or coffee, and it was only as she was driving across Putney Bridge that she realized she had no gardening gear, not even a pair of gloves. Well, it wouldn't hurt her to get a few blisters, and hopefully Doug had at least bought a spade.

The day had turned bright and hot, and even though the shower had made her feel considerably better, she still had a nagging headache. Tea. She needed tea, the great restorative. There was a Starbucks on Putney High Street, just round the corner from Doug's house. She'd take him a cuppa, too, as a peace offering.

A few minutes later, mission accomplished, she'd parked in Lacy Road and had managed to maneuver the two paper cups of tea out of the car when her mobile rang. "Bloody hell," she muttered, trying to set the tea safely on the bonnet and retrieve her mobile from her handbag. When she saw who it was, she almost didn't answer. The screen read simply "Mum." If Melody didn't answer, her mother would keep ringing. She took a breath and tapped Answer.

"Mum," she said warily. "I'm just in the middle of—"

"You're always in the middle of something, darling. Did you forget Sunday lunch again?" Lady Adelaide asked, disapproval evident in her tone.

"Oh, sh—" Melody caught herself. She *had* forgotten. Again. And it was her family's weekly ritual, not to be missed on pain of death. "Sorry, Mum." Taking a sip of her tea, she winced as it scalded her mouth. "Look, I do have other plans, and besides, I'm not the least bit presentable for lunch."

"Come anyway." There was a hint of steel in Lady Adelaide's voice. "You haven't been here for weeks, and your father is getting quite cross."

Ivan Talbot was not referred to as "Ivan the Terrible" at home and at the paper without reason. But while Melody could easily weather one of her father's temper tantrums, she knew his feelings were hurt, and that was much harder to ignore. As was her mother's displeasure. Addie Talbot had enormous charm and impeccable breeding, and she used both to ensure that her husband's life ran as smoothly as possible.

"Look, Mum, I promised a friend. I'm gardening—"

"Gardening? Don't be silly, darling. You don't know a thing about gardening. Just have a wash. You can change into something when you arrive. I'll tell your father you're coming."

The connection went dead.

This time Melody swore loudly and long. A woman pushing a pram down the other side of the street gave her an affronted look and walked faster. When the woman glanced back, Melody raised her hand in a little wave of apology.

She looked a right idiot, standing in the street muttering to herself. But there was no point in ringing her mother back.

She would go, then, but it would bloody well be in her own time. First she had to at least speak to Doug.

Collecting herself, she shouldered her handbag and picked up both cups of tea. The blinds in Doug's front bow window were open, but she'd seen no sign of activity. Reaching the front porch, she awkwardly pushed the bell with her elbow. The ring was clearly audible through the door, but there were no answering footsteps. She waited a moment, then set the cups down on the step and pounded smartly on the door itself. Dead silence. Nothing moved behind the green-and-gold stained glass set into the door's upper half.

"Damn you, Doug Cullen, if you're pouting," Melody said aloud. Taking her mobile out again, she dialed his number. There was no answer, and she didn't hear the phone ringing in the house. If he'd come back from the river and gone out in the garden by himself, why wouldn't he pick up?

Unless he was hurt . . . Or he'd done something stupid and fallen. Again. Her palms started to sweat.

The house was terraced. There was no access into the garden except through the house, and she didn't have a key. Now her hands were trembling. If only she could make sure he was okay. Maybe the neighbors had a key, or there was a way through their gar—

No. Melody took a breath and flexed her hands, forcing herself to relax. That was stupid. Of course he was all right. For all she knew, he'd turned his mobile off when he was out on the boat. Or he'd decided to stop in one of the riverfront pubs for a drink and hadn't heard the ring tone. Assuming he'd not had an accident in the boat . . . No, she thought again. She'd sat on Putney Bridge for ten minutes waiting for the traffic light to change. There had been nothing on the river but some rowing eights and coaching launches. No accidents. She was being ridiculous.

Fishing in her bag for a piece of paper, she scribbled a note to Doug on the back of her Starbucks' receipt. She hesitated for a moment, then took the much-creased and folded garden plan she'd drawn from her bag and put it and the note by the doorsill, weighting them both with the cup of now-cooling tea.

Refusing to let herself glance back at the house, she walked back to the car, got in, and drove to Kensington.

When she reached the town house, she stopped for a moment to gaze at it. With its own small gated front garden and white stuccoed facade, it looked plain enough. If you weren't familiar with London property values, you wouldn't guess that only someone very well-off could afford such a place. Ivan Talbot, owner of one of the most successful newspapers in London which had its premises just round the corner, certainly fell into the well-off category. But he hadn't been born to money, and he'd never made a secret of the fact that he'd grown up a working-class lad in Newcastle.

The black wrought-iron gate buzzed open before Melody could touch the intercom button. Her mother had been watching for her, having had no doubt that she would turn up as requested.

The glossy black front door swung open as Melody reached it and Addie Talbot gathered her into the house with a hug. Addie was, like her daughter, just a bit over five feet tall, but her delicate bone structure made her feel fragile as a child beneath Melody's hands. Melody kissed her smooth cheek and stepped away, taking in her mother's cream linen trousers and teal silk blouse—her mum's idea of casual wear.

Addie examined her at arm's length. "Darling, you do look a fright."

"I told you I wasn't presentable," said Melody, unable to keep the defensive tone from her voice. "And if you've invited anyone else, I'm leaving."

Her mum had a very bad habit of using Sunday lunches as occasions to trot out what she thought were eligible bachelors, making it clear that her parents felt she was in danger of becoming an old maid. Melody had not yet got up the nerve to bring Andy here— nor to tell Andy anything about her parents other than that her dad was in the newspaper business.

"Darling," said Addie, her forehead creasing in the deepest frown she ever allowed herself, "what on earth have you done to your hair?"

"Oh." Melody ran a hand across the top of her head. She'd actually forgotten her mother hadn't seen it. "I cut it."

"You cut it? With a pair of kitchen scissors? Surely Jean Paul would never have done that to you."

"No. I didn't cut it myself, Mum. I went to a salon. I just felt like a change." Melody had never worn her hair much longer than chin length, but a few weeks ago she had walked into a salon in Brixton on her lunch hour and had walked out with her dark hair as short as a boy's. Shorn like a pilgrim, she'd thought to herself when she looked in the mirror. She felt naked—and surprisingly unfettered. She wasn't at all sure that was a good thing.

"If you wanted a change, you might have bought a new outfit," her mother said, but now there was a hint of amusement in her voice. "I think it rather suits you, but I've no idea what your father will say."

"Where is he?"

"Downstairs, putting lunch together. It's just cold salads, but I think he has a special treat in mind for you."

Ivan Talbot, who could afford to eat at the best restaurants in London, and often did, had never forgotten his Newcastle roots. He liked to potter in the kitchen, making what he referred to as ordinary food.

"We should go down," Addie went on. "He'll be wondering what happened to us." The town house kitchen and adjoining living area were in the basement, overlooking the back garden. The ground-floor sitting and dining rooms were seldom used except for formal entertaining.

"Let's face the music, then." Melody led the way.

The stairs that led down to the basement were bare Portland stone, the treads slightly worn in the center. In the town house's heyday they would have been covered with a durable runner to muffle the sound of the servants going up and down from kitchen to dining room. But Melody's father had insisted they be left uncovered. He liked, he said, to see the bones of the house.

"Hi, Dad," said Melody as she came to the bottom of the stairs and stepped down into the kitchen. Tall as a Viking, fair hair going a distinguished gray, Ivan Talbot stood at the work top, wearing an apron. It should have looked silly on his large frame, but he managed, as he did most things in life, to carry it off with aplomb.

He gathered her into a hug and for a moment she let herself relax against his broad chest. "It's about time you showed your pretty face, lass." His northern vowels were still strong, even after more than thirty years in London. Although Melody was sure his sharp eyes missed nothing, he made no comment on her hair or her clothes. Her mother had come in behind her and begun gathering plates and cutlery.

"Cold ham, cucumber salad, beetroot, potato salad," he said when he had released her, pointing to the dishes set out on the work top. "I thought we could picnic in the garden, as fine as it is. And"—he gave her a boyish grin and pulled a dish from the fridge—"my smoked whitefish spread. We'll make the toast to have with it at the last minute. The bubbly is chilling." "Bubbly" to Ivan meant the Veuve Clicquot nestled in a silver ice bucket.

The doors at the end of the sitting room stood open and the space beyond glowed like a green gem. It was an elegant design, the plants in multiple shades of green fading to whites, arranged artfully around a patio of the same pale gray Portland stone used inside the house. And it was as different from the glorious, shaggy flower border that Melody had envisioned for Doug Cullen's little garden as night from day.

"Are you quite all right, darling?" asked Addie, pausing with a tray in her hands. "You had the oddest look for a moment, as if you'd lost something."

Melody blinked and shook her head. "No, I'm fine. Really."

"I thought you might be upset about your chief superintendent. Such a dreadful thing."

"What?" Melody stared blankly at her mother, not comprehending.

"I thought you'd have heard at work," said Ivan.

"I haven't been in all weekend." Melody felt suddenly woozy, as if all the blood had drained from her head. "What are you talking about? Has something happened to Superintendent Krueger?" Diane Krueger was her and Gemma's superior at Brixton Police Station.

"No, no," her father shook his head. "Your mother meant your friend Kincaid's guv'nor. Or ex-guv'nor, I should say. At Scotland Yard. Chief Superintendent Childs. Apparently he was attacked last night near his home. Left for dead in a churchyard. They're not certain he'll make it."

CHAPTER FIVE

"What do you mean, left for dead?" said Melody. "Is he going to be all right?"

"I've no idea, love, or I'd have said." Her father frowned. "I didn't mean to surprise you. I really did assume you'd have heard."

Forcing herself to unclench her hands, Melody tried to speak more calmly. "I told you I hadn't been in to work this weekend, and no one's rung me. Do you know what churchyard, or where he was taken to hospital? Was he—was he"—she swallowed hard—"shot?"

"I don't know." Ivan put the champagne he'd been holding back into the ice bucket and came over to her, placing a large, cold hand on her shoulder. "It just came across the news desk. I told them not to run it without more information. Do you want me to see what else I can find out?"

"Oh. No, Dad, but thanks." The last thing she wanted was for

Ivan to stick his newspaperman's nose into police business—or for Ivan to do anything that might make their connection public. "I was just . . ." She swallowed again, then managed, "Curious."

Her mother looked unconvinced. "You really do look quite peaky, Melody. You should take more care of yourself. I always said this police job was a bad idea. And after what happened to you—"

"Mummy," Melody broke in. "Excuse me for a minute, okay? I have to make a phone call." Before her mother could protest, Melody walked outside. There was a swatch of perfect green lawn beside the rectangular lily pond, but she kept going until she reached the bottom of the property. Her parents had built an outdoor fireplace into the stone wall at the very back, with two chairs and a small table. It was their favorite place to enjoy a drink on chilly evenings. Today, however, the sun beat down with full force, reflecting searing sunlight from the stone underfoot. Melody felt exposed, as if the rays might reveal her very bones.

She pulled her mobile from her pocket. But then she hesitated, her finger poised over the keypad. Her first instinct had been to call Doug. Childs had been his boss, too, as well as Duncan's.

But . . . no. She had left her peace offering for Doug, and she couldn't bear to be rejected again. Nor was it her place to tell him. That should fall to Duncan.

Moving her finger, she touched the most familiar number on her phone screen. Gemma.

Kincaid hadn't believed it when Gemma told him. It had taken a call to Tom Faith, who'd informed him that what Melody had said was unfortunately true. Denis Childs had apparently been set upon in the churchyard of St. James Clerkenwell sometime the previous evening, and was now in the Royal London Hospital's traumatic brain injury ward with a severe head injury. Faith didn't know more than that, and was planning to go to hospital himself.

"I'll meet you there," Kincaid said, and it was not until he'd rung off that he realized he'd just told Gemma he would stay with the children while she went out with MacKenzie.

"Go," Gemma told him. "I'll work something out."

As he drove across north London, he replayed last night's meeting over and over. Why had Denis been so cagey about the pub, choosing a place where neither of them would be recognized? Had he been afraid he was being followed? And if that were true and someone had trailed him to the Duke, had they seen Kincaid, too?

He frowned as he passed St. Pancras Station. As if he needed a reminder of Ryan Marsh. It had been Marsh who had helped Melody Talbot aid the victims of an exploding white phosphorous grenade in the station concourse. It had been Marsh who'd thought he might have been the intended target, Marsh who'd feared that he was being watched or followed by someone within the force itself. But Marsh was dead. And Denis Childs was lying in hospital after voicing the same sort of conspiracy hints.

If Denis was being followed, was Kincaid putting himself at risk by being seen to have a further connection?

Swearing, Kincaid slammed on the brakes to avoid running a red light. The hot exhaust fumes rolling in the open windows of the old Astra were making him feel woozy and he shook his head to clear it. He was being bloody paranoid. Bonkers.

Surely Denis had been attacked by a random mugger. And of course he should visit him. The man had been his boss and his colleague for years.

Glancing in the rearview mirror, he glimpsed Charlotte's car seat in the back and felt a sudden shiver of cold in spite of the heat of the day. What if, just if, he wasn't crazy? He had his family to think of.

He had to know more. He had to talk to Denis if he could. There was too much at stake for him to just stick his head in the sand and hope he was imagining things.

MacKenzie's husband, Bill, once again came to the child-minding rescue. But Charlotte, already disappointed by Kincaid's abrupt and unexpected departure, clung to Gemma's legs and cried when Gemma took her into the Williamses' house. It had taken some coaxing on Gemma's part before she agreed to go outside and swing in the garden with Toby and Oliver.

"I'm so sorry," Gemma said to MacKenzie as they got in the car. "Bill's a saint to put up with a sniffling three-year-old."

"That never happens at our house," MacKenzie answered with a grin, then sobered. "And he needed a break. He's been working nonstop trying to book another model and reschedule the catalog shoot." She made a rueful face. "That seems awfully callous, doesn't it, to be inconvenienced by Reagan's death? But it's not just the models—there are loads of people to reschedule, and we had to find a new venue. The one we had booked yesterday was only available for the day. Bill's been pulling his hair out."

"Fortunately, life goes on," Gemma said. "You can't feel guilty about it." She drove back past her own house and turned right into Clarendon Road.

"You would know, I suppose," MacKenzie said slowly. "I'd never given it that much thought—that you have to deal with families of victims. I don't know how you do it."

Gemma glanced at her friend before she spoke. "I won't say it gets easier. But, often, people want to talk. So you give them the opportunity. It helps them."

"I have no idea what to say to Reagan's mother. I've never met her, and it's been hard enough talking to Nita."

"The words will come. And the important thing is that you've made the effort." Slowing, Gemma turned into Blenheim Crescent. "We should have walked," she said, eyeing the parked cars lining both sides of the street. But, miraculously, she spied a gap and in a few moments had squeezed the Escort into it.

This was familiar territory, just north of Kitchen and Pantry on the corner at Elgin Crescent, and their friend Otto's café on Elgin Crescent, too, nearer Portobello Road. A 52 bus barreled past on Kensington Park Road, but Blenheim Crescent itself was quiet, as if the residents were napping after their Sunday dinners.

"It's back this way," MacKenzie said when they got out, gesturing towards the north side of the street. She touched Gemma's arm, halting her. "I keep thinking . . . what if it was Oliver . . ."

"You mustn't." Giving her a quick hug, Gemma didn't add that there was nothing she dreaded more than talking to parents who had lost a child. "Now, which house?" she asked, determinedly cheerful.

Taking a breath and giving her a slightly shaky smile, MacKenzie led her a few doors back. The sun glinted off the parked cars, making Gemma narrow her eyes against the glare.

MacKenzie stopped, nodding towards a house midway down the terrace. "This one."

Unlike its more colorful pastel neighbors on either side, the house was a pale gray with a glossy black door. And unlike some of its neighbors, the house was not divided into flats. Steps led down to a barred basement area, and up to the front door. The curtains were open in the ground-floor bay window, and Gemma realized she could see straight through the rooms and into the garden at the back.

"Notting Hill vanity," whispered MacKenzie, following her gaze. "If you have a garden house or flat, you want people to know it."

"It must be like living in a goldfish bowl," Gemma said, although she guessed that most families spent their time in the usual basement kitchen/sitting areas rather than in the more formal first-floor rooms.

They climbed the steps, the sun hot on their backs, and MacKenzie rang the single bell.

The woman who opened the door wore expensive exercise clothes, yoga bottoms and a fitted T-shirt, the sort of thing that Gemma couldn't afford and wouldn't have time to wear if she could. She was thin, with an angular face that was striking rather than pretty, and wore her light brown hair in a feathered collar-length cut. "MacKenzie," she said, drawing them into the entrance hall and skimming MacKenzie's cheek with an air kiss. "Thank you for coming. Reagan's mum is here," she added more softly as she closed the front door. "I'm feeling a bit desperate." Gemma saw that under the flawless makeup her eyes were red-rimmed and puffy.

"Nita, this is my friend Gemma James," MacKenzie told her. "I thought she might be able to help. Gemma, Nita Cusick."

Nita took Gemma's hand in a firm, dry clasp. "That's good of you," she said to Gemma. "Any help is appreciated. Did you know Reagan?"

"No, I'm afraid I didn't." Gemma was about to add that she'd met Nita's son the previous day, but Nita was already opening the door into the sitting room.

Entering behind her, Gemma's first impression was that she had stepped straight into a bower. The room's sofas and armchairs were covered in a pale lemony yellow floral, a pattern that was repeated on the walls but in more neutral tones. Scattered vases held bunches of white hydrangeas. Light poured in from the large windows overlooking the rear garden.

But any exclamation of pleasure Gemma might have made was stopped by the sight of the woman sitting in the corner of one of the long sofas. In Nita Cusick's elegant sitting room she seemed as out of place as a dandelion in a hothouse. She was, Gemma guessed, not much older than Nita, but her clothes were ordinary and there were threads of gray in her dark hair. If she had worn any makeup it was long gone, and her face was swollen and blotched from weeping.

"Gwen," said Nita, "this is my friend MacKenzie Williams. And her friend Gemma—"

"I'm Gemma James," broke in Gemma, having seen the blank look on Nita's face. "I'm very sorry for your loss, Mrs. Keating."

Gwen Keating nodded at Gemma, but all her attention was on MacKenzie. "Mrs. Williams," she said. "Reagan talked and talked about you. She thought you and Mr. Williams hung the moon." Her voice was soft, her accent lightly Welsh.

"Oh, we thought she was wonderful, too." MacKenzie, her eyes brimming with tears, sat down beside her on the sofa and took her hand. "I'm so sorry. I still can't really believe it."

"Did you know my daughter?" Gwen Keating asked, looking up at Gemma. When Gemma shook her head, Gwen pulled a crumpled catalog from her handbag. "Here. Look. She said Mr. Williams loved the way she photographed."

Sitting down on her other side, Gemma took the catalog. It had been folded open to a photo of a dark-haired young woman sitting on a brick wall. She wore jeans and an Ollie signature floral print shirt, and looked into the camera with an engaging half smile. Gemma recognized the picture—she had the same catalog at home somewhere in her kitchen. "Oh, I've seen her. She's lovely," she murmured, gazing at the photo, and realizing only as she spoke that she'd used the present tense. The girl radiated vitality—it seemed impossible that she was dead.

Gently, she pressed the catalog back into Gwen Keating's hands. Nodding, Gwen hugged the catalog to her chest with one hand and raised the other to her chapped lips.

Gemma looked round, hoping for tissues and a glass of water for the grieving woman, but the adjacent coffee table held nothing but a low bowl of white roses, their scent strong in the warm room. Nita Cusick hadn't joined them, but stood near the door, looking as if she might bolt at any moment.

"Nita," she said, "I wonder if Gwen might like a cup of tea? I'd be glad to make it."

"Oh. Of course." Nita looked so surprised that Gemma wondered if people in her social set didn't drink tea. "Right. I'll just pop down and put it together."

"Let me help," Gemma offered, standing.

For a moment she thought Nita might refuse, but then Nita nodded and said, "Thanks."

Gemma gave MacKenzie an encouraging smile as she followed Nita back into the central hall, where an elegant staircase led up and a slightly narrower one on the left led down.

"The kitchen's this way," Nita tossed over her shoulder as she started down.

Reaching the bottom, Gemma stepped down onto a stone-flagged floor and looked round with interest. Like the sitting room upstairs, the room stretched from the front of the house to the back. And like the wallpaper upstairs, the room was done in soft neutral tones, but here there was no pattern. The street windows were covered in tailored shades, but the large back windows were exposed. They framed the view so that the outside scene might almost have been a painted mural, and the reflected greenish light gave an underwater cast to the room.

The kitchen fittings were obviously bespoke and, Gemma suspected, very, very expensive.

"It's Wilkinson and Barley. The kitchen furniture," said Nita, who had turned and seen Gemma running a finger along the edge of the marble-topped center island.

"Oh, yes, I know it," responded Gemma. She had indeed seen the Notting Hill showroom, but that didn't mean she had ever been inside it.

"They're my clients."

Gemma must have looked slightly at sea, because Nita went on, "My firm's clients. I do public relations and marketing for them."

"It's beautiful. Really lovely," said Gemma, making an effort to redeem herself. And it was, but the room didn't look as if anyone ever cooked in it, and in her opinion it cried out for at least a spot of color.

Nor, she noticed, was there a kettle on the enormous black six-hob Aga, although a coffeemaker and an espresso machine were among the few things to mar the pristine work tops.

"I don't drink tea," said Nita, confirming Gemma's guess. "But there's an electric kettle and"—she paused as she opened a cupboard near the garden windows and reached inside—"this." When she turned back, Gemma saw that she held a chipped red teapot. "It was Reagan's," Nita continued. "She missed having a teapot so she picked this one up at the market. I have her tea, too." Nita opened a drawer as if to look inside, but stopped and pressed the teapot against her chest. "I—I don't know if it would be right to use it. Her mother—would she recognize it? I wouldn't want to cause her more distress."

"Here." Gemma went to her and gently took the pot and placed it near the kettle. "I'm sure it will be fine. Let's see that tea." Looking in the drawer, Gemma found a box of Tetley's English Breakfast tea bags tucked neatly in beside coffee-making oddments. She debated over three bags or four for the pot, then went for strong. They all needed it.

Nita stepped aside as Gemma put the bags in the pot, then filled the kettle from one of the two sinks in the center island. "What about mugs?" she asked when the kettle had begun to heat, but Nita again had the dazed expression she'd worn upstairs. Gemma touched her arm. "Nita?"

"Oh, sorry." Nita seemed to make an effort to smile, but when she began to take white mugs from an upper cupboard, Gemma saw that her hand was shaking.

"Nita, maybe you should sit down for a bit." Looking round, Gemma saw nothing that might offer a little support—the bar stools were metal and backless.

"No. I'm fine. Really," Nita said, but she turned her back to Gemma and leaned on the work top with both hands. "I'm used to dealing with crises, for heaven's sake. My clients count on me to handle any sort of emergency. But this"—she shook her head—"I just can't seem to focus. I keep thinking I'll ask Reagan to do this or that, and then I remember . . ."

"It must be a terrible shock." The kettle came to the boil and Gemma poured the hot water into the teapot. "Were you close? How long was she with you?"

"Two years." Seeming to recover some of her composure, Nita straightened and moved to fetch a tray for the tea things. "Mac-

Kenzie will tell you—Reagan was . . . Reagan was a lovely girl. I just can't believe . . ."

Gemma waited for the words she was sure would follow, but Nita didn't say the expected. Instead, Nita went on, haltingly, "The police said . . . they said they had to check to see if alcohol or drugs were involved. I can't believe that." Nita shook her head. "Not Reagan. I don't know what they've told Gwen. But Reagan was living in my house, so I feel . . . responsible . . ." For the first time, there were tears in Nita's eyes, and Gemma thought she could understand why Nita had been so awkward and scattered upstairs with Gwen.

MacKenzie hadn't told her this, but then MacKenzie wouldn't have known unless Nita had shared it with her. "If it's a suspicious death, of course they will want to—" Gemma began, but stopped when it occurred to her that it also seemed that MacKenzie hadn't told Nita her friend was a police officer. It wouldn't do to blurt it out suddenly, or to know more than a civilian. "I'm sure the police will have been very gentle with Gwen," she amended. "Under the circumstances. And as for being responsible, Reagan may have been living under your roof, but she was how old?"

"Twenty-four."

"Then she was a grown woman and responsible for her own behavior."

"Well, yes, I suppose, but . . ." Nita stopped and gave Gemma a tremulous smile. "I can see that you're right. I saw her. Did Mac-Kenzie tell you?"

"Yes, MacKenzie did tell me. It must have been terrible for you."

"I'm glad Gwen was spared that. But she said, when she came in, that she'd been to the mortuary straightaway. To see the . . . the body. And I wasn't sure what would be worse . . ."

"That's not a choice anyone should have to make." There was much that Gemma would have liked to ask, about Reagan, and about what Nita had seen. But the tea was getting cold and Mac-Kenzie would be wondering what had happened to them. She saw that Nita had only put out three mugs. Moving them to the tray, she asked, "Are you not having any?"

Nita made a face. "I've had too much caffeine today."

"We'd better go up, then. Here, let me," Gemma added, taking the tray. As she turned towards the stairs, she noticed a big basket, tucked away between the bottom of the staircase and the cupboards. Out of it poked a pair of muddy trainers and a football. She realized what had been bothering her since she'd first entered this house—there had been no sign that a boy lived here.

She thought of her own sitting room and kitchen, scattered with an ever-changing array of toys and junk. And usually Toby's muddy trainers as well, which were the same brand as these but a few sizes smaller.

Did Jess live with his father, then, and only visit here? But then why the nanny, Reagan? Or had she somehow got everything all wrong?

Turning to Nita, she said, "I met your son yesterday. Jess. At ballet. I think that's why MacKenzie asked me to come today. How is he doing with this?"

Nita frowned and rubbed a hand across her eyes. "I don't know. He won't come out of his room. He won't talk to me. He seems to think that this is somehow my fault."

"So you've decided you don't like my whitefish?" asked Ivan Talbot, watching Melody put a little of the spread on a cracker, then set the cracker down again.

"It's not that, Dad." Melody forced a smile. She had managed a bit of the cucumber and a bit of the cold potatoes, but she couldn't bear even the thought of the ham, and the whitefish was running a close second. She pushed the food around on her plate, hoping to disguise her lack of appetite. Her mother, she knew, had missed nothing, but so far hadn't commented. "It's the heat, I think," she said. "And I have a bit of a headache."

"We could go inside," suggested Addie.

"No, no. This is lovely." Melody shook her head, a bit too violently, and winced.

Now her mother was frowning at her. "Perhaps you should go have a lie down."

"No, really, Mummy. I'd rather be out here." That much, at least, was true. They were sitting at the table on the flagstone patio just outside the kitchen. The house shaded this part of the garden from the afternoon sun and there was a little breeze. She just couldn't seem to get food down, and she couldn't sit still, which was made worse by the fact that she knew how much her mother hated fidgeting. The champagne she *had* managed to drink, however, and she didn't stop her father when he topped up her glass.

"If you're worried about your chief superintendent," said her father, "we should listen to the news. I'm curious to see what the Yard is going to release." Before Melody could protest, he got up and went into the house, returning with the brown kitchen radio and tuning it to BBC1.

It was ten to two and the hourly update would be coming on soon. The song in progress finished and then came Sunday-afternoon host Alice Levine's familiar voice, burbling on about something that Melody only half heard.

"I'm not at all sure the Met press office will say anything,"

Melody told her father, abandoning even the attempt to eat the whitefish spread.

Unless he dies, thought Melody, and felt her heart skip painfully in her chest. Could Gemma have learned anything yet? She crumpled her napkin in her lap and shifted in her chair. What had happened? She couldn't just sit while—

Alice Levine's voice faded and the music started again, but this time Melody felt a jolt of recognition at the first note. It was the one song she avoided on the YouTube videos. Andy and Poppy had been playing it live when the grenade had gone off in St. Pancras Station.

She stood and reached across the table, fumbling to switch off the radio, knocking it over in the process and starting her champagne glass toppling. Her father grabbed the glass, his quick reflexes saving it, but both parents were looking at her as if she'd suddenly gone mad.

"Melody, what on earth?" said her mother, frowning as she righted the radio. "And I like that song."

Oh, God. Her mother, a fan? Should she say, "Oh, by the way—that guy, the one who was playing at St. Pancras? He's my lover." It was all she could do to hold in a strangled laugh. "I'm sorry," she said hurriedly. "I just remembered. There's something I have to do. At work." She leaned over and kissed her mother's smooth cheek, then gave her father a quick hug. "I'll ring you. Thanks for the lunch."

"But, darling," her mother said, pushing her chair back as if to stop her, but Melody was already ducking into the kitchen. She hadn't missed the speculative look in her father's eyes, and she ran up the stairs and out the front door like an Olympic sprinter.

She didn't stop until she'd turned the corner into the east side of the square. When she halted, gasping, she was suddenly aware that people were staring at her.

The sunlight seemed too bright. Her head was pounding, and her heart was still racing. For a moment she thought she might be sick. She grasped the top of the garden's fence and the iron felt cool under her hand.

Better, she thought. Better. Then she heard a siren in the distance and suddenly she couldn't get her breath at all. Her vision blurred. A wave of terror gripped her, wrenching at her gut. Panting, she clutched the fence now with both hands. Was that smoke she smelled?

She could hear Andy and Poppy's song playing in her head. Then people were shouting and crying. The sirens were getting nearer. The smoke burned her eyes and seared her throat, then the ground seemed to tilt beneath her feet. Christ, what was happening to her?

Suddenly, she felt a hand on her shoulder and a woman's voice said, "Melody? Melody, is that you? Is something wrong?"

Spinning round, Melody caught a glimpse of a red dress, then tried to focus on the worried face before her. "Hazel?"

CHAPTER SIX

Kincaid's route had taken him down City Road and then Commercial Street, into the heart of Whitechapel. Even though Brick Lane was one street to the east, with the Astra's windows down he could swear he smelled halal chicken and curry mixed with the exhaust fumes from the traffic.

The stark spire of Christ Church rose ahead as he neared Spitalfields Market on the right. And just before Christ Church on the left came Fournier Street, where Charlotte had spent most of the first three years of her life. The impulse to turn and drive down the street was almost irresistible, but that would take him into Brick Lane, which was one way in the opposite direction, and he didn't want to backtrack.

But in his mind's eye he saw the tall, narrow Georgian house with its blue door and heavily shuttered windows. Charlotte's parents, Sandra and Naz Malik, had bought it when no one wanted to live in Whitechapel and had restored it with much love and little money. When they'd died, the house had sold for more than they could have dreamed, and that money had gone into trust for Charlotte.

This was Charlotte's heritage, he thought, the bold graffiti and the women in silks bright as butterflies, the accents of the passersby mingling Cockney, Punjabi, and Urdu. How much did Charlotte remember, even now?

Her mother, Sandra, a brilliant fabric artist, had used the colors and textures of the East End in her work. Her father, Naz, a second-generation Pakistani, had been a lawyer who'd made a good practice representing local clients.

After their deaths, unwilling to let Charlotte go to maternal relatives who were both grasping and criminal, Kincaid and Gemma had petitioned social services to allow them to foster Charlotte. Although Louise Phillips, Naz's law partner and the executor of Naz and Sandra's estate, was fond of Charlotte and assiduous in looking after her financial affairs, she'd had no desire to take on the everyday care of a small child.

The thought reminded him that he'd been neglecting to check on Louise, who was recovering from a case of tuberculosis—and on Tam, Louise's friend and neighbor, who'd been badly injured in the grenade explosion at St. Pancras. He felt, for the first time in his life, overwhelmed by others' troubles.

And now this. He shook his head, forcing himself to concentrate as he turned into Whitechapel, nearing the hospital. But he was afraid of what he would find.

The Royal London Hospital was, in Kincaid's opinion, an architect's nightmare. The classical eighteenth-century frontage had grown additions over the years that ranged from Victorian to the latest in postmodern glass blocks, all jumbled together as if they'd been dumped from a grab bag. But the sight of the bright red air ambulance on its pad cheered him, and he thought that one day he must bring the children to see it.

And how lucky for Denis—or so Kincaid hoped—that he had been injured so near London's major trauma hospital and hadn't needed the air ambulance to get him here.

Once he'd managed to park the car and find his way to the main desk, a receptionist pointed him to the Adult Critical Care ward and he found it quickly enough. As he entered the ward's waiting area, Detective Chief Superintendent Tom Faith rose to greet him.

Faith wore golfing clothes, the sportiness of the attire incongruous with the worried frown on his face. "Duncan. Good of you to come." He clasped Kincaid's hand in a firm grip, then sat again, motioning Kincaid to an adjacent chair.

"How is he?" Kincaid asked, looking around the waiting area. There was an anxious-looking middle-aged couple in the far corner, but no one familiar. "Is there no family here?"

"Diane is sitting with him. They allow two people in the room, but I—" Faith shook his head and grimaced. "I thought they might need some time alone. And what good can I do in there?" He gave an eloquent shrug of his thin shoulders. "But I thought I should be here for Diane when the consultant comes to give her an update. She—"

"Denis is conscious?" Kincaid interrupted with a spring of hope.

"No." Faith shook his head. "They've induced a coma to reduce the swelling on his brain."

Glancing at the couple across the room, Kincaid lowered his voice. "What exactly happened?"

"We don't know. A couple of teenagers found him lying in the churchyard at St. James Clerkenwell. Girls cutting through the churchyard after dark," Faith added with a grimace. "At first they thought he was drunk—he was mumbling and trying to stand—and they hurried by. But then one of them thought he looked ill and went back to check. Thank God. They called 999. The medics found him unconscious. Blow to the back of the head."

It was Kincaid's turn to frown. "Mugged?"

"Not unless the muggers were interrupted. And that seems unlikely since they took time to kick him. His wallet and phone were still in his pockets."

"Did the girls see anyone?"

"They said not."

"Time?"

A sharp look from Faith reminded Kincaid that he was interrogating a senior officer—his senior officer. "Sorry," he said, making an effort to sit back in his chair.

"I understand you're concerned." Faith's reply was not exactly a reprimand but held a note of warning. He went on, "It was about nine, just fully dark. But it's doubtful he'd been there long. The churchyard is a regularly used pass-through."

Kincaid tried to think back. He'd met Denis at eight. How long had they talked? He hadn't looked at his watch when Denis left. Had it been more than half an hour? And even assuming that, how long did it take to walk from Roger Street to St. James Clerkenwell?

However you figured it, he might have been the last person to see Denis Childs before the attack.

"Diane says he left their house in Sekforde Street about half past seven for a walk, but we have no idea where he went." Faith might have read his mind.

Kincaid heard the rush of his own heartbeat pounding in his ears and sweat prickled under his collar. Across the room, the woman gave a soft little hiccoughing sob. Did he trust Faith enough to admit that he had been with Denis?

But Faith shifted in his chair, glancing at the door into the ward and then his watch, and the moment passed.

"It was a good thing he still had his wallet," Faith said. "Not that the ambulance service wouldn't have rushed him into trauma care under any circumstances, but knowing he was a police officer certainly didn't hurt. And when they called Diane from A and E, she told them about the transplant straightaway. They'd kicked him in the sides. We don't know yet what that might have done to his new liver," Faith added, and Kincaid saw that his fists were clenched.

Kincaid considered Faith's presence at the hospital, and his obvious closeness to both Denis and Diane Childs. "I'm sorry." He cleared his throat. "I knew Denis thought very highly of you as a colleague. I didn't realize you were such close friends."

"We were at the academy together. Our wives were best friends for thirty years. That's how they met." Glancing at Kincaid, Faith answered the question Kincaid had begun to formulate. "Linda died of cancer two years ago. I don't know how I'd have got through it without Denis and Diane . . . Well, never mind. But I would do anything for either of them. Of course I'm here." His voice was fierce.

Oh, Christ. Kincaid rubbed a hand across the Sunday stubble on his chin. So Denis had sent him into safekeeping with his most trusted friend, and he in turn had spent the last few months seething with resentment. If only he had—

The ward door opened and they both turned as if jerked by

magnets, then stood. It was Diane Childs. When she saw Kincaid, she smiled and came to him with her hand outstretched. As he took it, she said, "Duncan. How lovely of you to come." Her hand felt childlike in his. Slender, her dark hair barely threaded with gray, she had always seemed tiny beside Denis's bulk, but today, alone, she looked even more delicate. She wore no makeup other than a brave bit of rose lipstick, and her eyes were a startling deep blue against her pale skin.

"Any change?" asked Faith.

Shaking her head, she managed a smile as she sank into a chair. "No. But that's good, they say." She pulled the edges of her sapphire cardigan together.

"Let me get you a coffee," said Faith, rocking on his feet as if he couldn't bear to sit.

"If I have any more coffee I'll take off like a rocket. But, maybe . . . hot chocolate?" She shivered visibly. "The room is warm but I feel a little chilled."

Faith's brows drew together in disapproval. "You haven't eaten."

Diane Childs laughed, the sound so startling in the waiting area that the couple across the room looked up, distracted from their worry. "Tom. Stop it," she said with evident affection. "Go fetch me some hot chocolate, please. And just to make you happy, a sandwich."

For a moment, Kincaid thought Faith would protest. But having at least won part of his argument, he nodded and went out the way Kincaid had come in.

He was still feeling bemused by the idea of his superior officer being ordered about when Diane fixed him with her disconcerting deep blue gaze and said, "Tom can be a bit of a mother hen. But then I imagine you know that. Best to let him have his way."

Touching light fingers on his arm, she added, "And I wanted a chance to talk to you."

Kincaid froze. Did she know Denis had met him? Did she know anything about the things that Denis had been hinting at last night?

He scrambled for a reply, but all he could think was that she smelled faintly like his mother's Cheshire borders in summer— sweet pea, that was it, the scent he remembered. "I'm sorry," he managed, "about what happened—"

Diane was already shaking her head as if impatient with the condolence. "Denis has never been very good at telling people how he feels—and the fact that it's not encouraged in the police hasn't helped. But he talks about you often—and about Gemma and your children, especially your little daughter. I think perhaps he envies you that."

Taken aback, Kincaid gaped at her. That was the last thing he'd expected. But then he thought of all Denis's smooth little questions, inserted so seamlessly into other conversations. He'd always assumed it was Denis's way of keeping tabs on his officers—a good guv'nor knew that his officers' home life affected their work and so kept up with it—but it had never occurred to him that Denis's interest might be personal.

But as he considered it, things began to take on a different coloration.

There was Gemma's transfer to Brixton, coming so swiftly after she'd been instrumental in unearthing a long trail of assaults against female police officers by a senior officer. Kincaid had half suspected that Denis had arranged it as a sweetener, a way of discouraging him from protesting about the outcome of that same case. But what if it had been, not a subtle bribe, but a means of putting Gemma out of harm's way?

Diane patted his hand, bringing him back to the present. "He would never admit it, of course. But I know he was not happy about losing you to Holborn, although there's no one he respects more than Tom Faith."

"Losing me?" Kincaid asked. "Is that what he said?"

Diane sat back and sighed. "Well, perhaps he didn't put it quite like that. He—" She stopped, looking up as the ward door opened.

It was a consultant, easily identified by her white coat and stethoscope. Kincaid felt Diane tensing beside him, and for a moment he hoped the doctor had come to speak to the couple across the room. But she came straight towards them, saying, "Mrs. Childs?" in a soft, slightly accented voice.

Diane nodded and Kincaid instinctively clasped her hand.

"Mrs. Childs, I'm Miss Cisse and I'm the consultant who will be managing your husband's case while he's in the critical care ward."

The consultant's skin was a deep mahogany, and the name, Kincaid guessed, was central African, perhaps Nigerian. She wore the tiny plaits of her thick hair pulled back with a colorful printed bandeau, a contrast to her serious demeanor.

When she looked questioningly at him, he released Diane's hand and stood for a moment to shake the doctor's. "Duncan Kincaid," he said. "I'm a . . . a friend of the family." Diane gave him a quick nervous glance.

The doctor sat beside Diane, taking a moment to scan a small tablet she carried with her, then looked up and began, "You know we are keeping your husband under sedation to minimize any swelling on his brain? He has a type of injury called an epidural hematoma, which required surgery last night. The surgeon also inserted a tiny device into the incision that monitors the intercranial pressure—any swelling of the brain," she clarified, glancing at them both to make certain they were following.

Diane nodded, and Kincaid guessed some of this had been explained to her last night.

"Your husband also hit his head when he fell forward, and the two blows have given his brain quite a jar."

"A concussion?" Kincaid asked.

Miss Cisse nodded and smiled at him as if he were a prize pupil. "Yes, exactly."

"But we were told that Denis was talking when the girls found him," said Diane, and Kincaid could tell it was taking an effort for her to keep her voice steady.

"That's very common with your husband's type of injury." Cisse gave her another encouraging smile, but Kincaid didn't feel better. He'd seen injuries like this, where after a blow to the head, the person remained lucid for as long as several hours before losing consciousness. His stomach lurched.

"Can you tell what caused the injury to the back of the head?" he asked.

The doctor's smile lost some of its wattage. "I can guess it was made by something hard and that the depression was about the width of your finger. I don't think we can determine more than that, Mr."—she paused to consult the notes on her tablet— "Kincaid. Now, if there's anything else—"

"How long will he have to be kept sedated?" Diane's rose lipstick looked stark now against her pallor.

"That all depends on whether there is any more swelling, Mrs. Childs. But he's comfortable, I assure you."

"When he wakes up, will he remember what happened?"

"I'm afraid it's quite common for patients to have no memory of the incident that caused their injury. I wouldn't worry about that just now."

What the doctor didn't say seemed to hang in the air like a specter.

It was also quite common for patients with severe brain trauma never to wake up at all.

Kincaid went into the curtained cubicle alone. The doctor had left just as Tom Faith returned with Diane's sandwich and hot chocolate.

Slowly, he moved to the foot of the hospital bed and gripped the railing. There was an ugly purpling lump on the right side of Denis Childs's forehead, and the stubble from two days' growth of heavy dark beard covered his cheeks and chin. An IV catheter trailed from his right arm and his mouth hung loosely around the breathing tube, the muscles slack. The monitors stood by, silently blinking guardians, and Denis's large frame seemed shrunken under the hospital sheet.

A strip of bandage ran rather rakishly just beneath Denis's hairline and Kincaid assumed it anchored the small probe placed in the back of Denis's head. It was frightening enough, Kincaid thought, to watch those one knew well sleeping, but still in the mumble and twitch and the flutter of eyelids there were signs of the personality that animated the body. Here, there were none. He realized that although Denis Childs's face had often seemed impassive, in reality it had conveyed a myriad of expressions, all of them unique. And his dark eyes had been filled with a lively and calculating intelligence. They were closed now, the dark lashes fanned against Childs's olive cheeks.

Kincaid gripped the rail until his knuckles showed white. He would find out who had done this.

He would find out what Denis had been trying to tell him.

And Denis was bloody well going to wake up.

"Reagan was an only child but she always had a special knack for kids," Gwen Keating said to Gemma. Gwen had gulped her tea as if she were parched and Gemma had refilled her mug from the dregs of the pot.

MacKenzie had stepped into the hall to ring Bill and check on the children. Nita sat perched on the edge of the sofa, tapping her foot and glancing towards the upper part of the house every few minutes.

Gemma wasn't sure if it was because she'd served the tea, or because she hadn't known Reagan, but Gwen seemed fixed on telling her about her daughter. "Her dad died when she was three," Gwen went on. "Cancer. So it was always just the two of us. We did everything together."

"What do you do in Cardiff, Gwen?" asked Gemma, hoping to steer the conversation towards something less personal.

"I teach English literature at a comprehensive." Gwen leaned towards her, frowning. "Listen, the police officer I spoke to said they thought Reagan's death could have been caused by an alcohol or drug overdose." She set her empty mug down and went on, "I don't believe it, not for a minute. Reagan might have had a few drinks with friends, but she didn't binge. And she would never do drugs. I know kids. I'm not a naive mum. I see kids every day at school, I know what sorts of things they get up to. That wasn't Reagan, I'm telling you."

Gemma had heard similar testimony from parents before, painful in its earnestness. Shocked and grieved, most didn't want to believe their children could have been at fault. But Gwen Keating was right, she did know kids, and nothing about the woman struck her as naive.

And then there was the way Reagan's body had been described, which suggested another possibility—one that Gemma was certain her mother would find even more painful—suicide. "I'm sure they'll have some answers for you soon," she said, knowing that there was no good outcome, although a natural death would surely be the least painful.

"I want to take her things home," Gwen said, gathering her handbag to her, the first step in leave-taking.

Nita's head snapped round towards her, as if she'd been somewhere else entirely until Gwen spoke. "You can't."

"What?" Gwen stared at her. "What do you mean, I can't? Why ever not?"

Nita said, "I'm sorry. I didn't mean . . . It's just that the police told me that her room should be left as it was until they'd done their initial investigation. They didn't tell you?"

"No. They did not." Gwen's lips were pinched tight.

Somebody at Kensington nick had made a right balls-up of this, thought Gemma, starting with mentioning alcohol and drugs to Gwen when they hadn't done a tox screen or a postmortem. If it had been anyone on her team, she'd have had their head on a platter.

Nita shot her a pleading glance.

The room had grown warmer and stuffier. Wondering why Nita didn't open the windows for a little air, Gemma resisted the urge to get up and crank the casements out herself.

MacKenzie's voice had been a low murmur from the entry hall. Now Gemma heard the front door open and close. Rising, she peered out the front windows and saw MacKenzie pacing the pavement, mobile held to her ear. MacKenzie looked up, waved, and smiled.

"She could see Reagan's room, couldn't she, Nita?" Gemma asked, finding herself unable to sit down again. The scent of the roses had grown stronger.

"But—I don't know if she should— And I don't think I can possibly—"

"I'll go with her," Gemma said, cutting off Nita's protest.

Nita frowned. "And you'll make certain—"

"Of course Gwen won't take anything." Gemma's patience was wearing thin.

"Well, all right, if you're certain," said Nita, acquiescing with less than good grace. "It's the front room on the first floor. Jess has the back. I'll be in the kitchen. I need to make some phone calls." She gave them a brisk smile and went out. The room was so quiet that after a moment Gemma heard her soft footfalls on the stairs.

She turned to Gwen. "Are you sure you want to do this?"

Gwen stood, nodding, and Gemma guessed she couldn't bring herself to speak.

"Then let's go up, shall we?" Leading the way, Gemma had to admit that, in spite of the circumstances, she was curious. She wanted to see more of the house. And she wanted to know more about Reagan Keating.

When Gwen hesitated outside the closed bedroom door, Gemma turned the knob and gave Gwen an encouraging little pat on the shoulder. "I'll be right beside you," she said, standing back to let Gwen enter.

It was a spacious room, with two large south-facing windows. The blinds were half drawn and the windows closed, so it was even warmer than downstairs. Scent lingered in the air, something fresh and slightly grassy. The double bed, covered with a bright orange-and-purple-flowered duvet, looked hastily made, and one of a cascade of decorative pillows had fallen on the floor.

Reagan had had an eye for color, Gemma thought, and had liked her creature comforts. There was a bookcase filled with paperbacks and magazines, an armchair with a beaded reading lamp beside it, and on the desk, a little tea-making station with a tin of tea, a tin of shortbread, and a chipped Brown Betty teapot.

A pair of jeans was thrown over the chair arm, and two summer dresses lay rumpled on the foot of the bed as if tossed there in a hurry. Were these the things Reagan had almost worn on Friday night, then discarded?

Gwen sagged onto the edge of the bed as if her knees had been suddenly cut from under her and gathered up one of the dresses. "I gave her this," she said. "For her birthday." She gave a sudden wracking cry, then her shoulders began to shake as she rocked, weeping, the tears streaming down her cheeks and the dress clutched to her breast.

Gemma sat down beside her and put an arm round her shoulders, murmuring, "It's all right, it's all right," as if Gwen were the child, all the while knowing that it wasn't all right and that it never would be.

When Gwen's sobs had subsided to hiccups, Gemma looked round for tissues, spying a roll of kitchen towels tucked neatly behind the tea kettle. Giving Gwen a squeeze, she got up to fetch the roll, but as she stood at the desk she couldn't help looking at the big corkboard above it.

It was covered with scribbled notes and photos and pages torn from the Ollie catalog. There was the photo Gwen had shown her, and several others that Gemma remembered glimpsing in her own copies of the catalog. The notes were written in a neat, round, fluid hand that made Gemma think that Gwen had taught her daughter proper cursive script when she was young. Most seemed to be simple shopping lists, or reminders to meet someone at a certain time—indecipherable unless you knew the code of the initials and abbreviations Reagan had used.

But it was the photos that interested Gemma most. It was unusual to see so many printed photographs these days, when most people stored photos on their phones. Checking the desk, Gemma spotted a small color printer tucked behind a stack of books. There was an empty space at the front of the desk that might have held Reagan's laptop.

Tearing a couple of sheets from the kitchen roll, Gemma went back to Gwen. Then, as Gwen nodded her thanks and blew her nose, Gemma turned again to the photos on the board. There was one of Reagan with Oliver, and another of Reagan with Oliver and Charlotte. She hadn't realized that Charlotte had known Reagan. There were dozens of photos of Jess—Jess dancing in practice gear, Jess dancing in full costume, and one of Reagan and Jess together. Her arm was thrown casually over his shoulders and they were laughing, making faces at the camera.

And there were photos of Reagan with her friends. Most were late-night-group-selfies-in-the-pub, fuzzy and unflattering. But there were several shots of a very good-looking young man, and their placement made Gemma think those had been looked at often. He was very blond, with straight hair cut collar length all round, full lips, and striking blue eyes. His gaze engaged the camera in a way that made Gemma think he was used to being photographed.

"Gwen," she said, turning back to the bed, "do you know who this is?" She tapped the photo.

"Oh, him? That's Hugo. Reagan is—" Gwen swallowed hard and tried again. "Reagan was going out with him. But I don't think they'd been seeing each other as much lately."

"Did she say why?"

"She didn't say—I mean she didn't say that they weren't seeing each other. It's just that I noticed she didn't seem to have mentioned him much lately."

Glancing back at the photo, Gemma asked, "Do you know Hugo's last name?"

Gwen shook her head. "I should. I know she told me. But I never met him and I—I should have made more effort—" Her face crumpled again.

"Shhh." Gemma sat down beside her again and gave her a hug. "I only asked because I wondered if anyone had got in touch with her friends."

"Her mobile," Gwen said on a rising note of panic. "Where's her mobile? She would never have left it." Pulling away from Gemma, she stood and went to the desk, then began rifling through things with a frantic energy.

"Gwen." Gemma followed and put restraining hands on Gwen's arms. "Gwen. We shouldn't touch things. We—"

The door flew open with a bang that made them both jump.

Jess stood in the doorway, breathing hard. "What are *you* doing in here?" he demanded. "This is Reagan's room. You shouldn't be—" He stopped, staring at Gemma. "What are you doing here?" In ratty jeans and T-shirt, his face red and swollen from weeping, he was barely recognizable as the confident boy Gemma had seen at ballet the previous day.

"Jess, I'm a friend of MacKenzie's. It was MacKenzie who got my son a place in the class at the Tabernacle. My name's Gemma."

Jess frowned, looking from her to Gwen. Before he could protest further, Gemma added, "This is Gwen, Reagan's mum. Your mother said we could come up."

"She didn't say you could go through her things."

"No, she didn't. But we thought we might find her phone so we could get in touch with her friends."

"It's not here."

Gemma studied him with a level gaze. "You already looked."

Jess ducked his head, his belligerence fading. "I thought . . . I thought she might have . . . left a message."

"A message?" asked Gemma, but gently.

Jess shifted from one foot to the other and looked away. "I heard my mum talking. She said . . . she said the police thought maybe Reagan had . . . hurt herself. But she wouldn't. She would never do that." He looked back at Gemma, his eyes reddening and his fists clenching.

Beside her, Gemma heard the gasp of Gwen's indrawn breath, but she kept her focus on Jess. "Jess, she could have been ill. And accidents happen, as much as we hate—"

"No." Jess glared at her. "I heard my mum say how she was . . ." He stopped, pressing his knuckles to his lips and blinking hard. "I heard my mum say how she was found," he went on, his voice stronger. "Ray didn't just lie down like that and die. She couldn't have. She would never, ever have done that."

"You remember I was working at the café on the corner?" Hazel Cavendish asked, still holding Melody's arm and looking concerned.

"Of course." Melody forced a smile. "Of course I do. I was just miles away. You're working this afternoon?" she added, glancing again at Hazel's red sundress.

"The thing is, I'm not working there anymore," Hazel explained. "But I'm baking for them, and for some other cafés as well. I'd just dropped off some pastries here for tonight when I saw you."

"That's great news, Hazel," said Melody with real delight. "You're quite the entrepreneur."

Hazel looked pensive for a moment. "I miss the distillery sometimes." When Hazel had separated from her husband, Tim, she'd moved to a remote village in the Scottish Highlands to run her family's distillery, taking her daughter, Holly, with her. She'd returned to London after a year, saying that an isolated Scottish moor was no fit place to raise a child. But although she was a licensed therapist, she'd taken a job serving at the café and moved into a little bungalow in Battersea.

As far as Melody knew, Hazel and Tim were still separated, but Hazel looked well and happy.

"But I don't miss the Scottish winters," Hazel added with a smile. "But how are you? Were you visiting your parents?"

Melody nodded. "The dreaded Sunday lunch."

"No wonder you look so peaky. Come on." Hazel took her by the arm again. "Let me treat you to a cuppa at the café. We can visit—it's dead as a graveyard this time on a Sunday afternoon."

Melody's first instinct was to refuse. But as she started to shake her head, the world tilted again and the edges of her vision went bright and an odd acid yellow. Suddenly she wasn't sure she could make it to her car unaided.

Giving Hazel a shaky smile, she said, "That would be lovely."

"Brilliant. Let's go, then."

When Hazel tucked her hand in Melody's arm, Melody didn't object.

The tiny café on the corner was as deserted as Hazel had predicted. The small, dark-skinned woman at the register in the back looked up from a magazine when they came in. "Hazel," she said. "What are you doing back? Did you forget something?"

"No. I bumped into my friend and brought her for tea. You can take a break if you like, Mary. I'll watch the shop."

"Would you really?" Mary flashed them a blinding smile. "I need to pick up a couple of things at Whole Foods and they'll be closed by the time I get off." She whipped off her apron. "Um, half an hour?"

"Go. Take your time."

When Hazel had waved Mary out the door, she turned to Melody and pulled out a chair near the back. "Here. Sit. Unless you'd rather take one of the outside tables? It's a bit stuffy in here."

The café did feel warm, but Melody was still squinting against the bright sunlight. "No, this is fine." She sat with her back to the door, which always made her uncomfortable, but it was better than facing the glare.

"Tea or coffee?"

Melody couldn't bear even the thought of coffee. The little food she'd eaten at her parents' had made her stomach churn. "Tea, please."

"The kitchen's downstairs," said Hazel. "I'll be back in a tick."

True to her word, she was back in five minutes with a steaming pot of tea, cups, and a plate of small brown biscuits. "My new specialty," she explained as she sat across from Melody and filled their cups. "Brownie biscuits. They taste just like brownies but they're crunchy like a good tea biscuit."

Feeling better after the brief respite, Melody took a little nibble to please Hazel. "Oh," she said, pleasantly surprised. "These are fabulous. How did you do that?"

"Trade secret." Hazel grinned and raised her cup. "Chocolate and tea. Cure for anything."

Melody took another bite, then mumbled through crumbs, "So how did you get started baking for the cafés?"

"I always baked. At home. In Scotland. Then, about the time I started working here, the pastry chef left and I made some things to stem the panic." Hazel shrugged. "Before I knew it, I was working my shifts and doing all the baking. Totally mad. Then one day the owner of another café came in while I was here on my own and asked who did the baked goods. I struck a deal."

"You're doing this out of the kitchen in your bungalow?" Melody, who was hard-pressed to heat a frozen pizza, was impressed.

"Mostly. It's not that difficult if you're organized. But sometimes I use the kitchen in Islington." Hazel colored a little and fiddled with her teacup.

Melody remembered that Gemma had lived for a while in the garage flat of Hazel and Tim's Islington house. Was Hazel thinking of getting back together with Tim? She was trying to think of a discreet way to ask when Hazel changed the subject.

"How's your bloke, then?" Hazel said, and it was Melody's turn to squirm.

"He's on tour. With Poppy. They're taking Germany by storm at the moment, or so I hear."

"Good for them." Hazel sounded genuinely pleased. "Has it gone to his head yet?" she added, grinning.

"No. Not a bit," Melody protested, perhaps a bit too quickly. She couldn't help thinking about last night's missed phone call. And about the screaming girls she'd seen in the videos.

She felt cold and a little queasy again. How was it possible to miss someone you had known only a few months so badly? She wanted to see Andy, to touch him, to smell the faint metallic scent his fingers picked up from his guitar strings. She wanted to curl up on the old futon in his flat and listen to him noodle on his guitar, Bert purring in her lap—

"Shit," she said. "Bert."

Hazel gave her a startled look. "Sorry?"

"Andy's cat." Melody took a breath, trying to slow her suddenly pounding heart. "His name is Bert. A neighbor in Andy's building is feeding him but I promised I'd look in on him on the weekends."

"Well, it's not too late, is it?" Hazel asked gently, and Melody wondered if her flash of panic had shown. It wasn't that she hadn't looked in on the cat, it was that she'd completely forgotten she'd meant to. "The last time I saw you," Hazel added, "Gemma was trying to talk you into taking a kitten." She rolled her eyes. "I take it that you were sane enough to refuse. I can't say the same."

The night came back to Melody with crystal clarity. It had been a Saturday. She and Gemma were celebrating a good result on the investigation into the murder of a young girl in Brixton. They'd met Hazel at the Mitre on Holland Park Avenue for a girls'-night-out glass of wine. Melody had been fizzing, elated by their success on the case, excited for Andy, and feeling certain she was well on her way to recovering from the effects of the grenade at St. Pancras.

It had been the last night that the world had seemed manageable. The next day they'd learned that Ryan Marsh, the man who had walked into the fire at Melody's side, was dead.

Gemma and MacKenzie drove Gwen Keating to Paddington Station. Gwen had insisted on going back to Cardiff.

"It's the only place I can feel her," she'd said, standing with them outside the Cusicks' house, hugging her arms to her chest. "I don't know this place, these people." She gestured towards the house. "I don't know this boy. Why would he say such a thing? Why would anyone want to hurt my baby?"

"He's just upset," Gemma told her.

But of course Jess was upset. He was only a little younger than Kit had been when his mother died, and Gemma knew firsthand how hard it was for children to cope with such a loss—especially if they had little in the way of emotional support.

MacKenzie had walked Gwen to her platform gate while Gemma stayed with the car, and had been uncharacteristically quiet on the drive back to Notting Hill. "I just can't believe it," she said at last, breaking the silence as Gemma stopped at the Notting Hill Gate traffic lights. "I can't believe Reagan would overdose, accidentally or deliberately."

"There's not much point in speculating before the postmortem results come back," Gemma cautioned. The afternoon was morphing into evening, the light going flat as low, thin clouds moved in from the west. She needed to get home. Bill Williams must be going spare stuck so long with her two little ones, and she was worried about Duncan, who hadn't rung.

Still. She drummed her fingers on the wheel as a 52 bus roared by, turning the sharp corner into Kensington Park Road. The whole scenario of Reagan Keating's death was bizarre. It had that feel of wrongness that set her instincts clanging and her palms itching.

It was not her business, she told herself as the lights changed and she put the car into gear. It wasn't her shout. She had a full enough plate at Brixton nick, as well as her own family to look after, and not enough time to do either properly. She would see Jess the next time she took Toby to ballet, and she would nod and smile and he would never know that she had walked away.

The thought made her flinch.

The lights caught them again at Ladbroke Road, just a few blocks from her old nick, Notting Hill Police Station. And her old boss, Marc Lamb, who was one of the best officers she knew.

Not her job, she repeated silently. Not her shout. No one would expect her to do anything more than she'd done today. But the images came back to her—Jess, dancing, his face lit with concentration and with the joy that came from knowing his own power. The photo on Reagan's bulletin board of the two of them, her arm thrown over his shoulders, both laughing silly buggers into the camera. Reagan Keating had loved Jess. Gemma was as sure of that as she was of anything. And what if, just what if, Jess was right?

When Kincaid walked back into the waiting area, Tom Faith and Diane Childs were standing talking to a woman in a well-cut charcoal suit. He didn't recognize her until she turned and held out a hand in greeting.

"Detective Superintendent Kincaid," she said. "I've just been checking on your guv'nor here." It was Evelyn Trent, deputy assistant commissioner of Specialist Operations, and he hadn't known that she even knew his name.

He shook her hand. "Ma'am." She was a handsome woman in her fifties—or so he guessed—fine-boned, with fair skin and sleekly cut platinum hair. He'd seen her speak on command courses and at large briefings and had been impressed.

"Assistant Commissioner Neville stopped by this morning," said Diane with a strained smile.

Kincaid understood then. The big brass—Trent, and Sir Richard Neville, the AC Crime, who commanded both Denis Childs and Kincaid directly, both paying their respects to an injured officer and his wife. They thought Denis was going to die.

"Commissioner Neville always spoke so highly of your husband, Mrs. Childs," said Trent. "A fine officer, one of the best."

A rush of anger made Kincaid fight to keep his voice level. "Yes. One of the best. And he will continue to be so."

Tom Faith gave a quick nod of agreement. "We all know Denis Childs is too stubborn to give up."

Had Denis been too stubborn for his own good? Kincaid suddenly felt he couldn't stay in the claustrophobic waiting room a moment longer. He apologized to Diane Childs, who said, "Of course, you must go. Denis will appreciate your taking so much time from your family on a Sunday." She, too, emphasized the present tense, and her smile was almost conspiratorial. Realizing that he liked her very much, Kincaid gave her a quick hug, then took his leave of the senior officers.

Once he was out of the building he found it easier to breathe. As he walked to the hospital car park, he went round and round the same series of events.

Denis Childs had been worried enough about something—or someone—that he had sent Kincaid an anonymous text on what must have been a burner phone, setting up a meeting in a place where neither of them was known. Once there, he'd been his usual cagey self, but had warned Kincaid against some shadowy people within the force and told him not to meddle in things he didn't understand. A few minutes later, he had been brutally assaulted.

It was wrong, all wrong, just like Ryan Marsh's death.

A roaring noise he'd been half ignoring grew louder. Looking up, his saw the distinctive red of the air ambulance as the helicopter descended towards the rooftop landing pad. Perhaps at that very moment someone else's life hung in the balance. Denis Childs had been given a chance. Ryan Marsh had had none.

Kincaid stopped, watching the helicopter set down, his mind only half engaged with the scene before him. One death, one attack that might yet prove fatal. What would happen next? Was he at risk? Was Gemma?

He had to get to the bottom of this, and he was beginning to believe that he had to start with the death of Ryan Marsh. But he needed help, and he didn't know where to turn or who he could trust.

The helicopter settled like a great brooding bird, its blades still. Kincaid wondered if whoever had arrived from the air would leave via the morgue.

The morgue.

Of course. He was an idiot not to have seen it.

He knew exactly who could help him, and exactly what he would ask.

CHAPTER SEVEN

May 1994

Someone was smoking a joint. That was always a ticklish situation at these little get-togethers. Most of them smoked hand-rolled cigarettes, and no one wanted to play the narc and give it the "So, who is it, then?" But the May night was unseasonably warm and the windows of the first-floor flat in Earl's Court were open to catch any breath of breeze. All they needed was for a neighbor or a passerby to report them.

While it was certainly not condoned, a blind eye was turned to minor drug use—they were, after all, supposed to stay in character, even here. But the lot of them getting arrested for something as petty as possession of a little weed would not go over well with the brass.

Not that any of them were drug dealers, mind you, that wasn't the mission. But they were rebels—anarchists, some of them—

and a little of this and a little of that came with the territory. Most of them didn't let it go further. At least as far as he knew.

He wondered if there was a snitch among them tonight. There was something about Mickey, the newest recruit, that rubbed him up the wrong way. The man had a bland, freckled face and hair like a puff of duck's down, and he was always bloody smiling.

They were an odd bunch, no doubt about it. Less than a dozen men—and at the moment, two women, although Sheila and Lynn hadn't shown up yet tonight—scruffy and earnest, they were Special Branch's darlings. And they were professional liars, the lot of them. They grew their hair—or shaved it, if their targets were skinhead groups. Thank God he hadn't had to do that—he'd look like André the Giant.

They changed their names. They spent one night a week at home with their families, and the rest living their cover lives, invented with histories and exit strategies that would have done Tolstoy proud.

But every Wednesday night they met in this run-down flat behind Earl's Court tube station, where the floor vibrated with the rumble of the trains beneath them. It was "An opportunity to share and de-stress," supposedly, but they were expected to stay in persona, even with their fellow undercover officers. It made for some strange conversations, and was anything but de-stressing. Nor was it comfortable. The ratty sofa and chairs had once been brown, the tiny kitchen didn't bear thinking about, and someone had hung a biohazard sign on the door to the toilet, which wasn't far from the truth. It might be safe but it wasn't much of a house, he thought, and smiled a little at his own lame humor.

"What's so funny, mate?" asked Mickey. "Want to share it with us?"

So he was watching, the little bugger, but for whom? His handler? If that were the case it would mean that somebody, somewhere up the ranks, didn't trust him. Not good news. "Not anything you'd understand, Mickey, lad," *he said easily, and saw the man's painful flush.*

"Fuck you," *Mickey countered, with his usual originality.*

The exchange drew a few looks. Jim Evans, a big, bald bloke from Essex, laughed and said to Mickey, "Have another beer, man. Chill, you know?" *The talk went back to murmurs, and Jim pulled another Carlsberg out of a paper sack, passing it to the man beside him, Dylan West.*

Dylan West, a poser if ever there was one. Tall and thin, with dark, brooding eyes that made women think he was deep, and an ingrained air of superiority. They'd been at the academy together. He hadn't liked him then and he liked him even less now. Trust the wanker to pick a name straight out of a bodice ripper.

There was a jaunty rap at the door and Jim jumped up to open it. "Sorry we're late to the party, boys," *said Sheila, holding up a bottle of wine in each hand.* "But I'm sure we'll make up for it," *she added, grinning as she sashayed into the room, followed by Lynn.*

Sheila was always in the lead. With her combat boots, short skirt, and the T-shirt hugging her small but obviously bra-less breasts, she fit the part, except that no one knew exactly what part that was. If they all walked a fine line between staying in character but not talking about their specific assignments, Sheila never crossed it. He sometimes wondered if she was playing a part at all. If so, it was as natural for her as breathing. And he wondered if Lynn minded.

He knew Lynn's brief because they'd begun at the same time and she'd confided in him. She'd been given a secretarial job at British Gas, then instructed to hang about on the fringes of a back-to-the-earth eco group, voicing timid doubts about the morality of her employer. He didn't think that in reality there was anything mousy about Lynn at all, but she managed to inhabit her character just as convincingly as Sheila did hers.

"It's about time things got interesting around here," said Mickey with an obvious leer, and someone else gave a wolf whistle. The temperature seemed to have gone up in the room right along with the level of testosterone. The atmosphere in the room had changed—he could feel it.

This whole thing was a very bad idea, he thought, looking round the room as wine was poured into paper cups and more cigarettes were lit. Someone turned up the sound on the cheap boom box on the coffee table and Aerosmith's "Livin' on the Edge" blared out.

He wondered that no one else could sense disaster in the air.

Monday morning, Melody was awakened by the light from the flat's east windows. She opened her eyes, squinted at the brightness, and closed them again. She lay still for a moment, trying to hold on to snatches of a pleasant dream, but it was gone. Oh, well, it had been nice while it lasted . . . There had been dancing in it somewhere, something she never did. With a little sigh of regret, she stretched and opened her eyes again, scooping her mobile from the coffee table to check the time. It was 6 A.M. She'd slept for twelve hours. And if she'd stayed on the sofa again, at least this time she'd had a pillow and a duvet, and there was an empty cup of hot chocolate on the coffee table rather than an empty bottle of wine.

Having left the café yesterday with a mumbled excuse to Hazel, she'd blindly set off walking, taking great gulps of air like a winded runner. She couldn't let herself think about Ryan. She couldn't let herself picture his blue eyes the way she'd first seen them in his smoke-smudged face. They'd gone into the fire at St. Pancras together, three months ago, and they'd both survived. And now he was gone.

Walking faster, she fought the nausea, concentrating on breathe in, breathe out. Slowing at last, she'd found herself outside High Street Kensington tube station. What the hell was wrong with her? She rubbed her palms against her cheeks.

She needed to get to Oxford Street. She'd promised Andy, before he left, that she'd look in on the cat, but she still felt too shaky to drive. Not to mention that it nearly required an act of God to find a parking spot near Andy's flat in Hanway Place. The tube, then, she'd decided, glad it was Sunday because she knew she couldn't have borne the weekday crush.

Bert, Andy's big ginger cat, had been happy to see her, butting against her ankles and purring madly. After checking his food, water, and litter tray, she sat down on the futon and lifted him into her lap. But the cat soon tired of the attention and stalked to the other end of the futon, settling down to groom his paws with great deliberation. Melody hadn't grown up with cats and it had taken some adjustment for her to learn that Bert's sudden rebuffs weren't personal.

They'd had dogs in the country house, a succession of spaniels and retrievers, but cats had been strictly relegated to the stables. "I should think you'd be glad of the company," she said aloud, but Bert flicked his tail and gave her a glint from his golden eyes.

Restless, she stood and roamed the flat, touching Andy's guitars, straightening posters, brushing the dust from the top of the turntable cover. She'd stayed here often when Andy was just out and about, but now she felt awkward, out of place. She'd slept here, too, for a few months more often than she did at home. A glance at the futon made her think of it open, the covers rumpled, and she felt hollow with sudden, fierce desire. Time to go.

Scribbling a note for the neighbor who was looking after Bert, she let herself out with a last long look round the flat, wondering if she would see it quite that way again.

Back in Kensington, she'd hurried past her parents' town house to retrieve her car, then driven the short distance to her flat just north of Notting Hill Gate. Her father owned this flat in the 1930s mansion block. Her living here had been their compromise when she took the job—a job her parents didn't approve of—with the police. They'd wanted to feel that she was at least living some-place safe. Melody had never particularly liked the flat, never in-vited anyone there, and had done nothing to make it seem as if it belonged to her. But suddenly she'd wanted nothing more than to shut herself in and lock out everything and everyone else . . .

Enough, she thought now. What good had running away done, other than getting her a decent night's sleep? She sat up and threw off the duvet. How humiliated would she be if anyone learned how she'd behaved yesterday? Hopefully Hazel wouldn't have said anything to Gemma.

She was fine, just fine. She'd only needed a rest, and a fresh start.

A run and a shower later, she put on her best red skirt and red silk blouse. No dark suits today. She was going to start as she meant to go on. Bold. No nonsense.

But before putting her mobile in her bag she checked for missed calls. She was early, but that didn't mean that something important couldn't have come in from work. There were no new calls. Nor had there been anything last night from Andy, or Doug, or Gemma. Shrugging, she popped the phone in her bag and let herself out of the flat. Why had she thought she needed any of them?

Melody walked out of the building with a deliberate attitude to her step, then stopped short. A late-model, gun-metal-gray Mercedes sedan idled against the curb. Through the tinted windows she made out her father, using the steering wheel as a prop for a folded newspaper. He was working the Times crossword. As he did every morning, in ink. He timed himself. He was bloody fast and seldom wrong. She'd always thought it odd that Ivan didn't play chess, but he claimed he had no patience waiting for someone else to make a move.

Glancing up, he saw her, put down the paper, opened the door, and stepped out. Ivan Talbot was dressed for work, early as it was, in a perfectly tailored Saville Row suit a shade lighter than his car. His well-barbered fair hair gleamed in the sun and Melody noticed that the silver was definitely overtaking the blond. An elegant man, her father, and a powerful one. Certainly a man not to be taken lightly when he had a mission.

"What are you doing here, Dad?" Melody eyed him warily.

Ivan kissed her on the cheek and she caught the spicy scent of his cologne. "You look bright as a poppy this morning."

She stepped back. "Dad."

"Considerably better than yesterday, I must say. You worried your mother. She asked me to check on you."

Worrying her mother was a cardinal sin in her father's eyes. "I'm sorry. I wasn't . . . feeling well. A bug or something. I'll ring her today."

Ivan regarded her, his face unreadable. Passersby parted around them and fleetingly Melody wondered what they must think. The well-off older man, the car, the younger woman. But Londoners were not a curious lot as a rule, and no one gave them a second glance.

Nodding as if that were settled, Ivan said, "You'd best do that. But I thought you might like an update on your chief super."

"He's not my—" she began, but the automatic protest died on her lips. "What? Is he—"

"Stable. But not conscious. And a little bird said that his wallet and phone were on him when he was found."

"How do you—" Melody stopped. There was no point in asking. Her father had more snitches than the Met.

"So if he was mugged, they were interrupted," Ivan continued.

"You don't think so." Melody frowned. "You think he was . . . attacked? But why?"

Ivan shrugged. "Random viciousness, maybe. But there have been rumors about Denis Childs for years."

"What rumors?" Melody managed to say around the cold knot that was forming in her chest.

"Oh, a checkered past. Friends in the wrong places. You know the sort of thing." He paused, as if considering his words. "I'm just wondering if maybe something caught up with the elusive Detective Chief Superintendent Childs."

Charlotte tugged hard on Gemma's hand and came to a dead stop in the middle of the pavement. "Mummy, I don't want Oliver to go live with somebody else."

"Lovey, Oliver isn't going anywhere. Remember, we talked about that?" That was an understatement, as they'd had the same conversation a dozen times since yesterday, and Gemma was struggling to hold on to her patience. She was late getting Charlotte to her school near Pembridge Gardens because all the kids had been cranky and uncooperative that morning, and Duncan, whose day it was to do the school runs, had announced he wanted to go into Holborn early. "You're going to see Oliver in just a minute, if we hurry," she said, determinedly cheerful.

But Charlotte was not going to be jollied. She tucked her head into Gemma's shoulder and wrapped her legs around Gemma's waist, clinging like a limpet and beginning to sniffle. "I don't want to go to school."

"I'm sorry, love, but sometimes we have to do things we don't want to do," said Gemma, and instantly hated herself for it. Of course it was true, but no one knew that better than Charlotte.

Charlotte had come home from the Williamses' distraught, and Gemma knew she couldn't have helped overhearing talk about Reagan Keating's death. For Charlotte, her parents' deaths had meant the end of everything that was familiar, and a new home, a new family. She'd obviously translated that into worry over losing Oliver.

"I don't want to," Charlotte wailed, the sniffles threatening to turn into sobs. "I want to go home. With you."

Just then, the town house door opened and the headmistress herself stood there waiting for them with a smile. "Now, Miss Charlotte," she said briskly, taking Charlotte from Gemma's arms. "We have some special treats this morning you don't want to miss. You can't have a treat if you're crying, can you?" Over Charlotte's head, she mouthed, "I heard. Go." She made a walking motion with her fingers. "Wave at Mummy, now," she instructed Charlotte, and as soon as Charlotte had given Gemma a teary salute, she stepped inside and closed the door smartly behind them.

Gemma stood for a moment, feeling ridiculously bereft, then shook her head and started back to the car. Of course Charlotte would be fine, and maybe if she was in charge of hordes of under fives every day, she'd have Miss Jane's knack with them. She pulled up her shoulder bag and started for the car.

But the removal of one problem allowed her mind to go back to the other, nagging worry—Duncan. When he'd come home from the London yesterday afternoon he'd only given her the bare details of his visit, then he'd been silent as a tomb the rest of the evening. She'd have put that down to simple distress over the condition of a friend, except that he'd admitted that he hadn't mentioned that he'd met with Denis.

"You haven't told anyone?" he'd said sharply when she'd brought it up.

"No. Why didn't you tell Chief Superintendent Faith?" she'd asked, frowning.

"Let's just keep it to ourselves for the moment, okay?" had been his oblique answer.

She hadn't pushed him. She knew he was keeping secrets, and she intended to make him level with her. But she needed some time alone with him, away from the kids.

Her phone rang. Juggling her keys, she pulled her mobile from her bag and glanced at the screen. It was Marc Lamb, her former boss at Notting Hill nick. And he was calling on his personal phone.

Gemma felt a rush of dismay. She'd meant to call Lamb, but in the chaos of Monday morning with an upset child it had slipped her mind.

"Sir," she answered a little breathlessly. "James here."

"Gemma. Have you got a moment?"

Leaning against her car, she said, "Of course, sir. I was just going to ri—"

Lamb didn't give her a chance to finish. "I had a call yesterday from Bill Williams," he said. "You know him, I believe." Lamb's tone made it clear it was not a question.

"Yes, sir. But I didn't realize you did."

"Williams is very involved with community safety initiatives. Ours paths cross," he said drily. And money talks, he might have added. "I understand you had some contact with the family and the employer of the girl who was found in Cornwall Gardens on Saturday," Lamb continued.

"Yes, sir." Gemma felt sure she was about to get a bollocking for interfering in an active case. "Sir, I was only there to offer MacKenzie Williams a bit of moral support."

"Yes, quite," said Lamb. "Mr. Williams is very concerned that the police are using every resource to investigate the girl's death. I've just rung the officer in charge at Kensington. The postmortem results should be in this morning, but in the meantime, she'd like you to stop in and have a word."

"Me? But, sir, I have to get to Brix—"

"DI Boatman asked for you specifically when I told her you had a connection."

"But I don't—"

"As did Bill Williams," Lamb said with finality, but Gemma hardly heard him.

"Kerry Boatman?" she said, frowning. "I know her."

"So she said. She's expecting you."

Kincaid needed some time to think without the distraction of driving in Monday-morning traffic. The clamor and bustle of Whitechapel Road did nothing to clear his mind, and when he neared his destination he was no closer to being sure he was doing the right thing. But as he came into the hospital precinct, he saw the helicopter on its pad, a blaze of red against the city's morning haze. The sight of it once again gave him an odd sort of comfort. At least it wasn't out on a crash mission at the moment. Maybe that was a good omen.

Except for the angle of the light, everything looked just as it had the previous afternoon. But this morning he was going nowhere near Denis Childs's critical care ward. He'd asked Diane to ring him if there was any change, but he didn't want to be seen visiting again. The less visible the connection between him and Denis, the better.

Today, rather than going up to the care wards, his route took him down to the lowest regions of the hospital, and as the lift dinged open at the mortuary level he wondered if he was too early.

He should have known better. Rashid Kaleem was one of the Home Office forensic pathologists serving central London, and had to fit in postmortems and reports between calls to the scenes of suspicious deaths. This morning Kincaid was in luck. The doctor was in.

When Kincaid rapped on the open office door, Rashid looked up from tapping on his keyboard, his eyes widening in surprise. "Duncan. You're a sight for sore eyes, mate. What are you doing here?"

"Hoping to see you."

Rashid stood and came round his desk to shake Kincaid's hand. "You're always welcome in my dungeon," he said with a grin, his teeth white against his light brown skin.

Clearing a stack of papers from the spare chair, Rashid gestured for Kincaid to sit. It had become a joke between them, the state of Rashid's office. "One of these days, they'll find your shriveled body buried beneath mountains of books and paper," Kincaid said. "I thought we were in the digital age, anyway," he added with a wave at Rashid's workstation, which was—at least what Kincaid could see of it—certainly state of the art.

"It's my security blanket, this stuff." Rashid gave a moldy-looking stack of books a fond pat as he returned to his chair. "I like things that can't vanish without a trace. And not everything is on the Internet, believe it or not. Sometimes the old anatomy books are the best."

Kincaid thought he might prefer things that did vanish without a trace—like any record of this visit. He pulled the lapels of his jacket a little closer as he took his seat, having refused Rashid's offer of coffee. It was always cold in here, and Rashid never wore anything other than a T-shirt, usually with a gruesome pathologist cartoon on the front.

"So, not a social call, I take it, as nice as it is to see you bright and early on a Monday morning," Rashid said. "Is this about the Camden shooting? I thought that was pretty cut and dried."

"Not about that one, no. And not a social call, exactly, but not on the record, either." Kincaid took a breath, wondering if he was jumping off a cliff, then went on. "There was another shooting, one that looked similar. In March, in Hackney. I think it went down as a suicide. The victim's name was Ryan Marsh. Was it yours?"

Rashid frowned for a moment, then shook his head. "No. I'd remember."

"Good," Kincaid said, feeling a surge of relief. "I think," he added.

Rashid's frown deepened. "It wasn't your case, or you'd know who the pathologist was. But why haven't you just looked it up?"

"Because I didn't want to leave bread crumbs."

They stared at each other for a moment, then Rashid nodded, once. "And you thought I might look up this case?"

"In the normal course of things. Yes. Perhaps comparing a similar shooting."

"Like the one in Camden? That wasn't a suicide." Rashid raised an eyebrow almost to his gelled black hair. "But then you said 'went down as a suicide,' didn't you? So, you don't want to be seen looking into it, but you think the determination was a wrong call. Why?"

Kincaid laced his fingers together to keep them still. "I knew Ryan Marsh. He was an undercover cop who'd gone off the grid because he thought he was in danger. I convinced him he was safe."

"Bloody hell," said Rashid, when the import had sunk in. "You don't think he would have killed himself?"

"He was working on an exit strategy, taking his family abroad. He had two little girls. He went back to his cover flat to pick up a few things. He never walked out."

"Do you have any supporting evidence?" Rashid was all business.

Kincaid shifted in his chair, his throat suddenly dry. "I was going to see him that night. I walked in on the scene." He shook his head. "Something wasn't right, but I can't tell you what it was. The uniforms were already there, but not the detectives. I didn't hang about."

Picking up a pen, Rashid began to doodle, drawing interconnecting circles on a scrap of paper. "You didn't want to be associated with the victim? I'm beginning to get that."

"No," Kincaid agreed with feeling, "I did not."

"And you think someone on the force might have been"—Rashid paused, as if choosing his words—"involved?"

"I don't know anything for certain. Maybe Marsh was depressed, more desperate than we realized. Maybe he did shoot himself." Kincaid grimaced at the memory. "Maybe the determination was totally clean. But I can't look at the file. Because if I'm right—"

"You're buggered," Rashid confirmed with a nod, then gave him a sharp look. "You said 'we.' Who else knew about this?"

Kincaid hesitated. Perhaps he'd already endangered himself by confiding in Rashid—did he dare bring the others into it? But Rashid would guess, and if he were going to trust him, he'd better go the full Monty. "Doug and Melody. And Gemma."

"Do they know you're talking to me?"

"No. And I don't want them to. I never told them I'd seen him."

He'd driven around London for hours that night, sickened and shocked, struggling to come up with a way to explain to the others how he knew Ryan was dead. At last he'd said that Ryan's wife, Christie, had called him with the news, and no one had questioned it.

"You should tell them." Rashid waggled a finger at him. "Playing the hero could get you into big trouble."

"I'm not—I don't want them—the more they know the more danger they could be in."

"Well, thanks for that," Rashid said, with a return of his grin.

Kincaid wasn't amused. "I don't want to put you in danger, either, Rashid. I can walk out of here right now and you can pretend you never saw me."

"Right." Rashid turned the scrap of paper towards him and Kincaid saw that one of the doodled faces had morphed into a cat with a huge, toothy smile. "Pathologists are insatiably curious. That's why we do it, most of us. Although maybe there are some who just like really bad smells and have no people skills."

This time Kincaid couldn't stop a smile. "True. But, seriously, Rashid—"

"You said Marsh thought he was in danger. Who—or what—was he afraid of?"

"I don't know. That's the thing. He'd infiltrated the protest group involved in the St. Pancras grenade blast." Rashid had been the pathologist on call and it had been a nasty death. "Ryan thought that grenade was meant for him, but he would never say why."

Rashid drew a few more interconnected circles, frowning. "It seems to me you don't know very much. Why get involved?"

Kincaid swallowed, then said as evenly as he could, "Because he said he was in danger and I didn't take him seriously."

"What could you have done if you had?"

Shrugging, Kincaid shifted again. "I don't know. But that doesn't make it all right."

"No. Of course not. But why dig this up now, after two months?"

"Because night before last, someone attacked Denis Childs and left him for dead."

"What?" Rashid looked up, startled, his pen still. "Chief Superintendent Childs? Is he okay?"

"No. He's in a coma. Blunt-force injury to the brain."

Rashid grimaced. "You're right. Not good. But what does he have to do with your dead copper?"

"I don't know," Kincaid admitted. "But Denis was afraid, just like Ryan. He said there were people in the force who wished him ill." Kincaid wasn't going to say Denis had been on the way home from meeting him, even to Rashid.

Rashid studied him for a long moment, his handsome face creased in a frown. "I've never known you to be fanciful," he said at last. "And I would hate for anything to happen to you. I'll look up your case. But you should tell Gemma what you told me. And"—he cut off Kincaid's protest with a wave of his pen—"you should talk to someone outside the Met. Surely there's someone you can trust."

CHAPTER EIGHT

It had taken half an hour in the shower with the water as hot as he could stand to get Doug Cullen moving without groaning. Even with his sore muscles eased a bit, his ankle was so tender he was tempted to put on the hated boot cast.

Examining himself critically in the mirror as he shaved, he realized that he was sunburned, too. The splash of aftershave stung his cheeks and his neck was red as beetroot. He'd spent all his Sunday afternoon digging in the garden, working with a sort of manic intensity, not stopping until the sun was easing towards the top of the garden wall and his shoulder muscles simply refused to lift the spade one more time.

He now had a back garden ringed by perfectly turned beds, and no idea what to plant in them.

When he'd at last cleaned himself up enough to pop out for a takeaway, he'd almost stumbled over the offering outside his front door. The cups of tea had long gone cold and scummy, and Melody's note, he guessed, had been tugged by the breeze until it was anchored only by a corner. He read it, frowning, then pulled his mobile from the pocket of his jeans.

It was switched off. He'd forgotten to turn it on when he'd come in from the river. Bugger.

Carefully, he'd unfolded the tattered garden plan that had been tucked beneath Melody's note.

She must have thought him an absolute prat, refusing to answer her knock. And he had been, to tell the truth. He'd eased the kink in his shoulder, hesitating with his finger poised over the phone keypad.

In the end, too exhausted to think of a decent apology, he'd pocketed his phone again and left the call for the morrow, but now, as he rode the tube into work, he was no further forward. He didn't look forward to Monday mornings at the Yard these days, but today it was a relief to have a distraction from worrying about Melody.

As soon as he entered the CID floor, however, he felt something slightly off. There seemed a suppressed air of tension, and when one of the department secretaries hurried by with an armful of files, she glanced up and then away, not meeting his eyes.

"Um, excuse me?" Doug said, struggling to think of her name.

She paused and turned back to him, a reluctant expression on her dark, round face.

It wasn't until he tried on a smile that he remembered the sunburn. Maybe that's why she was staring at him with what looked like dismay. "Where's the fire?" he asked.

"Sorry?" She looked at him blankly.

"I mean, you seemed in a bit of a rush."

"Oh. No, it's just the AC wants these and he's in a mood. Everyone is, with the news about Detective Chief Superintendent Childs."

"What? What news?"

"I thought you'd know. It was in this morning's *Chronicle*." She lowered her voice and gave a conspiratorial glance round. "Someone attacked him on Saturday night. He's in hospital. Dying, the rumor is." Tightening her grip on her files, she added, "I've got to go or the AC will kill me."

Doug watched as she hurried off down the corridor. The chief? Dying? He couldn't believe it. Slowly, he made his way to Chief Superintendent Slater's office. Slater was his nominal boss, since Kincaid had been transferred to Holborn, and Doug disliked him intensely.

"Sir," he said, tapping on Slater's door just as Slater was hanging up his phone. "I just heard—is it true about Chief Super Childs?"

"If you mean that some bugger jumped him in the bloody churchyard, yes."

"But I heard that he was—"

"Dying?" Slater shook his head. "Induced coma. According to the AC." An unfamiliar expression crossed Slater's heavy face. "In any case, he won't be coming back to the Yard anytime soon, which means more work for the rest of us. So I suggest we get on with it."

Doug took the dismissal with a nod. When he was out of sight of Slater's office, he took out his mobile. Did Kincaid know? He dialed Kincaid's number but it went to voice mail, as had all his calls the last few weeks. Damn the man. What was wrong with him?

He rang off without leaving a message. Then he punched Melody's number without a thought for his apology.

The last time Gemma had seen Kerry Boatman, Boatman had been a detective inspector at Lucan Place Police Station in Chelsea. But Lucan Place was gone, sold off for its real estate value by the Met. Boatman was now at Kensington, the divisional station, and she had advanced to DCI. The station, a solid, utilitarian, redbrick block near the top of Earl's Court Road, had none of the charm of Victorian Lucan Place.

Gemma entered through the front doors. It had been some time since she'd seen the public side of a police station, and she was always a little amused by how innocuous police stations seemed. Like most modern London stations, from the lobby Kensington Police Station could have been mistaken for any ordinary business or government office—at least until you noticed the blue uniform blouses of the two female officers behind the glassed-in reception area. And assuming you didn't know that the glass was bulletproof.

When Gemma had introduced herself at reception, one of the officers made a call, then buzzed her in and escorted her up to DCI Boatman's office.

Boatman stood to greet her, coming round her desk to shake Gemma's hand. She looked much as she had when Gemma had last seen her, a small, slightly stocky woman with a friendly smile. Her dark hair was a bit longer, and there were a few threads of gray at the temples, but Gemma would have sworn she was wearing the exact same navy suit.

"Thank you for coming," said Boatman with a smile. "Would you like something? Tea? A coffee?"

The office was spacious, and there was a blur of green treetops visible beyond the window. Kerry Boatman had done well for herself. "Coffee would be great," Gemma answered. "Thanks."

As Gemma took the proffered chair, Boatman stepped out the door and murmured a request to a uniformed officer. Then she returned to her desk and leaned against its front edge, arms casually folded. "How are you?" she asked. "Family doing well? You have boys, if I remember."

Gemma nodded. "That's right. Two. And a daughter now as well. She's three."

"Oh, congratulations." Boatman smiled but looked a bit puzzled, and Gemma guessed she was wondering how Gemma had managed to acquire a three-year-old since they'd worked together last year.

"Foster daughter," Gemma explained. "You'll know about girls, I expect," she added, remembering the two grinning girls in the photos on Boatman's desk at Lucan Place.

"For my sins, yes. They're ten and twelve now. Frightening how fast they grow up." Boatman appeared very practiced at putting people at ease, but her deliberate manner had the opposite effect on Gemma. She sensed she was being played and she didn't like it.

There was a tap on the door and the uniformed PC brought in a coffee tray with all the accoutrements. When Boatman had done the honors, Gemma took a sip and raised an eyebrow in appreciation. "Proper coffee. That's lovely."

"I'd never get through the day, otherwise." Boatman took her cup and returned to her chair, an obvious signal that it was time to get down to business. "About this nanny in the garden," she said. "Chief Superintendent Lamb rang up first thing this morning, wanting a progress report." The slight narrowing of Boatman's eyes made Gemma think she didn't appreciate being manipulated any more than Gemma.

"It seems that the girl had some very well-connected friends," Boatman went on. "And that you knew her. When I heard your name I thought you might have some insight on events."

"I didn't actually know her," Gemma corrected. "She looked after a friend's son occasionally, and she also did some modeling for her catalog."

"So you never actually met Reagan Keating?"

Shaking her head, Gemma said, "No. But MacKenzie Williams was very upset by the news. She asked me to go with her to the Cusicks'. I thought it was the least I could do."

"Quite right, although I doubt it was a pleasant visit. Who did you speak to?" Boatman settled back in her chair, cradling her coffee cup, as if she had all the time in the world for a friendly gossip.

"Nita Cusick, Reagan's employer, and Reagan Keating's mum, Gwen." Gemma didn't mention Jess.

Boatman sipped her coffee and stared into space for a moment, obviously thinking. When she looked back at Gemma, her gray eyes were razor sharp. "Did either of them know you were a police officer?"

"It didn't come up. I've no idea if MacKenzie had mentioned it earlier. I was there as a friend."

"Of course." Boatman held up a hand in an apologetic gesture. "I understand. I just thought you might have got a little less . . . guarded . . . impression of the situation than we might, officially. You know how barriers go up when people know they're talking to the police. Even the most blameless souls start thinking about the parking ticket they forgot to pay."

Gemma smiled. "Exactly what situation are we talking about here?" she asked. "Gwen Keating said the officer she spoke to suggested that Reagan's death was drug or alcohol related. Is that true?"

"Did he? Damn," Boatman added under her breath, looking irritated. "Sergeant Enright is a clod with no common sense and fewer people skills. He had no business sharing assumptions with a shocked mother." Before Gemma could remind her that she hadn't answered her question, Boatman added, "Mrs. Cusick and the mother, how did they take the suggestion that the girl's death might be down to drugs or alcohol?"

"About as well as you can imagine. The mother was adamant that her daughter would never have overdosed on either. So was Mrs. Cusick." Gemma set her coffee cup down on the desk with a click. "Look, DCI Boatman, what's going on here? I was there as a guest. I can't offer you any kind of a professional opinion on Reagan Keating's habits."

"It's Kerry, Gemma. I thought we were on a first-name basis." When Gemma didn't respond, Boatman sighed and added, "Apparently, Mrs. Keating and Mrs. Cusick were at least partly correct. I've had the preliminary report from the pathologist. According to the initial tests, her blood alcohol level was quite high."

"But, you just said they were correct." Gemma was surprised as well as puzzled. She realized she'd been putting more weight on the assurances from MacKenzie, Nita, and Gwen Keating than perhaps she ought. "I don't understand."

"Nor do I. The pathologist says it's unlikely the girl's alcohol level was high enough to kill her. She did, however, find some other indications of foul play. What, I don't know yet." Boatman raised a hand before Gemma could interrupt. "I was just on my way to the mortuary. I'd appreciate it if you'd come along."

The exterior of Holborn Police Station was as unwelcoming as ever, its glass and dull concrete facade not improved even by the bright May morning sun. As Kincaid climbed the front steps, he pulled his lanyard from his jacket pocket and slipped it on. Entering reception, he almost bumped into Chief Superintendent Faith coming out.

"Sir," he said automatically, then felt a little jolt of apprehension. Why was Faith leaving the building first thing in the morning? "Sir, is there . . . any news?"

"No, no change." Faith looked tired, the hollows under his cheekbones more pronounced than they had been yesterday. "I'm just going to check on Diane." Frowning, he seemed for the first time to focus on Kincaid. "Have you been to hospital already?"

For an instant, Kincaid wondered if someone had seen him at the London. But that was ridiculous. He'd gone nowhere near the critical care ward. "No, sir. Not since yesterday. I thought I might stop in later."

"Oh, right. Good man." Faith clapped Kincaid on the shoulder and turned back towards the doors. Only then did Kincaid notice the man behind him.

"Duncan. Good to see you." Nick Callery held out his hand and gave Kincaid's a firm shake.

Kincaid had worked with Callery, a DCI in the counterterrorism unit, while investigating the St. Pancras grenade death. It was the case that had led him to Ryan Marsh, but he'd never shared anything about Marsh with Callery or his unit. Callery wore what Kincaid thought of as his usual attire, a silvery gray suit that matched the color of his short silver hair. He was, Kincaid guessed, in his forties, with a trim, athlete's build, and his lightly tanned face was unlined.

"Yes, you, too," he responded, with more warmth than he felt. He'd found Callery a bit overbearing.

"I was sorry to hear about what happened to Denis Childs. I'd just stopped in to ask the chief here if he'd had any news. I understand you worked with Childs for some time."

"Yes. Yes, I did." That was as much as Kincaid found himself willing to say.

Callery didn't seem to find his abruptness odd. "Your friend," he went on, "the officer who responded to the grenade. Talbot, wasn't it? How is she?"

Kincaid hadn't expected Callery to remember Melody, much less to ask after her. "She's fine. I'll tell her you asked after her when I see her next." He noticed Callery had a small bandage on his left hand.

Following his glance, Callery smiled. "Kitchen accident. I'm a clumsy bastard. Good to see you. We must have a pint sometime." He nodded at Kincaid, then followed an impatient-looking Faith out the main doors. Watching the two men walk down the steps, Kincaid couldn't tell if they were leaving together. He shrugged and continued on his way up to CID.

His team were all in. Detective Sergeant Simon Gikas, his crime scene manager, was as usual hunched over his computer keyboard. Detective Inspector Jasmine Sidana, his second in command, was on the phone. And Detective Constable George Sweeney was, quite literally, twiddling his thumbs, with his feet propped up on the rubbish bin at the side of his desk. None of them had the air of being particularly busy, although the room hummed with the expected Monday-morning activity.

"Boss," said Gikas, looking up with a grin. "We were beginning to think you'd skived off for the day."

"You should be so lucky."

Ending her phone call, Sidana gave him a nod of greeting. "Boss."

If not as effusive a welcome as he'd got from Gikas, the nod was at least friendly. They'd come a good way since he'd started at Holborn back in February. Sidana had felt she'd deserved a promotion to DCI, along with the leadership of the team, and she'd resented him bitterly. Perhaps she still did, Kincaid thought, but they'd progressed to the point where she seemed willing to work with him civilly. She was still prickly and as starchy as her trademark white shirts, but she was a good officer. He'd come to like her and to value her insights on a case.

Sweeney, who seemed in no hurry to take his feet off the rubbish bin, was the thorn in his side. The man was arrogant and his work slipshod at best. Kincaid couldn't figure out how Sweeney had been promoted to detective constable, or placed on this team.

Before he could reprimand him, Kincaid's phone rang. His first thought was that it was news about Denis, but when he glanced at the caller ID he saw that it was his mother. He walked into his office and closed the door as he answered.

"Mum? What's up?" It wasn't like Rosemary Kincaid to ring him at work. "Are the kids okay?" He worried about his sister Juliet's two, especially Lally, who was only a few months older than Kit and had a talent for trouble.

"The children are fine," said Rosemary, and he heard a little tremor in his mother's warm voice. "It's your father, darling. I didn't want to worry you, but he's had a little . . . episode."

"An episode?" he repeated, not comprehending. "Mum, what are you talking about?"

"It was last night, late. He said his chest felt a bit odd. He didn't want to make a fuss—you know how your father is—and he was sure it was just indigestion. But it didn't go away. Finally, I made him ring Jim, and Jim admitted him to hospital right away."

Jim Strange was his family's GP as well as one of his parents' closest friends.

"Is he okay? Why didn't you call me?" Through the glass of his inner-office window, Kincaid saw Jasmine Sidana glance up at him and he made an effort to lower his voice. "Where is he now?"

"There was no point upsetting you last night," said Rosemary. "He's fine. He's just going to have to have a little procedure this afternoon. A stent, the doctor says."

"A stent? But that's—"

"Very routine these days, according to the cardiologist." Rosemary seemed to be making an attempt at her usual brisk manner, but the tremor was still there. "I'll ring you as soon as he's out of the theater," she added. "I promise, I—"

"No," Kincaid interrupted. "Mum, I'm coming up."

"Don't be silly, darling. I'm sure there's no need. You can't just leave work at the drop of a hat—"

"I'll see you in a couple of hours."

CHAPTER NINE

As she reached the Chelsea and Westminster Hospital in Fulham Road, Gemma was still trying to work out if she'd been asked or ordered to accompany Kerry Boatman. The Chelsea and Westminster had the best burn unit in London, and she'd become quite familiar with the hospital when their friend Tam Moran, Andy Monahan's manager, had been badly burned in the St. Pancras grenade fire.

The curved awning over the hospital's front entrance had always made her think of a bus stop, and there was Kerry, waiting for her beneath it as if this was any ordinary meeting on any ordinary spring day. Gemma had a moment to study the other woman, unobserved, as she waited to cross the road.

The pleasantly neutral expression Kerry had worn during their interview had been replaced by a frown. She glanced at her watch and checked her phone twice before looking up and spotting Gemma.

When Gemma reached her, she said without preamble, "Gemma, look, I'm sorry to have hijacked you on this. I didn't want to talk about it at the station, but I'm in a bit of a pinch here. My regular partner is out on maternity leave. I've got pressure from the brass to look into this, thanks to your posh friends"—Kerry softened the comment with a half smile—"and I've been assigned a sergeant who can't open his mouth without putting his foot in it. If the pathologist is right about the foul play, this case could turn into a real political balls-up."

"So you thought you'd make me the football?" Gemma said, eyebrows raised.

Kerry gave her a sheepish shrug. "Well, maybe a little. But I honestly thought I could use your help. And that you might have a personal interest in finding out what happened to this girl."

As she did. "Then let's see what we're dealing with, shall we?"

When they were led into the mortuary's glassed-in viewing room, the pathologist was sitting at a desk in the postmortem room itself. She was writing notes, her back to them, her straight black hair just brushing the shoulders of her scrubs and swinging a little when she moved. She must have heard their arrival because she turned just as Gemma said, "Kate?"

"Gemma!" Dr. Kate Ling stood and came towards the glass barrier, a smile on her face. It had been some time since Gemma had worked with her, but she thought Kate—who had always had the sort of delicate frame that made Gemma feel large-boned and awkward—looked thinner, and her face looked drawn. Kate's smile, however, seemed to reflect genuine pleasure.

"How are you?" asked Kate. "And the family?"

"Everyone's well. We haven't seen you in donkey's years. I thought perhaps you'd taken a post somewhere else."

Kate gave a little grimace. "I took some time off. My mum's been ill."

"Sorry to hear that," Gemma said. She'd have asked more but Kerry shifted beside her. Guessing the two weren't acquainted, she hurried to make the introductions. "Dr. Kate Ling, this is DCI Kerry Boatman."

"Nice to meet you," said Kerry, but Gemma could sense her irritation with the niceties. "I understand you've found some irregularities with our unexplained death," Kerry went on.

"You could say that," Kate answered. "Let's take a look." She slipped on her headset and a pair of gloves while they stepped right up to the glass. "I wanted you to see what I found on my external exam before I opened her up." Her voice was amplified now, as if she was in the room with them, and she gave Gemma a little sideways smile. No doubt she remembered occasions when Gemma had been a little squeamish.

When Kate lifted the sheet from the form on the nearest table, Gemma recognized the face she'd seen in photographs. She thought she'd been prepared for that, but still it shocked her to see the resemblance to the woman she'd met yesterday, Reagan Keating's mother, Gwen. It made Reagan, as the living, breathing person she had been, seem suddenly very real.

"My guess is that your young woman suffocated," Kate went on. "First, she has classic petechiae." She pulled back an eyelid with her gloved finger, but Gemma couldn't actually make out the tiny red dots in the eye caused by bleeding of the capillaries.

"You're sure she wasn't strangled?" asked Boatman.

"There are no marks on her throat. Of course it's possible that something may show up on the internal exam, but I'm inclined to doubt it." Kate glanced up at them. "There were trace fibers in her nose—fibers that match the skirt of her dress."

Gemma thought about it. "Couldn't she have wiped her nose with her skirt?"

"Hard enough to cut the inside of her lip with her tooth, and to leave bruising in the tissue on the inside of her mouth?" Kate shook her head. "I don't think so. There was another fiber caught on the edge of the same tooth, and there was a tiny spot of blood on the hem of her skirt."

"So you're thinking that someone held her own skirt over her nose and mouth? Any signs of a struggle?"

"There was a bit of grass under her fingernails, but no foreign tissue or fiber. There are other scenarios that might account for the cut and bruising in her mouth and the fibers in her nose. But that's not all I found. Look at this."

Kate folded back the sheet and pointed to faint purple marks on Reagan Keating's bare left shoulder. "Bruising. There's more on her right thigh."

Gemma tried to visualize the scene. "So you're suggesting someone knelt on top of her, holding her down while they smothered her with her own skirt?"

"Someone right-handed," Boatman put in thoughtfully. "Using their right knee and left hand to keep her down. But wouldn't that take a great deal of strength?"

"That would depend on a good many other factors."

"Including the girl's physical condition." Boatman frowned. "You said her blood alcohol was high. So she was drinking."

"That's an assumption. But, yes, according to the initial tests, I'd definitely say she would have been impaired. And of course we won't know about drugs until the tox screen comes back."

"Was she sexually assaulted?" asked Gemma.

"No. Although there were signs of fairly recent intercourse, but not immediately before she died."

"Still," mused Gemma, "she might have had an argument with a boyfriend." She was thinking of the blue-eyed blond in the photos on Reagan's corkboard.

Kate shrugged. "It's possible. But I can tell you that argument or no, whoever smothered her straightened her clothing and composed her body afterwards. She didn't lay herself out like a sleeping princess."

Kincaid stood on his own doorstep, the sound of the taxi's tires fading away in Ladbroke Road. This little part of London might have been a ghost city. Not a car moved in the silent streets. There was not even a dog walker or pram pusher to disturb the leafy peace. The air was filled with birdsong, and the trees in the big garden were coming into the full, ripe green of summer.

Fishing out his key, he unlocked the cherry red door and stepped inside. The house was even quieter than the street. Then Geordie gave a startled yip, as if he'd been awakened from a nap, and a moment later the dogs trotted into the hall, tails wagging and noses quivering. "Some use you'd be if I really was a burglar," he said, scratching Geordie behind the ears, and giving Tess a quick rub on her wiry head. The house felt odd, too, devoid of human presence but haunted by the smell of coffee and burnt toast.

He knew he'd left Gemma in the lurch that morning. He also knew that any irritation she harbored would vanish when he told her Hugh was ill. He'd meant to ring her as soon as he reached the house, but now found he didn't think he could cope with hearing her sympathy. Not yet, at least. He'd ring her from the car, once he was well on the way, once he'd had a little more time to get used to the idea.

With midday traffic, it shouldn't take him more than a couple of hours to reach southern Cheshire. His parents and his sister lived in the market town of Nantwich, but the nearest hospital was in Crewe, five miles away.

The dogs followed him upstairs as he went to throw a few things in an overnight bag. A clean shirt, his shaving kit, a warmer jacket. Just because it was balmy in London didn't mean it would be warm farther north. He stood for a moment, wondering what he'd forgotten, and felt the house settle around him. It was odd that the empty house made him feel the presence of Gemma and the children so strongly. It was as if their daily lives had left an imprint in the air, while he felt insubstantial.

His whole life seemed suddenly insubstantial, as if everything that mattered to him might vanish like smoke on the wind. He could not imagine his dad ill. He knew his parents were getting older, of course he did. But Hugh Kincaid had more energy than anyone he knew. Always full of the next project, the next enthusiasm.

His mum had said Hugh's heart problem was minor—perhaps he was letting his worry over Denis color his concern for his dad. That was one thing, at least, he could hope he was right about.

All the way into Brixton, Melody worried over whether to tell Gemma about her father's veiled hints concerning Denis Childs's past. Just what had Ivan been getting at? And why had there been no news from Gemma or Duncan?

She'd decided to take the tube, and on the walk up to the Notting Hill Gate station she'd stopped in a newsagent's and bought, not only the *Chronicle*, but all the major dailies. Thumbing through them on the train, she found brief mentions of the attack on Denis, but only the *Chronicle* had asked for information from witnesses.

By the time she reached Brixton, she'd decided to keep Ivan's innuendos to herself, at least for the time being. Heaven forbid she carried tales from Ivan that she might have to document to senior staff. She left the stack of papers on an empty seat and saw the other passengers reaching for them before she'd stepped off the train.

The police station was a short walk from the Underground station, north along Brixton Road past the Station Road Market. It was quiet on a Monday morning, most of the stalls shuttered, but it still looked cheerful in the bright sunshine. She passed a dreadlocked young man who glanced at her red outfit, then gave her an approving grin and murmured, "Sweet." The little encounter boosted her confidence and she walked into the police station a few minutes later still wearing a smile.

The smile, however, only lasted until she got to CID. There was no sign of Gemma, and their boss, Superintendent Krueger, wore an expression that promised a blistering for some unlucky peon. Krueger was on the phone. Ending the call, she glanced round the CID room, and when she saw Melody her frown made it clear that Melody was the one who was in for it.

"Sergeant." Krueger motioned Melody into her office. "In here." Krueger was a slender, dark-haired woman in her forties. Rumor had it she had a wicked sense of humor when she'd had a few drinks, but Melody had never seen it.

She closed the door with some trepidation. "Ma'am."

Krueger didn't sit. Not a good sign. "Your guv'nor, Sergeant, has somehow managed to get herself seconded to another case."

"Ma'am?" Melody had no idea what she was talking about.

"I've just had it from the chief super at Notting Hill. Something about having connections with the victim." Krueger made "connections" sound like a dirty word.

"Connections?" Melody repeated blankly. "What connections? What victim?" She heard herself, knew she sounded a stupid cow, but her mind had gone into overdrive. Was it someone they knew? Or did this have to do with Denis? But Notting Hill had no connection with Denis. And Denis wasn't—

Krueger interrupted the whirlwind of Melody's thoughts. "I can see that DI James has not seen fit to inform you of this development. Perhaps she'll fill you in when she decides to grace us with her presence. In the meantime, you're in charge."

Taking that as a dismissal, Melody said, "Ma'am," once more, then turned and escaped to her desk.

DS Shara MacNicols, the detective sergeant on their team, glanced from Melody to Krueger's door and rolled her eyes, muttering, "Warpath," under her breath.

"Do you know anything about this?" Melody whispered.

"Not a thing." Shara shook her head and beads on the ends of her tiny braids made a faint clicking sound as they bounced. They were blue today, Melody saw.

She tapped her computer to life and tried to look busy. Thank God their only active investigation was into the death of a homeless man whose body had been found in Battersea Park. The pathologist's report was in her inbox. Glancing through it, she took a little breath of relief. Malnutrition, hypothermia, kidney and liver failure from chronic alcoholism. Natural causes, then. Poor old bloke, but his demise was not something that required Gemma's immediate presence.

With a surreptitious glance at Krueger's office, she held her mobile below the level of her desk and pulled up Gemma's number. "What the hell is up, boss?" she typed. Then, "Where are you?"

There was no reply.

CHAPTER TEN

"I want to see the crime scene," Gemma said to Kerry Boatman as they left the mortuary.

"But I thought you were there yesterday." Kerry, who had been checking her phone, glanced up at Gemma with a frown.

"I was in the Cusicks' house. I didn't have any reason to go into the garden. I'd have looked like some sort of voyeur."

"Aren't we all, though," muttered Kerry absently, then she gave Gemma a sharp look. "What's this about the victim's boyfriend?"

"I saw a photo of him in Reagan's room. Her mother says his name is Hugo, but she doesn't know his last name. And she got the impression that Reagan had gone off him lately."

"So they argue and he kills her?" Kerry shrugged. "Possible. But he'd had to have had access to the garden."

"Isn't there a gate?"

"No. There's a heavy, locked door in a brick wall at the Ladbroke Grove end. It would take a ninja climber to get over it."

"Someone could have had a key," suggested Gemma.

"I suppose it's possible someone could have got hold of a key," Kerry agreed. "But I think it's much more likely our perpetrator was either a resident or someone who had access through one of the houses. I've got an appointment with the gardener in half an hour. We'll find out about the key."

Gemma heard the inclusive "we" and shook her head in protest. "But I've got to get to Brixton—"

"Not to worry. I had a chat with Chief Superintendent Lamb on the way over. By now, he's had a chat with your guv'nor."

"Bloody hell," said Gemma. Krueger would be having kittens. "You really have hijacked me."

"You could always say no."

"And get in Marc Lamb's bad graces?" Gemma could tell from Kerry's self-satisfied expression that she knew she had Gemma well and truly fixed.

They met Clive Glenn at the Ladbroke Grove end of Cornwall Gardens. It had grown warmer as the morning progressed and Gemma could feel the sun hot on her cheeks and the bridge of her nose. If this weather kept up, she was going to have to start wearing sunblock.

Clive Glenn was certainly tanned enough. He was also good looking in an American advert, outdoorsy way. In his late thirties or early forties, Gemma guessed, with hair and a short beard just beginning to gray. That he was fit was evident, given his jeans and tight T-shirt. But when he spoke, his accent was as posh as Melody Talbot's, and Gemma had to stop herself looking surprised.

The glint in his eye as they finished their introductions made her think he'd seen her slight start and was laughing at her.

He'd arrived before them and they found him leaning against the tail of a small truck parked near the garden entrance. The truck's bed was filled with equipment and bags of what looked like mulch.

The entrance itself was as Kerry had described it—a wooden door, painted a soft blue, and set in a high redbrick wall that stretched between the two houses on either side. It was impossible to see into the garden, and it would take a ladder or climbing equipment to get over the wall.

"This is the only entrance?" Gemma asked, sounding sharp even to herself. She wanted to wipe the amusement from Glenn's face. "What about the Kensington Park Road end?" she added. Of course she'd walked or driven past it often enough, but she couldn't remember ever noticing the garden, much less an entrance.

"It's an iron fence. Ten feet high, and grown over with very prickly Cecile Brunner roses. No gate." It seemed to Gemma that there was still a slight mockery in Glenn's voice, but if Kerry noticed it as well, she didn't react.

"So how do you get in this end, then?" said Kerry.

Glenn pulled a key from the pocket of his jeans. It was a tarnished brass lever lock and was nearly as long as his hand.

"Is there only one key?"

"This is the original," Glenn answered. "Mrs. A has a copy."

Gemma frowned. "Mrs. A?"

"Mrs. Armitage. She's the chair of the garden committee. It was Mrs. A who found your body, and let your people in and out."

"Right," said Kerry, as if she knew this, but the corners of her mouth were pinched and Gemma suspected she had not. "Let's have a look, then."

"Do you know Mrs. Armitage well?" Gemma asked as Glenn led them to the gate.

He shrugged. "I guess you could say she's my boss. She's all right. A bit fussy, but then most of the committee chairs are the same."

"You take care of more than one property?"

Glenn threw her that amused look over his shoulder as he fitted the key in the lock. "I'd hardly have a business if I didn't."

"But surely you can't do all that work yourself?"

"I'm a landscape designer, Sergeant. I hire contract labor for the big jobs. But I like doing the routine maintenance myself."

Gemma didn't bother correcting him on her rank, because they'd stepped through the gate onto an interior path. The pea gravel was inches thick and shifted like wet sand beneath their feet. If anyone had come in this way, they wouldn't have left usable prints.

Shrubs and the trunks of large trees blocked their view of the garden proper but golden sunlight filtered in from either side. The space felt secret and a little claustrophobic. Following Glenn and Kerry down the right-hand path, Gemma stepped out into the open and said, "Oh."

The view down a long expanse spread before them. The path on which they stood ran all the way round the perimeter, as well as into the garden's center where it outlined more formal beds. Thick-trunked, mature trees were scattered throughout the green turf at the nearer end, punctuated with banks of glowing rhododendrons.

There was no sign of crime scene tape.

"Where was she found, exactly?" Kerry asked, and Gemma realized for the first time that Kerry had not actually seen the body in situ. "This just landed on my desk this morning," she said to

Gemma, sounding defensive. "And I'm going to kill Enright," she added under her breath.

Clive Glenn led them to a particularly large plane tree at the edge of a sweep of lawn. A shed just large enough to hold gardening tools stood nearby. In the stronger light, Gemma could see the fine lines around his gray eyes and she revised her estimate of his age up by a few years. "She was under this tree," he said. "Just there." He pointed to a spot on the lawn side of the tree. "It was the weirdest thing I've ever seen." For the first time he sounded less than sure of himself.

"But you didn't find the body," said Boatman, glancing at her phone as if to check a note.

"No. It was Mrs. A. But I got here just after—before the police. The residents use the space quite a bit on Saturdays, and I like to make sure it's at its best. Sometimes rubbish blows in, or kids have a bit of a party and leave things lying about."

"Any particular kids?" asked Gemma, thinking instantly of Jess. But Jess was far too young to be hanging about late at night in the garden. Then she remembered, uncomfortably, that Jess's mother had said she'd taken a sleeping pill and gone to bed early. Who knew what Jess had been up to?

Glenn shrugged. "No. I don't know any of them. But I do find things. Beer cans. Used condoms. Cigarette ends. You assume it's kids, but . . ."

"Was there anything like that around Reagan Keating's body?" Kerry asked sharply.

"No. I'm just saying it happens."

"That must have been really upsetting, finding her like that. For you and Mrs. Armitage," Gemma said, trying to keep him talking.

"She was in a right state, Mrs. A. No phone—she doesn't hold with them—so I suppose she was going to wait until someone came out. She came running towards me when I came in the gate, white as a sheet. I was afraid she'd have a heart attack."

"Do you remember what she said?"

His eyes half closed, Glenn turned the key in his fingers as if it was an aid to memory. "'There's a girl. The nanny. She's dead.' I thought she was off her head, but I followed her. And then when I saw her—the girl—I knew she was dead. But I checked for vital signs anyway"—he looked at Gemma, as if she'd doubted him. "You don't run landscape crews without some first-aid training. I know how to find a pulse. But"— he gave an almost imperceptible shudder. "She was cold."

"Then what did you do?" Gemma asked.

"I rang 999. Then I sent Mrs. A to wait at the gate. One of us had to let them in, and I didn't want to leave her with the . . . girl."

So Clive Glenn had been alone with the body. As had Mrs. Armitage, Gemma reminded herself. "Did you know her? Reagan Keating?"

For a moment, Gemma thought he wasn't going to answer. Then he lifted one shoulder in a little shrug and slipped the key into his jeans pocket. "I'd seen her a few times. With the kid she looked after."

"Did you talk to her?"

"No. I didn't even know her name." He shifted his weight from one foot to the other. "Do you mind if I get to work now? I've a schedule to keep." He added that they could make arrangements with Mrs. Armitage to use her key, and described her house to them so that they could find it from the inside.

After asking him to leave the gate open until they could get a key sorted, and not to work near the area where the body had been found, Kerry thanked him. Then, as he turned away, she said suddenly, "This rubbish you find, Mr. Glenn. Are you sure you don't know any more about that?"

"Look." He swung back towards them, both hands jammed in his pockets. "I don't live here. There are probably close to thirty houses on this garden, and a good few of those are broken up into flats. I've spoken to maybe half a dozen residents in the five years I've looked after the place."

He hadn't met Kerry's eyes, and when he'd glanced at Gemma he'd looked away. There was something he wasn't telling them. "But?" prompted Gemma.

Glenn withdrew a hand from his pocket to scratch his beard. After another moment's hesitation he seemed to come to a decision. "I don't want to tell tales. But it's light very early in the summer and I like working that time of day, before the heat. I've seen—I think there's a bit of musical houses that goes on."

"Musical houses?" Kerry looked blank.

But Gemma understood. Although she'd never caught anyone at it in their garden, she'd heard rumors about the goings-on in communal gardens since she'd first come to work in Notting Hill. "Hanky-panky between neighbors. Sneaking into each other's houses. Or," she added, thinking of the used condoms, "maybe meeting in the garden for a quickie."

Glenn nodded, looking pleased with her. "Yeah. Exactly."

Kerry, on the other hand, seemed anything but happy. "Who have you seen, Mr. Glenn? Playing musical houses. Was it Reagan Keating?"

He shook his head. "No. I don't know. It's just an impression. Shadows moving in the dim half-light. The sound of doors closing. I shouldn't have said anything. I've never recognized anyone."

"But you've seen which houses the people came from?"

"No. Not even that. I can't help you." His answer was flat, final, his clamped lips making it clear he meant it.

Gemma knew he was lying.

"I'm getting the crime scene team on this," Kerry said when Glenn had left them. "Although I think there's a snowball's chance in hell that there's anything left to find." Putting her phone to her ear, she walked away from Gemma and began to pace up and down on the gravel path as she talked.

Gemma moved into a patch of shade and stood, gazing at the spot where Reagan Keating's body had lain. Why this spot, at the edge of the glade? Did it have some special significance? Was there any possibility the body had been moved here? Kate Ling hadn't mentioned lividity. Pulling out the little notebook she still carried in her bag, mobile notwithstanding, she jotted a reminder to herself to check.

The tree was beautiful, as perfect as a drawing in a children's picture book, set against the green sweep of lawn. What was it called in some of the old books Kit read aloud to Toby? Greensward, that was it. It had an Old English sound that made Gemma think of knights and enchantments. Or maybe she was just associating it with the way the girl had been described—laid out like a sleeping princess. She needed to see the crime scene photos for herself.

The turf showed no evidence of a struggle, although she did find a length of foot-wide parallel indentations at the edge of the path. Gemma thought it likely they had been made by the mortuary gurney, but there was always a possibility that it had been something else—a cart or a wagon, used if the body had been moved. She made another note, then looked up, trying to see how this spot related to the entire area. Was it visible from the nearby houses?

She thought the trees and shrubs would have screened it completely from the houses on the left. On the right, the small private patios were dense with shrubs and flowering plants, although she thought it might be just possible to see the patch of lawn from the upper windows of the nearest houses. That left the approach from the center of the garden.

There, casual beds of azaleas swooped down towards the formal beds in the garden's center, the riot of color punctuated by clumps of spent tulips and daffodils. Gemma thought a witness would have to have been quite close to have had an unimpeded view. She wondered how much light there had been late on Friday evening. The tall houses themselves would block any illumination from streetlamps in the surrounding area.

It had been a very private place to die.

She'd pulled her mobile from her bag, intending to take some quick photos, when Kerry finished her call. "They're on their way," she said as she rejoined Gemma. "However much good it will do. And I've had them radio the beat constable to come keep an eye on things until the SOCOs get here. Again"—she rolled her eyes—"not that I think it likely to make much difference when everyone and their dog has probably been tramping over the place all weekend. But I'm hoping the officer on duty is the one who took the initial call."

Wrong shift, Gemma thought, but didn't correct her.

"What do you think of the gardener?" Kerry asked. "Right out of D. H. Lawrence, isn't he?"

Gemma thought it over. "He could have known her better than

he admitted. There's definitely something he's not telling us. But he's not exactly a bit of rough, if that's what you were getting at."

"Dishy enough that a twenty-something might fancy him."

"Yes, but there's a big gap between her fancying him—or him fancying her—and him having a reason to kill her," Gemma argued. "If he's married, he doesn't wear a ring."

"We'll find out. I've got his particulars. And I'd like to know if he was making up the whole midnight shenanigans story out of whole cloth, or if he's protecting someone."

"I'd say start with his Mrs. Armitage. He seems to admire her. We'll find out if it's mutual." Gemma gazed at the surrounding houses. Clive Glenn had been right about the number of residents, and she knew from her own communal garden that many of them probably didn't know one another. Even if the lack of access limited the number of suspects, finding connections to Reagan Keating was going to be a daunting proposition.

The constable arrived, but it was not the same officer who had been called to the scene on Saturday morning. Kerry, frowning again, gave him instructions on where to wait until the crime scene team arrived, and asked to be notified immediately when they did. "No point cooling our heels here in the meantime," she said to Gemma. "But I think when we speak to residents, we should keep it to suspicious death, at least for the time being. I'd not like the girl's mother to hear that her daughter was murdered before I have a chance to speak to her. I tried ringing her a few minutes ago but got voice mail."

"Gwen Keating told me she meant to go back to work today. She said she couldn't abandon her students this close to the end of term. And what else would she do?" Gemma added. "I don't think sitting home alone would be bearable."

"I'll ring her again this afternoon, then." Kerry looked unhappy.

Clive Glenn had told them Mrs. Armitage lived on the north side, near the Kensington Park Road end, but they'd only walked a few yards when a woman came out of the nearest house on the left.

"Can I help you?" she called, stopping at the low iron fence and gate that separated her patio from the gravel path.

"We're police officers, ma'am." Kerry took her warrant card from her bag as they joined the woman.

"Detectives?" The woman studied Kerry's ID, then returned it. "Are you here about the girl who died? I saw you from my study window, talking to Clive." Slender and sensible looking, with short, mouse brown hair and a pleasant voice, she reminded Gemma of a younger version of Kincaid's mother, Rosemary.

"We are looking into her death, yes," Boatman answered. "And you are?"

"Marian Gracis."

Gemma extended her hand over the gate with a smile that she hoped hid her irritation with Boatman for not introducing her. "I'm Detective Inspector Gemma James. Did you know Reagan Keating, the young woman who died, Mrs. Gracis?" Using "Mrs." with a stranger was always tricky. Women who were not married or had kept their own names could be offended, but to Gemma, "Ms." always sounded casual to the point of rudeness.

"To speak to," said Marian Gracis. "She seemed a very nice girl. What a terrible thing to happen. Do you know anything yet?"

"We're looking into it," Boatman told her. "And of course we're interested in talking to residents here in Cornwall Gardens. Did you see or hear anything unusual on Friday evening, Mrs. Gracis?"

Marian Gracis frowned. "But I understood that Reagan just . . . died. What would I have seen?"

"Perhaps she was with someone earlier?" suggested Gemma. "Someone who might have known if she was feeling ill. Or . . . odd in some way."

"If you're implying that Reagan took drugs, I don't believe it." Some of the woman's friendliness had evaporated. "Nor do I believe she took her own life. Oh, yes," she added, as if they'd expressed surprise, "rumors are going around the garden. My boys heard it from one of Roland's sons. And of course Mrs. Armitage is buttonholing anyone who has the bad luck to run into her." Her expression made it clear that she didn't hold Mrs. Armitage in the same regard as Clive Glenn.

"Your sons," said Gemma, "are they friends with Jess Cusick?" She thought Marian Gracis was about the same age as Nita Cusick.

"Not friends, exactly. They're a good bit older. Fourth and sixth form. But Jess did tag after them when he was younger and he wasn't so tied up with his dance classes." Marian shook her head. "He's such a talented boy. This must be so awful for him. Especially after that poor boy's death last year."

"What boy?" asked Gemma. No one had mentioned anything about another death.

"Henry Su. He was in Jess's year, but I don't think they were exactly friends."

"What happened to him?" asked Kerry.

"Asthma attack. All the neighbors were searching for him when he didn't come in that night. They found him in the old toolshed at the back of the Sus' house. Apparently the door was stuck and he couldn't get out. He must have panicked, poor kid, and triggered his asthma. Anyway, it was all dreadful, but now the Sus have torn down the old shed and are building a huge extension, and Mrs. Armitage is on the warpath." Gracis sighed. "Rightly so, but I don't think anyone else has the heart to tackle the parents on it."

"When did this happen?" asked Gemma.

"Oh, before Christmas. It was bitterly cold. No one could imagine what the boy was doing in the shed."

"You said this boy—Henry—and Jess weren't exactly friends. Why was that?" Gemma thought that Toby would be thrilled to have another boy his age close by.

Marian Gracis looked uncomfortable. "I don't want to speak ill of the dead, especially a child."

After a moment, Gemma prompted her. "But?"

Gracis hesitated a bit longer, then gave a rueful shrug. "You want to like children, to think the best of them. You really do. God knows my boys were insufferable sometimes. But the truth is that Henry Su just wasn't a very nice child. I think somehow that made it all the more horrible. People felt guilty because they didn't feel worse, if you know what I mean."

"Not nice in what way, exactly?" asked Gemma, even though she could sense Kerry's impatience.

Gracis bit her lip, then grimaced. "Honestly, Henry Su was a bully. But you should ask Roland. He has a son the same age and Henry made the boy's life a misery."

When Melody's mobile rang, she fumbled it off her desk in an effort to silence it before Krueger, who was standing in the door of her office with her back to the CID room, heard it.

"About time," she whispered when she got the phone to her ear, sure it was Gemma calling.

"For what?" said Doug Cullen, sounding puzzled.

"Doug. I thought—" Melody caught herself, lowered her voice.

"Hold on, okay?" Leaving the CID room, she ducked into Gemma's office. After all, DS Krueger had said she was in charge. She shut the door and sat at Gemma's desk. "I thought you were Gemma," she said, dropping the whisper. "She's gone walkabout this—"

"Denis Childs was attacked," Doug broke in, sounding breathless. "He's in hospital. He's in a coma."

"I know."

"You know?" Doug's voice rose another octave. "And you didn't bother to tell me?"

"I seem to remember that you weren't speaking to me."

"Oh, that. My phone was turned off." When Melody didn't respond, he added, "Look, sorry. I didn't—it was stupid, all right?"

"You could say that," Melody agreed, knowing she was being annoying and enjoying it.

"Can we talk about this later?" Doug's frown was evident in his voice. "Does Duncan know? About Denis?"

"I told Gemma. I assume she told him, but I haven't spoken to her since."

"Wait a minute. Then who told you?"

Melody hesitated. There were voices in the corridor now. "I can't talk here," she whispered. "I'll take an early lunch. Meet me at the Caffè Nero across from Brixton tube." She disconnected before Doug could argue.

Melody loved the old Morleys department store. She supposed one day it would either be tarted up or torn down, but for now she could enjoy the feeling of being transported back a few decades whenever she walked through the door. The Caffè Nero was on the first floor, so she entered through cosmetics and took the stairs to the coffee shop.

She bought a small latte, then found a table by the front window with a view of the Brixton Underground sign. Peering down at the street, she spotted Doug coming out of the Underground station. His jacket was slung over his shoulder and the knot on his tie was pulled down. He was limping, and as he paused to search for the café, he pushed his round glasses up on his nose.

He disappeared from view and a few moments later came into the café, his limp more pronounced. "Bloody stairs," he said, sinking into a chair with obvious relief.

"There is a lift, you know."

Doug scowled at her. "Bloody nuisance trying to find it."

Melody wasn't sure if he meant the lift or the café, but neither one was difficult. "What have you done to yourself?" She nodded towards the ankle.

His frown grew deeper. Doug Cullen, with his blond, fine hair and Harry Potter glasses, was much too baby faced for such a glare. "I'll get you a coffee while you think about it," Melody said.

When she came back with his drink, his expression had relaxed a bit. He wasn't just hot, she realized as she studied him, but sunburned. "Bit too much rowing," he said in answer to her question from a moment earlier, taking the coffee with a nod of thanks.

"Surely you weren't out long enough to get that burnt."

A blush turned his face an even deeper red. "I may have done some digging."

Melody gave him a skeptical eye. "May have? Some? How much some?"

He shrugged. "All the beds. I guess I . . . um . . . got a little carried away."

"Good God. No wonder you're limping. You are a prize idiot, Doug Cullen."

"Yeah, well." Sipping at the coffee, he winced, then took off the lid and blew across the top. "Maybe so." He met her eyes for a moment. "Look, I am sorry about yesterday. I was an ass."

"I'll say," she muttered, then added, "I was worried about you." It was her turn to fidget and she turned her cold paper coffee cup. "Can we just forget about it?"

Doug looked relieved. "Okay. Fine. I'm fine with that." Suddenly he squinted at her. "What on earth have you done to your hair?"

Melody started to laugh. She couldn't help herself. When the patrons at the next table gave her disapproving looks, she clamped a hand over her mouth until she managed to get control. "Some detective you are," she sputtered.

"I knew something was different," Doug protested, turning red again. "It looks . . . nice."

"God preserve me from fulsome compliments," she said, rolling her eyes.

"I didn't mean—"

"Of course you didn't. Just stuff it, okay?" She crossed her arms and leaned back in her chair. "So you wanted to talk to me?"

Now Doug had to lean towards her and lower his voice. "I want to know how you knew about the chief. And what you know."

"My father told me. He said it came across the news desk."

But Doug was sharp, and he'd picked up on her hesitation. "You think your dad got it from someplace else?"

"He has a lot of . . . contacts. For all I know he heard it from the commissioner himself. But . . ."

"But what?"

Melody wrapped her hands around her cup. This was what she'd decided not to tell Gemma. But surely she could tell Doug.

Maybe he'd tell her she was crazy and then she could forget the whole thing. "He—my dad—came to see me this morning. He was—well, you know what Ivan is like when he knows things—"

"I don't, actually," interrupted Doug. "Since you never see fit to introduce your lowly friends."

"It's not that at all," Melody said, stung. "Do you want me to go on or not?"

"Yeah. Sorry." Doug did not look suitably abashed. Or convinced by her excuse.

"About Den—the chief." She leaned in, elbows on the table. "My dad was hinting that he had a checkered history. And that maybe his past had caught up with him."

Doug just stared at her. "I don't believe it," he finally said. "Not the chief super. But . . ." He sipped at his cooling coffee as he thought. "Things have been really weird the last few months. Gemma's transfer. Duncan's transfer, without a word. And mine—although I think I was just collateral damage. The chief disappearing for months. And then this. It's hard to believe he turns up back to work at the Yard and just randomly gets mugged and nearly killed. Or—" Doug blinked.

"What do we know about him, the chief super, really?" Melody said slowly.

Doug shook his head. "I can't—I don't believe he would do something—"

"Just because you don't believe doesn't mean you can't look."

They stared at each other. Then, Doug took off his glasses and rubbed the bridge of his nose. The lenses had protected the skin around his eyes from the sun, leaving it oddly pale against his red face. Putting his glasses back, he said, reluctantly, "Yeah. Okay. I can look. If only to prove your dad wrong. But you can, too."

"I suppose I can," Melody said slowly. She knew she could

access the newspaper's files—she'd done it before. What the hell were they getting themselves into, if the attack on Denis Childs had not been random?

She looked at her friend across the table and he seemed suddenly very vulnerable. "Doug?"

"What?" he said, sounding startled by her tone.

"Just don't get caught."

JUNE 1994

He kissed his wife goodbye and walked the three blocks to the more commercial street where he'd left his Ford Transit overnight. Every week, he tried to see that ordinary walk as the transition between his real life and his other life, but he found it was getting harder to make the distinction.

The day was already warm when he climbed into the van. It reeked of sweat and old food wrappers left behind by the load of protesters he'd driven to last weekend's demonstration. He wrinkled his nose in disgust and wound down the windows.

The Transit was almost ten years old but its unglamorous exterior disguised a 3.0 liter V6 engine. It was powerful and reliable, both essential for a cover vehicle. Useful transport meant you were much more likely to be accepted into the hierarchy of a protest group. Of course, then it was necessary to have a cover that explained his need for the van. His was that of an odd-job gardener and landscaper. He was big enough, and fit enough, for the job to be credible, but he'd had to learn enough to be able to talk plants, and to help out members of the group who needed work done. The job also explained his easy availability for those things in which he wished to be involved, and gave him a good excuse to bow out of those he wanted to avoid.

Turning on Radio 2, he drove north through central London.

When the remake of "Love Is All Around" came on, he switched the radio off with a grimace and went back to thinking about what he'd say when he met up with his group that night.

All the undercover officers had elaborate cover stories to explain their weekly absences from their groups. His was a father dying of cancer in Norwich, an old man with no one else to look after him.

In reality, those who were married—and most of them were—went home to spend one day a week with their families. He was sure that Special Branch recruited married officers deliberately, considering they were at less risk of "going native." In spite of which, although it was not officially condoned, cops on long-term undercover assignments were encouraged to "cultivate useful relationships." In other words, to sleep with the enemy. For many, he knew, their initial access to a group came through forming a sexual liaison with a female member.

So far, he'd managed to avoid that sort of entanglement. It had taken patience to insinuate himself into his little group, but he had no shortage of that. For months, he'd hung around the community center in Notting Hill where his targets assembled, casually joining in conversations, then displaying a wary interest. Eventually, over bottles of cheap wine in the flat he'd taken just across the canal in Paddington, he told them that he was widowed, his young wife lost tragically in a motor crash. The story made him cringe, and in his lowest moments he wondered if he was somehow jinxing his wife as well as his hale and hearty father who was living happily in Hertfordshire.

But it seemed he'd told the tale convincingly. He was fussed over by the women and clapped on the back by the men. After that, he'd begun to be included in the distribution of leaflets and the planning of a few demonstrations.

His campaigners were a loosely knit collection of antidiscrim-ination protesters, some white and some black, brought together and galvanized by the brutal murder of a young black man named Stephen Lawrence in south London the previous spring. On the twenty-second of April 1993, eighteen-year-old Lawrence, an athlete and a good student who had hoped to become an architect, was walking home from his uncle's house in Plumstead with a friend, Duwayne Brooks.

Lawrence, walking ahead to see if a bus was coming, was set upon by five white youths and stabbed to death.

The failure of the Metropolitan Police to properly investigate the crime, or to provide substantial evidence against the perpe-trators, who had been identified by witnesses, had caused a huge public outcry. By April of 1994, Stephen Lawrence's family had initiated a private prosecution against the two initial suspects and three others, and the Met was in turmoil.

Special Branch had been tasked with discovering what evi-dence the Lawrence family had uncovered. It was feared that more unwelcome revelations about the force's failure to solve the Law-rence case could lead to widespread civil unrest.

And it was rumored that some of his small group of campaign-ers had connections with the Lawrence family and might be privy to inside information on the Lawrences' plans to discredit the police.

The trouble was, the more he listened and learned, the more he liked his group, and the more he agreed with their agenda. And the more he helped out, the more he found himself actually suggesting ideas for leaflets and plans for actions.

Both of which were strictly off the rule book.

CHAPTER ELEVEN

Following Clive Glenn's directions, Gemma and Kerry easily found Mrs. Armitage's house. They let themselves in through the wood-slatted gate and looked round curiously. The small patio was even more manicured than the communal area and Gemma wondered if she had someone—Glenn perhaps—to help with it, or if she did all the work herself. She knew enough to tell that most of the roses were antique varieties rather than hybrid teas. The roses lined all but the front of the small plot, and in the sun the scent was dizzying. Although there were two teak chairs and a small table on a patch of carefully laid flagstones, it was not a space where Gemma could imagine anyone sitting out with a drink or having a barbecue.

They knocked on what Gemma guessed was the door to a mudroom, but there was no answer. There was no sound of a radio or television, and the room overlooking the garden was shuttered.

After a few moments, Kerry shrugged and turned away. "We can go out to the street and round the front, but I don't think she's at home."

"What about giving this Roland bloke a try?" Gemma asked. Marian Gracis had told them that Roland's last name was Peacock and that he lived in the house just to the north of the gate. "He might have seen something, if someone did try to get in through the gate or over the wall." Gracis had also told them that Roland Peacock worked from home, so Gemma thought he might be a useful source of information about all of the residents, not just Reagan Keating and the boy who had died.

Kerry gave an irritated glance at her watch. The SOCOs still hadn't arrived. "We might as well."

As they walked back towards the gate, they had no trouble recognizing the Sus' house. The unfinished steel-and-glass extension protruded from the ground floor, completely covering what must once have been the private garden, patio, and toolshed. The thing was a blight on the landscape, and Gemma was certain it was in violation of council building regulations. She could only imagine the horror with which such a thing would be met on their own garden. Why had no one other than Mrs. Armitage complained?

"Good God." Kerry stopped, gaping. "I'm surprised no one's murdered *them*. And how have they managed to get away with it?"

"Bribing someone on the council?" Gemma suggested, only half joking. "I'll ask MacKenz—" Too late, she remembered that the Williamses were not on Kerry's list of favorite people at the moment. She was rescued by the ringing of Kerry's mobile.

Kerry listened, then said to the unfortunate caller, "Another hour? You're taking the piss. What the hell are they doing, having a ladies' lunch?" She stomped a few feet up the path, her back to Gemma. "You'll have to get another constable to relieve the poor sod I've had twiddling his thumbs at the scene for half the morning—"

Half the morning was an exaggeration, but still it startled Gemma into looking at her watch. It had gone twelve. She realized she'd never checked in with Brixton, which she should have done no matter Kerry's assurances that her absence had been cleared. And then she realized that she'd never switched on her mobile's ringer since she'd muted it at the mortuary. What if Charlotte's school had tried to reach her, or the boys had needed her?

She pulled her mobile from her bag and checked it. She'd missed a text from Melody, and two calls from Kincaid, but he hadn't left a message. Her heart skipped. Was there bad news about Denis?

Catching up with Kerry, she tapped her on the shoulder, then mimed making a call. When Kerry nodded, Gemma turned and walked back towards Mrs. Armitage's house as she dialed Kincaid's number.

It rang half a dozen times before he picked up, his voice a barely intelligible mumble.

"Where are you?" she said. The road noise from the old Astra was unmistakable. "Are you in the car? I thought you took the tube this morning."

"I'm on the M6."

"What? Why?"

"My dad—" His voice faded. Clearing his throat, he went on with a heartiness that sounded forced. "It's my dad. He's had a heart problem. I'm on my way to Cheshire."

Gemma stopped, swayed. It was only the fact that her feet seemed rooted in the gravel that kept her from toppling.

She thought she'd coped with Denis Childs's injury, with knowing that he might not survive. She'd coped with Gwen Keating's grief, and with an unexpected sense of familiarity with the murdered girl.

But she suddenly felt that a support had gone from her world, that this was one more thing than she could bear. "Oh, no," she said. "Not Hugh."

"Are you okay?" Kerry had finished her call and walked back to Gemma, who stood, her phone still clasped in her hand.

"It's my father-in-law," said Gemma. "He's had some chest pains."

Kerry looked concerned. "Is he okay?"

"I don't know. My husband's on his way there. They—my in-laws—live in Cheshire, in Nantwich."

"Do you need to go? Of course, I'll understand if you do," Kerry added, but without a great deal of conviction.

"No. Not now, at least. Duncan said he'd ring when he got there and knew more."

"Well, I think we should take a break. Let's get some lunch—it'll do you good." Kerry gave Gemma a slightly awkward pat on the shoulder. "What's good around here?"

Kitchen and Pantry was close enough.

"Are you sure this is a good idea?" Boatman asked, wincing at the sound of a crying baby as they squeezed by the parked push chairs and the frosty ice-cream case in the café's entrance.

"We might have to—oh, wait," Gemma said, spying a free space by the window. "There's a spot. If you'll choose what you want from the board, you can stake it out while I order for us."

A few minutes later, they were settled on sofas just inside the open window overlooking Kensington Park Road, plates of jacket potatoes on their knees and coffees balanced rather precariously on a small, wobbly table. The baby had mercifully stopped crying.

Gemma had chosen roasted vegetables on her potato, and Kerry, mushrooms in a cream sauce. Watching the plume of steam rise from her lifted fork, Gemma thought better of trying her first bite of potato.

Kerry, having been less cautious, was waving a hand in front of her mouth as if that would help cool her scorched tongue. "Bloody hell," she said when she could speak. "Maybe we should have gone for the ice creams."

"Good thing the coffee's cold, then," said Gemma, attempting a levity she didn't feel.

They both pushed bites of potato about on their plates in an attempt to cool it, then took tentative nibbles. Kerry soon polished hers off, but Gemma found she'd lost her appetite and the cheese drizzled over the veggies was congealing unappetizingly.

After watching her for a moment, Kerry said, "I'm going to get us some more coffee, and see if this time they can make it hot."

With Kerry gone to the counter, Gemma gave up on her lunch and stared idly out the window. Then a passing figure caught her eye. It was Nita Cusick, looking very businesslike in a skirt and heels, scowling and talking intently on her mobile as she walked by. Even though the window was open and she passed within a few feet of Gemma, she didn't look up. Gemma thought that if they'd meant to talk to Nita again that afternoon they might not find her at home, as she'd been walking away from Cornwall Gardens, towards Notting Hill Gate.

Kerry returned with two fresh cups of coffee, but before Gemma could mention Cusick, Kerry eyed her barely touched plate disapprovingly. "So tell me about your father-in-law. Are you close? I didn't think you'd been married for that long."

"Not that long, no, but Hugh——" Gemma stopped, unsure of how to begin to describe Hugh Kincaid. She remembered when she'd met him, that first Christmas in Nantwich. She'd met Rosemary before, but she'd been nervous—terrified, really—about meeting the rest of Kincaid's family, afraid she wouldn't live up to their expectations. Or to their memories of Kit's mother. But Hugh had taken her under his wing. He'd done everything to make her comfortable, showing her the town and asking her questions about herself. And he'd listened to her with interest and with respect, something she'd never experienced with her own father. She shook her head as her eyes threatened to fill. "Hugh is . . . just Hugh." And then she realized she'd have to tell the children.

The crime scene officers had arrived when Gemma and Kerry returned to Cornwall Gardens. The constable who had been guarding the scene had moved to the gate, and Clive Glenn was packing up his tools. Kerry stopped him before he could leave.

"I need that key," she told him.

"I can't give you my key. I thought Mrs. Armitage——"

"Mrs. Armitage isn't in, and the police must have access to this garden." They'd tried Mrs. Armitage again, this time from the front door, on their way back from lunch. "I've got crime scene technicians in here, for heaven's sake," Kerry went on. "Who do you think is going to lock up after them? Don't be a wanker."

Gemma almost laughed at the expression on Glenn's face. He took a deep breath and she could see the red flush under his stubble and his suntan.

"But——"

"Key." Kerry held out her hand. "Or I'll take it in as evidence and then you'll likely never see it again."

The two stared at each other, but Gemma had no doubt by this time who was going to win this pissing contest.

Glenn shrugged, then pulled the key from his pocket. He rubbed his large, calloused fingers along the barrel, then dropped the key into Boatman's outstretched palm. "On your head be it, then, Detective Chief Inspector. If anything happens to this"—he shook head—"well, I'd not want to be on the wrong side of Mrs. A."

With that, he climbed into his truck and roared off.

Kerry tucked the key into a pocket. "Now, let's have a word with this Mr. Peacock."

It was the house on the left-hand side of the gate, built of dark brown brick that, unlike most of the houses on the garden, had not been covered with stucco. The brown brick continued into the wall that met the gate itself, so that the whole impression was for-tresslike. The house sat close to the street, with only a low hedge to separate it from the pavement. The door was painted a glossy black.

"The place is downright funereal," Kerry muttered as she rang the single bell. The house was not divided into flats, then. They could hear it, loud as a klaxon, echoing through the house. After a moment, they heard footsteps and a man's voice muttering something unintelligible.

"Whatever you're selling, you can bugger off," he said as he opened the door. "I don't want—" He broke off in midsentence, staring at them. "Who the hell are you?"

Gemma would have introduced herself first, but Kerry was ever ready with the warrant card. "Police," she said smartly, holding it up. "Can we have a word, Mr. Peacock?"

Roland Peacock was tall and thin and obviously farsighted. He peered at the card, then shook his head. "I need my glasses. I'll take your word for it. The two of you don't look like insurance salesmen." Smiling at his own humor, he motioned them in. "But if this is about that parking complaint, I'm impressed they've sent detectives. You are detectives?" he asked, glancing back at them. Kerry, in her navy suit, certainly looked the part, but Gemma was more casually dressed in tan trousers and a lightweight, yellow poplin jacket.

She held out her hand. "Detective Inspector Gemma James. And this is Detective Chief Inspector Boatman."

Peacock's eyes went wide. "Definitely not about the parking, then. You'd better come in." He turned and led them in. They passed a formal living room and a dining room on either side of the hall, as well as a wide staircase sweeping upwards. The front rooms were done in a dark chocolate with cream molding, but the room they entered at the back of the house was a deep terra-cotta. The ceilings were very high, and floor-to-ceiling bookcases filled much of the space not taken by the windows overlooking the garden. At one end, there was an open-plan kitchen and a comfortable-looking family dining area. There were books and newspapers scattered about on tables and sofas, and a reassuring smattering of the debris left in the wake of boys.

In the living area, a scuffed leather armchair was positioned with a view into the garden. Beside it was a shaded lamp. Papers, an open laptop, and a pair of wire-framed glasses were thrown casually over the ottoman. "We've obviously caught you working, Mr. Peacock," said Gemma, determined to take the lead. After all, if Kerry Boatman wanted her on the case, she was bloody well going to do more than take notes. "You're neighbor Mrs. Gracis—

Marian—gave us your name. We're looking into the death of Reagan Keating."

"Oh. That. Of course. I heard about it, but I thought she'd over-dosed or something. Why are the police investigating?" Peacock had put on his glasses. His eyes were sharp and very blue.

"For the moment, we're treating it as a suspicious death," said Kerry. "Mrs. Gracis told us you worked from home. We thought that if there had been anything odd going on, you might have no-ticed."

"But she died during the night, poor girl. Or so I was told."

"It's our job to look into things thoroughly when something like this happens." Kerry was more conciliatory than Gemma had heard her before. "Which means we'd like to speak to as many of the residents as possible. Could we—"

"Oh, of course. Sorry." Peacock gestured towards a slightly worn pair of velvet sofas. He shifted the ottoman aside and folded his length into the armchair. "But I don't know how I can help you."

Gemma perched on the edge of the sofa nearest him. "What is it that you do, Mr. Peacock?"

"I'm a journalist. Freelance. I write on economics. I have a proper office upstairs, but I like working down here, especially on fine days." The windows were open, but the heavy plantings at the west end of the garden made the house seem very private.

"And your wife?"

"She's an architect. Her office has subsidiaries in the States and Germany, so she travels a good bit."

So Roland Peacock was home alone during the day—at least while his sons were at school—and sometimes at night, if his wife traveled. He was, she realized, a very handsome man. Not in a film-star way—his face was too long, his hairline receding—but there was something extraordinarily attractive in the way his features fit together. And his blue eyes, now slightly shielded by the spectacles—were mesmerizing. She could certainly imagine a younger woman being smitten. "Did you know Reagan Keating, Mr. Peacock?" she asked. "I understand one of your sons is the same age as Jess Cusick."

"Yes, my Arthur is the same age as Jess. They were friends."

"Were friends?" Gemma asked, wondering if something had happened to the boy.

"I suppose they still are," Peacock clarified. "But Arthur's away at school now, so they don't see each other much. And after the— there was a tragedy here, last year. I can understand if it put the boys off doing ordinary things."

"You're talking about the boy who died?" asked Gemma, glad he had brought it up.

"Henry, yes. Henry Su."

"The three boys were friends?"

"No, they weren't friends." Peacock was surprisingly adamant. "They were the same age, and Arthur and Jess always got along well. But . . . Henry was . . . different."

"Different, how?" Kerry spoke sharply enough to make Peacock give her a startled glance. He might have forgotten she was there. When he hesitated, she added, "Don't say you don't want to speak ill of the dead. The dead are dead and it won't hurt them."

"But I can't see—"

"Nor do you know how any information you have might help us."

Roland Peacock looked at her. After a moment he took off his glasses and rubbed his face. "Henry Su was a bully and a troublemaker. Hard to say if that was due to being horribly overindulged by his parents, or just his natural inclination. He teased the other kids mercilessly. To be honest, that was one of the reasons we decided to send our Arthur away to school. Henry was in the same year at the local school and was making his life a misery there and at home."

"What exactly happened to Henry Su?" Gemma asked, wanting to confirm what Marian Gracis had told them.

Peacock grimaced, then put his glasses on again so that Gemma couldn't quite read his expression. "Henry liked to hide. I suppose it was a way of getting attention. Usually, the kids would ignore him, glad to be shut of him for a bit. If they'd looked, that day . . ." He shook his head. "Things might have been different.

"Henry was asthmatic, you see. He managed to lock himself in the little shed where his father kept tools and gardening things. I suppose when he couldn't get out, it triggered his asthma. He didn't have his rescue inhaler. He—he wouldn't have been able to get his breath."

"He suffocated?"

"He was unresponsive when we found him—by this time it had got dark and his parents were frantic. Everyone was out searching. They kept him on life support for a week before the doctors convinced his parents to let him go. But they didn't donate any of his organs." Roland shook his head again, his mouth set in a grim line. "I suppose I can understand that. It was tragic. But perhaps his death wouldn't have been so pointless if it had allowed someone else to live."

Gemma thought suddenly of Denis. His sister's unselfishness had given him a new chance at life, only to have it now hanging in the balance.

"To make it worse," Peacock went on, "now his parents are building a bloody great extension where the shed was. It's illegal, and it's horrible, but no one really wants to take them on because it seems insensitive. Except Mrs. Armitage, of course, the head of the garden committee." Peacock's expression relaxed into a smile. "She doesn't suffer from delicacy."

"She found Reagan Keating, didn't she?" said Kerry.

"So I heard. Poor kid. What do you think happened to her?"

"So you did know Reagan?" asked Gemma, well aware that he had not answered their original question.

"I'd met her, of course. I remember how cut up she was the night Henry was found. But I've not seen her much since Arthur went away to school, and I can't say I ever knew her well."

"Is there anyone on the garden who was a particular friend of Reagan's?"

Roland Peacock thought for a moment, frowning. "You might speak to Asia Ford, in the house next to the Cusicks' but one. She seemed quite friendly with the girl at the garden party."

"Garden party?" Gemma repeated.

"Two weeks ago. Our annual spring fling. Games and refreshments and punch. Silly games like egg-and-spoon races. Although, in fact, there was more than punch. Asia was touting her home-made limoncello. Tasted like bathroom cleaner, if you ask me." He waved his hand in a dismissive gesture. "The whole thing is a chance for the new money to trot themselves out in front of those of us who are middle-class professionals, or worse, have inherited our houses. We are a nuisance they'd like to be rid of. Then their property values would go up."

"All good mates, then." Kerry gave him a sharklike smile. "We've been given to understand that sometimes there's a bit of, um, hanky-panky that goes on in the garden at night. Illicit activity, if you take my meaning. Residents visiting other residents, that sort of thing."

"Hanky-panky? God, I haven't heard that in years. And, no, Chief Inspector, I don't know anything about any *illicit activities*. My wife would kill me."

Then Peacock seemed to realize what he'd said and looked, for the first time during the interview, truly horrified.

Roland Peacock had told them they'd recognize the house by the wisteria growing over the small patio. Indeed, Gemma had noticed the flowers when they'd walked along the south side of the garden that morning. The scent, heavenly on the morning air, was even stronger now in the heat of the day. The plant grew on a pergola anchored by the two brick walls separating Asia Ford's patio from its neighbors on either side. It made Gemma think of a purple-roofed cave.

Beneath the clustered blooms there was a bricked area with worn, comfortable-looking wicker furniture, and a small greenhouse. Almost every available space was filled with pots and plants and gardening tools, but shelves in the greenhouse held a beautiful array of glass bottles. Strings of fairy lights hung beneath the pergola.

As in most of the houses, a low iron fence and gate separated the private patios from the larger space. Gemma hesitated at the gate—it seemed an intrusion to just walk into a space so personal.

Kerry, who had stopped to check on the SOCOs, had just joined her when the house door opened and they were spared the dilemma.

A woman came out, greeting them with a smile. "Were you looking for me? I saw you from the kitchen window."

"Are you Asia Ford?" asked Gemma, although she was certain it must be she. The name, with its combination of the exotic and the commonplace, fit her perfectly. With her loosely tied hair, cotton T-shirt, and flowing skirt, Gemma at first thought her young, perhaps Reagan's age. But as she came into the brighter light by the gate, Gemma saw that there were silver sparkles in her light brown hair and that her face was lightly lined.

"I am. Can I help you?" Asia Ford took in Kerry's very official jacket and skirt and her smile faded. "I saw the people in boiler suits. Is this about Reagan?"

"I'm afraid it is," Gemma said, and introduced them. "Can we have a word?"

"Oh, dear." Ford touched her fingers to her lips, but the gesture only partly covered the spasm of distress. "Such a dreadful thing." She shook her head as she unlatched the gate. "Please, come and sit. I was just making some lemonade. I'll bring the pitcher out."

Kerry started to protest but Gemma quickly said, "Thank you. That would be lovely." The jacket potato and coffee at lunch had left her thirsty, and it was getting very warm. She sank gratefully into one of the wicker chairs and Kerry followed suit although with obvious reluctance. It was cooler under the purple canopy and the sweet scent of the blossoms hung about them like a physical presence.

After a moment, drawn by curiosity, Gemma stood up again and went to the door Ford had left standing open. "Can I help?" she called, looking into a kitchen cum sitting room.

Roland Peacock's living area had been scattered with things in everyday use, but beneath the surface clutter the rooms had been modern and expensively designed. Asia Ford's kitchen and sitting area, however, might have existed in a time warp.

An enormous old cream-colored Rayburn dominated the room,

and Gemma thought it might heat the entire house in the winter. There was a scarred Welsh dresser, more of the same wicker furniture as that on the patio, a table covered with a floral oilcloth, and beside the Rayburn, a sofa of indeterminate age and color draped in cashmere shawls. A farmhouse sink and oak work tops stood below the window.

The walls—what could be seen of them beneath an assortment of prints, paintings, and posters—were the same pale green as the walls of Gemma's childhood flat. Every surface in the room seemed filled with odd bits of china, books, and jugs filled with fresh-cut flowers.

It ought, thought Gemma, to have been claustrophobic, but instead she found it immensely charming. "What a wonderful room," she exclaimed.

Ford looked up from the mismatched glasses she was setting on a tin tray. "Do you like it? The house was my parents', and I've never been inclined to do it up. Or had the money, truthfully, with what it costs these days to refit things." To the tray, she added a clear pitcher afloat with sliced lemons, a small bowl of ice cubes, and a vase filled with the same trailing, pale pink roses Gemma had seen at the bottom of the garden. "Climbing Cecile Brunner," Ford said, following her glance. "Clive Glenn cuts them for me. I love the scent. You could hold the door for me," she added, and together they took out the refreshments.

Gemma remembered what Peacock had said about the new money wanting to get rid of the residents who'd inherited their properties. She could just imagine a builder slavering at the thought of tearing out that kitchen and putting in all the mod cons, and it made her sad. Not that either Ford or Peacock were old— she would put Ford perhaps in her fifties and Peacock in his forties, although it was hard to judge men in those mid years.

"Your parents—did they live here a long time?" she asked.

"My mother was born in this house. Her father was a factory manager, very respectably middle-class although Notting Hill had declined from its heyday by then. My parents were missionaries so the house was rented out piecemeal over the years," Ford added as she put two ice cubes in each glass and topped the glasses up from the pitcher.

Gemma had been expecting a fizzy drink or lemonade made from a tin, but what she tasted when she lifted her glass was fresh, cool, and tart enough to make her mouth pucker. She drank half of it down in a gulp. "That's wonderful."

"I grow my own lemons," said Ford, with a gesture towards the little greenhouse. Beyond the glass bottles, Gemma glimpsed the glossy dark green foliage of lemon trees, and remembered Roland Peacock's comment about the limoncello.

"Miss Ford," she said, "Roland Peacock said you were friendly with Reagan Keating. He said the two of you were chatting at the garden party."

"Please, call me Asia. 'Miss Ford' makes me feel like a spinster aunt." The animation faded from her face and she sighed. "Reagan liked to help me with things. And she loved it here." Her gesture took in the patio. "We were so looking forward to the summer and picnics. Silly things."

"You spent quite a bit of time with her, then?" said Gemma.

"I think Nita's house was not . . ." Asia Ford winced. "I don't mean— It's just that I think Reagan was homesick. I know she missed her mum. There was always just the two of them and they were close. Her mother must be devastated. Have you spoken to her?"

"I met her yesterday," said Gemma, without explaining the circumstances. "But I believe she's gone back to Cardiff."

"I'll write to her. I'm sure Nita has her address." Asia shook her head. "I just can't believe Reagan is gone. Such a beautiful, healthy girl, dying like that. What could have happened?" She looked directly at Kerry. "You must have some idea."

"We're looking into it," Kerry told her. "That's our procedure with unexplained deaths."

"Reagan would never have harmed herself," Asia Ford said, as if something in Kerry's tone had suggested it. "She was a positive person. Interested and engaged, with a plan for her life."

"Did she confide in you about things?" Gemma asked. "Do you know if anything was troubling her? Please," she added, seeing Asia's hesitation. "You never know what might be of help."

Asia refilled their glasses, then spent a moment wiping down the pitcher with a cloth. "I think she'd had a falling-out with her boyfriend," she said at last. "A blond boy. Very good looking. Although I don't think that was the reason Reagan liked him. Or at least not the only reason," she added with a smile.

"Was that Hugo?" asked Gemma.

"Yes, that's right. Reagan brought him to visit a few times. He was very charming." There was a distinct lack of enthusiasm in the comment.

"You didn't like him?"

"I wouldn't say that, exactly. He's a well-brought-up young man with good manners. He was always perfectly polite. But—" Asia made a face. "I don't think he thought much of me. I'm not exactly what you would call up and coming. At any rate, I could always sense . . . something . . . I don't know . . . condescension, perhaps, beneath the nice manners."

"Is that why Reagan fell out with him?" Kerry asked.

"I doubt Reagan noticed, and I certainly never said anything. It was just me being overly sensitive, I imagine. And then there were the bricks."

They must have looked puzzled because Asia nodded towards a small pile of bricks by the door to the greenhouse. "I'm trying to finish paving the greenhouse floor to match the patio. Reagan suggested he could help. He didn't come with her to visit after that." She grinned at the memory, grief momentarily forgotten.

Gemma could imagine such a pretty boy being horrified by the thought of a little manual labor. "Was it that Brit caused the problem between them, do you think?"

"Oh, I think that would be overestimating my importance in Reagan's life." Asia swirled the liquid in her glass as she considered. "Reagan could be very definite about things. A bit of a straight arrow." She looked up at them and Gemma saw that her eyes were an unusual color, a gold that was almost amber. "I think," Asia said slowly, "that he'd done something she didn't approve of. And that she was considering breaking things off."

Asia Ford wasn't able to tell them much more about Hugo. He'd only been introduced to her by his first name. She'd gathered that he was a student at one of the London universities—a business degree, she thought. And his familiarity with the Notting Hill area had made her think that perhaps he lived nearby.

They'd meant to try Mrs. Armitage again, but as they were leaving Asia had told them that it was Jean Armitage's bridge day. Jean, said Asia, usually made a day of it by doing her weekly shopping afterwards.

"Are you friends?" Gemma asked, curious since she'd got the impression Mrs. Armitage was rather starchy.

"United in loving this place. It's funny. Jean and her husband bought their house when I was a teenager. I was quite terrified of her. Now I see that she wasn't all that much older than me and no doubt I threatened her authority. Who'd have thought we'd both still be here?"

Gemma would have asked more, but Kerry had had a call from the crime scene techs so they said goodbye and hurried back towards the top of the garden.

One of the SOCOs, a round-faced man with red-blond stubble, met them at the perimeter. "Detectives," he said, nodding at them. "We've found some indentations in the grass that might have been made during a struggle. We'll do our best to match them up with the position of the body. But here's an interesting thing." He held up a plastic evidence bag. In it was a white blob, about two inches in diameter. "There was a puddle of candle wax in the grass. No container, no wick. Just wax."

"Relation to the body?" Kerry snapped.

The SOCO glared at her. "As we weren't called to the scene with the body in situ, I can only extrapolate from the photos taken by the attending officers." Having made his point, he turned back towards the scene. "However, I would guess the wax was two or three feet from the victim. We're going to extend the perimeter," he added, "but I don't think it will be worth getting in the lights and generators."

Glancing at the lengthening angle of the sun, Gemma gasped, checked her watch, then took Kerry aside. "I've got to go. Duncan's in Cheshire and I haven't made other arrangements for collecting my daughter from school."

"And I have to ring the grieving mother," Kerry said. "We'll start again in the morning."

By the time Gemma had arrived home with Charlotte, Kit and Toby were there as well. She still hadn't heard from Kincaid, and when she'd tried ringing him, his phone had once more gone to voice mail. But even without news, she'd have to tell the children something.

Corralling them in the kitchen with the promise of a snack to hold them until dinner, she took some cheese from the fridge and cut it into cubes, then began slicing apples. When she had the plate ready, she sat the little ones at the kitchen table and called Kit in from the living room. If asked, Kit would have said he was too old for after-school snacks, but he scooped up half the cheese and apples and started out of the kitchen again.

"Kit—"

"I've got homework—"

"I know you do, lovey, but just wait a minute, please. I need to talk to you all. Your dad's not going to be home tonight—"

"That's really a news flash," Kit broke in, apple halfway to his mouth.

"Don't be cheeky," Gemma snapped back, irritated. "I mean that he's gone away. To Cheshire. To see your grandparents."

"What? Why?" Kit frowned. "Why didn't he tell us?"

"Because he just found out this morning." Toby and Charlotte were squabbling over the cheese, so Gemma spoke directly to Kit. "Hugh had some chest pains yesterday. They're doing a procedure this afternoon. A stent. It's a—"

"I know what a stent is," Kit interrupted. "Are they just doing one? How bad is it? Are they going to have to do a bypass?" His cheeks had gone blotchily pink and his voice rose as he added, "They'll have to crack his chest if they do."

Toby, picking up the strain in his brother's voice, let go of the last cube of cheddar and looked up. "Crack whose chest? Granddad's? Why? Is he going to die?"

"No, he's not going to die, sweetie," said Gemma. "Of course he's not. He's just had some discomfort and they're going to make him feel better. I'm sure your dad will tell you all about it when he rings. You and Charlotte can take the dogs out for a little run, and I promise I'll let you know as soon as your dad calls."

When she heard the French door bang behind them, she thought suddenly of Henry Su. She'd never worried about the children when they were playing in the communal area, but perhaps it wasn't as safe as she'd thought.

Turning to Kit, she said, "Darling, would you tell them to stay close to the patio? I—"

"You tell them," said Kit. "I've got to work on my project." But he had his phone out as he stomped out of the kitchen, and Gemma felt sure he was already texting his cousin Lally in Nantwich. She knew he was angry because he was frightened and she didn't have the heart to reprimand him.

Sighing, she'd started for the patio doors to check on the children when the front bell rang. "What now?" she muttered, changing direction and yanking open the front door.

Melody Talbot stood on her doorstep, looking every bit as sullen as Kit had a moment before. Before Gemma could speak, Melody blurted out, "Where the hell were you today?"

CHAPTER TWELVE

"You'd better come in," said Gemma, frowning. She realized she'd never had a chance to ring Melody back that day, but she didn't understand why Melody seemed so upset. Or why Melody looked so bedraggled. Her red silk blouse was half untucked, and her short, dark hair looked damp and disheveled. "Where's your car?" Gemma added, glancing up and down the street.

"Walked from Holland Park tube."

Gemma bit back more questions as she ushered Melody in. "I'll just put the kettle on. I think we could both use a cuppa." What Melody needed, she thought, was a glass of Asia Ford's lemonade, but tea was the best she could do. As she walked back through the house, she realized she could no longer hear the children. "Hang on a sec," she said. "Let me check on the little monsters."

When she peered out the French doors, the children were farther away from the house than she liked. Charlotte was in the tree swing, with Geordie running in excited circles around her, his ears flapping. For a moment, Gemma didn't see Toby and her heart gave a little skip. Then she spied him, crouching down and digging at something in the ground.

"Charlotte, be careful," she called. "Toby, stop whatever it is you're doing. And stay on the patio where I can see you. Both of you. I mean it."

Melody had come up behind her. "Practicing my fishwife," Gemma told her, a little embarrassed to have been heard shouting at them. "But I'm feeling a bit overprotective today. If you don't mind, we'll bring our tea back in here where I can keep an eye on them." She thought it better not to talk on the patio where the children could overhear them, and it was cooler in the house.

Gemma made the tea quickly, splashing hot water onto Yorkshire Gold tea bags and adding milk as she dunked the bags in the mugs. Melody, usually so helpfully capable, stood silently, watching. By the time Gemma carried the mugs into the sitting room, she was feeling awkward as well as concerned. She checked on the children again, then sat in the armchair and tucked her feet up under her. Melody took the sofa and perched on the edge, as stiff-backed as a child called to the head's office, her tea untouched on the side table.

"I'm sorry about today," Gemma said. "It was—"

"Krueger called me into her office for a bollocking," Melody broke in. "Because you weren't there. She said you'd been seconded to another team."

"Not exactly," Gemma began, but Melody interrupted.

"And what about the chief super?"

Gemma realized that she hadn't spoken to Melody since Duncan's visit to hospital. "Duncan went to the London yesterday, after you called. They've put Denis in a coma, to reduce the swelling from the head injury. And they're worried about his liver."

"His liver? Why?"

"Because of the transpla—" Too late, Gemma remembered that they only knew about the transplant because Denis had told Duncan when they'd met on Saturday night. And that Duncan didn't want anyone knowing he'd seen Denis just a few minutes before he was attacked.

But surely other people knew about the transplant, like Chief Superintendent Faith. They must have talked about it at the hospital.

"What?" Melody demanded. "What are you talking about?"

Gemma couldn't take it back, so there was nothing for it but to go forward. She took a breath and said, "Denis Childs had a liver transplant. That's why he was away, apparently."

"But— But that's bonkers." Melody frowned. "Although I can believe he was ill. He hasn't looked great, the last year or two. But why all the cloak-and-dagger?"

"I suppose he didn't want people knowing he was ill." Gemma hated not telling Melody everything. Trying to mask her discomfort, she shifted in her chair and said, "Have you heard anything about his condition today?"

Picking up her mug at last, Melody shook her head without meeting Gemma's eyes. "No, nothing. But you'd know better than I. Surely Duncan's heard—"

"Duncan's not here," Gemma blurted out. "He's gone to Cheshire. His dad had chest pains last night." She'd been composed for the children, but now, talking about it to a friend, her eyes filled with unexpected tears.

"Oh, no. I'm so sorry." Melody sat forward, instantly contrite.

Drops of tea sloshed onto her red skirt, but she didn't seem to notice. "It's Hugh, isn't it, your father-in-law? Is he going to be all right?"

"I don't know. Duncan hasn't rung since he left this morning. And he should have been there hours ago."

"Don't worry. I'm sure he's just caught up in family stuff. And here I've shown up on your doorstep acting an absolute cow, when you've this on your plate. I really am sorry."

"No, you couldn't have known. And I didn't know this morning. That's not why I wasn't in today."

This time, Gemma did tell Melody everything. About meeting Jess at the dance class, about MacKenzie asking her to meet Reagan Keating's mother at the Cusicks' yesterday, about the call from Marc Lamb on her way into work that morning. She told her about the meeting with Kerry Boatman, the postmortem, and about visiting the scene of the girl's death.

Melody listened with widening eyes. "Crikey," she said when Gemma had finished. "You have been a busy bee. This DCI—Boatman—you said you'd met her before. Is she okay? Or is she just covering her arse?"

"I think . . ." Gemma said, considering, "I think she's a good detective. I don't envy her being pressured by Lamb and the Williamses. But on the other hand, Bill and MacKenzie were right to push for a thorough investigation. They knew Reagan, and their instincts were right. She didn't die of natural causes."

"So you have a locked-garden mystery," Melody mused.

"I don't see anyone getting in that gate," Gemma agreed.

"It all sounds quite creepy, with the white dress, and the candle wax in the grass. Some kind of ritual gone wrong, do you think?"

Gemma frowned. "From what I've learned about Reagan Keating so far, I can't imagine her being involved in anything like that. And it wouldn't explain her missing phone."

"Did she have a computer?"

"There was a photo printer on her desk, but no desktop or laptop. If she had either, it's missing, too. We'll find out tomorrow."

Melody looked suddenly stricken, as if realizing that the "we" didn't include her. "Good luck, then," she said, glancing at her watch, then giving Gemma a bright smile and gulping what must now be stone-cold tea. "But I've got to run——"

"Boatman is obviously short-staffed," broke in Gemma. "If there's any way I can swing getting you a temporary assignment——"

But Melody was already shaking her head. "You didn't see the guv'nor's face today. She was livid. I think I'd like to keep my job. And besides, I'm in charge in your stead." This time her smile seemed more genuine.

"Stay for dinner," Gemma offered as Melody stood, not wanting her to go.

Melody hesitated for just a moment, then made a little rueful face and said, "Can't. Meeting someone. But thanks."

"A date? I thought Andy was in—where, Germany?"

"Your guess is as good as mine." Melody's shrug seemed deliberately offhand. "And, no, it's not a date. Unless you count meeting Doug at the Jolly Gardeners for a drink. Which I certainly do not."

After Melody left, Gemma had brought the children in from the garden, settling them in the dining room with a game of Jenga and hoping to hold off the pre-dinner demands for telly or video games. The game of stacking tiles was too hard for Charlotte, so

Gemma anticipated a meltdown any moment. And she'd already had to scoop the kittens off the table when they tried to bat at the tiles.

Rose, the tortoiseshell and white kitten, came into the kitchen as if summoned by the thought, wrapping herself around Gemma's ankles. She was an affectionate little thing, not as much of a troublemaker as her brother Jack, and Gemma was developing a decided preference. Stooping, she picked the kitten up for a cuddle. "Girls," she murmured, stroking the soft little head, "should stick together, yeah? But don't say I said so." Rose had black patches over her eyes and one was larger than the other, giving her a piratical look. In between the black patches her fur was ginger, and then white around her very pink nose. Kit had given Gemma more than one lecture on the genetics of cat coloration, but she had to admit it had gone in one ear and out the other. All she remembered was that only females were tortoiseshell.

The kitten apparently decided she was more interested in prawns than adoration and squirmed towards the work top. "No, you don't," Gemma told her firmly and set her down. She'd just begun chopping shallots when there was a crash of Jenga tiles from the dining room and the rising sound of a squabble. It was a relief when the doorbell rang.

"Pick those up," she admonished the children as she crossed the hall. She was already preparing to say, "Changed your mind, then?" to Melody as she opened the door.

But it wasn't Melody, it was MacKenzie Williams, with Oliver, who was holding tightly to his mother's hand and leaning his curly head against her leg. "Gemma," said MacKenzie, "I'm so sorry to barge in again like this. But I needed to talk to you."

Oliver tugged on MacKenzie's hand. "Mummy, I want to go in."

"Not unless you're invited, darling," MacKenzie admonished.

"Of course he is." Gemma gave Oliver a pat. "Go on, then. Charlotte and Toby are playing a game in the dining room. The grown-ups can talk in the kitchen," she added quietly to Mac-Kenzie.

"We can't stay long," MacKenzie murmured as Oliver ran inside. "I told Bill we were going to the shops for something I forgot."

As her friend followed her into the kitchen, Gemma saw that there were dark hollows under her eyes, and that the mass of her dark hair was drawn back haphazardly with a clip, as if she hadn't bothered to brush it.

"Could I have one of those?" MacKenzie asked when she spied Gemma's glass of wine.

"Of course." Gemma filled a glass for MacKenzie, glad she'd had a full bottle on hand. Joining MacKenzie at the kitchen table, she raised her own topped-up glass and tapped it to MacKenzie's. "Cheers."

MacKenzie took an obligatory sip but then set her glass on the table and leaned forward. Her shoulders looked tight with tension. "Listen, Gemma. I didn't mean to drop you in the shit today. Bill told me he called your boss this morning and asked that you be included in the investigation into Reagan's death. He can be a bit overbearing when he gets the bit between his teeth, and he was very fond of Reagan. But he had no right to demand that you be put on the case. Or to cause any awkwardness for you at work."

From what Melody had told Gemma about Detective Superintendent Krueger's mood that morning, Gemma suspected it would be more than awkwardness. But she said, "Don't worry about that, it's not your—"

MacKenzie waved a hand to stop her. "No, really, hear me out. I feel like I presumed on our friendship. I had no idea, when I asked you to go with me yesterday, that it would be so . . . so complicated. And I'm sure I overreacted, that Reagan was just ill, or maybe took too much of something she didn't realize would hurt her. And now I feel a complete fool—"

"MacKenzie," Gemma said softly, aware of the little voices— and little ears—across the hall. "I'm sorry. But you *weren't* wrong. The pathologist did the postmortem this morning. I'm afraid Reagan was murdered."

MacKenzie stared at her, gaping, then whispered, "Oh, Christ." She touched her glass with a trembling hand but didn't pick it up. "Are you sure?"

"I'm afraid so. It will take time for the labs to come back, but the postmortem results were pretty conclusive. We have enough to go on with."

"But— How?" MacKenzie whispered.

Gemma hesitated. The information would come out soon enough. She'd like to keep the advantage of that knowledge in interviews for as long as possible, but she didn't see any reason why she shouldn't tell MacKenzie. "Please don't share this with anyone except Bill," she cautioned. "Reagan was suffocated."

"Suffocated?" MacKenzie sat back, blinking, her white skin like parchment against her black hair. "Oh, my God. Why . . . Why would someone do that to her? Was she—" She didn't seem able to finish the thought.

"No, no." Gemma grasped her friend's hand. "Reagan wasn't sexually assaulted." MacKenzie was so pale now Gemma was afraid she might faint. "Are you all right, MacKenzie? I know this is a shock."

"I just can't imagine . . ."

"Nobody can. And when you know someone, well, nobody can be prepared for something like this." Gemma pushed MacKenzie's wineglass towards her. "Here. Have a good sip. Or I can get you some water. Or a cup of tea."

Shaking her head, MacKenzie lifted the glass and took an obedient sip. Then she made a face and pushed her glass away. "I don't think I can . . . I'm sorry. I feel a little ill. I keep thinking . . ."

Rising, Gemma filled the kettle. "You have a cuppa before you go. It will help with the shock." Another crash of tiles and a high-pitched shriek came from the dining room. Gemma wasn't sure if it had come from Charlotte or Oliver, but in either case she predicted impending chaos.

MacKenzie recognized the signs as well. "No, I'm fine. Really. We'd better go. I will tell Bill I spoke to you—although I still don't think he should have put you on the spot like that. But Gemma, do you . . . Do you have any idea who might have . . . done this to her?"

"We've heard she wasn't getting on with her boyfriend, that's all. But we only have a first name for him—Hugo."

MacKenzie stared at her. "Hugo?"

"Blond. Pretty. At least I think that must be him. Reagan had photos on the corkboard in her room."

"I don't believe it." MacKenzie's eyes widened and she put a hand to her mouth.

"What?" Gemma stared at her. "Don't tell me you know him?"

"Hair like this?" MacKenzie brushed a hand just below her jawline.

"Yes."

"But— She never— I had no idea . . ."

"MacKenzie. Look at me." Gemma reached across the table and

patted her friend's hand. She understood shock, but she was impatient now. "Do you know him?"

MacKenzie nodded, slowly. "It has to be Hugo. Hugo Gold. But I had no idea they were seeing each other."

"How do you know him?" Gemma asked, trying to keep her voice level.

"He modeled for us."

As Kincaid drove north, the clouds moved in from the Atlantic like a blanket flung across the sky. With a shiver, he cranked up the heater in the Astra. Even though he'd known not to count on the fine London weather holding, the chill made his spirits sink. He tried to concentrate on the rolling Cotswold landscape—at least what he could see of it from the motorway. The spring fields looked a shockingly brilliant green against the flat gray horizon.

The rain set in in earnest at Birmingham. But by the time he took the turnoff for Nantwich, the downpour had ceased and patches of blue were appearing in the western sky. He told himself it was a good omen. Not, of course, that he usually thought of himself as superstitious, but the last few days had set him grasping at titbits.

Leighton Hospital sat north of Nantwich, on the A530. It seemed small, provincial even, compared to the warren of the London, and he found the cardiac unit easily enough. His mother was the only person in the waiting area. He stopped for a moment, just on the other side of the glass door, observing her. Rosemary Kincaid was a handsome woman, with the fine bone structure that grew more defined with age. Usually, she dressed well if not elegantly—Nantwich was, after all, a country town and a bookshop didn't call for much in the way of finery—and she was always careful of her appearance. Today, however, she was in what she referred to as "farm clothes"—jeans, a cardigan that he recognized as his father's, and the pair of old brogues she wore for gardening. He thought she must have put on whatever came to hand.

Glancing up, she saw him and sprang to her feet. "Darling," she said as he pushed open the door, and the exhaustion was momentarily smoothed from her face by a smile. When he reached her, he wrapped his arms around her in a hug. It surprised him still that his mother's head fit into the hollow of his chest, as if the memory of looking up at her was imprinted on his consciousness.

"Mum." He stepped back to look at her but kept his hands firmly on her shoulders. "How are you? How is he?"

"I was just trying to decide whether to ring you, but I thought I'd wait a bit longer. He's had a stent put in, just one, and he's still a bit groggy from the procedure."

"But he's okay?"

"They say he's fine. That they caught it before the blockage was too severe. No thanks to him, the stubborn old coot." Her voice wavered at the last. Guiding her back to her chair, he sat down beside her and took her hand. He felt a little giddy with relief.

"Tell me what happened," he said.

"It was about four last night. He was rubbing at his arm. His left arm." She mimed the gesture, then shivered. "He insisted I drive him to hospital, that he wasn't going to look a fool for nothing.

"Dear God. It was raining, and the roads were like pitch. I thought *I* was going to have a heart attack," she added, managing a smile.

"What was he doing yesterday?" Kincaid asked suspiciously, knowing his father all too well.

"Building a fort for Sam."

"Bloody hell," he said in disbelief. That was over the top, even for Hugh.

"I know. Don't tell Juliet. I said he was working in the barn."

"Where is Jules?" he asked.

"Here, until an hour ago. She's expecting you for dinner tonight. Although of course you'll want to sleep at the farm."

"What about Dad? When are they sending him home?"

"They want to keep him overnight. And I'm not letting him out of my sight."

Hugh Kincaid was dozing in his hospital bed. The sight gave Kincaid a jolt of déjà vu, but unlike his visit to Denis Childs, when his dad opened his eyes they sparkled with recognition.

"Son. They shouldna have dragged you all the way up from London." Hugh's voice was thready, his Scottish accent more pronounced.

"You shouldn't have put yourself in hospital," Kincaid teased, pulling up a chair. "What were you thinking? Isn't Sam too old for a fort?"

Hugh shrugged a bit apologetically. "Even teenagers need a retreat."

Kincaid stood, reluctantly. His dad was sounding tired. "You get some rest. And behave yourself, or I'll hear about it in the morning."

Hugh reached for Kincaid's hand. "You're coming back, son?"

"Of course I am. Just try to stop me." On impulse, Kincaid leaned down and kissed his dad's bristly cheek, something he hadn't done since he was a child.

CHAPTER THIRTEEN

He sat in the café across from Earl's Court Station, watching the door uneasily. Usually he reported to his handler by phone several times a week, particularly when there had been a meeting of his protest group. But this morning he'd been summoned. Especially as it was the beginning of his one day off and he'd been planning to make the most it, perhaps take his wife for a drive in the country to enjoy the fine weather.

He'd come deliberately early. The place was a working man's café, Formica tables, scuffed lino floor, the food ordered and served from the counter. But the café was clean and was known for its good food and generous portions. After a week of the vegetarian life in Paddington—he didn't dare be seen eating meat by his new friends, who were vegetarian or vegan all—he'd ordered the full fry-up, bacon and sausages and, horror of vegetarian hor-

rors, *black pudding. Now he was on his second mug of industrial-strength tea, sitting where he could watch the door and the bustle of the street beyond.*

So it was that he saw Red before Red saw him, and the unguarded expression on his handler's face made the food he'd just eaten turn leaden in the pit of his stomach.

Spotting him as he came in the door, Red crossed the café briskly—he was always brisk, a man going places and in a hurry to get there—and stopped at his table. "Need a refill?" Red asked, nodding at the mug, but it was perfunctory.

"No thanks. I'd float." He tapped his still-full second cup for emphasis, then watched as Red went to the counter and got himself a coffee. The man looked like a copper even in his casual clothes. His posture was ramrod straight, his clipped little ginger mustache something only a policeman or a soldier would sport, his summer polo shirt tucked too tightly into his pressed trousers, and his sports jacket just a bit too tailored.

Returning, Red made a pucker of distaste as he mopped up a few drops of a previous customer's spilled tea with a flimsy paper napkin. As he sat, he glanced round the café. The place was emptying, entering the lull between breakfast and lunch. Red frowned, assessing him. "You look like shit."

If that meant he no longer had the proper spit and polish, that was true enough. He'd learned to achieve a certain level of stubble, and had let his dark hair grow over his ears and his collar. He wore a denim shirt, the sleeves rolled up to the elbows, and sturdy canvas work trousers. He was, after all, supposed to be a jobbing landscaper. "Thank you, sir."

"Don't be a smart-ass with me," said Red, obviously not appreciating his humor. With a frown, he leaned across the table and lowered his voice. "Now, what sort of progress are you making?"

He blinked. "Progress? I've told you. We've some new leaflets and we're joining in a march in south Lon—"

Red waved a hand dismissively. "You know very well that's not what I mean." The handler checked again for eavesdroppers. It made him look furtive. "What have you learned about the Lawrences? Have they got anything new?"

Ah. Light dawned. He should have known. It was only a few weeks ago he'd learned that one member of his group was meant to be his particular target. Twenty-seven-year-old Annette Whitely was an actress, just beginning to get better parts in film and on television. She was mixed race, her father West Indian black, her mother white. She'd grown up in Notting Hill and was fiercely devoted to stamping out racial discrimination. Horrified by the handling of the Lawrence case, she'd spoken out publicly several times. It was hoped by the Met that her minor celebrity would give her some access to the Lawrence family's private investigation into their son's death. "Not as yet," he said carefully.

Red bristled. "This is taxpayers' money you're wasting, sonny, lounging around and eating your nut loaves and curries."

He thought, not for the first time, that if the taxpayers had any idea where their money was going they would be horrified. "Sir." He kept his tone reasonable. "You know these things take time."

"Don't patronize me, sonny," Red hissed, and the color of his face made it clear the nickname had to do with more than his hair. "Things could go pear shaped and we are counting on you."

There'd been another story in the Chronicle that week, further detailing the Met's incompetence in the Lawrence case. "Sir," he said even more quietly. Anyone who knew him well would have recognized his even voice as a sign of rising temper. "I can't just make up things out of thin air."

"Then I suggest you try harder. Or things might get very difficult for you."

He stared at the little man across the table. "Are you threatening me, sir?"

Red gave a little smirk, not quite hidden by his mustache, and
leaned back in his chair. "It would be a shame if your pretty wife
found out you were shagging one of your unwashed protesters, now
wouldn't it?"

"What are you talking about? I've never—"

"Only because you're too much of a wimp to take advantage
of what's under your nose. A surprise, a big fellow like you." Red
shrugged. "But what does it matter whether you did or didn't?"
He pulled a snapshot from his pocket. "Do you think your wife
would believe you if someone happened to show her this?" He slid
the photo across the table.

He stared at it in disbelief. "You've got to be taking the piss."
The photo had been taken on the street, near the Tabernacle. The
group had been tacking up handbills. Annette, working beside him,
had been bumped by a passing pedestrian. He'd put out a hand
to steady her and that had been all there was to it. But what he
saw in the photo was his hand grasping her shoulder as she leaned
into him, and her laughing happily as she looked up into his eyes.
There was an intimacy to it that he hadn't recognized at the time.

And what made it worse was the fact that Annette Whitely was
absolutely, stunningly beautiful.

"What man wouldn't fancy that?" Red asked, pocketing the
photo again. "And what man's wife wouldn't believe he did?"

By the time Melody had walked across Putney Bridge and made
her way to Lacy Road, she was warm and her red outfit felt wilted.

The little sheds in the front of the Jolly Gardeners were already occupied—they were quickly staked out by smokers—but she was able to snag a table inside by the big front windows. The open casements let in the warm evening air along with a drift of cigarette smoke.

The pub was a detached building in a road of small terraced houses just off Putney High Street. Victorian or Edwardian, the place had been updated well, with bare floors and simple, mismatched furniture that set off the high ceilings and the lovely large windows. In winter, coal fires burned in the period fireplaces, but this was an evening for being, if not in the garden, as close to it as possible.

She gazed out, fidgeting with the glass of white wine she'd bought at the bar. After her rush to get here, Doug was late. Before coming into the pub, she'd glanced up the street at his house. Dusk was drawing in, but no light shone through the green-and-gold glass in his front door. Doug was usually Mr. Punctual. She dug her mobile from her bag, double-checking she hadn't missed a call or a message, then laid it on the table.

Then, with a sudden shake of her head, she picked up the mobile and slipped it back into her bag. What could possibly look sadder than a woman alone in a pub, desperately checking her messages?

The pub was filling up now and standing patrons were eyeing the empty place at her table. She forced a smile and put her bag firmly on the chair. Half her wine was gone, and if she got up, she'd lose the table. She took a tiny sip, then pushed her glass aside. Where the hell was Doug?

She should have stayed at Gemma's. But she'd felt awkward there, too. Uninvited, a stray. Gemma's world seemed complete in itself, brimming with children and dogs and even the bloody cats, a life full and always in motion. She thought of her own flat, empty and uninviting, and wondered how she'd got to such a place in her life.

Then she remembered Gemma's face as she'd told her about her father-in-law, and she chastised herself for being selfish.

She'd taken her mobile out again to send Gemma a text when, from above her, Doug said, "Sorry. Bloody tube."

"Jesus!" She dropped her mobile for the second time that day, and had to grope for it on the floor as Doug moved her bag and collapsed into the chair. "Where did you come from?" she asked as she sat up again, mobile in hand.

Doug nodded at it. "You were busy."

"I wasn't—" She shook her head. "Let's not argue. Get a drink."

He touched her glass. "Another round?"

She started to say yes, then realized she just felt terribly thirsty. "Just some sparkling water, please. With ice."

Doug raised an eyebrow at that, but got up again and threaded his way to the bar. They knew him here, the place was his regular. She saw the barman smile as he took Doug's order. Where, she thought, did she go that anyone knew her?

It had been different when she and Gemma had worked out of Notting Hill. She'd known the best coffee shops and sandwich shops and bakeries, and had in turn been recognized and welcomed. She'd met mates from work for drinks at the pub near the station, where the staff greeted her with smiles and knew her usual. None of those things had happened at Brixton—somehow her routine there had never gelled. She felt . . . displaced. With Andy gone, Doug and his house and this pub were the closest things she had to familiar territory.

Doug came back, balancing a pint in one hand and a large bottle of San Pellegrino and a glass in the other. Melody took the glass gratefully. She filled it from the bottle and drank most of it down.

"Are you okay?" Doug gave her a concerned look as he slid into his chair.

"Yes, just—it was warm today and I've been back and forth across the city."

Doug looked surprised. "You went home?"

"No." Melody drank more water. "I went to see Gemma. I wanted to know why she didn't come in today. Krueger was furious, said Gemma had been seconded to some big case. I hadn't heard a word from her and I was—" She stopped, not wanting to admit how betrayed she'd felt.

"Did you talk to her? What happened?" Doug put down his pint and absently wiped the foam from his lip. For a moment, he looked like a little boy eating an ice cream, and Melody was tempted to smile.

"Well, it wasn't exactly like that." She told him about Reagan Keating, the girl who had been found dead in the garden, and about Gemma's connection through her friends. "So Gemma got a bit steam-rollered, and I suspect Superintendent Krueger was royally hacked off because Marc Lamb didn't even consult her before borrowing her from Brixton."

"It will be Gemma who takes the fallout, not Lamb," said Doug.

Melody nodded. "I'm afraid so. But I wish . . ."

"What?"

She shook her head. She wasn't going to admit, even to Doug, how much she wanted to be back in Notting Hill, working on a case with Gemma.

"It's never a good thing when people start calling in favors. You're well out of it," said Doug, and she knew that he knew exactly what she'd been thinking.

"Yes." She poured more San Pellegrino into her glass. The ice was gone, and the water had done nothing to slake her thirst.

Doug leaned towards her, his face intent. "What about Denis? Did they know anything?"

"It wasn't 'they.' Duncan's in Cheshire. His father's ill. But," she said, before Doug could interrupt her, "Gemma said he went to see Denis yesterday, at the London."

"But he can't talk. Denis, I mean. If he's in—"

"An induced coma, apparently. Because of the blow to his head. But, Doug, Gemma told me—" Melody paused, not certain she was supposed to repeat this, but Gemma hadn't cautioned her against it. "Gemma said that Denis had a liver transplant. That's why he was away."

Doug looked at her like she'd gone bonkers. "What are you talking about?"

"You didn't know either?"

"Of course I didn't know. I'd have told you." He thought for a moment. "How did he keep something like that quiet at the Yard? And how did Duncan and Gemma know? Is that why he's been avoiding me?"

Melody could hear the hurt in his voice. She thought about how badly she'd felt, shut out by Gemma for one day, and for the first time really understood how Doug must have been feeling the past few months. "No," she said, "I don't think— I got the impression they didn't know, either. Someone must have said something at the hospital."

Doug sat back, sipping at his pint and frowning. "Cagey bugger," he said at last. "And that's not the only thing Denis Childs has kept quiet."

"You found out something." Melody's pulse gave a little flutter. She wasn't sure if it was excitement or dread. "Tell me."

"You know I didn't see any of this. For the record."

"Just tell me." She found she was gripping her glass.

"I did a thorough search on the Web—you'd be amazed at what's out there," Doug said. "Denis Childs was a perfect candidate for a cop on a path to the top. University—Oxford"—this he threw in with a pleased little smile—"where he read Classics. Then, Hendon, graduated top in his class. After that, the usual couple of years in uniform, then a transfer into CID, where he quickly made detective sergeant."

Melody waited, wondering if strangling him might be worth going to prison.

"He moved around a bit, again, not unusual, and did his courses. Then"—Doug paused for another sip of his beer—"he vanishes. Boom. Just like that. There's no record of any posting for three years. Then he reappears, in central London, promoted to DI."

They sat staring at each other. Finally, it was Melody who whispered, "Bloody Special Branch."

"That would be the logical assumption."

"It doesn't necessarily mean counterintelligence," Melody said. "He could have done anything. Protected the queen, even."

Doug grinned. "That would explain your father's hints about a checkered past, all right."

"Oh, ha bloody ha," said Melody, but he'd made her laugh. "Can you find out anything else? Maybe you could, you know, get a look at their files."

He was already shaking his head. "Hack Special Branch personnel? Just exactly how daft do you think I am?"

Hazel Cavendish had spent the afternoon baking at the Islington house. Not that the kitchen was professional, by a long chalk, but it was a good deal bigger and better equipped than the kitchen in her little bungalow in Battersea. Since she'd taken the contracts to provide baked goods for a half dozen West London cafés and restaurants, she'd been picking up her seven-year-old daughter, Holly, after school and coming here several afternoons a week.

"*The Islington House,*" she murmured to herself as she washed up the last of the sheet pans. She thought of it in italics. Not as *Tim's house,* or as *their house.* Although technically it was, still, their house, even though she hadn't lived in it for two years.

It was two years almost exactly, she realized, since she had run away to Scotland. She had taken Gemma with her on that ill-fated trip, but not even Gemma had been able to save her from a disaster of her own making.

As she dried the last pan, she gazed out the window at the shadows lengthening in the garden. The garage flat was dark. Neither she nor Tim had wanted to rent it since Gemma and Toby had moved out, although she knew the money would have been helpful. Tim had managed to keep the house up without her income—had even helped her a bit—and had never complained. How, she wondered, could she ever learn to deal with her guilt when her husband seemed set on sainthood?

Tonight he'd invited them to dinner, and had gone to the shops while Hazel finished up the last of tomorrow's tarts. Holly was playing with a friend down the street and Tim had promised to collect her on his way home.

Hazel avoided seeing their neighbors, with whom she had once been close. She found her situation hard enough to explain to herself. Separated, but still married. "Co-parents," she supposed, a term she hated. Friends, yes. She thought they had become so, over the past two years, which was very odd. They talked about things now in a way they had never done when living as husband and wife.

And lovers . . . yes, sometimes. The thought made her color. Folding her tea towel, she took down a glass and poured herself white wine from the open bottle in the fridge. She wandered out the back door and sat on the terrace, where she and Gemma had sat and gossiped so often on warm summer evenings while the children played in the garden. She'd been avoiding Gemma lately, too, she realized. She thought Gemma must know what was going on with Tim, but she was embarrassed to admit it even to her closest friend.

She and Tim hadn't made love here, in the bed they'd shared for years, but only in her little bungalow, when Holly was at school or sleeping over with a friend. Then, it felt like they were teenagers, stealing a few hours for illicit sex, and it was better than she ever remembered. What would it be like if they lived together again? Hazel wondered. Would ennui set in? And if it did, would she be content with it?

A shout from the gate saved her from pursuing that thought. Holly came charging in, brandishing a scraggly doll. "Mummy, Amanda gave me her Barbie," she said when she reached the terrace. "Can I keep her, please? Amanda said she's old and she doesn't want her anymore."

"What did Amanda's mummy say?" Hazel asked.

"She said I could keep her. Amanda's getting a new Barbie. A curvy one, but Amanda thinks that's stupid."

Hazel looked up at Tim, who'd come in through the house and brought his own glass of wine. She rolled her eyes at him as he sat down beside her, but said to Holly, "Darling, why does Amanda think curvy Barbie is stupid?"

"Because Barbie doesn't look like that, Mummy," said Holly with a seven-year-old's disdain for the obvious.

"But—" Seeing Tim's grin, Hazel stopped. They'd never told Holly she couldn't have a Barbie, on the theory that the forbidden became more desirable, but they'd never bought her one, either. "Okay, sweetie," she amended, trying not to grimace at the doll's deformed body and feet. "Go play with her, then." She ruffled her daughter's dark curls.

When Holly had run happily off, Tim touched his glass to hers and said, "Good call."

"Not tackling gender and body stereotyping during cocktail hour?"

"Ooh," he said, laughing, "I like it when you talk like a therapist."

Hazel smacked him on the arm. "Shut up."

"Seriously, she'll get tired of her, and Barbie will be *so* over."

Holly's singsong voice drifted to them from the bottom of the garden. When Hazel looked, she saw that Holly had managed to loop one of Barbie's feet in the swing rope, and was now hanging the doll by one leg, upside down. She and Tim both started to laugh. "Sooner rather than later, I think," Hazel managed through giggles. "You're right, as usual."

"I try to live with it," he said, still teasing, but Hazel went quiet, gazing out over the garden, and thinking they should put a light on a timer in the garage flat.

She and Tim had both been family therapists, with separate practices. But when she'd come back to London after their separation, she hadn't felt she had any business counseling others. "Physician, heal thyself," she murmured.

Tim gave her a sharp look.

"I was thinking I could use a therapist's advice," she said, grasping for a logical change of subject.

She saw the sudden tension as his fingers tightened on his glass. "What about?" he asked, so levelly that she knew the effort had cost him. He was afraid she was going to drop some kind of bombshell on him.

"It's about Melody Talbot." She touched his arm lightly in assurance and felt him relax. "I saw her yesterday. It was very strange and it's been nagging me since." She told him about running into Melody in Kensington Square. "She seemed frantic, and almost . . . I don't know . . . disassociated. The only reason she gave was she had been to her parents' Sunday lunch and wasn't feeling well."

"That sounds reasonable. Especially if her family is difficult."

"But it wasn't reasonable," Hazel insisted. "You know how it is when something is really wrong—you can feel it."

Tim was silent for a moment, watching Holly, then he said, "Melody had a bad time with that fire in St. Pancras, didn't she? She could be dealing with some degree of posttraumatic stress."

Hazel nodded. "That's what I was thinking. But I wondered— do you think I should say something to Gemma? As a friend?"

"Melody's friend, or Gemma's friend?" Tim asked, frowning. "You may not be practicing, but you're still a therapist, and that feels a bit like tale-telling to me."

"Damn." Hazel leaned back and sipped at her wine. "I was afraid you were going to say that."

"I think that you should have more faith in your own judgment. You'll think of something."

Hazel considered this. "The first thing is to get her to talk to me. I'll ask her to lunch."

"So what happened with the dishy detective constable?" Kincaid asked.

DCI Ronnie Babcock snorted into his beer so forcefully that he had to wipe his face with the back of his hand. "Dishy? Jesus, Duncan, are you even living in the last century, much less this one? And she better not hear that you ever uttered that, or she'll probably take out a contract on you."

Kincaid and his old schoolmate had retired to the Bowling Green, the comfortable pub in the shadow of St. Mary's Church in the center of Nantwich, and just a short walk from Kincaid's sister Juliet's house. Rosemary had rung to say that Hugh was resting well and Kincaid had promised to help her get him settled at home in the morning.

The constable in question was Detective Constable Sheila Larkin of the Cheshire Constabulary, who had been Babcock's very capable assistant in the case Kincaid and Gemma had become involved in Christmas before last. "I thought you fancied her," Kincaid said, unperturbed.

"Not everyone can carry off going out with a coworker. And besides," Babcock said, a little bashfully, "I had a better offer."

Kincaid raised his glass and clinked it against his friend's. "I'll drink to that." While Babcock might have flirted with DC Larkin, he'd shown real concern for Juliet's welfare when she was going through a difficult time. It was obvious that concern had blossomed into considerably more. "So do you have any, um, plans?" he asked.

"Don't tell me you're going all brotherly and asking what my intentions are towards your sister?" Ronnie sounded only half mocking.

Kincaid shrugged. When Kincaid had shown up for dinner at Juliet's, Ronnie's presence had merely confirmed what Kincaid already knew. "Just curious. You two seem well suited. And Juliet deserves some joy in her life." Kincaid felt awkward, afraid he'd crossed the line into maudlin.

But Ronnie said, quite seriously, "We're just taking things slowly. We've both been through hard divorces and Juliet's been through worse than that. The kids don't need any big changes for a while, either." He grinned. "Just getting to the point where I could officially spend the night was milestone enough."

"That's probably more than I want to know," Kincaid said, laughing.

"How's your Gemma, then?" asked Babcock.

Gemma, Kincaid remembered, had been so taken with Ronnie Babcock that he'd felt a spark of jealousy. "She's fine. Busy." He'd rung her from Juliet's before dinner, and while she'd obviously been relieved to hear that Hugh was doing well, she was just as obviously unhappy with him for not telling her sooner. He'd try her again that night, but first he wanted to talk to Ronnie. The problem was, he didn't know where to start.

"Are you okay?" asked Ronnie, frowning at him. "You're not having an affair, are you?"

"Bloody hell, Ronnie." Kincaid stared back, horrified. "Of course not. What made you think that?"

"You've had that distracted look all night. Checking your watch, checking your phone."

"No, no, it's nothing like that," Kincaid said, shaking his head. "My boss—my former boss—is in hospital. I was hoping for news."

"He's ill, then?" Ronnie had relaxed, his expression sympathetic again.

"No. Well, not exactly." Kincaid told Ronnie first about the attack on Denis, then about Denis's odd behavior since the autumn. "The investigation into the murder of a female senior officer—a rower—led us to uncover years' worth of wrongdoing by a recently retired deputy assistant commissioner, Angus Craig. Then, we found that the DAC had raped and killed another senior female police officer.

"My guv'nor, Denis, had us hold off overnight making the arrest." Kincaid could feel himself beginning to sweat, although the evening was cool and the pub windows were open to the breeze. He cleared his throat. "In the early hours of the next morning, Craig, and his wife, were found dead, shot, their house burned around them."

"Murder/suicide?" asked Ronnie.

"All the hallmarks. I felt Denis was culpable because he held off on the arrest."

Kincaid was suddenly aware of the sounds in the pub, the murmur of conversation, the clink of glasses. Had he been speaking too loudly? No one at the nearby tables seemed to have taken any notice. But Ronnie Babcock was watching him intently, a slight frown on his prematurely creased face.

"And then what happened?" Ronnie asked.

"That was my last case before I took leave to look after Charlotte." They had talked about Charlotte at dinner with the children. He'd shown them photos, and Juliet had made him promise to bring the whole family for a visit when the boys started their summer break. He drank a little of his beer and went on. "When I came back to the Yard, my office had been cleared out and there was a transfer letter on my desk, signed by Denis. I was reassigned to the murder team at Holborn Station. And Denis was unreachable. There was no explanation. I thought"—he grimaced—"I thought it was a punishment for questioning his judgment. I was furious. But . . ." He'd got to the part that no one but Gemma knew, and he was reluctant, now that he'd come to it, to go on.

But Ronnie just watched him steadily, and in some small part of his mind Kincaid thought, Good copper. Silence was the unfailing interview technique, and in the face of it he at last went on.

"On Saturday, I found out Denis was back at the Yard. I tried to see him. Then he texted me, asking me to meet him at a pub in Holborn that night. He said he'd been away for health reasons, and that there were certain people in the Yard who wished him ill. He said he transferred me for my own good, so that I'd have less association with him. And he told me to keep my nose out of things if I knew what was good for me."

"A bit dramatic," Ronnie ventured, but his expression didn't display skepticism.

"So I thought. But a few minutes after he left me that night, he was attacked and left for dead." Kincaid grasped his pint in both hands. "I haven't told anyone except Gemma that I met him that night."

"And he's—"

"Unconscious. Induced coma. They're not sure if he'll recover."

"But you don't think it was random?"

"No, I don't believe it was a random mugging. Nothing was taken. If some schoolgirls hadn't happened upon him, he'd have died."

"Coincidence, then?" Ronnie asked.

"I don't know. Maybe. But if it wasn't, and someone saw him

meeting me . . ." Looking down, Kincaid realized his pint was empty. But when Ronnie mimed a refill, he shook his head, wanting his wits about him.

"A wee bit paranoid, perhaps," said Ronnie. "Unless"—he gave Kincaid his most intense blue gaze—"there's something you're not telling me."

"I—there was—" Suddenly, Kincaid changed his mind about another round. He wasn't going to get through this without a little Dutch courage. Without a word, he took Ronnie's glass as well as his own to the bar. He came back, not with beer, but with two double measures of the pub's best whisky.

He took a swallow. When his eyes stopped watering and he could get his breath, he told Ronnie everything he could remember about Ryan Marsh, ending with the night Ryan Marsh died. "I found him. I didn't tell anyone that I was there. Not even Gemma. And I hope to God none of the duty officers recognized me."

Ronnie sat quietly, sipping his whisky, his gaze unfocused. Drained, Kincaid closed his eyes, so that he was startled when Ronnie said softly, "You don't think it was suicide, do you, mate?"

"No. I don't believe it. I never did. I've asked a pathologist friend to double-check the postmortem results."

Ronnie considered for a moment, then tapped his forefinger on the table. "So. Let me get this straight. You have two cops who seemed to be afraid of someone within the force. You suspect one was murdered—although you have no proof—and that one was the victim of a murder attempt—although you have no proof. You also think that you might be connected by the perpetrator—or perpetrators—with one or both of these men."

Kincaid nodded, reluctantly. "You think I'm bonkers."

"You've always been bonkers, at least according to your sister,"

Ronnie said with an unexpected grin. Sobering again, he added, "However, in this case, I think maybe you are . . . not."

"What?" Kincaid frowned. "You're telling me I'm not crazy?"

"First of all, unless you've suddenly taken leave of your senses, you have good instincts, and good judgment. You should trust both." Ronnie looked Kincaid in the eyes. "And there's something else. There was a cop coming in here for a while. Early retirement from the Met, he said, moved back here to his home county for his health—although I got the impression that his health problems included drinking large amounts of alcohol on a regular basis. He was a DCI, he said, and when he'd had a good deal of booze, he muttered things about knowing too much and being turfed out because of it. I haven't seen him lately. Maybe I should look him up. His name's Frank Fletcher. Ring any bells?"

When Kincaid shook his head, Ronnie went on. "Coincidence, probably. Alcohol-induced paranoia, a drunkard making excuses for his failures. But, when we talked about the job, I'd have sworn he was a good cop." Ronnie shrugged. "There are always rumors about corruption within the Met—and any other force, for that matter. Mostly bunk, but—"

"No smoke without fire?" The words had slipped out, but the adage brought unpleasant memories to Kincaid's mind. He took another sip of his whisky, trying to vanquish the taste of ash.

"So." Ronnie tapped the table again. "If your pathologist friend says he thinks your undercover cop did not commit suicide, what exactly do you intend to do about it?"

Kincaid blinked. "I don't know."

Ronnie shook his head. He leaned towards Kincaid, elbows on the table. "You're shooting in the dark. I don't like it. You don't know enough about either of these men. You don't even know if your undercover cop was rogue or still on the Met's payroll. Is there any connection between these two, Childs and Marsh?"

"No. Not that I know——" Kincaid stopped, thinking furiously. "Wait. Ryan Marsh was inserted into the antidevelopment protest group in Camden months before Denis arranged my transfer there. That night, when we met, Denis said he sent me to Holborn because he trusted DCS Faith. But what if——what if he knew Ryan Marsh would be on my patch? But then he'd have to either have known Marsh, or known something about the group——" He stopped, rubbing his face. "That really is bonkers. You're right. I'm running blind. I'd never go into a case this way."

Ronnie was so close now that Kincaid could feel his breath on his face and smell the tang of whisky. "You need to learn every single thing you can about this Marsh, and about your guv'nor," Ronnie said, jabbing him in the chest with a forefinger. "And, listen, mate, you have got to tell Gemma. Now. Or you are going to be in a world of trouble."

CHAPTER FOURTEEN

Gemma woke on Tuesday morning no less cross than she had gone to bed the night before. When Kincaid had rung for the second time, the children had been in bed and she'd been taking the dogs out. She had, of course, left her mobile on the kitchen table, so had missed his call by minutes. When she listened to his message, he said he was staying the night on Juliet's sofa rather than going to his parents' farm. He'd sounded a bit slurred.

She hadn't rung him back.

She slept fitfully, tossing and turning and waking to look at the clock. In spite of the cocker spaniel and the two kittens curled on her feet, the bed felt empty and cold.

When the sun rose, she was glad of an excuse to get up. As she got herself and the children ready for the day, she found herself looking forward to morning coffee and a chat with Melody. Then she realized she wasn't going to Brixton, wasn't seeing Melody. She had a different agenda.

After MacKenzie had given her Hugo Gold's name and phone number the night before, Gemma had rung Kerry Boatman with the information. Kerry had rung back a few minutes later, saying that Gold had agreed to see them at nine that morning, at Bill's in Kensington.

She and Kerry decided to meet at the entrance to the Kensington High Street tube a few minutes beforehand, as the café was in the tube station arcade.

It was another bright day and Gemma's temper improved as she stood outside the station, watching the bustle of Kensington High Street and enjoying the sun that—for the moment at least—felt pleasant. When Kerry appeared, coming from the direction of Earl's Court Road, she looked more relaxed than Gemma had seen her.

"I walked," Kerry explained when Gemma told her she looked well. "Clears the cobwebs." She slipped back into the navy suit jacket she'd slung over her shoulder. "And at least we have a place to start this morning, thanks to you."

"This seems an odd choice for an interview." Gemma gestured at the arcade.

"His suggestion. He said he lives in Holland Park and would be on the way to his university classes. Sounded quite cut up about the girl's death."

"He knew about Reagan?"

"Not until your friend Mrs. Williams rang him last night—or so he says, anyway. Let's see what he has to say."

"Do you know this café?" Gemma asked, gesturing at the arcade.

"I stop there sometimes on my way home for a latte. It's a nice place to sit for a bit and think—between one fray and the next, if you know what I mean."

"Where do you live?" Gemma asked.

"Peckham Rye. The heart of suburbia, I know. But my husband works for Lambeth Council and it gives him an easy commute." Kerry glanced at her watch. "Let's see if they're here."

Gemma followed Kerry through the door and breathed in the smell of coffee and bacon.

It was a comfortable space, done in wood and brick and leatherette banquettes, with a spiraling iron staircase to an upper level. There were colorful enamel teapots, empty biscuit and oatmeal tins holding cutlery, and overall a cheerful hum. Gemma thought it would be a pleasant place to meet friends for a meal or a cup of tea, or to come for a bit of a think. She could understand why Kerry liked it.

She recognized Hugo Gold immediately, sitting on a banquette near the back. He looked older and thinner than he had in the photos on Reagan's corkboard, and Gemma wondered if the hollows under his eyes were chronic, or due to a sleepless night. Still, with his blond hair in its slightly feminine cut and his regular features, he was striking. A young man and a young woman sat at the table with him.

"That him?" Kerry murmured as she waved off the seating host. When Gemma nodded, she said, "Recognized him from your description. Looks like he brought reinforcements."

They crossed the room, weaving past tables. Hugo Gold looked up at them blankly, then, when he realized they were heading for him—Kerry's navy suit screamed cop—Gemma saw him stiffen. The young man, who had been speaking to him earnestly, stopped and turned to look.

"You must be Hugo," said Kerry, reaching the table first. "I'm DCI Boatman." She held out her hand and he half-rose to shake it. "And this is DI James. Do you mind if we sit?"

There was room on the banquette beside Hugo. When he nodded to his friends, they vacated their seats, the young man moving round beside him and the woman pulling an unused chair from another table. Gemma found it interesting that it was the young man who sat beside Hugo. He was rather plain, and made more so by the contrast with Hugo. His mousy hair was a little long, like Hugo's, but unstyled and, although Gemma put him in his early twenties, his face still showed a scattering of spots.

"I'm Sidney. Sidney Wyatt," he said, with a hint of belligerence. He wore a stained brown T-shirt that bore the faded logo of a band Gemma didn't recognize. Hugo, on the other hand, had thrown a royal blue blazer over a white T-shirt and looked as though he'd stepped out of a fashion advert.

In a soft voice, the young woman introduced herself as Thea Osho. Her skin was a deep, burnished black. She had full lips and high cheekbones. Her dark eyes, which slanted upwards at the corners, were accentuated by expertly applied eyeliner. Her head was shaved on one side and the rest of her hair fell in long, tiny braids that had brightly colored metal discs attached to the ends. It was a look that no one ordinary could have pulled off. She greeted them with a smile that seemed genuine and a glisten of tears in her eyes. "We want to know what happened to Reagan," she said. "We're her friends, too."

So, not there as emotional support for Hugo, Gemma thought, or at least not on Thea's part.

When the waitress came to the table, Kerry ordered a latte, but Gemma shook her head and took out a little notebook. She wanted to listen without the distraction of a drink.

"You didn't know that Reagan was dead?" she asked, directing her question to Thea.

Thea shook her head, the little discs on the ends of her braids jingling. They were bottle caps, Gemma decided, that had been pounded flat. "I'd been texting her, then ringing her since Friday," Thea said. "At first I thought she was just busy with Jess's dance classes and her modeling."

"But you didn't hear from her," Gemma said, when she paused.

"No. Then her voice mail filled up. I was a little worried about her, but I never thought . . ."

"You didn't go to her house?" Kerry asked, having accepted a beautifully designed latte from the waitress, who called her "love" with a familiarity hinting at visits more regular than Kerry had admitted.

"Oh, no. I wouldn't have done that." Thea sounded surprised. "Reagan didn't really like her friends coming there. And to be honest, I never felt welcome." She shrugged a dark shoulder, exposed by the thin strap of her tank top. "I don't think her boss approved of me," she added with a little grimace and a finger touched to her cheek, making it clear she meant the color of her skin. Her movements were so fluid that Gemma thought of Jess, and wondered if Thea danced, too. And if she'd at first wondered if there was anything between this girl and Hugo Gold, she decided that there was not. He was gazing past her, his face blank, and there was no spark of intimacy between them.

"Hugo." Kerry, fortified by a sip of coffee, sounded ready to get down to business. "When did you see Reagan last?"

He seemed to bring himself back to them with an effort. "It was Friday." His accent was quite posh but his voice, thought Gemma, was just a bit too high to be pleasant. "We all went to the piano bar on Friday night," he added, looking at Sidney and Thea as if for confirmation. They both nodded.

"The piano bar?"

"Kensington Piano. It's across the road," said Hugo, gesturing towards Kensington High Street. "Upstairs."

Although she'd never been in, Gemma had often walked past its tiny frontage with the black downstairs door.

"I understood you were a couple," Kerry said. "You didn't try to reach her over the weekend?"

Hugo shifted in his seat. "No. We had a bit of a row at the club and I thought she was still cheesed off with me. I thought she'd text me when she'd had a chance to cool off. You know, to apologize."

Kerry looked surprised. "Reagan needed to apologize to you? Why was that?"

He shrugged. "She was just having a bad night. Pissed off with everybody. I told her to chill, it was Friday night and we were out to have a good time, and for that she bit my head off."

"Was she drinking?"

He shrugged. "She had one, maybe two drinks. But Reagan isn't—wasn't—a big drinker."

"Then what happened? Did you see her home, Hugo?"

"No. She just left. It was only about half past ten. She said she had a headache."

"Did Reagan have her mobile with her?" Gemma put in, still bothered by the missing phone.

"Well, yeah, I'm sure she did," said Hugo, but he sounded uncertain. "I mean, why wouldn't she?" From his tone, Gemma might have asked if Reagan had gone out without an arm.

Thea spoke up. "She did. I saw her texting."

"Any idea who she was texting?" Gemma asked.

Thea shook her head. "No. Maybe it was work. Or her mum."

Gemma had the feeling Thea knew, or guessed, more than she

was saying. And neither Nita Cusick nor Gwen Keating had mentioned hearing from Reagan on Friday night. "Do you know any other friends that she might have been in contact with?"

"We were her best friends," said Sidney, joining in for the first time. He sounded truculent, as if Reagan hadn't had any right to other friends. Thea gave him a glance filled with what Gemma would have sworn was dislike. So these three were definitely not the Three Musketeers.

"Is there any chance she left her mobile at the club?" asked Gemma.

"I don't think so." Thea frowned. "But I suppose she could have dropped it and not realized. It was mad in there. It always is on the weekend, but on Friday there was an engagement party as well as a birthday party. It was an absolute crush—you couldn't move for the people. Reagan wanted to go someplace else, but no one was listening," Thea added, her tone accusing.

Hugo bristled. "Reagan knew what the place was like when we made the plans. She'd been before."

Gemma guessed that he didn't like being criticized. She knew Kerry was thinking the same thing when Kerry said, suddenly sharp, "So your girlfriend wasn't feeling well in a crowded club, and you just let her go home by herself, Hugo? You weren't worried about her?"

He glared at Kerry. "Why should I have been? She was a grown-up. All she had to do was get the bus up the hill."

Gemma gaped at him. What charm had Reagan seen in Hugo's utter self-absorption?

It was Thea who turned on him. "Except she wasn't okay, was she, Hugo? She died. Died! If you'd gone with her—if any of us had gone with her—she might have been okay." She looked from

Gemma to Kerry. "And you still haven't told us what happened to her. MacKenzie Williams just told Hugo she'd been found dead in the garden. How did she die? Something terrible happened to her or you two wouldn't be talking to us. You don't get two senior detectives doing interviews for a natural death."

Gemma said merely, "Had you all been to the Cusicks' house? Even though you say Reagan didn't encourage visitors there?"

They all nodded, if a little reluctantly. Hugo glanced at Sidney before saying, "We went to pick her up a few times. When she wasn't quite ready, or Nita was late getting home and she couldn't leave the kid, she invited us in. And I went over a few times when Nita was out. But it was all very up front and proper," he added, as if they'd accused him of impropriety.

"Thea?" Gemma asked, turning to her.

"Well, yeah, I've been to the house a few times. More than that, I guess, but usually when Nita was out."

"You'll have gone in Reagan's room?"

"Yeah, of course."

"Did Reagan have a computer?"

Thea nodded. "A nice one, too. She was saving money—that's one of the reasons she took the job, because it meant not having to pay rent on a flat—but she splashed out on a few things like the computer and her little printer." She gave Gemma the brands of both.

While Gemma was making notes, Kerry said, "What about the garden? Did you go in, any of you?"

"We had drinks on the patio once or twice," said Thea. "But the whole place—the house, the patio—was bloody sterile. It was never comfortable. Nita doesn't even like Reagan cooking in the kitchen." She didn't seem to realize she'd used the present tense.

"Hugo?" asked Kerry.

He looked wary. "Yeah, a few times. We walked around. Where was she—" He stopped, swallowing. "You know."

Instead of answering, Kerry asked, "Did she show you the gate?"

"No." He frowned. "Why would she? We always went through the house."

"And you didn't go there to talk things over with her after she left the club on Friday night?"

"No. I told you. There was nothing to talk about," Hugo said, his voice rising.

"Okay, okay, calm down." Kerry smiled, which Gemma didn't think Hugo would find the least bit reassuring. "We have to ask these things. It's best if you just answer and get it over with. Where did you go after you left the club on Friday night?"

Hugo glanced at Sidney, then said, "We hung out with some mates at UCL. Student accommodation. We got thoroughly pissed, if you must know."

"This was all three of you?"

"No, just Sidney and me. Thea had her own thing."

"Can your mates corroborate this?"

"Well, yeah, I suppose. But I'm not sure how much anyone will remember. Or that they'll be thrilled to talk to the police." For the first time, Hugo looked a little frightened. Gemma wondered if there had been drugs involved in his get-together, as well.

"We'll try not to make them too uncomfortable," said Kerry, with such sincerity that Gemma had to hide a grin. "Thea, what about you?" Kerry added.

"I went to my boyfriend's. I'd had enough noise for one night. We stayed in and watched telly." Unlike Hugo, she seemed relaxed. "I still wish I'd checked on Reagan. Maybe I could have done something . . ."

"You can't know that," Gemma told her, although she couldn't blame her for feeling that way.

"I'll need all your particulars, and contact information for your friends"—Kerry nodded at Hugo and Sidney—"and your boyfriend," she added to Thea. "As well as the times you left the club. Did you go together?"

"Yeah," said Thea. "We all took the tube back to Euston Road, then split up from there."

"I'll need each of you to come into Kensington Police Station and make a written statement of everything you've told us here." Before any of them could protest, Kerry added, "I understand if you have lectures or commitments this morning, but I'd like for you to do this today. We don't want to have to send a panda car for you, now do we?" With that, she drank the last of her latte and signaled for the bill.

When Kerry had paid, she and Gemma took their leave. Before they reached the restaurant door, Gemma looked back. The three heads were bent together over the table, and as she watched, Sidney lightly rested his fingertips on the pocket of Hugo's blazer. It was an oddly intimate gesture.

They'd reached the street when Thea came running out the arcade doors, calling out to them. "I told them I was late for a class," she said, glancing back at the arcade. "But I thought you should know. I think Reagan meant to break it off with Hugo. She was seeing someone else."

"Do you know who?" asked Gemma.

"His name is Edward Miller. He's a client of Nita Cusick's."

Kincaid woke on Tuesday morning feeling a little the worse for wear, as well as stiff from sleeping on Juliet's sofa, which was a foot too short for him. Juliet was dashing round the house, shouting at the kids to hurry or they'd be late to school, and he couldn't believe he'd managed to sleep through the chaos.

"And I've a building site to get to," Juliet added, handing Kincaid a cup of tea as he wandered into the kitchen. She filled a thermos for herself from the teapot and added milk and sugar. "You can use my shower," she added, giving him a critical eye. "I take mine after work." She wore her builder's overall, and looked all the more feminine for it.

Sam and Lally trooped noisily in wearing their school uniforms, shrugging into backpacks, and Kincaid felt a sudden searing homesickness. He'd missed telling the children goodnight last night when Gemma hadn't returned his call, and now he was yet again missing their morning routine.

He was wondering why Gemma hadn't rung him back when Juliet gathered up her things and gave him a quick kiss on the cheek.

"You will look after Daddy this morning, won't you?" she asked.

"Of course." He pulled her into a hug. "And you keep me posted on things, okay?" What he didn't want to say in front of the children was that he was counting on her to tell him the things that his mother would not.

"Do you have to go?" asked Sam, long-faced.

"I'm afraid I do. I have to go to work, and your cousins miss me." He tousled Sam's hair and resisted the urge to do the same to Lally. Instead, he leaned down and kissed her very gently on the cheek. "You look after your mum, okay?"

Lally nodded, blushing, and pulled something from the pocket of her jeans. She handed him a folded piece of paper. "Will you give this to Kit?"

"Yes, of course." He tucked it carefully into his shirt pocket.
"It's origami. I've been practicing."

"I'll tell him. He'll be——"

"Must run," interrupted Juliet, hustling the children towards the door.

"Jules," he said, and when she turned back he added, "Thanks. For everything. And"—he grinned—"keep Ronnie Babcock in line."

Although his father was now stable and settled at home, worry over his parents consumed the first hour of Kincaid's return journey. But by the time he reached Birmingham, his night was catching up with him. The car was warm and he was beginning to nod. He rolled the windows of the old Astra down farther and turned up the radio, but nothing helped the sleepiness. "As bad as drink," he mumbled, and pulled off with relief at the first motorway services.

Stopping in an empty spot at the edge of the car park, he turned off the car and was asleep within seconds.

He woke with a start a half hour later. His mouth felt like old leather and his head was pounding. Sprucing himself up as best he could, he went into the shop and bought a coffee. Then, realizing that he hadn't eaten since the night before, he added a sandwich and a bottle of water. A few minutes later, back in the car, he'd polished off the sandwich and the bottle of water. Feeling much more alert, he took a sip of the coffee, then started the car and eased back onto the motorway.

As he drove, he found himself thinking about his conversation with Ronnie Babcock the night before. Ronnie was right, he realized now. With everything that had happened to Denis and to Ryan Marsh, he'd been so emotionally involved that he'd failed to do basic police work. But how could he go about any proper investigation now without leaving tracks that could endanger him and his family?

As he gazed once again at the rolling hills of the Cotswolds to the west, a flicker of half-formed thought nagged at him. He'd almost grasped it just before he woke from the deep sleep in the car, he remembered now. Had he been dreaming? Had it been to do with Ryan? He glanced at the overhead motorway sign—he was coming up on the exit for Oxford. And south of Oxford, there was the cottage near Sonning where he and Doug and Melody Talbot had visited Ryan Marsh's wife, Christie. Was she still there? he wondered. If so, would she still be watched? It was too dangerous, he thought, to pay her a visit.

And then he thought of the island, Ryan's hideaway on the Thames, near Didcot. Christie Marsh had known roughly where it was because she'd followed her husband as far as the river, and it had been Christie who had told them about it. It was where he and Doug had found Ryan and convinced him to come with them. If they hadn't, would Ryan still be alive?

Had Christie managed to find the island after Ryan's death? If not, what might Ryan have left there?

With sudden decision, Kincaid swung the car into the lane for the Oxford exit. He meant to find out.

CHAPTER FIFTEEN

After leaving Bill's and the tube station arcade, Gemma and Kerry tried the piano bar, on the other side of Kensington High Street. The place was locked up tight, its hours stating that it didn't open until five. "We'll have to come back," Boatman said. "Maybe about half past four, see if we can catch the staff before the punters start coming in." Gemma agreed, but also thought it was going to be another long day, and she'd not had a word from Kincaid about when he might be home to help with the kids.

From there they walked back to Kensington nick, retiring to Kerry's office for a strategy session and, in Kerry's case, more coffee. Gemma decided the woman must have caffeine for blood.

"So what did you think of our little trio?" Kerry asked, leaning against the edge of her desk as she had the day before.

"Unlikely," Gemma said after a moment's thought. "On all fronts. Reagan seems to have been a sensible girl. I can't imagine what she saw in Hugo Gold. Although he was different in the photos," she added. "Maybe since they modeled together, she saw the persona he generates in front of the camera."

"Yes, good point. But Sidney is rather unpleasant, wouldn't you say?" Kerry added with an expression of distaste.

"I got the impression Hugo rather enjoys Sidney's adoration, although I doubt he returns it. And Thea—what is a girl like that doing with either of them?" Gemma shook her head, adding, "I'd like to talk to MacKenzie Williams about Hugo." Taking out her notebook, she jotted "talk to MacKenzie" on her running list.

"I'll get someone checking their alibis for Friday night," Kerry said. "Although I suspect that Sidney would happily cover for Hugo."

"And I suspect Sidney is happy to have Hugo to himself," Gemma mused.

Kerry's eyes lit up with the spark of possibility. "Could Sidney have killed her, do you think?"

"Out of jealousy? Maybe. But how?"

"He strikes me as a sneaky bastard," Kerry said. "Maybe he figured a way to get in through the house. Or over the wall—although we haven't found any evidence of a climber." Then she sighed and shook her head. "But I can't see Reagan Keating sitting down for a tête-à-tête with him in a secluded spot."

Gemma nodded agreement. "And nothing we've heard explains her high blood alcohol. If she wasn't a drinker, and she only had a drink, or possibly two, at the club, how did she end up practically comatose?" she asked.

"Maybe Hugo talked her into a meeting. I can see that. Then they started arguing about the new boyfriend. He got angry. They struggled. He suffocated her, then cleaned up any evidence."

Gemma could tell from Kerry's dreamy expression that she liked this scenario, but she had to burst the bubble. "That still doesn't explain the alcohol. Especially not if she was already cross with him and didn't feel well. And that's assuming Hugo was familiar enough—and comfortable enough—with the house to have removed any evidence, and possibly her computer, then let himself out without anyone noticing."

"So maybe the girl was a secret drinker." Kerry sounded peeved. "You can't take everything people say about someone who's died at face value. Maybe she didn't have a headache. Maybe she just wanted an excuse to leave the bar. Maybe she was meeting the new boyfriend."

She was right, Gemma knew, although she was loath to give up the impression she'd formed of Reagan Keating. "We need to talk to this Edward Miller," she said. "And that means a visit to Nita Cusick first."

"And before that"—Kerry gulped the last of her coffee, then walked round her desk and picked up a heavy old-fashioned key—"we need to return the gardener's key to Mrs. Armitage. The crime scene techs are finished, so we don't need access. And I'd quite like to talk to the lady."

This time they parked on the north side of Cornwall Gardens. Gemma blinked as she got out of the car. The sun was already fierce, and the shade cast by the terraced houses was welcome. As she looked up, she thought how secret the enclosure seemed, completely hidden behind its formidable terraces and high gates.

The frontage of Mrs. Armitage's house was a pale rose pink, and having seen her patio, Gemma couldn't imagine her having chosen anything else. The front door gleamed with new black paint, and the brass had been polished to within an inch of its life. The house had the same large front windows as Nita Cusick's, but unlike Nita's, which allowed a view from the street straight through the sitting room, Mrs. Armitage's windows were discreetly covered with net panels.

When they reached the door, they could hear a radio through the partially open casement downstairs. It seemed that this time they were in luck. Mrs. Armitage was at home.

Kerry lifted the knocker, and a moment later they heard a woman's voice saying, "I'm coming. Hold your horses." Then the door swung open and Jean Armitage surveyed them without surprise.

"Mrs. Armitage?" said Kerry. "I'm Detective Chief Inspector Boatman and this is Detective Inspector Gemma—"

"I know who you are," said Mrs. Armitage. "I've been wondering when you would manage to get to me. You'd better come in."

"We did try yesterday, Mrs. Armitage."

"So I heard. It was my bridge afternoon—you couldn't expect me to wait around twiddling my thumbs while you talked to half my neighbors."

As Gemma's eyes adjusted to the dimmer light in the hall, she took in the old but sparkling-clean lino and the gleam of the stairway banister. She smelled beeswax and lavender, and something delicious baking.

In layout, the house was a mirror image of the Cusicks', but there the resemblance ended. Glancing into the sitting room, she saw furniture covered with a floral chintz that did *not* match the floral wallpaper, a worn Persian rug that looked nonetheless of fine quality, and a surprisingly large and modern flat-screen television. The windows overlooking the rear were covered with the same net panels as those overlooking the street, but Gemma found she could see out quite well. It was a comfortable and lived-in space.

As for Mrs. Armitage herself, she was not at all what Gemma

had expected. She might be either side of seventy, Gemma thought, but well-preserved in a way that had nothing to do with makeup or cosmetic surgery. Her graying hair was thick and simply cut. She wore tan twill trousers, belted at a neat waist, and a lightweight white cotton blouse. Her skin was only faintly lined and her eyes were a bright, sharp blue. All in all, an attractive woman, Mrs. Armitage, and Gemma had a better idea of why Clive Glenn, the gardener, had spoken of her with both respect and admiration.

"We'd better go down to the kitchen," Mrs. Armitage said. "I've been baking some tarts for Nita Cusick. Such a shock for her, poor thing."

Kerry said, "Yes, of course," not making it clear whether she was agreeing with the invitation to the kitchen or the shock to Nita Cusick, but following Mrs. Armitage obediently down the stairs with Gemma trailing behind.

The kitchen was of the same vintage as the sitting room, comfortable and obviously well-used. A pan of tarts sat cooling on the work top, and on the table lay reading glasses, a pen, and the *Times* crossword, half-finished in ink.

"Keeps the brain fit," said Mrs. Armitage, following Gemma's gaze. Gemma remembered Melody telling her that her dad did the *Times* crossword in ink every day and she suspected his brain, too, was plenty fit. "Now, I was just about to have my elevenses," Mrs. Armitage went on. "Will you have tea and a tart?"

"Yes, please, that would be lovely," Gemma said quickly, not giving Kerry a chance to demur. "Can I help?"

"Plates and cups in that cupboard." Mrs. Armitage nodded to the right of the sink. "I'll just put the kettle on."

Doing as she was told, Gemma glanced out the windows over the basin. They had the same net panels as the windows upstairs, but here afforded a softened view of the patio and, through a gap in the roses, the vista beyond. It was lovely, but it was unfortunately at the opposite end of the garden from where Reagan Keating's body had been found. A door to the patio stood open, letting in a welcome drift of cooler air. The kitchen was warm from the baking and the heat of the day, even in the basement.

Kerry had taken a seat at the table and was checking her mobile, earning her a disapproving glance from their hostess. Gemma hoped fervently that she'd left her own phone on Silent.

"Use the good stuff, mind," said Mrs. Armitage, when she saw Gemma reaching for some ordinary pottery mugs.

The good stuff, Gemma saw, was white bone china bordered in gold. Proper teacups and saucers, and small plates, all simple and elegant. "How pretty," she exclaimed, setting the cups carefully on the table.

"We entertained a good deal when my husband was alive. I don't get much opportunity now, except when it's my turn to host the bridge group." For the first time, Mrs. Armitage sounded less forceful.

"I'm so sorry," said Gemma. "How long since you lost your husband?"

"Two years. Just after our fiftieth. Heart attack."

Gemma pushed away thoughts of Hugh. "It must have been difficult for you, all on your own like that and finding Reagan Keating's body," she told Mrs. Armitage.

"Oh, well, I take things in my stride, Harold always said." Mrs. Armitage gave a little shake of her head, but she looked pleased by the sympathy. "Sit, sit," she added, putting a filled teapot and a plate of tarts on the table.

"Did you know Reagan well, Mrs. Armitage?" Gemma asked

as she accepted a filled cup and a tart. Kerry, she gathered from her face, was not a tea drinker, although she took the offered cup without comment, then spooned heaps of sugar into it.

"Not well, no. But she was kind to me when Harold passed. She'd only worked for Nita a few months, but she brought me a card and homemade biscuits. Very well brought up, I'd say, was Reagan. And such a pretty girl, too."

Although she might not have cared for the tea, Kerry had accepted a tart with alacrity. With a tart halfway to her mouth, she asked, "Did you see anything unusual on Friday night, Mrs. Armitage? I'm sure you're very observant."

Gemma had managed a nibble while Mrs. A—as she couldn't help thinking of her, Clive Glenn's nickname having stuck in her head—was speaking. The tarts were mincemeat, tangy with citrus and rich with spices. The pastry was flaky and delicate, made with lard, Gemma guessed, baker's daughter that she was. She could not imagine Nita Cusick succumbing to such temptation, and hoped Jess liked mincemeat.

Mrs. Armitage smiled at the compliment, then shook her head with apparent regret. "I do like to keep an eye on things, but no, I'm afraid in this case I can't help. I watched the news at ten and went to bed. I like to keep to my routine, and I'm a sound sleeper." She looked at them over her cup. "She was murdered, wasn't she? Reagan?"

"We believe so, yes," said Gemma. She knew Kerry had spoken to Gwen Keating, but they hadn't yet had a chance to inform Nita of the postmortem results. "Did someone tell you that, Mrs. Armitage?"

"Nita. I saw her this morning. She'd been on the telephone with the poor girl's mother and she was that upset." Mrs. Armitage looked a little shaken herself. "Are we to think that someone came into our garden and did this . . . this terrible thing?"

"We've examined the gate, and we've spoken to Clive Glenn," said Kerry, finishing off her tart. "We haven't found evidence of forced entry through either end of the garden, so it seems more likely Reagan Keating was killed either by someone who lives on, or has access to, one of the houses—"

Mrs. Armitage was already shaking her head. "I can't believe that. No one in Cornwall Gardens would do such a thing."

"Do you know all your neighbors, then, Mrs. Armitage?" Kerry asked, sounding skeptical.

"Well, no. Some of the houses are divided into flats. And some are only occupied part of the year. But we've never had anything like that here," Mrs. Armitage insisted.

"But I understand you have had some unpleasantness lately," Gemma said. "Over your neighbors' extension."

"Oh, them." Mrs. Armitage drew her mouth into a tight line. "I didn't consider them."

"I understand they're Asian?"

"Chinese. Or he is. But that has nothing to do with it. It's the fact that they don't have any consideration for their neighbors. Or for rules."

"You mean because of the extension?"

Mrs. Armitage nodded. "It's an abomination. I know they've had their difficulties—quite tragic—but that's no excuse."

"I understand their little boy died," said Gemma. It occurred to her that the Sus' child had also suffocated. "Did Reagan have any dealings with the Sus?"

Mrs. Armitage frowned. "Not that I know of. Although I did see her reprimand the child a few times, when the two boys were outside. And rightly so. He was as inconsiderate as his parents, and a bully." She looked a little abashed. "I don't mean to speak ill of the dead, but it's true."

Could the Sus, Gemma wondered, have held Reagan responsible in some way for their son's death, and avenged him by suffocating her? They had access, certainly, but it was hard to make the rest of the scenario work.

"If you're thinking of talking to them, you'll have to come back. They're both out at work the entire day. I don't know when they think they'd use that monstrosity."

Gemma thought about the little boy who by more than Mrs. Armitage's account had been unpleasant and disliked—and whose parents were never home. She felt her usual pang of guilt over what she feared was her neglect of her own children, and shrugged it off with an effort. "You're observant, Mrs. Armitage. What other neighbors did Reagan know?"

Mrs. Armitage thought for a moment, then said, "She was quite chummy with Asia. Asia Ford, on the Blenheim Crescent side."

"Yes, we met her," said Kerry. "Seems an odd friend for a young woman."

Mrs. Armitage bristled. "Asia is an interesting woman. Well read, well traveled. I don't think it odd at all."

Gemma took a different tack. "Reagan was an attractive young woman. Do you know if she was particularly friendly with any of the men?"

After pursing her lips for so long that Gemma had decided she wasn't going to answer, Mrs. Armitage sighed and said, "I don't like to talk out of turn." In spite of Mrs. Armitage's hesitation, Gemma heard little reluctance in her voice. She waited in expectant silence.

"I did see something," Mrs. Armitage admitted at last. "It was Roland Peacock. Such a nice man. He was paying rather a lot of attention to the girl at the garden party. I don't think he meant anything by it—there was a good deal of champagne punch going round as well as Asia Ford's limoncello, and people were jolly—but it was obvious that his wife wasn't pleased." She shook her head. "Pamela Peacock. Makes you think of one of those old Beatles' songs, doesn't it?"

Gemma nodded. "Quite. What's she like, Mrs. Peacock?"

"A right bloody cow," said Mrs. Armitage with startling vehemence. "He's a nice man, Roland Peacock, as I said. I wouldn't be surprised if his wife drove him to look for a little comfort elsewhere."

The river looked different in spring.

Rather to Kincaid's surprise, he'd found the little marina easily enough. He'd hired a canoe, smiling to himself when he thought of Doug Cullen's earnest insistence on rowing the skiff they'd hired on their previous visit, notwithstanding his injured ankle. He hadn't had the heart to remind Doug that he'd grown up on Shropshire canals and rivers and had handled boats of all sorts since he was a lad.

Paddling in the direction he remembered from their previous excursion, he scanned the curves of the river for the little island, separated from the shore by a wide channel that had not been visible until they were almost upon it.

Everything was softened now, the sinuous curves of the river seeming unfamiliar in their cloaks of lush spring growth. Yet when he came round a long bend and saw the brushy jut of land, he knew it immediately. He paddled in, beaching the canoe in the same little notch he and Doug had used that day, soaking his trainers in the process. Then he stood, orienting himself to the landscape. In February, it had been eerily silent except for the occasional birdcall. Today the air was filled with raucous birdsong, but there was no sense of human presence. Kincaid remembered Ryan saying that there was no mobile phone reception here, and he felt suddenly very alone.

Closing his eyes, he forced himself to concentrate on his recollections, then opened his eyes again. There, he thought, there had been the campsite, through that little break in the trees. Carefully, he made his way through the undergrowth to the area he remembered, marveling at how quickly nature took back its own. The site of Ryan's fire pit was a mere indentation among the weeds and nettles. Surely, he thought, Ryan had left more behind than this?

It was hard to believe this had been a man's hideaway, complete with tent and cooking fire and makeshift benches. He knew Ryan hadn't taken the tent that day. Had someone come along and, finding it, considered it abandoned and fair game? Suddenly, he had a horrible feeling that he'd wasted his time coming here. It had been a whim, born of need and regret, and indulged when he should have been back in London trying to find out who had attacked Denis Childs.

He stood for a moment, gazing absently at the remains of the camp, imagining the echo of voices and the smell of wood smoke. Then he remembered the rifle. Ryan had greeted them that day armed with a rifle. When he'd come with them, he'd left it behind, but there was no sign of it now. Had it gone the same way as the tent?

Still, he began to look more carefully, starting in the center of the camp and widening his perimeter in careful traverses. There was no sign of the gun, rusting in the undergrowth. But as children, he and Juliet had pretended to be archaeologists, searching for "artifacts" their father had buried for them. That early recognition of disturbed earth had served him well as a policeman on cases he mostly didn't care to remember. Seedlings liked the softened earth, and in those places the growth was sometimes a paler green. His pulse quickened when he found one spot, some yards from the main campsite. It was oblong, perhaps a yard long and half as wide. Progressing more carefully, he soon found another. When another circuit turned up nothing further, he looked around for a digging tool, cursing himself for having come so unprepared. In the end, the best he could do was a sharp stick.

It was well past noon now, and as he began to dig in the first spot, he could feel the midday sun scorching the back of his neck. He kept on, but when he reached the depth of about a foot in the area he'd selected, he stopped, leaning on the stick and wiping the sweat from his eyes. He couldn't believe Ryan would have stashed something any deeper.

Wishing he'd bought a water bottle at the marina, he moved to the second spot and began working at the earth with his stick, more scraping than digging. He'd dug a few more inches when he struck something solid. And smooth. Clearing another few inches at the same level, he began to glimpse the obstruction. White, smooth, slightly rounded. PVC pipe, he decided, when he'd cleared a little more, and it certainly wasn't plumbing.

He scraped and cleared with more enthusiasm, down on his knees at the end and using his already sore hands. Tossing the stick aside when the entire pipe had been freed, he lifted the tube out and examined it. It was about two feet long and six inches in diameter, sealed at one end with a glued cap, and at the other with a screw-on cap.

Carefully, he unscrewed the removable cap. The end of the tube had been stuffed with a bundle of blue cloth, filled, Kincaid found as he eased it out, with something heavy and granular. From the feel, he thought the contents were desiccant, the sort you bought in bulk. He looked again at the cloth. It was a bandanna, he realized, dark blue, Indian cotton. Ryan had been wearing it—or one just like it—the day he'd left the island with them.

He sat back on his haunches, suddenly reluctant to pull more of the contents out willy-nilly. Instead, he smoothed a level space on the pile of soil he'd removed. Then he canted the tube at the sealed end and gently tipped the contents onto the ground. There were two cloth bags with drawstring ties. The first contained a notebook, which seemed to be filled mostly with lists of camping supplies, a passport with Ryan's photo under the name of Roger Meadows—Ryan had liked his initials, and his nature references, apparently—and a tight elastic-banded wad of one-hundred-pound notes.

Kincaid guessed what was in the second bag from its shape. He eased the bag free, and was glad he hadn't dumped the contents without care. It was a handgun, a Walther nine millimeter, with a spare clip. He stared at it, frowning. If this was Ryan's, where had the gun that had killed him come from?

He looked at the bandanna again. It was certainly possible that Ryan had had more than one of the cotton handkerchiefs. But he had left the island wearing one, and he'd not had one on when he died. If he'd only owned one, had he come back to the island?

Ryan had stayed with Doug for a week in February, during which he'd certainly not been a prisoner, and Doug had been gone all day at work. So Ryan had hours every day, unaccounted for. But if he'd come back, how the hell had he got here? Hitched?

Hired a car? He'd had the cash to do the latter, as evidenced by the wad of bills. In that case, had he hired a boat? Or stolen one, so as not to leave a record?

If Ryan had come back, what, Kincaid wondered, had he taken away with him? Or, he thought, perhaps more important, what had he left behind?

Spurred by this thought, he picked up the last item in the tube, a peppermint tin, perhaps two inches by three and half an inch deep. Opening it, he saw miscellaneous camping oddments— some stick matches, a ball of drier fluff useful for starting fires, a little coil of twine, a mini Swiss army knife. Beneath them, he caught a glimpse of something small and flat and dark blue, perhaps the size of his thumbnail, in the bottom of the tin. Pushing the drier fluff aside, he lifted the little rectangle. It was a memory card.

Despite Mrs. Armitage's advice, Gemma and Kerry had tried the Sus, then the Peacocks. Mrs. Armitage had also said that she thought Roland Peacock went in to his newspaper on Tuesdays. Mrs. Armitage was, of course, correct, so after finding no one at home, they then went on around to Blenheim Crescent and rang the bell at Nita Cusick's. When there was no answer there, they walked round the corner into Kensington Park Road, looking for the address Nita had given them for her office. It was a small, elegant space, sandwiched between a gourmet provision shop and an Italian bistro, and only a few doors from Kitchen and Pantry. There was no sign advertising the business, only a small brass plate by the door identifying it as CUSICK PUBLIC RELATIONS. Through the window they could see a front room that looked more like a chic sitting/conference room than an office.

When Gemma opened the door, a bell chimed, and Nita came hurrying out of a room at the back. "Oh, it's you," she said, and Gemma wondered who she'd been expecting. She looked, Gemma thought, as if she'd aged five years since she'd seen her on Sunday. Then, she'd looked thin but fit. Today, the flesh seemed to have melted from the bones in her face, and in her fitted sleeveless dress her shoulders looked almost obscenely skeletal.

"Can we have a word, Mrs. Cusick?" Kerry asked, but Gemma heard the concern in her voice.

"Oh." Nita looked baffled for a moment, as if processing the request, then said, "Of course. Come into the back." She led them into a windowless office which, while not exactly untidy, looked more inhabited than anywhere Gemma had seen in Nita's house. The back wall was lined with black-and-white photos of Jess dancing. In some, he was even younger than Toby, and Gemma was fascinated by the progression in his grace and posture.

Although Nita didn't offer them seats, Gemma and Kerry took the two visitors' chairs.

"I understand you've heard the news about Reagan," Kerry began without preamble.

"Gwen Keating called me first thing this morning." Nita shivered, even though it was warm in the office, and slipped into a cardigan that had been thrown over the back of her chair. "I still can't believe it. It was bad enough that Reagan was dead . . ." She shook her head. "But murdered? There must be some mistake."

"I assure you there is not, Mrs. Cusick. And that we're doing everything possible to find out who was responsible. Now, if we can just—"

Nita didn't let Kerry finish. "Her . . . body. Gwen wants to make funeral arrangements. Now that you've done . . . whatever it is that you do . . ." She seemed unable to finish the thought, and looked so ill that Gemma felt sorry for her.

"I promise we'll let both you and Mrs. Keating know as soon as Reagan can be released," said Gemma.

"Gwen wants to have the service there. In Cardiff. Which is understandable of course, but Jess . . . I don't know what to do about Jess."

"Does he want to go to the funeral?" Gemma asked.

"I don't know. He won't talk to me."

Gemma heard the indignation in Nita's voice and a little of her sympathy evaporated. She couldn't help but think of Kit at almost the same age, trying to find a way to deal with his shock and grief over the loss of his mother. "He's only ten," she said. "This must be very hard for him."

"Yes, of course." Nita nodded. "His father thinks Jess should stay with him for a few days, but I said he'd just have to come home and deal with it all over again."

She had a point, Gemma supposed, although she was inclined to agree with Jess's dad.

"Mrs. Cusick," said Kerry, "we've been given to understand that Reagan knew one of your clients, a Mr. Edward Miller."

Nita frowned. "Edward? Of course she knew Edward. He and Thomas come to the house occasionally."

"Thomas?" asked Gemma.

"Edward's brother. They own a boutique gin distillery. Very up and coming."

Gin, Gemma wondered, or the brothers? "According to Reagan's friend," she said, "Reagan and Edward Miller had been seeing each other socially." Silently, she cursed Kerry for having infected her with police-speak.

"What?" Nita looked as if a bomb had fallen in the room. "If you mean she was going out with Edward, that's absurd. Edward and Thomas come from a prominent family—"

"So you're saying Reagan wasn't good enough for Edward Miller?" said Gemma.

"No, of course not. Reagan was a perfectly nice young woman. But their backgrounds are very different. Reagan attended business college, Edward went to Harrow and Oxford. And if this is true—which I doubt—it was very unprofessional of her." She couldn't have made it clearer that the help had no business fraternizing with above-stairs.

"Where could we find Mr. Miller?" asked Kerry, seemingly unconcerned with the social niceties.

"On the premises of the distillery, I should think," said Nita, grudgingly. "Red Fox Gin, in Shepherd's Bush. But I'd really prefer you not bother him."

Back at the marina, Kincaid returned the canoe, telling the chatty marina owner that, yes, he'd had a pleasant and uneventful paddle. Then he squelched back to the car and took his already worn but dry socks from his overnight bag. He sat on the edge of the backseat as he changed his socks and shoes, gazing at the river beyond the marina car park. It did look peaceful, he thought, but his mood didn't match.

He'd stood for a long time, staring down at Ryan's cache, deliberating. In the end, he'd put everything back into the tube except for the memory card. He'd had the tube half buried when, on impulse, he'd opened the end once more and, dumping out the desiccant, removed the bandanna. Then he'd finished refilling the hole, and had camouflaged the spot as best he could with leaves and brush.

Now, he looked down at his hands, which were raw and red. What was he going to do with what he'd discovered? What had Ryan been planning, and what was on the memory card that he'd gone to such pains to keep safe?

Did he dare look at the thing even on his home computer? He wasn't at all sure he had the expertise to protect activity on his computer from scrutiny, if someone should decide to look at it.

But the worst thing was that he needed a sounding board, someone he could trust, to talk to. He was beginning to see that he'd kept things to himself for far too long. And that he had better start working on his apologies.

Taking out his mobile, he dialed Doug Cullen's number.

CHAPTER SIXTEEN

JULY 1994

He'd kept his temper, that day in the café, and hadn't given Red an answer. He'd never been one to act precipitously, and so he'd gone about his daily routine for a few days, doing odd jobs, showing up at the Tabernacle for cups of tea and gossip. In the end, he decided that since he had no intention of doing what Red had instructed, the best way to counteract his threat was to neutralize it.

He went home on an unscheduled day, following his usual routine of parking the van several streets away and walking to the house. But this time he was as concerned about being spotted by one of Red's minions as by someone from his undercover life.

On his last visit home, he'd walked right past a neighbor, un-recognized. It surprised him how much small things changed peo-

ple's perception. He'd let his hair grow shaggy and kept his beard trimmed at just past stubble length, and he'd traded his suits for flannel shirts, T-shirts, and jeans. Clothes did indeed make the man, it seemed. A good thing, he supposed, as it was less likely his cover would be blown if he ran into a friend or an acquaintance, but it also made his visits home awkward. He didn't want the neighbors thinking his wife was entertaining strange men.

So he made a pretense of knocking, then let himself in with his key. The house reeked of turps. Following his nose, he found his wife on a ladder in the kitchen, stripping old paint off the wall beside the cooker.

She turned, startled, then said, "Darling! What are you doing here?" Jumping lightly down, she came into his arms with a smile.

He held her tightly, then stood her at arm's length, keeping his hands on her shoulders while he looked her over. She wore old paint-spattered jeans with a tank top, and had tied a scarf over her dark hair. "You smell of turps," he said. "And you don't look like a policeman's wife."

"Just as well, since you don't look like a policeman." She laughed up at him. This had become their stock routine. "But, really, darling." She searched his face. "What are you doing here? Is everything all right?"

"I think," he said, "that we should have a cuppa."

What Red hadn't counted on was that he'd never kept anything from his wife. Sitting at their kitchen table, amid tins of paint and a floor covered with spread newspapers, he told her about Red's demand.

"But that's awful," she said. "Those poor people, the Lawrences, lost their son. Why would the Met want to make up bad things about them?"

"Because the Met buggered the investigation very badly, and they hope that by discrediting the boy's family they'll draw attention away from their failure." He didn't say that he suspected the officers in the Lawrence investigation might have been guilty of more than ineptitude. His group of campaigners were convinced that at least one officer had been bribed by the father of one of the original suspects in Lawrence's murder.

"That's despicable." She was incensed, and he loved her for it. "But they can't make you, can they?" she added, sounding suddenly a little frightened.

Taking her hand, he told her about Red's threat, and the photo. He'd described the campaigners to her on his weekly visits, so she nodded when he mentioned Annette Whitely. "It would have been hard work to have got even one shot that might be interpreted as intimate," he added. "Which means that they've been following me."

Her eyes widened. "But that's dreadful. Can't you just quit? Tell them you don't want to do this anymore."

"I can't just quit. Not if I ever want to work as a copper again." He squeezed her hand and smiled. "Well, I might get a job as a constable in Upper Footing . . ."

He'd made her laugh. "There's no such place and you know it, Den. But, seriously——"

"I'm a police officer, love. This is what I do. And if I quit, they'd just put in someone they know would be willing to discredit the Lawrences. There has to be a way round this, some sort of compromise."

She looked at him for a long moment. A puff of warm breeze from the open window stirred her hair, and her eyes were blue as cornflowers. He didn't see how he could bear to go on being sepa-

rated from her, taking his one night a week like a starving man's
ration, but he didn't see a choice. "You just said it yourself, dar-
ling," she murmured at last. "You're a police officer, not a diplo-
mat, and compromise isn't your job. Promise me you'll be very,
very careful."

The address Nita Cusick had given them for Red Fox Gin turned
out to be a very ordinary lockup garage in a very ordinary subur-
ban road in west London. "Are you sure this is it?" Gemma asked
Kerry, who was driving.

"This is the right number," said Kerry, when she'd maneuvered
into a parking space. "And look." She pointed at a small metal
plaque by the garage doors, on which was depicted the head of a
red fox, wearing a smile. "Clever."

Possibly, thought Gemma, but the place was not what the "boutique" in "boutique distillery" had conjured up in her imagination.

The only thing that marked the premises as different from the
surrounding houses and garages was the glossy red paint on the
garage doors. There was also a side door next to the lockup doors,
and beside it, a bell, and, they discovered, a small brass plate that
read RED FOX LONDON DRY GIN, DISTILLERS.

Kerry glanced at Gemma, said, "Right place, then," and rang
the bell.

After what seemed an interminable wait, a young woman answered. She was short, slightly stocky, had blue-tinted spiked hair,
and wore a white cotton tank that showed off her brightly colored
wrist-to-shoulder tattoos. "Sorry," she said, in an unmistakable
East London accent. "Bit understaffed today. And we're not really
open to the public."

"We're not public." Kerry produced her ID. "We'd like a word with a Mr. Edward Miller."

The young woman stared at them, then said, a little fiercely, "Edward's not seeing visitors today. If you can leave a num—"

"I'm sorry." Gemma stopped her with a smile. "But we really do need to see him. It's important," she added gently.

"Well, okay," said the young woman, after another moment's hesitation and a shrug of a colorful shoulder. "You'd better come in, yeah." Opening the door fully, she led them into a room that seemed to be a combination of product display and shop. One wall was lined with glass shelves filled with perfectly aligned bottles of different varieties of Red Fox gin—at least half a dozen, to Gemma's surprise. There was also a counter, and a seating area furnished with comfortable-looking modern furniture.

There was a door that Gemma guessed led into the garage proper, and another that she thought must lead to a room overlooking the small gated parking area they had seen to the right of the garage.

Suddenly the second door banged open and a man strode through it into the display room, saying, "Agatha, tell whoever it is to bugger—" He came to a halt as he seemed to realize the visitors had already intruded. He was tall, with a shock of unruly red hair. Unlike Gemma's coppery locks, his hair was true ginger, the color that got you teased in the school yard. And, now, as he ran his hands through it, making him look a bit unhinged. "Agatha," he said again, "I said I didn't want—"

"Edward, they're from the police."

"Mr. Miller," said Gemma, "we need to speak to you about Reagan Keating." She told him their names, but she wasn't sure he'd taken them in.

Agatha took charge. "Why don't you take the visitors into the office, Edward. I'll bring in some tea, yeah?" She put a hand on Edward Miller's arm and he nodded slowly.

"Thanks, Ag," he said. To Gemma and Kerry, he added, as if he owed them an explanation, "Administrative assistant, Agatha. Runs the place." His eyes, Gemma saw, were red-rimmed and puffy. She had to assume that Nita Cusick had given him the news about Reagan.

He led them into the room he'd vacated so hurriedly and sank into the chair behind a paper-littered desk. Behind the desk was a serving cabinet which held a bottle of each of the liquors Gemma had seen in the display room, as well as some clean tumblers.

The only other seating was a short sofa in front of the desk, so that Gemma and Kerry Boatman were forced to sit side by side in sardine fashion. "Sorry," said Edward. "Usually we have our meetings out there, or in the garage. But . . ." He trailed off, look- ing at them blankly, as if having trouble remembering why they were there.

After a glance at Kerry, Gemma took the lead. "Mr. Miller, we understand you were friends with Reagan Keating. You do know that she's dead."

Grimacing, he nodded. "Nita called me. I still can't believe it." He shook his big head.

Edward Miller was good-looking, Gemma thought, with strong bones and, rather incongruously for a big man, a slightly upturned nose. She guessed that he was not that much older than Hugo Gold. But where Hugo seemed like a boy, Edward Miller looked very much a man. As if to prove it, he seemed to make an effort to recover himself.

Swallowing and giving his head another shake, he said, "Why are you here?"

"We need your help," Gemma told him. "You can start by telling us when you saw Reagan last."

Edward thought for a moment. "It was after the garden party. So Monday last, I think."

"Had you spoken to her since then?"

"Yes. I was—we were going to get together on Friday night. I had a distillery event—we often have tours on Fridays—but Reagan said she'd meet me after. She had to—this is awkward—" He stopped as Agatha came in, carrying a tray with a mismatched assortment of mugs and a chipped teapot. She poured for them, efficiently, giving Edward a concerned glance.

"Thomas rang," she said. "He's coming in to deal with the run. So you can go home as soon as you like."

"And do what, exactly?" he snapped at her, then immediately apologized, shaking his head. "I'm sorry, Ag. It's just—I can't— I'd rather be here."

Agatha seemed unoffended. "Well, think about it, anyway." She gave Gemma and Kerry a nod and left them to their tea.

"Thomas is your brother?" asked Gemma.

"And my partner. He'll be— Oh, Christ, Ag will have told him, then, when she rang him. He'll be gutted, too. He's—he was— fond of her." Edward pushed aside his untouched tea and rubbed at his face.

"You've known Reagan for a while, then?"

"Since she came to work for Nita. Nita helped us get off the ground here, when everyone thought we were crazy." He stood, restlessly, taking a bottle from the cabinet and sloshing the liquid into one of the tumblers with a shaking hand. "Best medicine," he said, raising his glass to them before taking a swallow. "Would you like to try some?"

Gemma caught the sharp, clean scents of juniper and citrus, and intriguing hints of spice. "We'd better stick to tea, but thank you," she said.

"But in spite of predictions, your business has been successful," said Kerry, straightening her back and shifting her thigh away from Gemma's, obviously finding it a struggle to seem professional when squashed into such intimate contact. Kerry was on a tack, and Gemma waited to see what it was.

"Yes. More than we ever imagined." Edward managed a smile. "We thought we were crazy, too. Now we've got two more stills ordered."

"You distill here on the premises?"

"Yes. We have one still now, our original copper-pot still."

"And you use strong alcohol in your distilling process?"

Edward frowned at her, as if he thought the question a bit daft, but he didn't seem concerned by it. "Yes, of course. We start with good-quality grain spirit—ours is barley—which is about sixty percent alcohol by volume. That goes into the still with our combination of botanicals. It macerates at an even temperature overnight, then the next day we distill it, slowly, so that the botanicals come off in layers." From Kerry's expression, he might have been speaking Greek. "That's why it's called 'small batch,'" he said. "It's nothing like the gin you get from the big distillers, which is made using concentrates—"

Kerry waved him to a stop with her free hand. "All to put in a glass of tonic?"

"Well, you can do a bit more than that." From the flash of amusement in Edward's face, he'd realized he was talking to someone likely to prefer bathtub to boutique.

Although Gemma thought Kerry wanted to know more about

the alcohol, she said instead, "You were telling us about Friday night. You were supposed to meet Ms. Keating. What happened?"

Edward shrugged. "She didn't show up."

"Surely you called her, or texted her?"

"Of course I did." Edward's face went blotchy, the unbecoming blush of the very fair-skinned. "No response. Some of the chaps were still here, checking on the next day's run. So I waited, and after a bit I texted her again. A few minutes later, I got this weird text back, and I thought she was blowing me off."

"Would you mind showing me?" asked Gemma. "Just her reply," she added, sensing his deepening embarrassment.

With a reluctant shrug, Edward scooped the mobile from his desktop and tapped the screen a few times before coming round the desk and handing it to Gemma. The text was highlighted by a pop-up box and tagged with a tiny photo of Reagan, which made her seem suddenly, eerily alive. Gemma read it aloud for Kerry's benefit. "'Sorry, headache, can't make it.'"

"And that was it?" she asked, looking up at Edward and resisting the temptation to scroll backwards or forwards on the screen.

Edward nodded, taking the mobile back and sitting again at the desk.

"And did you try to get in touch with her after that?"

He took another swallow from his glass, not meeting their eyes. "No," he admitted. "At least not until yesterday, and then her voice mail was full. Look, as I said, this is a bit awkward." His blush deepening, he went on, "Reagan and I, we liked each other. But we weren't . . . sleeping . . . together, if that's what you think. She'd been seeing someone else, and she said she had to break it off with him completely before she—before we . . ." He cleared his throat, then said, as if challenging them, "She was a nice girl, damn it."

"I'm sure she was," agreed Gemma. "So when she canceled on you, and then didn't get in touch, did you think she'd changed her mind about breaking it off with her boyfriend?"

"I didn't know what to think. I mean, isn't 'a headache' the classic excuse when a girl doesn't want to see you?"

"Possibly. But Reagan told some other people that night that she had a headache. It may be that she really didn't feel well."

"But that's not why she died, is it?" said Edward. It was the first time he'd asked anything specific about Reagan's death.

"Mrs. Cusick didn't tell you?" asked Kerry.

He shook his head. "No, she just said that Reagan was . . ." He swallowed. "Dead. That she was found murdered. I assumed—I couldn't bear to think . . ."

"She wasn't raped," Gemma said. "Nita didn't tell you that?"

"No. Nita was not exactly chatty. That's the other thing that's awkward."

Gemma frowned. "I'm not following you."

Edward hesitated, then said, "Look, of course I was worried when I didn't hear from Reagan. It wasn't like her to just leave things hanging with no explanation. I thought if she'd decided she didn't want to go out with me, she'd at least put me out of my misery.

"I'd have called the house to check on her, but Nita . . . Reagan didn't think Nita would approve of her seeing me, so of course I didn't want to drop her in it. She meant to tell Nita. And she said that if Nita wasn't comfortable with us seeing each other, she'd quit the job. She was ready to move on. The only reason she'd stayed as long as she had was because she was worried about the kid."

"Jess?" asked Gemma, frowning. "Why?"

"He was under a lot of pressure with tryouts for the ballet

school. She wanted to at least get him through that. She said he depended on her. He hadn't dealt well with his parents' divorce. The dad has a new girlfriend, too, which hasn't helped." Edward stood again. Moving to the drinks' cabinet, he began lining the bottles up more precisely, his movements jerky. "Now, I think if I'd just called her that night, or gone to the house, or something, she might not have . . ." He kept his back to them.

"Mr. Miller," said Gemma. "Edward. What time did you get that return text from Reagan?" She hadn't held the mobile long enough to check the time stamp.

He turned around, sniffing. "I don't know. The chaps had gone home. It must have been well after midnight."

"I think you shouldn't worry too much over what you might have done," Gemma said, but a little absently. She was wondering how certain the pathologist could be in determining whether Reagan had died before or after midnight.

Doug Cullen had not been easily convinced to talk, much less meet.

"Why didn't you tell me Denis was back?" he said, before Kincaid got further than a half-formed request to meet for a drink.

"I didn't know—"

"You must have heard he'd been attacked, then. Why didn't you have the bloody courtesy to tell me that?" Doug's public school vowels grew stronger, as they did when he was really upset. "And why have you been treating me like a pariah the last couple of months? Now all of a sudden you want to meet for a bloody pint?"

"Look, Doug, it's complicated. I'm in—someplace near Wallingford. If you could just meet me after work, I'll let you know when I'm—"

"What are you doing in Wallingford? That's where—"

"I know where Wallingford is." Kincaid was getting irritated himself. "Just meet me. I don't want to talk about this on the phone. Make some excuse to get out of work, but don't tell anyone you're seeing me. No one. Got it?"

"Why all the cloak-and-dagger? Don't you think that's a little extreme?" But now Doug was curious—Kincaid could hear it in his voice.

"I'll explain everything," he said. "I promise. Meet me at"— he thought for a moment—"the Scotch Malt Whisky Society. You know where it is. I'll text you when I'm in the city."

Kincaid disconnected. It was the only way to stop Doug once he got started talking.

He'd put the car into gear and was pulling out of the marina when his phone rang. Not Doug calling back, he saw when he glanced at the screen. Rashid.

"Rashid, what have you got?" he asked, clicking on. Then, with a spike of panic, "It's not Denis, is it?"

"No. I've not heard anything," Rashid assured him. "It's that other matter. I think you'd better come in—"

"I'm outside London at the moment. Can't you just tell me—"

"No. I'd rather not." Rashid was unusually brusque. "And there are some things you need to see. I'm off the rota for the day, but I'll wait in my office until you get here."

London traffic was heavy. Kincaid was sweating and tense by the time he finally reached the hospital. He wondered if Rashid would have waited for him, but the pathologist was in his office, as he'd promised.

"Duncan," he said, and stood. His usual dry smile was missing, and for the first time that Kincaid could remember, he closed his office door. "Thanks for coming." Waving Kincaid into his usual chair, Rashid sat again behind his desk. "Sorry to have brought you in like this."

Kincaid's alarm bells ticked up another notch. "Rashid, what the hell is it?"

Rashid had picked up a pen. Turning it in his fingers, he said, "I thought—I know you've had a rough few months. I thought maybe you were being a tiny bit paranoid when you told me about your friend. And I apologize."

Kincaid sat still. Whatever Rashid had found, it must be bad.

"I need you to look at some photos, if you don't mind coming round the desk," Rashid said, clicking his computer mouse a few times with his free hand. Kincaid stood and went to stand beside Rashid. "You'll have seen gunshot wounds, yeah?" The slip from the pathologist's normal and somewhat formal English into Cockney patois was even more unnerving.

Mouth dry, Kincaid nodded.

"Okay, look at this." Rashid opened a photo on one of the two large monitors on his desk. "This is a self-inflicted gunshot wound to the head. We see them often enough. Normally, people hold the gun right against the skin. On the temple, or sometimes under the chin. Now, here, see the bubbling under the skin around the entry point?" He used his pen as a pointer. "That's blowback, caused by the gases created by the projectile. Now, here's your mate's photo," Rashid said, swiveling to the other monitor.

Kincaid blinked, trying to disassociate himself from what he'd seen that night. "Okay." It could have been anyone, he told himself, this close-up view of a head and the dark point where the bullet had entered.

"No blowback, you see?" Rashid tapped the screen with the pen.

He did see. "So what does that mean?"

"It means that very few suicides manage to hold the gun away from the skin. In the midst of an argument, maybe. Or maybe they have a last-second change of heart but the reflexes can't catch up. Highly unlikely, at any rate. And then—" He zoomed in the photo until the gunshot wound looked like an alien landscape, and Kincaid let out a little breath of relief. "Look at this. There are plastic shards in the wound. You see?" He used his pen as a pointer again. "And that means—" Rashid looked up at him, as if expecting a response from a prize pupil.

"A silencer. A drink-bottle silencer. Homemade."

"Exactly." Rashid sounded pleased. "It's not impossible for a suicide to use a silencer, granted. I've seen it once. Guy lived alone, maybe didn't want to disturb his neighbors. It was weeks before someone complained about the smell."

"But not likely in this case. What else?"

"The angle of the wound is off. Not to mention that your guy was found in the middle of his sitting room. Not sitting on the chair or the sofa, not lying on the bed. How many people top themselves standing up? Again, it's not impossible. I've seen that, too, with a bloke who was drunk and in a slanging match with his wife. But even he managed to press the gun to his scalp before he pulled the trigger. See what I mean?" Rashid tapped and another photo came up.

Kincaid's stomach lurched. It was a photo of the body in situ, taken with the crime scene tech's wide-angle lens. Ryan lay sprawled in the middle of floor in the cheap sitting room Kincaid remembered, his face turned to one side, his arms splayed, a dark pool spreading beneath his head. The fingers of his right hand were curved in the grip of a semiautomatic handgun.

For an instant, the smell hit Kincaid again. There was the warm coppery scent of fresh blood, and beneath that, excrement. He stuffed his hands in his pockets to stop them trembling.

And then, as he stared at the photo, the room surrounding the body seemed to come into sharper focus. It was the cheap sitting room, yes, but it was not exactly as he'd seen it. "There's no backpack," he said.

Rashid looked up at him, dark brows raised in a query.

"I remember now. I wasn't in the room more than a minute. I saw that he was dead, and I knew I couldn't be connected with him. But I've never been quite sure how I knew that it wasn't suicide. There was a backpack, half open, by the sofa. He'd been packing. Whatever he'd left in that flat, he'd come back for it. And between the first responders and the SOCOs' photos, somebody took it."

"There you are, then," said Rashid. "You were right. I'd never have ruled this as a suicide."

"But—" Kincaid made an effort to collect himself. "How, then? How did this scene get passed as a suicide?"

"Pathologist's call," Rashid said, grimacing.

"Rashid, who was it? Who was the pathologist?"

"Kate Ling."

The sheet was too tight, binding him. He tried to pick at it, but found he couldn't move his hands. Were they tied? He tried to struggle, but his body seemed unable to obey.

"Just take it easy, Mr. Childs," said a voice that seemed vaguely familiar. "You're in hospital, do you remember?"

Of course, he thought, the surgery. He remembered he was having surgery. Was it over? Where was his sister? "Liz? Where's Liz?" he tried to say, but his mouth didn't work, either.

Gagged, he must be gagged. They'd found him out. Panic set in. He had to free himself. They would hurt Diane. Craig had said so.

"Mr. Childs, don't struggle. We'll have to increase your sedation again if you don't calm down."

Sedation? Why was he sedated? His heart pounded wildly and he tried again to free his hands.

The voice said, distantly, "His blood pressure and heart rate have shot up. We'll try again this evening, when his wife's here."

And then the fog descended.

CHAPTER SEVENTEEN

"According to the pathologist, she was having sex with someone," Kerry Boatman said as she and Gemma drove back towards Kensington. "Assuming—and that's a big assumption—that Mr. Miller is telling the truth about not having slept with the girl, was it Hugo Gold? Maybe she wasn't as fed up with Hugo as everyone seems to think. Or she decided to give him a farewell shag."

"You're a bloody cynic," said Gemma, amused.

Kerry flashed her a grin as she braked two inches from the back of a Transit van. "Goes with the job. So what if she did meet Mr. Miller when she left the club? A romantic tête-à-tête. He brought some of his poncey gin with a little extra punch to it, thinking he'd get in her knickers at last."

"And?" asked Gemma, hoping that Kerry could theorize and keep her eyes on the road at the same time.

"She confesses that she's just shagged Hugo. Poncey's romantic evening is in ruins. Nice girls don't do that. He means to have her himself, so he holds her down and tries to keep her quiet. Then, poof, she's dead. So he lays her out like an unsullied princess." There was anger beneath Kerry's mockery.

"What about the text?" asked Gemma.

"He sent it himself. From her phone, which he likely tossed in a bin on the way back to wherever it is he lives." Kerry accelerated away from the traffic light as if she were driving at Le Mans.

"Um," said Gemma, as mildly as she could. "It sounds as if he might have an alibi, up to midnight or so."

"So he met her after that."

It was obvious that Kerry had taken a dislike to Edward Miller. But that didn't make her right. Before they'd left Red Fox, they'd got the contact information for Edward's brother Thomas, and for the others who'd stayed behind after the tasting. Agatha Smith had been one of them. Even if Gemma had been disinclined to believe Edward, she had a hard time imagining Agatha as a liar. "We need to pin down Kate Ling on the time of death," she said. "And we need to verify what time Reagan left the club in Kensington."

Screeching to a halt again as they came up to the Shepherd's Bush station, Boatman nodded at the car clock. It was just past four. "We should be able to catch someone at the piano bar by the time we reach Kensington." She accelerated smoothly away from the light into Holland Park Road. In spite of her little burst of temper, she was a good driver.

Gemma was intrigued by the temper. What was it about Edward Miller that had ticked Kerry off?

They ducked under the half-rolled-up door of the piano bar and started up the narrow stairs, Kerry already cursing. Gemma wondered if she were subject to claustrophobia. When they pushed through the door to the first floor, Kerry gasped like a swimmer coming up for air.

The space was long and narrow, with a big window overlooking the street and framing the grand piano. Bistro-style tables and chairs and a few banquettes lined the wall, leaving a free center aisle. The place smelled faintly but not unpleasantly of booze and sweat. Gemma did not miss the days when a bar like this would have reeked of morning-after ashtrays.

At the back was the bar itself, presided over for the moment by a barman wiping glasses with a cloth.

"Oy," he said, looking up. "We're closed until five. Didn't you read the sign?"

Kerry flashed her ID at him, her attitude still in evidence. "Police."

The barman raised a sardonic eyebrow. "Weights and measures?"

"CID," Kerry snapped. The barman's eyes widened a fraction.

Putting down his cloth, he said, "No need to get your knickers in a twist. What can I do for you ladies?" His receding hair was pulled into a ponytail and his tight black T-shirt was strained by the beginnings of a paunch. Still, there was charm in his grin, and Gemma guessed he was accustomed to using it.

Before Kerry could threaten him with cuffs, Gemma gave him her biggest smile. "Tell us your name, for starters."

He hesitated for a moment, then shrugged. "Darrell. Darrell Byrd. Like the band. With a *y*."

"Were you working this last Friday night?"

"I'm always working Fridays and Saturdays, darlin'. Me and one or two others. It's a madhouse in here. What's this in aid of?"

"Just a few questions relating to an investigation we're pursuing." Gemma suspected he wasn't averse to a little drama, and she didn't want the weight of "murdered girl" to color his account. She held up her phone with Reagan's photo on the screen. "Do you remember seeing this girl on Friday night?"

Darrell wiped his hand again with the bar cloth, then took the phone from her and studied the photo. "Yeah, I remember her, though I couldn't have told you whether it was Friday or Saturday."

"Why do you remember her? Was she a regular?"

He shook his head. "No. But she was pretty, you know, in a girl-next-door sort of way."

"Did you serve her alcohol?" Kerry asked.

"Of course I served her alcohol. It's what I do." Darrell gave her an unfriendly look. "And she was not underage, if that's what you're thinking."

"No, not at all," Gemma assured him. "So, she did have a few drinks?"

"One. A specialty cocktail. I made it myself. She made a face when she tasted it, so I don't think she cared for it." Darrell looked a little hurt.

"And that was it?"

"Unless someone else served her, but I don't think they did. She left not long after that. She was having a bit of a row with a bloke. I noticed because they were standing back by the loo"—he nodded towards a narrow corridor that led back from one side of the bar—"and I had to go to the storeroom to get another case of vodka."

"Could you tell what the row was about?"

"Not really." Darrell thought a moment. "She said something to him about 'cheating.'"

"She said he was cheating? Not the other way round?" Gemma asked, thinking Hugo might have found out about Edward Miller.

"That's what I remember. I couldn't imagine what she saw in the guy, anyway." Darrell rolled his eyes. "Little wanker, if you'll excuse my language."

Gemma frowned and saw Kerry wearing a perplexed expression. "A blond bloke, with hair like this?" She held her hand parallel to her jawline. "Very good looking, like a model?"

Darrell looked as confused as Kerry. "No. A weedy little guy. Needed to eat his spinach. Mousy hair. And spots."

Kincaid left his car at the hospital and took the tube from Whitechapel to Farringdon. From there, he walked the short distance down Greville Street to the Scotch Malt Whisky Society, tucked above the Bleeding Heart Tavern.

For some time, he'd used the club as a retreat. When he'd transferred to Holborn, and the club had become within walking distance, he'd come more often, but he'd never taken anyone there from his team at Holborn nick.

Now, he was glad to have a place where he could feel—at least temporarily—safe, and where he could think. It was nearing five by the time he reached the Bleeding Heart and there were already crowds spilling out of some of the Hatton Garden pubs. Ducking down the little alleyway beside the Bleeding Heart, he pushed the buzzer at the whisky society's door. When it released, he climbed the open-tread stairs to the first floor.

The society rooms were directly above the pub. The large main room held the bar as well as seating at comfortable tables and sofas. Bright, modern paintings adorned the white walls. There was a fireplace in the room's center, cozy in winter but unused now, and large windows on two of the room's sides, open to catch any hint of breeze. To one side of the bar was a much smaller room, the Snug, with a single long table and walls lined with racks of the society's special bottles.

Kincaid signed in at the bar, then ordered a sandwich to be sent up from the pub. "Choose something for me," he said to the barman. "Something bracing."

"Bad day?" asked the young man.

"You could say that."

"Hmmm." The barman thought for a moment, then poured a measure from a numbered bottle. "This should do it," he said, handing Kincaid the small snifter. "Cheers."

Kincaid thanked him and, drink in hand, headed for the low table in the very back corner. He wanted the spot where he would be least likely to be overheard. He'd texted Doug as he walked from Farringdon and had received a terse reply saying that Doug had been hung up at the Yard but was on his way.

After some thought, he texted Gemma, saying merely that he was back in London and would be home soon. He wasn't ready to talk—he didn't know where he would begin, or how he'd explain where he'd been that day. He missed her and the children with an almost physical ache, but he couldn't let himself think about that now. He had to concentrate on making sense of what he'd learned.

Raising his glass, he took a swallow of the whisky, neat. What tasted like liquid smoked peat seared his throat and he blinked away tears. Bracing didn't begin to describe the stuff. He lifted the glass again and inspected it. The liquid was pale gold with a slight green tint. Adding a drop of water from the jug provided on the table, he sipped again, gingerly. This time he got sweetness beneath the smoke, and butter, and medicinal herbs, with a last lingering hint of dark chocolate. Sipping again, he sat back, feeling some of the tension drain from his body. When he glanced up, the barman grinned at him and Kincaid gave him a thumbs-up.

His sandwich came, and by the time Doug walked through the door, he'd finished his meal and his drink and had ordered coffee for them both. He had an instant to examine Doug while Doug searched the room for him. It had been almost two months since he'd seen his friend, and he was shocked at how drawn Doug's face looked beneath the familiar round glasses. Drawn, and sunburned. What the hell, Kincaid wondered, had Dougie Cullen been doing? He wasn't wearing a jacket, and with his tie loosened, his shirt-sleeves rolled up, and a satchel over his shoulder, he looked more like a schoolboy than ever.

Then Doug saw him and crossed the room without a smile. Kincaid stood and held out his hand. Doug hesitated, then gave it a brief shake. It felt awkward, and Kincaid's hands were sore from digging.

"Thanks for coming," Kincaid said, when Doug had taken the offered chair. "I've ordered coffee for us both. I thought we'd need clear heads. But have something else as well, if you like."

"Coffee's fine."

"What have you done to yourself?" Kincaid asked, gesturing at Doug's pink face. "Costa del Sol?"

"Gardening." Doug's scowl made it clear that small talk was out.

The barman brought the coffee. Thanking him, Kincaid poured, then watched as Doug added generous doses of sugar and cream. He waited, and when he had Doug's full attention, he began as he'd known he'd have to begin, with the night of Ryan Marsh's death and what he'd seen.

"You were there?" said Doug. "You saw him? Why didn't you tell me?"

"Because . . ." Kincaid looked round, making certain that the people at nearby tables were deeply engaged in their own conversations. "Because I was bloody terrified. I knew Ryan was afraid for his life. He thought the grenade in St. Pancras had been meant for him. And I knew that night that something about the scene was wrong."

"But—"

"I thought I had to make sure that no one knew any of us had any connection with Ryan. I thought you would be safer if you thought it was suicide. And, then, after a few weeks, I thought maybe I was crazy. But I couldn't"—he paused, staring at his hands and scrubbing one thumb hard against the other—"I couldn't make myself talk about it." He looked up at Doug, and after a moment got a slow nod of understanding.

"It was bad?"

Kincaid nodded. "Yeah. It was bad."

"So why are you telling me now?"

"Because I found out I wasn't crazy." Kincaid explained what Rashid had learned.

Doug was shaking his head before he'd finished. "Why now? Why ask Rashid now? Why tell me, after months of keeping me in the dark?"

"Because of Denis."

Doug stared at him. "What does any of that have to do with Denis?"

Kincaid looked round again, then lowered voice. "I met Denis. Saturday night. I think I was the last person to see him before he was attacked. He asked me to meet him at a pub in Holborn. He thought he was being watched, and followed, just like Ryan. He hinted there was something rotten going on in the force, and he warned me off asking any sort of questions, for my safety, and my family's. And then someone tried to kill him as he walked home."

"Christ," whispered Doug. "Does anyone else know you met him?"

"I told a friend in Cheshire. A cop. He's a good guy, and I needed to talk to someone with no connection to the Met."

"Cheshire?" Doug looked a bit whiplashed.

"My dad had a little health scare. I had to make a quick visit."

Frowning, Doug said, "That still doesn't explain why you're telling me all this now."

Kincaid took a breath. "Because I realized it's not my right to try to protect you without your knowledge. That I might actually be putting you in more danger by keeping you in the dark. And because . . ." Kincaid drank the rest of his cold coffee, fortification for the last hurdle. "And because I need your help."

"So were they lying about Reagan arguing with Hugo? Or did she have rows with Hugo *and* with Sidney?" asked Kerry. "And why would she accuse Sidney of cheating?" They were standing a few doors from the piano bar in Kensington High Street. Gemma wished she could have a sit-down and a coffee in the shade at Carluccio's, but Kerry was obviously not in the mood for chatting over a cup of espresso.

"I'm going to give Thea Osho a ring." Gemma pulled out her mobile. "I'm sure she knows more about what was going on that night than she's told us." But there was no answer at the number Thea had given them. She texted, asking Thea to ring her back as soon as possible, then noticed she'd missed a text from Kincaid while they were in the bar.

"Bugger," she said aloud when she'd read it.

"Something wrong?" asked Kerry.

Forcing a smile, Gemma said, "Husband's gone walkabout. Are you ready to call it a day? If not, I'll need to make arrangements for my kids."

Kerry gave a sympathetic *tsk*, but shook her head. "I can't believe that this girl was completely without faults. No one is, in my experience. We know from the postmortem that she'd had sex recently with someone, but until we get the DNA profile from the semen, we can only assume it was Hugo. I can't imagine that it was that weedy Sidney, although I suppose stranger things have happened. And if Mr. Poncey Distiller is telling the truth that it wasn't him, we need to look at our other options. We haven't ruled out the gardener, who has no alibi. Or Roland Peacock." She glanced at her watch. "I wonder if we could catch his wife at home now?"

The woman who answered the Peacocks' door was thin and blond and had the sort of elegance that made Gemma feel horribly wilted after a day spent doing interviews in the heat.

"Mrs. Peacock?" asked Kerry, and introduced them. Looking more irritated than concerned, Pamela Peacock led them into the house they'd seen yesterday.

"Roland said you'd been round about that girl," she said over her shoulder.

If Edward Miller had irritated Kerry, this woman, with her middle-class drawl, set Gemma's teeth on edge. "You mean Reagan Keating, ma'am," Gemma corrected. "She was twenty-four. Hardly a girl."

"She was a nanny." Mrs. Peacock gave Gemma an amused glance. "And anyone under thirty is a girl to me— Sergeant, is it?"

"Detective Inspector," Gemma responded, as pleasantly as she could manage. She put Pamela Peacock in her early forties, and as well-preserved for her age as Nita Cusick. It was amazing what money could do. Her own mother at forty had looked every inch of it.

They'd reached the kitchen. Something delicious smelling was cooking in a Le Creuset casserole on the hob. Gemma found herself hoping that it was Roland Peacock's doing, and that this woman hadn't managed to put together a gourmet meal without marring her perfect linen outfit or her flawless makeup. The chair where Roland had sat yesterday was empty and his work had been tidied away.

"Is Mr. Peacock at home?" asked Kerry.

"No. Our son had a rugby practice. Sit, do." She gestured at the dining area, but didn't offer them tea or coffee.

"Well, that's fine," said Kerry as she and Gemma sat on dining chairs, "as it was you we wished to speak to."

Pamela Peacock raised a plucked eyebrow. "How can I help you, then?"

"We're trying to learn a little more about Reagan. That helps us put together a bigger pic—"

"I've heard she was murdered. Jean Armitage told Roland. Frankly, I think that's preposterous. Surely, you've made a mistake. The girl probably overdosed on drugs."

"Why would you think that, Mrs. Peacock?" asked Gemma.

"Well, those things happen." Pamela Peacock shrugged. "We all know it."

"Is this based on your personal knowledge of Reagan's habits?"

"No. I hardly knew her."

"But your husband was quite friendly with her, I understand. They were chatting quite recently, at the garden party, Sunday before last."

Pamela had been leaning casually against the kitchen island. At that, she straightened and crossed her arms. "You've been talking to Jean Armitage. Roland was nothing but polite. Parties are parties. He's a man of considerable charm, and I can see how a young woman would be flattered by his attention. And I'd warn you not to pay too much attention to Jean Armitage. She enjoys her little dramas."

Finding she trusted Jean Armitage's account considerably more than Pamela Peacock's, Gemma translated this as, Everyone was smashed on punch and limoncello. Roland was flirting outrageously with Reagan Keating, who didn't slap him, and Jean Armitage is a meddlesome bitch.

"I'm sure you're right, Mrs. Peacock," said Kerry with an understanding smile, pouring oil on the waters. "But what can you tell us about last Friday evening? I understand your son was ill?"

"Stomach flu." Pamela looked as if even the thought made her want to vomit. "Roland sat up with him. I'd just come back from a grueling business trip. Besides, I don't do sick. That's always been Roland's forte."

Thinking of nights spent sitting up with one child or another, Gemma almost envied her easy delegation. "Um, can you confirm that?" she asked.

"Of course I can. We had to call the damned GP out."

Gemma wondered where they had managed to find a GP who made house calls, not to mention in the middle of the night. "How's your son?" she asked.

"Just allowed back at school today." Pamela's voice softened a bit. "Poor Georgie. That's why Roland wanted to keep an eye on him at rugger practice."

"Your husband told us that your other son—is he the elder?—is away at school this term."

"No, George is the elder. It's Arthur, our younger son, who's away at school." Pamela shook her head. "It seems a bit pointless now. We think we'll bring him home next term.

"To be honest, it has been a bit hard for him. I suppose that if your child has been bullied, boarding school is perhaps not the best option." Pamela's smile was weary. "But we couldn't see what else to do." When they didn't immediately respond, she added, impatiently, "Surely Jean Armitage has told you about Henry. Henry Su."

"I believe your husband mentioned him," said Gemma. "This was the boy who died?"

Pamela made a face. "It was horrible. But he'd made life such a misery for Arthur that we'd already decided to send him away next term."

"I understand he was difficult. Didn't he tease Jess Cusick, too?"

"You'd think that with his dancing, Jess would have been an easier target than Arthur. Arthur is only a swot, and a bit delicate at games. Jess, however, seems to be made of sterner stuff. Per-haps his dancing has made him tough." There was no malice in her voice, only an unexpectedly revealed fondness for her son.

"I've met Jess," said Gemma. "He seems very focused."

Pamela's laugh held no humor. "You could say that. Focused enough to let the nasty business of Henry Su's death roll off his back. They blamed him, you know, the Sus. And they blamed the nanny. Reagan."

"Reagan?" said Gemma, startled. "Why?"

"They said if she'd been watching Jess properly that day, she'd have realized Henry was missing and sounded an alert."

"But Henry wasn't her responsibility."

Pamela Peacock sighed. "I'm not sure that makes much difference to parents who have lost a child and are looking for anyone to blame but themselves."

"You bugger," said Doug with feeling, when Kincaid had explained what he'd done that afternoon. "So that's why you were in Wallingford. I'd have gone with you." He looked as disappointed as a child denied Christmas.

"I know. It was a spur-of-the-moment thing."

"So what did you find?"

Quietly, Kincaid told him.

"He was going to bolt," said Doug, after considering for a moment. "He never meant to kill himself."

"No."

"Maybe he'd made connections among campaigners he'd infiltrated. Maybe he thought he could take the family and disappear abroad, where no one had any idea who he really was." Doug frowned, swirling the sugary syrup in the bottom of his coffee cup. "Most of the undercover cops have elaborate exit stories planned years in advance. They're intended to be put to use when they go back to the regular job, but maybe Ryan really meant to enact his." Doug seemed somehow to find the idea comforting. "You remember," he went on, "how we found Ryan in the Met's records, first as uniform and then as CID, and then he disappeared off any active roster?"

Kincaid nodded, not sure where this was going.

Doug glanced at him, then back at his coffee, as if uncertain how to go on. "You know it was Melody's father who first heard that Denis had been attacked. He . . . suggested . . . to Melody that perhaps something from Denis's past had come back to haunt him."

"Denis's past?" Kincaid said in surprise.

"Well, that's what I thought, too. But, then, I thought, why not have a look, so I did. The pattern is easy to spot once you've seen it."

"What pattern?"

"One like Ryan's. Exemplary record. Uniform to CID in record time. A year as a detective sergeant in Hackney. Then, poof. Nothing for three years. Zip. Nada. Then, suddenly Denis Childs reappears, as a DI, posted to Charing Cross nick."

Kincaid sat back, staring at him. Finally, he said, "Shit. Denis was undercover. I'd never have thought . . ."

"No. But it might explain some things. Those connections Ivan Talbot hinted at—could they have been people in whatever groups he infiltrated? Or old mates from Special Branch?"

Kincaid recalled his earlier thought. "Is it possible," he said to Doug, "that Denis knew Ryan Marsh? Or knew about Ryan Marsh? When he transferred me to Holborn, Ryan had already been in place with Matthew Quinn's little group for months."

"I'm beginning to think that anything is possible. And Denis was very good at gathering information." Doug pushed his glasses up on the bridge of his nose and reached for his satchel. "Did you bring that memory card? Let's have a look. Maybe Ryan will tell us."

With another glance round the room—he was beginning to feel like a bloody spy—Kincaid slipped the little rectangle from his wallet and handed it to Doug.

As he watched Doug put his laptop on the table, Kincaid's phone buzzed in his pocket. Taking it out, he saw that it was Jasmine Sidana, his DI from the team at Holborn. He frowned, debating whether to take the call, but he knew Sidana would never ring him for something trivial. Scooting his chair back a bit, so as not to disturb Doug, he answered.

"Sir," said Sidana. "I know you're tied up with family matters. But we've just pulled a body out of the canal at King's Cross. And there's something I think you'll want to see."

"I'm back in London, actually." Kincaid glanced at his watch, calculated how long it would take to walk from the club to the station. "I could be there in about half an hour."

When he rang off, he found Doug frowning at the computer screen. "What is it?" he asked.

"The memory card. It's just pictures. A jumble. Makes no sense to me." He slid the computer round so that Kincaid could see the screen.

Kincaid scrolled through the dozen images. As each photo popped up on the screen, his dismay grew deeper. He recognized the cluster of buildings in the village center. He knew the pub. And the church, with its distinctive lych-gate. "Dear God," he whispered. "It's Hambleden. It's Angus Craig's house."

It was the house as he'd first seen it, unscathed by fire, and the leaves on the trees surrounding it were the russet of late autumn. Doug, he realized, had only seen the aftermath, when the Craigs were both dead, and the house a smoking ruin.

CHAPTER EIGHTEEN

JULY 1994

They had made love on the kitchen floor, amid the spread news-papers and tins of paint. It had felt illicit, and so consuming that when he turned up at the Tabernacle hours later, his body was still tingling.

It left him totally unprepared for the long faces of the group hunched over their coffee cups in the Tabernacle café. Annette Whitely was there, and Marvin Emba, a studious-looking black man, as well as half a dozen other regulars.

"What's happened?" he asked, sitting down, his coffee order forgotten.

"Where have you been?" Marvin challenged him, his chin thrust out. "We've rung your flat half a dozen times."

"I had a job." He was unprepared for this, too, and he hated not having a scenario worked out. "North London," he added, rubbing at a suddenly noticed paint smudge on his hand and trying not to think about how it had got there. "What's happened?" he asked again, doing a mental head count. None of the regulars were missing.

"It's Whitewatch," said Annette. Whitewatch were the most extreme of the smaller fascist groups that had popped up in London recently, and one he was sure Special Branch had an eye on. "They've said they're going to march at Carnival. People are going to get hurt."

"We have to do something," Marvin chimed in. "Protest. That's what we're about."

"Then someone really will get hurt," Denis said, as calm as he could make it. Notting Hill Carnival had been plagued by racial violence since its inception. This year's celebration was only a few weeks away. The police would be out in force, but they couldn't stop every flare-up from turning into a vicious brawl.

"You know what they're like, Den." Annette, usually his ally, was glaring at him. "We can't just do nothing."

Whitewatch was not only as racist as their name implied— they also particularly targeted biracial people, calling them "abominations." People, he thought, like Annette. "Look," he said. "Engaging with these people is like throwing petrol on a fire. It's what they want. We know that. The only effective message we can send is a peaceful one."

"Then we can march peacefully," said Deirdre. A school-teacher, with the frizzy hair and huge glasses popular a decade earlier, she liked to feel she was in charge. The others, however, looked at him expectantly. He'd never wanted—or meant—to be considered the leader of the little group. But he'd found—as he suspected had most of the undercover cops—that being a *policeman gave one a natural authority that was difficult to camouflage.*

"We can march," he agreed, "but I think we'd be better served getting out leaflets and handbills, encouraging people to keep things peaceful. Nothing will get better if there's a riot." There were reluctant nods, but he sensed mutiny brewing. "Where did you hear this?" he asked. "Are you sure it's not just a rumor?"

"My brother," said a woman called Beverley, "works in an auto repair shop with a bloke who hangs round the group. This bloke was bragging about how they were going to kick heads at Carnival. And, get some, you know . . ." Beverley, like Deirdre, was white, and the white members of the group were always uncomfortable repeating racial epithets.

"Maybe it's just talk, then. But we'll keep our eyes open, right?" This time the nods were more enthusiastic, but he didn't trust any of them, even Annette, not to start spreading the rumor. And the more talk, the more the potential for violence would rise.

As much as he hated to, it was time he made a report to Red Craig. It was his job.

Leaving the Peacocks', Gemma and Kerry walked along Cornwall Crescent. As they approached the Sus' house, Gemma's spirits felt inexplicably heavy. She wasn't looking forward to talking to this couple who'd lost a child and whose method of dealing with their grief seemed to be making enemies of all their neighbors.

The front of the house was architecturally identical to the others on that side of the terrace, but while most had some adornment, polished brass knockers or topiaries or window boxes, the Sus' house was stark. It felt like a blind eye.

Kerry charged up the steps and pressed the buzzer. She had to press a second time before there was an answer.

Gemma had been expecting both the Sus to be Chinese, but the woman who answered was white, as blond and thin as Pamela Peacock, but with none of her natural elegance. Her face was hard, and her mouth was compressed into a thin, red, unwelcoming line. When Boatman introduced them and showed her warrant card, she looked at them blankly, then said in a high, strident voice, "This is too bloody much. Who did they pay off to get detectives to harass us?"

It was Kerry's turn to look blank. "Mrs. Su?" she asked, recovering. "Mrs. Lisa Su?"

"You know perfectly well who I am or you wouldn't be here. I'm not talking to you—"

"Mrs. Su, there seems to be some misunderstanding. What is it that you think we're here about?"

"The extension, of course."

Lisa Su, Gemma decided, might have been pretty if not for what seemed a perpetually angry expression. Her eyes protruded slightly, as if pushed out from the pressure within.

"This has nothing to do with your extension," said Kerry. "Is your husband at home?"

"Yes, but I don't want to disturb him." Mrs. Su looked suddenly uncertain. "Really, can't you just tell me what this is about?"

"Do you mind if we come in?" asked Kerry. They were still standing on the doorstep and she gave a pointed glance at Jean Armitage's house, two doors down. "And it really is important that we talk to you and your husband."

"Oh, all right." Mrs. Su ushered them ungraciously into the hall. And there she left them while she went down the stairs into the basement. They heard her call, "Ben? There's—" The sound was cut off by the thud of a closing door.

The doors to the sitting room were closed as well. There was nothing on the walls, just as there had been nothing about the exterior of the house to give a clue as to its inhabitants.

Ben Su preceded his wife up the stairs. Gemma's first thought was that she hadn't expected him to be so good looking. He was tall and lithe, with thick dark hair just beginning to gray a little at the temples. His handsome face was, like his wife's, set in lines of anger. But while Lisa Su looked petulant, he looked . . . dangerous. Gemma took an instinctive step back, but there was nowhere to go.

"What do you want?" he asked in precise, unaccented English.

"We're investigating the death of a resident here on the garden," said Kerry. "Reagan Keating. I believe you knew her."

"What are you talking about? We don't know of any death. We can't—"

"The nanny?" his wife said, interrupting him. "The nanny? She's dead?"

Kerry glanced at Gemma. Was it possible that they really didn't know? She supposed it was. They had no friends among the neighbors, as far as Gemma knew, and they seemed to be away from home all day. The monstrous unfinished extension must block any view of the garden from the basement and ground-floor rooms.

"Yes, the nanny," Gemma answered, by now thoroughly irritated by the pair. "She was killed sometime Friday night, in the garden. We understand you held her in some way responsible for the death of your son."

The bulge of Mrs. Su's eyes grew more pronounced. "Who told you that? We only said that if she'd been more careful—"

"Lisa, that's enough," barked her husband. To Kerry and Gemma, he said, "We know nothing about this, and neither of us spoke more than half a dozen words to the girl. Now, if you don't mi—"

"Mr. Su. Mrs. Su." Kerry was looking pinched. "We're sorry to take up your valuable time. But a young woman has been murdered. Did you see anything, or anyone, out of the ordinary on Friday night?"

Lisa Su shook her head. "I was staying the night with my sister. In Milton Keynes."

"Mr. Su?"

For a moment, Gemma thought he wouldn't answer. Then he said, "Out with clients from the bank. I was late back."

"How late?" asked Boatman.

Again, the slight hesitation. "About three."

"Can you confirm this?"

"Of course I can confirm it. But you can talk to my solic—"

"It was that boy," broke in Lisa Su. "The dancer. That was what Ben said to her. If he hadn't bullied our Henry, Henry wouldn't have hidden in the shed. I know he wouldn't. Henry didn't like tight spaces. And he'd never have lost his inhaler if something hadn't upset him. Ben told her that."

"You told Reagan that?" Gemma asked Ben Su. "When?"

But it was Lisa who answered. "At the stupid garden party. Where no one talked to us." Her big eyes glistened with tears.

"Wait." Gemma had to stop herself giving Lisa Su a shake. "Are you saying that Jess Cusick bullied your son?"

"Christ, what an unpleasant couple," said Kerry as they walked away. "The question is, are they that horrible *because* their son died? Or was the son a little twat because his parents were worse twats? And now they're even more awful than they were before?"

"I don't believe for a minute that Jess Cusick bullied Henry." Gemma was still furious. On the back of a card, Ben Su had scribbled the names and numbers of his colleagues from the bank, and of his wife's sister. Then he'd added his lawyer's number and told them to contact the solicitor with anything further. It had been all Gemma could do to keep a civil tongue in her head.

Kerry looked over at her as they reached the car. "I think we need a drink. That was hazardous duty."

Gemma had to agree. She'd already arranged for Wesley Howard to watch the kids. That left Kincaid unaccounted for, but Gemma wasn't going to ring him to tell him that she was going to be late.

Kerry's pub of choice was The Hansom Cab on Earl's Court Road, next to Rassells garden center where Gemma had been the previous Saturday, and just a few steps from Kensington Police Station. The pub's front room was small and unpretentiously relaxed, with comfortable furniture and an impressive center bar. The clientele seemed to be local, and regulars. Boatman chose a table in the corner and sank into an upholstered chair with a sigh of pleasure.

"My feet are killing me," she said, surreptitiously slipping her shoes off under the table. "This place has quite a history, you know." She gestured round the pub. "Although you wouldn't think it to look at it now, Piers Morgan was a co-owner for a while, along with his brother, Rupert, and another posh bloke called Tarquin Gorst. Can you believe that? Piers, Rupert, and Tarquin. Poncey gits. It was a celebrity hangout. Thank God that's a thing of the past. Now, this is just a decent pub with good beer and very good food."

The waitress, a friendly girl with tattoos to rival Agatha Smith's at the distillery, came to take their orders. Boatman went for bitter on tap. Gemma, studying the bar, spotted a familiar logo. "I'll try the Red Fox gin. With tonic."

"You liked him, didn't you?" said Kerry, when the waitress had gone.

"You mean Edward Miller?" Gemma thought about it. "Yes. I suppose I did. Although that doesn't mean I'd rule him out as a suspect. But I take it you didn't care for him."

Kerry shrugged, her expression rueful. "Old prejudices, I suppose. Nothing against him personally." When Gemma waited expectantly, she sighed and went on. "I was a bright girl. My parents scraped together nearly every penny they earned to send me to a fee-paying day school so that I'd have a good education. So I spent six years being looked down on by people with accents like his, who didn't think I was good enough to be there."

"A big chip, then," said Gemma, with an understanding grin.

"Beer-sized," agreed Kerry when the waitress had brought their drinks. She lifted her pint glass. "Cheers. Here's to getting to the bottom of this damned case. I'd really like to pin it on one or both of the Sus, but I suspect their alibis will pan out."

"I don't think they can possibly have anything to do with Reagan's murder," said Gemma, tasting her gin. "I can't come up with any believable scenario where Reagan would have gone into the garden alone with either of them."

Frowning, Gemma thought a little more about dark and brooding Ben Su. The man exuded power as well as anger. And he was very good looking. "Well, maybe I'll take that back . . ." She sipped some more, liking the herbal tang of the gin, then said, "What if Lisa *was* away at her sister's? What if Reagan was feeling guilty about Henry's death? What if she took Ben Su up on an invitation to meet in the garden, thinking she'd have a chance to apologize?"

"I can see that," agreed Kerry.

"And when he wanted more of an apology than she was prepared to give, he smothered her," said Gemma. "I suppose it's possible, but would Reagan, who by all accounts wasn't much of a drinker, really have drunk that much alcohol with him?" she asked.

Kerry, who'd been studying the dinner menu, set it down with an air of decision. "Try the chicken pie. It's their specialty."

"Oh, but I didn't intend to—" Gemma stopped. The children were looked after, and Kincaid was off doing heaven knew what. She felt suddenly rebellious. "I'll have the chicken pie," she said as the waitress came back to the table with her pad at the ready. "And another G and T."

Kerry raised an eyebrow.

"I'm fine," said Gemma, although she realized her tongue felt a bit numb. "And I'm not driving."

"Strong stuff, gin." Boatman nodded at Gemma's glass. "Can't abide the taste of it, myself. According to your mate, Mr. Miller, what goes into that still is even stronger. What if he mixed a little of the high-proof stuff into what Reagan thought was a normal drink? Or a couple of drinks? She wouldn't know what hit her."

Gemma had texted Kate Ling, asking her to give them a more definite time of death, but she hadn't heard back. "I suppose it's possible. But I think you're going to find that Edward Miller was well occupied until after Reagan was killed."

"There is the damned text." Kerry frowned into her beer. "I don't like it. And I don't like that the Three Musketeers lied about her arguing with Sidney at the bar."

"Maybe Hugo and Thea didn't know," suggested Gemma. "But whatever happened between Reagan and Sidney, I do not believe she met him in the garden. Until we get all their alibis confirmed, we're treading water. And we don't have enough hish—" Her tongue was definitely not cooperating, but her mind felt clear as a bell. "History. On Reagan. Nita Cusick didn't approve of Reagan's friends, and seems to have had absolutely no interest in her personal life. But there's someone we haven't talked to."

"Who?" asked Kerry, sounding a little owlish.

"The ex-husband. Jess's dad."

Kincaid led the way. Doug had insisted on walking with him as far as Holborn Police Station. "You don't want to be seen with me," Kincaid told him. "Especially with that memory card on you."

"I'll get the tube from Holborn. You don't think someone's going to jump me for my laptop?" Doug sounded amused. Then, when Kincaid nodded at the street sign and Doug realized where they were, he said, "Shit."

They were walking along Clerkenwell Road, the way Denis must have walked on Saturday night, going to and from the pub in Roger Street. It was after six o'clock now and Clerkenwell was crowded with pedestrians, commuters heading home or to the pubs.

"This was Denis's route," said Doug. "But it was dark when he was attacked. And it wasn't in an open street," he added, but after that he looked around warily. "Do you suppose Denis was carrying something?"

"Nothing seemed to have been taken."

"But what if it was something no one knew he had?"

Kincaid considered, shook his head. "I think whoever attacked Denis heard someone coming, probably the girls who called 999. Otherwise they'd have cleared out his pockets. And I think they'd have made sure he was dead."

He was distracted, still thinking about the photos Ryan Marsh had hidden. Looking at the last one again, he'd recognized Edie Craig, wearing the same green scarf she'd worn the day he'd talked with her, outside the village church. And he'd caught, in the background, a glimpse of Edie's little whippet, Barney, running off the lead. He would have sworn that the photos were taken just before the fire. Did that mean that Ryan had been there? Had he known the Craigs?

Could Ryan have worked for Angus Craig, either on or off the books?

There was another possibility that explained those photos, nagging at the edge of his brain, but he didn't want to think about it. Not now.

"Duncan, are you okay?" Doug put a hand on his arm, stopping him. "I've been talking to you for five minutes. If I'm not going into the station with you, I'd better go on ahead."

Kincaid realized that Clerkenwell had changed to Theobald's Road, and the hulk of Holborn Police Station at the corner of Lamb's Conduit Street was in sight. "Sorry," he said. "Look, you're going to talk to Melody, aren't you?"

Doug looked uncertain. "Well . . . should I not?"

"You already have." Kincaid attempted a grin. "So you may as well tell her the rest. I want to know what her father was hinting at. Ivan Talbot has ears in all sorts of places and sources we can't touch. And I want to know anything that either of you can dig up on Kate Ling."

"Right. I'll ring you."

As Doug started to turn away, Kincaid said, "Dougie." This time he had no trouble summoning a smile at the expression on Doug's face. Doug despised the nickname. "Thanks for coming."

For once, Doug seemed at a loss for something to say. He gave a half-sketched salute and turned away, his satchel slung over his shoulder. Kincaid watched him until he disappeared in the crowd, and hoped he hadn't just sent his friend into terrible danger.

The CID room at Holborn looked just as it had when Kincaid had walked out yesterday morning, on his way to Cheshire. A glance down at his jeans, now dried a little stiffly, assured him that time had indeed passed. He ran a hand across his chin. The stubble felt well past five o'clock, but there was nothing for it. His face felt warm, too, and he wondered if he was as sunburned as Doug. Then, Jasmine Sidana looked up from her desk and spotted him. He could have sworn he saw relief flash across her face.

Simon Gikas sat studying his computer monitors, as usual, and DC Sweeney had, apparently, gone home. Just as well, Kincaid thought. When Sidana said "Boss," Simon looked up, too.

Rising, Simon said, "Guv. Are you sure you should be here? How's your old dad?"

Kincaid realized to his dismay that he had not even checked in with his mum since he'd left Nantwich. "Fine. He's doing well. They've sent him home."

"Did you get in a little fishing on your way back, then?" asked Simon, eyeing his bedraggled clothes.

Closer than he might have guessed, Kincaid thought, but said, "So what's going on?"

Sidana stood, glancing round the room at the few other detectives who were working late. "Maybe we'd better go in your office, boss."

Kincaid led them into his office and closed the door. No one sat. He couldn't imagine what necessitated such secrecy but his stomach knotted with tension. "What the hell is it?"

Simon Gikas looked at Sidana, who gave him a nod. "We pulled a floater out of the Regent's Canal at King's Cross today, near the *Guardian*. Nasty bit of business. Been in for a couple of days, from his condition. It wasn't until they got him to the mortuary that they saw it was more than a drowning. He'd been stabbed."

"And?" Kincaid asked.

Sidana took it up. "His wallet and phone were in his pockets. Driving license identifies him as one Michael Stanley, age fifty-two, white male. His license covers commercial vehicles, so maybe a lorry driver. But when the mortuary ran his prints, they came back as Michael Stanton. They were in the Met database. He's a cop."

"What?" Kincaid stared at them. This suddenly sounded all too familiar.

"Yeah," said Simon. "Or he was. Not showing as retired, but hasn't been posted anywhere in ten years. And his record, what I could find of it, shows some disciplinary issues."

"What about his phone?"

"Toast, probably, after extended time in the canal. And I'd guess it's a burner anyway. Cheapest model."

"Home address on the license?"

"An estate in Hackney, but there's no such flat number in that location."

Kincaid liked this less and less, and Hackney rang big alarm bells. Ryan Marsh's cover flat had been in Hackney. "Where in Hackney, exactly?" He said it so sharply that Simon and Sidana both started.

Frowning, Simon told him the name of the estate. It was not the one where Ryan had lived, but it was not dissimilar.

"Who's the pathologist?" Kincaid asked.

"The body went to the London," Sidana told him. "I don't know if anyone's been assigned to do the postmortem yet."

"I want Rashid Kaleem on this one. And, Simon, find a real address. He's got to have left a trail somewhere."

"Sir," said Sidana, sounding unusually hesitant. "We were wondering. We haven't yet informed Chief Superintendent Faith that the victim's prints were in the Met personnel database. He seems to have a lot on his plate at the moment."

"Yes, I know." Was he just being paranoid, thinking they had another undercover cop on their hands? But it fit the pattern. And if there was even a possibility that it was true, the fewer people who knew, the better. He trusted these two. And Tom Faith. But once Faith was told, the information would be passed up the chain of command, and that thought made him uneasy. "Let's see what we can find before we bother the chief super," he said, and both Sidana and Simon looked satisfied.

"Have you got photos?" he asked.

Sidana passed him a folder she'd carried in with her. Opening it, he found copies of the crime scene shots. He recognized the section of the canal where the body had been pulled out. The canal path was busy in the daytime, he guessed, but probably deserted at night except for the occasional jogger. Of course, the bloke hadn't necessarily gone in where he'd surfaced . . .

Had the victim been stabbed from the front or the back? Kincaid wondered. In a fight, or in an unguarded attack from behind?

He flipped to the close-up photos of the corpse. The entry wound was beneath the left rib cage. It would take the postmortem to show whether the knife had been angled upwards, a deliberate blow. Next, he studied the man's face, but he couldn't tell much because of the bloating. There was a small mark on the neck, but from the photo he couldn't determine whether it was a bruise or a birthmark, or perhaps a tattoo.

The next page showed him an enlarged copy of the driving license with its photo. An unremarkable man looked back at him. Thinning fairish hair. A rather old-fashioned-looking mustache, which he had not sported when he'd gone in the canal. Eyes, brown; height, five feet, ten inches. And, yet, there was something in that unremarkable face that made Kincaid think he'd not have turned his back on this man.

"Can I keep these?" he asked Sidana.

"Your copies, boss."

"Then see how soon Rashid can do the postmortem."

"You look all in, boss," said Sidana. From her, it was the height of personal concern. "You should go home."

Yes, he thought. He should. But he had a lot of talking to do when he got there, and he was not looking forward to it.

CHAPTER NINETEEN

AUGUST 1994

He had prayed for rain. The day of Carnival, however, dawned bright and clear. It promised to be hot, and heat always escalated the potential for violence. Notting Hill Carnival was a policing nightmare, with close to a million people jammed into a few streets, and most of the crowd partaking liberally of alcohol.

It was the first day, Sunday, so he didn't expect the crowds to be quite as dense, or as rowdy. But he still had to push his way through people just to get to the Tabernacle, where the group had agreed to meet.

He'd talked them out of carrying placards, thank God. "Carnival's always been about cultural harmony," he'd told them. "It's not the place you have to make that point."

"Tell that to Stephen Lawrence," Marvin had said and the rest had nodded in agreement.

It was Annette who'd come up with the idea for badges. She'd had them made, half with just Stephen Lawrence's first name, half with his photo. They agreed they'd wear them on their clothes, and on ribbons and sashes, and that they would hand them out to festivalgoers.

When he arrived at the Tabernacle he found them decked out like human Christmas trees, buttons clanking and jingling. Annette, who ordinarily straightened her hair, had put it in tiny braids festooned with beads and ribbons. She handed him a large sash, covered in the big badges. "I made this for you," she said.

He held it up. "But . . . it's pink," he said, and grinned. Their excitement was contagious, as was the steel band music already pulsing from the giant speakers set up along the carnival route. Dutifully, he put on the sash, and they checked each other's makeshift costumes, giggling like kids getting ready for a party.

"Remember to stay together," he said, when they were ready. "And stay out of trouble, okay?"

"You're such a mother hen, Denny." Annette laughed up at him. "Are you sure you're not a schoolteacher? We'll be good, we promise. And you remember to have some fun." He thought she'd come closer than she realized, and he'd better at least look like he was in the spirit.

By that afternoon, he'd discovered it wasn't hard. Notting Hill was a kaleidoscope of sound and color and movement. DJs spun reggae from the great stages, steel bands marched, the costumes were an outrageous blaze of color, and everyone danced. In between, they ate jerk chicken, and corn, and Jamaican peas and rice from the stalls. They'd long ago given away all their badges. There were more black faces than white in the crowd, and everyone seemed moved by a spirit of bonhomie. Strangers danced together in the sun, the women with the morning's cardigans tied round their waists like Caribbean skirts. On Elgin Crescent, three uniformed constables broke into a dance routine. They'd obviously practiced their choreography, and the bystanders cheered with approval when they finished.

The police presence had been friendly and conciliatory, and if there had been any scuffles, he hadn't seen them.

At last, tired and thirsty, they'd decided to head back to the Tabernacle. The smells were getting to them—not just the street-stall foods, but sweat, and spilled rum and beer, and most of all the eye-watering stench of urine. The Carnival provided temporary toilets, but there were never enough, especially for the beer drinkers. The pavements were littered with cigarette ends, spilled food, and crushed cans of Red Stripe.

The group had turned into Westbourne Park Road when he felt something slippery under his shoe. Looking down, he saw a crushed ice cream cornet and a puddle of melted ice cream. He was wiping his sticky shoe against a clean spot on the pavement when a prickle at the back of his neck made him look up.

They wore white T-shirts emblazoned with scarlet interlocking Ws, the symbol for Whitewatch. Five abreast, walking westward down Westbourne Park Road, swinging beer bottles held loosely in their fingers. Five, he thought, like the five men who had attacked Stephen Lawrence. Five white men. They wore chains in their belt loops.

He stood, slowly, instinctively reaching out to thrust back the people nearest him. Annette. And Marvin. The constant thump from the steel bands seemed to fade until he heard the thud of his own heart. Then, he focused on the man in the middle. His brain froze, stuttered, refusing to match the face to the situation.

It was Mickey. And Mickey was looking straight at him, grinning.

"Nice pink sash you've got there, girlie," Mickey called, and the others hooted and laughed. They were drunk, or high. Or both. He could see it in their unsteady swaggers, and in their glazed eyes. For a wild moment, he wondered if he'd been targeted. He'd known Mickey had been put in a right-wing group, but he'd never dreamed it was this one. He'd told Red Craig his protesters meant to march at Carnival. Was this the response?

And, then, he wondered if Mickey meant to out him.

"A pansy, playing with coloreds and half-breeds," said the man on the right. They all laughed, and there was an ugliness to it that made his hair stand on end. Mickey, he thought, what the hell are you doing?

He felt Annette step forward, heard her draw breath to speak. He shoved her back.

"Bugger off, you lot," he said to the men, but he looked straight at Mickey. He kept his posture nonconfrontational, his voice even.

"You gonna make us?" jeered the man on the right.

A black man stepped out of the now-silent group of onlookers, right in front of the gang. He was young and thin, his face ashy with anger. "You bastards," he shouted at them. "You don't belong here. This is our Carnival. Get out."

Mickey's eyes went cold. Denis had an instant to think, Jesus, he's lost it.

There was a flash in the corner of his eye. He turned his head, glimpsing a professional camera held by a large fair-haired man, his face half obscured by the camera body.

He threw an arm up, half in fury, half in protest. Then, just as the halo cleared from his vision, he saw the bottle fly from Mick-

ey's hand. It struck the young black man in the head. The man fell to the curb, writhing and moaning, blood pouring from his scalp.

There was a great collective sound from the crowd, a gasp of outrage, and people surged forward. Denis shouted at them to get back, the command voice instinctive. In the distance, police whistles began to blow. Mickey rocked on the balls of his feet, still looking triumphant, ready to take on a fight, but the others were shifting uneasily. As the whistles grew louder, they began to back away. Mickey gave him a last look and turned on his heel.

Denis knelt by the fallen man. He looked for something, anything, to staunch the bleeding from the head wound. His hands were already bright with blood from trying to assess the extent of the injury. Something white landed beside him and he saw that it was Annette's cardigan. Groping for it, he felt a jab to his hand. When he looked down, he saw that he'd sliced it open on a shard of the broken bottle.

Ignoring the cut, he did his best to wrap the man's head, shouting, "Someone call 999." Then a pretty black woman knelt beside him, holding a toddler by the hand. "Wes," she said, "let's give the man your T-shirt, love."

He started to caution her to get the child back, away from trouble. But when he looked up, Mickey and his gang had melted into the crowd.

As soon as Melody arrived, she could tell Doug was full of news. But she made him show her what he'd done in the garden first, while there was still light. "No wonder you got a sunburn," she said, gazing at the pristine slate of newly dug beds in the twilight.

"You'll still help me, won't you?" Doug asked.

"Of course I will," she said, but all her ideas and her energy for the project seemed to have vanished. Filling those empty beds now seemed an insurmountable task. "We'll talk about it at the weekend."

They went in, and only when she had her tea did she let him begin.

Doug told her everything he'd learned that day from Kincaid.

She couldn't take it in. Shaking her head, she said, "Ryan didn't kill himself? But . . ." She felt numb. Ryan Marsh taking his own life had been the overriding fact of her existence for nearly two months. She'd dreamed of him putting the gun to his head, seen his blue eyes gazing at her from his smudged face as he pulled the trigger. She'd wondered, over and over, if there was something she might have said or done that would have stopped him. She'd wondered, if he'd been so haunted by the horror of the death in the fire at St. Pancras, if she would ever escape it.

Suddenly, she was furious. "Duncan didn't tell us? Why didn't he tell us?"

"He hadn't any proof. And—"

"We could have found proof. We could have—"

"And that's the other reason he didn't tell us," Doug broke in. "He was afraid that if Ryan had been murdered, and we started digging, we'd be in danger, too. Now look what happened to Denis."

"But there's no connection between Ryan and Denis," Melody argued. "Other than the fact that we know—or think we know—that they both worked undercover."

Doug, straddling his ottoman, waved his beer at her for emphasis. "They both thought they were being watched. And Ryan might have had some sort of connection with Angus Craig."

"I don't believe it," Melody said hotly.

"He had photos of the Craigs' house. Maybe he was working for someone who was watching Craig."

"But who—"

"There's something else. Duncan rang me while you were on your way here. Camden pulled a body from the canal at King's Cross today. According to his fingerprints, a cop. But his ID was false and he'd no record of any posting in the Met for at least ten years. His address was false, too, no such number in that estate. But the estate was in Hackney, not far from Ryan Marsh's cover flat."

Melody's curiosity started to take over. "You said 'no posting in at least ten years.' How old was this guy?"

"Fifty-two, according to the fake driving license. Duncan said his record showed 'disciplinary issues,' but when I looked at his files, there was more than that." Doug got up and went into the kitchen, pulling another beer from the fridge. This time, when he held it out towards Melody, she nodded. He grabbed another for himself and brought one to her.

She didn't drink, but held the cold bottle to her face while Doug returned to his perch on the ottoman. It was growing dark. Through the open slats of the shades, she could see the lights coming on in the street. With a sudden shiver, she got up and closed the shades with a snap. "What else?" she asked, turning back to Doug.

"This guy, Michael Stanton, disappeared more than once. He was a DC, with twelve years in the force and no further promotion. Then, in the summer of '93, he just vanished. He doesn't show up again until three years later. After that, he moved from department to department, with repeated cautions for excessive force, and complaints of sexual harassment from female colleagues. Until he disappeared again, this time for good."

"Summer of '93?" Melody frowned. "Wasn't it '94 when Denis

dropped off the map for a couple of years? Could there be a connection?"

"Between Denis and this scumbag? I don't see what."

"It's too much of a coincidence." Melody started to pace. "I don't believe in coincidence. What the hell was Denis Childs doing in 1994?"

"You know someone who might know," Doug said a little hesitantly.

"What?" Melody frowned at him, beer bottle half lifted to her mouth. "What are you talking about?"

"You mean 'whom,' not what. Your father."

The house was dark and quiet when Kincaid came in the front door. It was well after nine now—of course the younger children were in bed—but something about the stillness didn't feel right. He told himself not to be silly, but he was relieved when he heard a woof and Geordie came running to greet him.

"Where's Mum, boy?" he asked, stooping to ruffle the dog's silky ears. Geordie, who certainly understood every word, led him straight to the kitchen. Gemma sat at the kitchen table, illuminated only by the small lamp on the work top, cradling what looked like a mug of tea.

"Gemma," he said, more sharply than he intended. "What are you doing in here in the dark? Where are the kids?"

"Charlotte is asleep. Toby is supposed to be reading for"— she glanced at the clock—"five more minutes. And Kit is doing his homework." She was enunciating with the sharp precision of anger. It did not bode well. "And I might ask where you've been," she went on. "Your mum rang ages ago. She thought you might like to know how your father was doing."

"He's all right, isn't he?" Kincaid said, alarmed.

"She says he's doing fine. A bit fretful is all."

"Oh. Good." Relief washed over him. "I'll just go check on the children, then."

"Not until you've told me what's going on." Gemma leaned forward, pointing at the opposite chair. "Sit." When the light caught her face, he saw that it was implacable.

"I'm not sure where to start." He went to the high cupboard where he kept his good bottle of Scotch, taking the bottle down, then pouring an inch into a tumbler. He held the bottle out towards Gemma.

She shook her head. "I've had enough tonight, thank you."

"Scotch?" he asked, confused.

"No. Long story. And I'm not telling it now."

When he'd put away the bottle and taken the chair she'd indicated, Gemma went on, conversationally, "You know, if you were anyone else, I'd think you were having an affair."

"An affair?" He stared at her, shocked. "But that's daft."

"Is it? You've been distant. You make excuses not to be home. When you're gone, you can't seem to explain what you've been doing. And today, after driving all the way to Cheshire to see your father yesterday, you couldn't even be bothered ringing your mother. Or checking your messages. So you had better tell me."

He took a swallow of the whisky, and when it had burned its way down all the way to his gut, he took a breath and began. He started, as he had with Doug, with the night Ryan Marsh had died. As he spoke, he watched her eyes grow wider. Her cheekbones looked sharp and her full lips were pressed tightly together. When he got to his conversation with Ronnie Babcock in Nantwich, she interrupted him.

"You told Rashid all this, and not me? And then you told Ronnie, and not me?"

"It wasn't deliberate, Gem. I didn't want to worry you and I thought maybe I'd just let things get to me—"

"Since when have you not trusted me to tell you if you were batshit crazy?" she interrupted.

"And would you have told me that?" he countered. "If I'd told you I saw Ryan dead that night? And that I didn't believe he'd killed himself, but I had no proof?"

Gemma sat back. After a moment, she said, "I don't know. I'd have thought you were understandably upset."

"You could say that." He heard the hard sarcasm and took another swallow of the whisky. "But I wasn't off my nut." He told her about his second meeting with Rashid, although he hesitated to tell her that the initial pathologist had been Kate Ling. He knew she liked Kate personally, as did he, and that she wouldn't want to hear it.

"Shit," Gemma whispered when he'd finished.

"Yeah." Getting up, he retrieved the whisky bottle and poured a splash into her empty teacup. "There's more," he said.

He told her about going to the island, and about finding the memory card. And then what the memory card contained.

Gemma looked puzzled. "Wait. How did you—" Light dawned. "You didn't have your laptop, and you'd never have used a computer at work. You asked Doug, didn't you?"

He nodded, reluctantly. "I rang him this afternoon."

"What about Melody? Does she know about all of this, too?"

Kincaid knew he was digging himself in deeper, but there was no help for it. "Doug was going to talk to her. We think her father knows something about Denis." He explained about the hints Ivan had dropped.

Absently, Gemma sipped at the whisky, then made a face and

pushed the cup aside. "Not everything that Ivan Talbot knows is necessarily the truth," she said. "And none of this explains why Ryan had photos of the Craigs. Do you think he was spying on Angus Craig? Who would have authorized something like that? And who could arrange a dodgy postmortem report on Ryan Marsh?" For the first time, she looked a little frightened. "That would take someone with both knowledge and authority—"

"Gem, the pathologist was Kate Ling."

"What?" She stared at him, her face blank with shock. "That's bollocks. I don't believe it."

"She signed the damned thing."

"But—Rashid must be wrong, then," she said, shaking her head.

"Have you ever known Rashid to be less than thorough? Or accurate?"

"No. But . . . Kate must have made an honest mistake, then." Gemma's chin went stubbornly up.

"More than one mistake? The report was full of them."

"It's subjective, any postmortem. You know that. And she's been—" Gemma stopped suddenly.

"She's been what?"

Gemma shook her head. "Nothing," she said, but she didn't meet his eyes. "What are you going to do, then?" she asked.

He realized he hadn't told her about the dead cop—or former cop—in the canal. But he was exhausted, and grubby, and he honestly didn't know what the hell he was going to do about any of it. "Keep digging, I suppose," he said, rubbing his hand across his chin. "There must be connections we're not seeing."

"Well, you'll have all your coconspirators to help you. A good thing, since you obviously haven't needed me."

Gemma got up and dumped her undrunk Scotch in the sink. "I'm going to bed," she said. "You can suit yourself."

CHAPTER TWENTY

September 1994

He'd demanded a meeting with Red Craig the day after the incident at Notting Hill Carnival. Not the café, he said. He didn't intend to be discreet. Holland Park, by the Kensington gates, he told Craig. And then he waited, pacing, cradling his bandaged hand, which was throbbing.

Craig was late, and when he did arrive, he looked, as usual, perfectly groomed, supercilious, and slightly amused. Furious, Denis walked into the park, forcing Craig to follow him to a spot away from passing pedestrians, before he spat out, "What the hell happened yesterday? Mickey has gone completely mental. Do you realize that? He assaulted a bystander."

"According to him," Craig said, flicking an early falling leaf from his collar, "he and his friends were threatened, by you and by the black man. He felt a need to protect himself. And in doing so, he established credibility."

Denis stared at him. "Credibility? Are you mad? That man could have been killed. Mickey's actions could have started a riot." He rubbed a shaking hand across his mouth. "A riot! And it would have been the Met's responsibility."

"You know we have no official connection with any officer in a deep-cover assignment."

He couldn't conceal his shock. "You mean you'd disavow him."

"Or you, if it was necessary." Craig smiled. "I suggest you make the most of your heroics yesterday with your group. We need some real information, something that will damage the Lawrence campaign. And if you can't get it, we'll find someone who will."

He hadn't gone to the weekly undercover officers' gatherings for six weeks after that. He'd checked in with terse messages, and he'd stewed, angry at Craig, at Mickey, at the force, and at his own inadequacy. After a month, his wife told him he was not fit to live with and she was glad he only came home once a week.

The only positive thing he felt he'd accomplished was keeping his group from any more clashes with Whitewatch. But the next time he showed up at the Tabernacle, Annette was waiting for him in the garden. The weather was beginning to turn and the dark was coming on earlier. Lights began to blink on in Powis Square as she took his arm, saying, "Let's take a little walk." For the first time, he was tempted to put his arms round her for comfort, and perhaps for more than comfort. But then she gave his arm a squeeze and let it go, swinging her gloved hands briskly against the evening chill, and the moment passed.

She glanced at him, then away, before she spoke again. "Denny, I know you want to look after us. I can see it in every-thing you do. And you were marvelous that day at Carnival. But there's not much point in us just meeting for coffee. The whole idea was that we should do something important."

"You want to be martyrs?" he said, his anger suddenly spilling over to include her, too.

"No," Annette answered, carefully. "I don't think any of us do. But we want to be a voice for the sort of injustice that let Stephen's killers go free. And we can only be that if we speak up."

Slowly, he turned to face her. He was floundering. If he agreed to help them, he might be putting innocent people in danger. If he refused, he was out of a job, and quite probably a career. And he would be putting Annette, and Marvin, and all the others in the hands of someone who would assuredly betray them.

He knew where his duty lay, and he knew what was right.

"Okay," he said at last. "Count me in."

Kincaid spent a restless night in uneasy, exhausted sleep, dreaming of water and blood, and always aware of Gemma, huddled on the far side of the bed. Sometime in the early hours of the morning, she rolled against him, relaxed in deep sleep.

Fully awake, he lay still, not daring to disturb her. But he was comforted by the warmth of her body and the steadiness of her breathing, and, eventually, he drifted to sleep again. This time, he dreamed of Hambleden, a jumble of images like the ones he'd seen on the memory card. He saw the house, whole and unscathed by fire. He saw the church and the lych-gate. He saw Edie Craig, trailing her green scarf in the dusk, but her face was always turned away from him. Somewhere out of his sight, her little dog barked and barked, and then Angus Craig shouted at his wife to shut the damned dog up.

He woke with a gasp. Dogs were barking, but he realized they were his dogs, and it was play barking, not alarm. It was morning.

The children were up, and Gemma was gone from the bed. From the bathroom, he heard the shower running. He lay still, trying to hang on to a fragment of the dream that was slipping from his grasp like tattered cloth. The dog barking . . . Edie Craig's dog barking. Why had Edie Craig's dog been out, and unharmed, the night the house burned? He sat up, blinking, and threw back the covers.

When he came down to breakfast, Gemma was still giving him the cold shoulder.

"I'm taking the children to school," she said, although he'd offered.

Kincaid had had enough. "Go get your backpacks," he told the kids, in a tone that brooked no argument.

When the kids had gone, Kincaid stood in the doorway, blocking Gemma's exit. "Gemma, stop it, okay? You were right. I was wrong. I should never have kept anything from you. I'm sorry."

She faced him, hands on hips. "What if something had happened to you? And I'd have known nothing. Nothing. About any of this. Now you've gone and done just what Denis warned you not to do—stuck your nose into things. And look what happened to him."

"What would you have me do? Stick my head in the sand and hope it will all go away?"

"No, but— Well, yes, maybe."

"And let whoever murdered Ryan Marsh get away with it?" Their voices had escalated to what Toby called "shouting whispers." He made an effort to tone his down. "You'd have me let whoever attacked Denis get away with it? I don't believe you."

Gemma stood, arms folded now across her chest, glaring at him. Then, after a moment, she sighed. "No. But don't you ever keep things from me again."

"No. I won't. I promise."

She let him put his hands on her shoulders and kiss her cheek.

From the doorway, Toby said, "Mummy, can we come in now?"

"In one minute," she called back.

"I'm not going in to Holborn this morning," Kincaid said, before she could ask. "Just so you know."

"What? Why not?"

"Because I'm going to Hambleden. To see a man about a dog."

Gemma dropped the children at their respective schools, then drove to Kensington Police Station, mulling over things as she sat waiting at successive traffic lights. She was still angry with Kincaid. Not as angry, true, but not happy, either.

But what would she have done if he'd confided in her the night he'd found Ryan dead? Told him he was imagining things? She could work out, from what Rashid had told him yesterday, what had triggered his unease. The half-packed backpack, the body in the middle of the room. Perhaps there had been other tiny subliminal clues. And Duncan had known Ryan. He should have trusted his instincts.

He *had* trusted his instincts, she reminded herself. He had been afraid, and his instinct had told him to run. What if he hadn't? What if he'd gone blundering in, asking inconvenient questions? Could he have ended up like Denis? Or like Ryan?

She shivered in spite of the warm morning. What was he getting into now? And what the hell had he meant by "see a man about a dog"?

Her mobile rang just as she was parking, and Kate Ling's name popped up on the screen. "Shit," Gemma said aloud. She should have told Kincaid she was working with Kate on this case.

Taking a breath, she answered with forced cheeriness. "Hi, Kate. What's up?"

Kate Ling sounded amused. "You asked me to call, remember? You're getting forgetful in your old age, Gemma."

"Oh, right, so I did." Gemma laughed, and it sounded awkward to her ears. "The time of death on Reagan Keating. We wondered if you could make a determination on whether it was before or after midnight."

Kate's sigh came clearly down the phone. "You know I hate doing that, Gemma. But if you want my unofficial opinion, I'd say before. But not long before. Okay?"

"Great. Thanks, Kate."

"Anything for you, Gemma," Kate said with an affectionate chuckle. She rang off before Gemma could thank her again.

Gemma sat, staring at the phone, feeling ill. How could Kate have got the postmortem report on Ryan Marsh so wrong? She'd argued with Kincaid last night, but, like him, she had utter confidence in Rashid's judgment.

A rap on her window made her jump nearly out of her skin. It was Kerry Boatman, peering in at her. Gemma switched off the Escort's engine and opened the door.

"I've been talking to you for five minutes," said Kerry. "You were completely in outer space. Are you all right?"

"Fine." Gemma grabbed her bag and locked the door. Looking at Kerry, she groaned. "Don't tell me we're walking again."

"It's not far. Just past Earl's Court tube. Nita Cusick's ex is meeting us at a hotel in Barkston Gardens. But he's just delayed our appointment by half an hour, so we might as well take our time. Besides, there won't be any bloody place to park."

In truth, Gemma was glad enough of the walk and a chance

to think. She wished she could confide in Kerry. Even more, she wished for Melody's comfortable presence.

Instead, she told Kerry about Kate Ling's phone call.

"Before midnight?" said Kerry, thoughtful. "In which case, Reagan Keating did not send that text to Edward Miller. And"—she stopped before Gemma could protest—"Miller's brother, Agatha Smith, and two other distillery employees all swear that not only was Edward at the place until at least one o'clock, he was too pissed from partaking of his own product to do much of anything but stagger to his flat down the road."

Gemma was relieved. She hadn't thought Edward Miller capable of murdering Reagan, but she'd been wrong before.

"Thea Osho's boyfriend confirmed her alibi," Kerry continued. "And Hugo's and Sidney's university friends confirmed that they both arrived at one of the friends' college lodgings about eleven o'clock."

"Damn," said Gemma, and Kerry grinned.

"My sentiments exactly. So where does that leave us?" They'd stopped at the Cromwell Road crossing, and the traffic whizzing by made it difficult to hear.

When the light changed and they were once again walking down Earl's Court Road, Gemma said, "Either of the Peacocks. Either of the Sus. The gardener. Some resident of the garden who hasn't come across our radar. Or someone completely unknown."

"Helpful." Kerry shot her a glance. "But that someone was not unknown to Reagan. Maybe the ex-husband can tell us something useful."

They passed the tube station and almost immediately turned into Barkston Gardens on the left. It was a pretty square with a gated garden in its center, a peaceful oasis after the roar of Earl's

Court Road. The surrounding buildings were the white-trimmed, redbrick terraces that Gemma associated particularly with Chelsea and South Kensington, and the hotel came up very quickly on their left.

"He's not staying here, is he?" Gemma asked as they walked through the pleasant reception area.

Kerry shrugged. "Beats me. All I know is he asked us to meet him in the dining room here."

The dining room, it turned out, was actually three connecting rooms, with a bar at the far end. Light poured in from the large windows facing on the street. Staff was clearing a huge breakfast buffet from the center table in the main area. There were a few diners lingering over their breakfasts, but more tables were occupied by patrons with laptops and files, and a few by groups obviously in business meetings.

A friendly red-haired man came to greet them. "We've just finished serving breakfast, I'm afraid," he said with a smile, and a definite Scottish accent. "But can we do something else for you?"

Even Kerry seemed charmed. Smiling back, she said, "We're here to meet someone. A Mr. Cusick."

"Oh, right. Chris is in the Snug. He told me to look out for you. I'll take you back."

They followed him to a small room tucked into the left-hand side of the rear dining area. It was a cozy space with comfortable furniture, low tables, and a wall of bookshelves at the far end.

A man sitting in one of the armchairs and typing busily on a laptop looked up, then put aside his computer and rose to greet them.

"Thanks, Darren," he said to their guide, holding out a hand to Kerry, then Gemma. "I'm Chris Cusick." He motioned them into adjoining chairs. "Please, have a seat. Would you like some coffee or tea?"

Gemma had seen a beautiful latte on a patron's table as they walked through the dining area. "I'd love a latte. Thanks." She'd missed her coffee that morning, as well, and was feeling it.

"Yes, the same," said Kerry, looking blissful at the thought.

Cusick stepped out for a word with Darren, then came back and sat down. He was tall, lightly bearded, with Jess's ash brown floppy hair, and he moved with a grace and intentness that reminded Gemma forcibly of his son. "Thanks for meeting me here," he said. "I'm sure you're wondering why."

"I thought you were a banker," said Gemma.

He grinned, his teeth white against the beard, but Gemma saw hollows under his eyes. "I am a banker. An investment banker. I spend most of my day on my computer." He waved a hand at the laptop, closed now. "Which I could certainly do at home. I live just at the top of the garden," he added, with another gesture that made Gemma want to focus on the movement of his hand. "But, my girlfriend, Parminder—my partner, if you will—is a flight medic for air ambulance. She works nights." Again, the flash of a smile. "That's when all the fun stuff happens, apparently, although I don't get it." He shrugged. "Anyway, I toddle along here most mornings to give her some peace and quiet."

"I can see why," said Kerry as Darren brought their coffees. She looked as if she might purr.

"You wanted to talk to me about Reagan," Chris Cusick said when they'd taken their cups. Gemma had the feeling that in spite of his genial manner, he was quite used to directing the conversation. She wondered how that had worked with Nita.

"I was absolutely shocked when Nita told me what happened,"

he went on. "Reagan was a nice girl. And she was great with Jess. I still can't believe she's dead. And now Nita says you think she was murdered." He watched them intently as he spoke. Gemma had the impression he was hoping they'd tell him he was mistaken.

"You didn't believe your wife, Mr. Cusick?" asked Gemma.

"Ex-wife," he corrected, sharply. "And Nita can sometimes be a bit . . . dramatic."

"You mean she makes things up to get your attention?" said Kerry, having drained half her latte in one swallow.

His eyes widened, but then he shrugged again. "She's been known to exaggerate things, on occasion."

"You two are in regular contact?"

"We have joint custody of Jess. And I own the Cornwall Gardens house."

Kerry nodded and drank more of her coffee. "Very generous of you, I'm sure, Mr. Cusick."

"It's Jess's home, too."

"You were still living there when Reagan came to work as nanny?" Gemma asked, earning one of Cusick's laser glances.

"Nita and I separated six months after Reagan started. If you're wondering, Detective, whether I had an affair with Reagan, I did not. We were friends, and I was very glad she was able to give Jess some support during the divorce. Parminder, my girlfriend, liked her very much, too."

"Mr. Cusick," said Gemma, "you know we have to ask. Can you tell us your whereabouts last Friday night?"

"Of course." He seemed not at all offended. "It was Parminder's night off. We had dinner with friends, then we came here for drinks, actually. The bartender makes a terrific passion fruit martini."

"And you left here about what time?"

Cusick shrugged. "Close to midnight, maybe. The bar can be pretty busy here on Friday nights, but it had emptied out. Then, we went back to the flat and watched a film. I try to stay up with Parminder on her nights off, if I can manage."

Kerry tapped his girlfriend's contact information into her phone and had started to thank him for his time when he interrupted her. "Have you seen Jess? Is he doing okay? This has to have been a terrible shock for him, but he's not returning my calls. Or Parminder's, and he usually wants to hear all the gory details of her call-outs. He's not due to stay with us until Friday and I'm worried about him."

"I have seen him," said Gemma. "He seemed quite angry and upset. Your wife told us he's not communicating with her, either."

"Poor little bugger." Cusick frowned, then set down his coffee cup with a decisive clatter. "I'm going over there to talk to him this evening. Weekday visits aren't in our agreement, but Nita will just have to lump it for once."

"Mr. Cusick." Touching his arm as he started to rise, Gemma asked the question that had been bothering her. "Do you by any chance know where your son was last Saturday morning? Apparently, he left the house early without telling his mother where he was going. She was frantic to find him missing, especially after she learned Reagan was dead. A friend finally tracked him down that afternoon at his ballet class at the Tabernacle."

"Nita didn't tell me that. Christ." He shook his head, his mouth pinched in irritation. "I can tell you exactly where Jess would have been. And why he didn't tell his mother. Jess takes classes several afternoons a week at the London Boys Ballet School in Finsbury Park. That's one of the reasons Nita insisted on keeping Reagan on, so that Reagan could drive him there, although I think he's old enough to go by himself, on the tube. The tryouts for the eleven-plus advanced program were on Saturday morning. Jess will have gone, and he won't have told Nita because she forbade him to do it."

"Why?" asked Gemma, puzzled. "I'd have thought the more opportunities for a boy as talented as Jess, the better."

"That's not the way my wife sees it. The London Boys Ballet School is the only all-male ballet school in the world, and they're doing terrific things. But nothing matters to Nita except the Royal Ballet. Nothing else has mattered to her since Jess was three years old and his teacher told her he had promise."

This was where it had all started, Kincaid thought as he slowed for the bridge in Henley-on-Thames. Seven months ago, he and Gemma and the children had been on their way back from a visit to Glastonbury when he received a call on his mobile from Chief Superintendent Denis Childs. They were still getting Charlotte settled into their home, and Childs knew Kincaid had requested a parental leave of absence starting the next week.

But it was a high-profile death, Childs said, perhaps accidental, and Kincaid was on the spot. So could he just take a look at things? A personal favor had been implied.

To Gemma's chagrin, Kincaid agreed. Kincaid's route that day had taken him just this way, through Henley, then north on the Marlow Road, following the winding course of the Thames downriver.

The victim's body had been found caught in the weir below the village of Hambleden. Kincaid now knew that Denis Childs had been aware that newly retired Deputy Assistant Commissioner

Angus Craig lived in Hambleden, and Kincaid now also knew that Childs had had good reason to think Craig might be a suspect in a suspicious death.

And Childs had dropped Kincaid in the midst of it.

During the course of the investigation, evidence had surfaced that implicated Angus Craig in another death, but Denis Childs had delayed Craig's arrest.

In the early hours of the following morning, the Craigs' house in Hambleden had gone up in flames. Craig's body, and that of his wife, Edie, had been found inside, an apparent murder/suicide.

It had seemed an open-and-shut case. Edie had been found in the kitchen, Angus in his study, both shot with the handgun that appeared to have been gripped in Angus's fingers. The remains were too damaged by the fire to determine much more.

But something about the events of that night had nagged at Kincaid. This morning, triggered by his dreams and the barking of his own dogs, he'd realized what it was. Edie Craig's little whippet, Barney, had been heard barking by a neighbor some hours before the fire started. The neighbor, getting no answer when he'd rung the Craigs, had left a message and taken the dog in for the night.

The idea that Edie Craig had had some premonition of what was to come, and had perhaps let the dog out to keep it safe, had haunted Kincaid ever since. But if that was the case, what had happened in the hours that had elapsed between the finding of the dog and the start of the fire? No scenario quite added up.

He remembered that the detective constable on the scene had said the neighbor's name was Wilson. The Craigs' house, a beautiful estate at the far edge of the village, had been Edie's, inherited from her family. The closest neighbor would be the house nearer the village, a good half mile from the Craigs'. He'd try there first.

He preferred not to leave a trail by asking the Henley police, although he'd have liked to see Detective Constable Imogen Bell again.

He'd only seen the village in the autumn. Now, it was even prettier, with the lush spring green of the trees a vibrant contrast to the dark stone and red tile roofs of the buildings. He passed the pub, where he had drunk a beer, and the church, where he had once met Edie Craig at the lych-gate. As he drove past the village center, the houses grew farther apart. Then, after a longer gap, came the place he remembered. The small bungalow sat back from the lane, its well-tended garden riotous with blooms. In the distance, where the Craigs' red-tiled roof had once marked the horizon, Kincaid saw nothing.

Spotting a wide place in the verge, he pulled up the car and got out. He'd dressed the part that morning, but his jacket had come off and his tie been unknotted as soon as he'd climbed in the un-air-conditioned Astra. Now, he slipped into his jacket, which was only lightly dusted with dog hair from the backseat, and pulled the knot on his tie up a bare half inch.

He'd opened the gate into the garden when the bungalow's front door swung open. A man came out, half pulled by two small dogs on leads. One was a Blenheim Cavalier King Charles spaniel. The other, he recognized instantly. Barney, Edie Craig's whippet.

"You kept him," he said.

"I'm sorry?" The man looked confused, and a little wary. "Can I help you?"

"Barney. Edie Craig's dog."

The dog, hearing his name, or perhaps dimly recognizing something in Kincaid's voice, began to wag his tail and strain at the lead. Kincaid squatted and the man, seeing that the garden gate was closed, let the dog go. Barney ran to Kincaid and, after an initial sniff, delicately licked his fingers.

"I'm sorry," the man said again. "But who are you?"

Kincaid gave the dog a last pat and stood, collecting himself. "My name's Kincaid." He pulled his warrant card from his pocket and held out the open folder just long enough for the man to see the Met seal and his name. He wasn't at all sure he wanted to identify himself as a detective superintendent. Slipping the folder back into his jacket pocket, he held out his hand. "You're Mr. Wilson, I believe?"

Nodding, the man shook Kincaid's hand tentatively. His fingers were damp. "Danforth Wilson. That's right. How can I help you?"

Wilson was a small man, edging past middle age. He wore gold-framed glasses and was dressed in a slightly fussy and seasonally inappropriate tapestry waistcoat. He squinted at Kincaid, looking more anxious since he'd seen the identification.

"Is there somewhere we can talk?" Kincaid asked. He stooped again to give the spaniel a pat. "That's a very nice Cavalier you have there, Mr. Wilson."

Wilson seemed to relax. "Thank you. Her name is Lola. I was just taking the dogs for their morning constitutional, but I suppose we could sit in the garden for a bit." He gestured at a bench set amidst a riot of roses. Kincaid wished he'd left his good suit jacket in the car. Following Wilson, he sat beside him, avoiding reaching thorns as best he could.

"Graham Thomas," said Wilson. "Lovely, isn't it?"

It took Kincaid a moment to realize he was referring to the fulsome yellow rose that was at that moment threatening his eyesight with a wayward tendril. "Yes," he agreed. "Lovely." The scent, in the sun, was headily sweet. He shifted sideways so that he looked Wilson in the eye. "Mr. Wilson—"

"How do you know Barney? You haven't come to—"

Kincaid was already shaking his head. "I met Barney once, with Edie Craig. I'm glad to see him happy here."

"There was no one else to take him, you see. Neither of them had any family. The estate is still tied up in probate." Kincaid must have looked surprised at his knowledge because he added, "It's common knowledge at the pub. No one claimed the dog. I didn't mind, and now I'm afraid I've grown quite attached to him. When you said you were with the police . . ."

"I did come to see you about Barney," Kincaid said. "I had met Edie and Barney once, and then I was called in after the fire. Today, I was passing through Henley, and I just wondered if the dog was all right. One of the officers told me you'd taken him in that night." That was, as far as it went, the truth. "I wondered if you could tell me exactly what happened."

The small man was quiet. Kincaid couldn't see his eyes behind the reflection in the gold-framed glasses. Wilson picked a petal from a drooping Graham Thomas bloom. "I don't like to think about it," he said at last, shredding the petal with his well-manicured fingers. "If I had known . . . If I had done something . . . But if I *had* gone over, and he . . . Craig . . ." A visible shudder went through Wilson's body. Kincaid didn't need him to elaborate.

"It doesn't bear thinking about," Kincaid said. "But that night— had Barney ever been loose at night before?"

"No. Never. That's why I— It was all very strange. I don't know why I didn't clip him on a lead and walk him back."

"Why don't you tell me exactly what happened."

"I was just going to take Lola out for her little bedtime ramble round the garden. My television programs had finished—I'm a bit of a night owl," he added, with a little glancing smile at Kincaid, as

if staying up late was a slightly naughty admission. "I heard barking. I couldn't think what was happening."

"What time would this have been?"

"Oh, I don't know, exactly." Wilson pushed at his glasses in a
gesture that reminded Kincaid of Doug. "My program finished at
a quarter to twelve, if I remember. I'd gone, you know, to the loo.
And made myself a little nightcap." Another little smile with the
guilty admission.

Kincaid waited.

"I thought if it was someone out walking a dog, they would go
on, so I waited a bit longer. But the barking didn't stop. I shut Lola
in the house and went out with my torch. There was Barney, just
standing in the meadow outside my fence, barking. He came when
I called out to him."

"Was the dog his usual self?"

"He was shivering, I remember. But it was a chilly night, and he
hasn't much coat," Wilson added, affection in his voice. "There was
no sign of Edie, so I took him in the house, and I—" He paused.
"To be honest, I couldn't think what to do. I had the Craigs' phone
number, but one didn't like to . . . I did think of taking him over
and putting him in their garden, but . . ."

"So, in the end, you rang the house?" Kincaid asked, encouraging.

Wilson nodded. "Yes. I left a message. When no one rang back
within half an hour, I put Barney in the kitchen with some water
and a towel for a bed. I thought I'd get up at first light and walk
him home. But—" He stopped and removed his glasses, twisting
the wire earpiece back and forth in his fingers. "But— The sirens
woke me, and the smell of smoke. At first I thought it was my own
little house and I panicked. And, then, I looked out the window
and . . . I could . . . see it burning . . ."

"That must have been terrible," Kincaid said after a silence. "What did you do?"

"I dressed and walked down the road, to see if there was anything I could do. But I was turned away, as if I were a mere onlooker." Grievance still echoed in Wilson's voice.

"But you did go back?" Kincaid asked.

"When it was light. They stopped me well away from the house again, but I told that detective to let Edie know I had Barney with me. It wasn't until I went to the pub later in the morning that I heard they were dead." Wilson put his glasses back on and sat with his hands folded in his lap, his gaze unfocused. "They said what had happened, but I couldn't—I couldn't imagine how someone could do such a thing."

Kincaid sat quietly, watching the dogs, which had come to lie in a patch of shade. Barney looked back at him, his bright-eyed little face alert and trusting. "No," he said. "Nor can I. Mr. Wilson, was there anything else at all unusual that night?"

"No. Not that I can remember. Other than the men in the car, of course. But that was earlier. And I did tell that constable."

Kincaid, who'd been preparing to rise, dropped back onto the bench and stared at Wilson. "What men?"

"The ones in the four-by-four. A Range Rover. New. It was odd, though, because the car was clean but the plates were mud spattered."

"Where," Kincaid said slowly, "was this, exactly?"

"Just before the pub. Lola and I—and Barney now, of course—go most evenings for a little visit, around half past five. I thought the car would stop to let us cross, but it didn't. Quite rude, I thought. The rear windows were dark tinted, but I could see the two men in the front seats quite clearly as they went past. They were going towards the Craigs', so I thought perhaps it was police business, but they didn't look at all like policemen. And the one nearest me, the passenger, gave me a look that could kill. I was going to call out to them, you know, to say they should mind their manners, but after that . . . I didn't quite like to."

"No," Kincaid said. His heart was pounding in his ears. "Mr. Wilson, could you describe these men?"

"I told that constable," Wilson answered, aggrieved again.

"Yes, but would you mind telling me?"

Wilson sighed. "The passenger was older. Not a nice face, that one. And he had a mark on his neck, just here." He touched the side of his neck. "A birthmark. Or perhaps an old tattoo."

Kincaid couldn't shake a growing dread. "And the driver?"

"Oh, he was younger. And much better looking. Short brown hair, with that bit of stubbly beard that's fashionable nowadays."

For a moment, Kincaid thought he might thank the man, shake his hand, and walk away. He sat, staring into space, until Barney trotted over to him and rested his long, pointed muzzle on Kincaid's knee.

"Mr. Wilson," he said, "you've been very helpful. Is there anything else you can remember?"

Wilson frowned, his face scrunched in concentration. "I can't say why, but I had the sense they'd been arguing. The driver looked startled, not as if he'd meant to almost run me over. And he was quite the dashing sort, really, with that bandanna round his neck."

CHAPTER TWENTY-ONE

Kincaid had almost reached the car when he remembered what he had on his mobile. Turning back, he met Mr. Wilson, who'd collected the dogs, at the garden gate. "Mr. Wilson," he said, "would you mind having a look at something?" He held out his phone. The photo on the screen was the one of Michael Stanton he'd sent to Doug the evening before, taken from Stanton's driving license. "Do you recognize this man?"

Wilson peered at the photo, frowning, then glanced up at Kincaid. "That looks like the man in the car. The passenger, not the driver. Who is he? I'd not like to think he'd come back here."

"Don't worry, Mr. Wilson." Kincaid slipped the mobile back into his pocket and forced a smile. "I can assure you that this man won't be bothering you again."

Back in the car, he gave Wilson a wave and made a U-turn in the lane. He didn't want to drive by the remains of the Craigs' house, and he wanted to get out of the village.

He drove back the way he'd come. As he slowed through Henley, he realized his hands were shaking. Turning off the main road, in a moment he found himself in view of the river. Having stayed in Henley for several days during the autumn investigation into the death of the rower, Rebecca Meredith, he knew immediately where he was—on New Street, by the Hotel du Vin. He pulled into a lucky parking space and got out, throwing his jacket and tie back into the car. A few yards farther on, New Street curved round at the river to meet Hart Street at the bridge. But between the road and the water, there was parking space and access to small boat docks. He walked down to the edge of the quay and stopped, staring across the river at the Leander Club, watching a few sculling crews out for a late-morning practice.

After a bit, he noticed the sun beating down on the top of his head and his face, but he couldn't seem to move. He saw, not the river, but the interior of the Craigs' house just before the fire took hold, as he'd visualized it so often in his imagination.

Edie lay dead in the kitchen. Her face was a blur—he couldn't see it. Didn't want to see it.

Angus was on the floor in his study, the room where Kincaid had interviewed him shortly before. He lay, like Ryan Marsh, in the middle of the room. In front of his massive, intimidating desk. Not collapsed in the leather chair behind the desk, nor on the floor beside the desk, where he might have toppled if he'd shot himself while sitting in the chair. His hand, like Ryan's, held the gun that had killed him, and had killed Edie.

But, what if, Kincaid thought, like Ryan, Angus Craig had not shot himself? Or his wife? What if it had been set up to look like a murder/suicide, just as Ryan's death had been set up to look like a suicide?

What if someone had come into the Craigs' house that night and shot Edie as she stood, unsuspecting, in the kitchen, then walked into Angus's study and shot him? If a silencer had been used, Angus wouldn't have been alerted by the first gunshot.

If either of them had struggled in a last moment of shock and terror, both the scene and the bodies had been too damaged by the fire for it to be obvious to the investigators.

Whoever had done this thing, it must have been someone familiar with the house—someone, perhaps, who had been watching it, and taking photographs.

The thought made Kincaid feel ill.

After a bit, he walked back to the car. Leaning against it, he rang Doug.

"I've put both Ryan and Stanton in Hambleden the evening of the night the Craigs died," he said when Doug answered.

"What? What are you talking about?" Doug sounded utterly baffled.

Kincaid told him.

After a long silence, Doug said, "I can't really talk. Let me ring you back." Five minutes later, Kincaid's mobile buzzed. He could hear street noise in the background and he guessed Doug had left the building. "Why didn't this Wilson bloke tell someone?" Doug asked without preamble.

"He did. Imogen Bell. But she had no reason to pass it on. Wilson is something of a fusspot. She probably thought he was manufacturing a bit of drama for the attention. And there was never any suggestion that Angus Craig hadn't killed himself and his wife."

Doug was quiet again. Then, he said, "You're not seriously suggesting that Ryan and this Stanton bloke killed them? And set the fire? I can't believe that Ryan Marsh was a murderer." He sounded as distressed as Kincaid felt.

"No." Kincaid thought about Melody's account of Ryan's actions when the white phosphorous grenade had gone off in St. Pancras station. Ryan had run towards the fire, not away. He'd been desperate to get people to safety, to do something to help.

But Ryan had then fled the scene, afraid he had been the grenade's target. Was it because of what had happened the night the Craigs died? Because of what he knew? Or because of what he'd done?

Kincaid thought of the time he and Doug and Melody had called on Ryan's wife. Ryan's old Labrador had come to him and put her head on his knee, just as Barney had done this morning. And when they'd brought Ryan to Kincaid's house, Ryan had immediately and affectionately greeted the dogs.

"Wilson said the two men were arguing," Kincaid told Doug. "What if Ryan knew—or guessed—what was planned? Maybe he knew what Stanton was capable of doing."

"Stanton had an obvious history of violence. Surely Ryan knew that."

"If I'm right about what happened to the Craigs, he was guilty of more than a short temper and harassing women," Kincaid said, working it out. "Craig's death must have been calculated, planned, at least from the time Craig became a serious suspect in Rebecca Meredith's murder."

"Damage control," said Doug. "In case he was guilty of killing Meredith?"

"Or in case other things came to light." Kincaid thought, watching the gulls wheel lazily over the river. "We found out that Craig had committed another murder. What if he was involved in things that we *didn't* uncover? Things that might have implicated other people."

"Things he might have used to bargain with, if the assaults or the murder had gone to trial?" Doug suggested, after a pause.

"It's possible. But Stanton—and Ryan, to whatever extent he was involved—were pawns. So who did Angus Craig's death protect?"

"Whoever it was, they must have killed Ryan. And Michael Stanton," said Doug.

Kincaid nodded, even though Doug couldn't see him. All their assumptions made sense, but his mind kept going back to Barney. "Edie Craig's dog was out at least two hours before the fire started. Why? Could it have been Ryan who let the dog out? Ryan would never have let the dog burn."

"Assuming the Craigs were already dead, hours before the fire was started. Maybe the fire smoldered."

Kincaid thought back to that morning. "The fire investigator told me that from the pattern of the blaze and the amount of accelerant used, the fire took hold very quickly. Petrol was splashed all over the damned place, then it was torched. So what happened in those intervening hours?" Kincaid made an effort to lower his voice. He was getting some odd looks from passersby.

"Maybe they were looking for something," suggested Doug. "Maybe the fire was set to cover up the evidence of a search. Or to cover up evidence, full stop."

"I think," Kincaid said slowly, running his hand through his hair in frustration, "that we may never know the truth. Everyone who could tell us exactly what happened that night is dead."

When Gemma and Kerry walked out of the hotel after saying goodbye to Chris Cusick, Gemma felt her mobile vibrate. Checking it, she saw that she'd just missed a call. She put a hand over her other ear, trying to shut out some of the traffic noise as she listened to a garbled voice message.

"That was Asia Ford," she said to Kerry when it finished. "Something about the high-proof alcohol she uses for her limoncello having gone missing. She sounded quite upset." Gemma tapped Redial on the number, but it rang half a dozen times before switching over to what sounded like an answering machine. She disconnected without leaving a message. "No answer. But in her message she said she'd be waiting to hear back from us."

"High-proof alcohol?" Kerry looked dismayed. "Christ. Don't tell me it was right under our noses the whole time. We'd better go have a word with her."

Now, Gemma regretted the walk back up the incline of Earl's Court Road, which had seemed gentle enough going down. Her legs were aching by the time they reached the police station, and even Kerry was puffing a bit. When they reached Gemma's car, she tried Asia Ford's number again. Still no answer. Her unease grew. "Let's take mine," she said, unlocking the Escort, and Kerry agreed.

"High-proof alcohol," Kerry repeated as Gemma drove. "Easily accessible to anyone who knew she used it. Not Edward Miller's raw spirits at all."

"You can't think Asia Ford gave it to Reagan?"

"I doubt she'd be calling us if she had." Taking out her phone, Boatman typed something in. "Listen. Here's a recipe: '151 proof grain alcohol. Lemon zest. Sugar. Water.' It says not to use vodka because even the strongest vodka has flavor."

"Everyone on the garden knew Asia made limoncello," said Gemma. "Or if they didn't, they knew after the garden party."

She tried to push her speed up a bit, but it was pointless in the congestion of Kensington High Street at near lunchtime. Handing her mobile to Kerry, she added, "Try again, why don't you?"

Kerry complied, then shook her head when there was no answer. "Maybe she forgot."

"Asia Ford may be a little eccentric, but she didn't strike me as the least bit dotty."

"Maybe when you didn't ring back right away, she decided it wasn't urgent."

"Maybe," said Gemma.

They rang Asia Ford's bell but there was no reply. They rang again and waited. Kerry was starting to look annoyed. "Really," she said, "if it was that impor—"

"Let's try Nita's," Gemma interrupted. "Maybe we can go through the garden."

They walked two doors up, but there was no answer at the Cusicks', either.

"How about Mrs. Armitage, then," suggested Gemma. "She's most likely to be home this time of day." It meant going round the Kensington Park Road end of the garden. As they walked, Gemma tried to see through the thick rose hedge that covered the garden's only area of iron fencing, along the street, but it was impenetrable. Sleeping Beauty's hedge, indeed, she thought.

Mrs. Armitage answered on the first ring, to Gemma's relief. "Detectives. What can I do for you?" she asked with a smile, ushering them in. "Have you come back for tea and tarts?"

"Could you let us into the garden?" Gemma asked. "I had a call from Asia Ford, saying she wanted to see us urgently, but now she's not answering her phone or her door. We thought perhaps she might be outside."

"Of course. Do come through. That's not like Asia," Mrs. Armitage added, frowning, as she led them down to the kitchen and out the back door. "Did she say why she wanted to see you?"

"Something about her limoncello," Gemma said, not wanting to elaborate until she had a better idea what this was about.

To Gemma's surprise, Mrs. Armitage led them, not by the path, but straight across the grass. "I don't think Clive will mind if we walk on the grass for once," she said. The garden seemed different today, Gemma thought, feeling the soft turf give beneath her feet. It took her a moment to realize that in the last half hour, clouds had come scudding in from the west. The light had gone soft and gray, making the colors of the grass and flowers seem more intense, and she caught the faintest scent of rain in the air.

There was no sign of Asia Ford in the communal garden. But as they drew nearer to her house, they saw that the little gate into Asia's covered patio stood open. "That's odd," murmured Mrs. Armitage. "Asia never leaves her gate open."

Gemma's uneasiness plummeted to dread. Hurrying, she was first through the gate, calling out, "Asia? Miss Ford?"

The kitchen door stood open as well. There was a faint sound from inside and Gemma hurried into the kitchen. Asia Ford sat on one of the wicker kitchen chairs, holding a tea towel to the back of her head. Her face was white as chalk and the look she gave Gemma was puzzled.

"Christ," said Kerry, coming up behind Gemma, just as Gemma saw that towel was stained with blood.

"Miss Ford!" Gemma ran to her. "What's happened? Are you all right?"

"I honestly don't know." Asia Ford started to shake her head, then winced. "I was just going into the greenhouse for something.

I don't remember now what it was. And, then, the next thing I knew, my face was on the bricks, and when I tried to move, my head hurt like bloody hell. Did I fall?"

"Let's have a look, shall we?" Gemma said. Mrs. Armitage, who'd been hovering, handed Gemma a clean tea towel and Gemma smiled her thanks. First, she looked right into Asia's eyes, and saw to her relief that the pupils were not dilated. Then, she moved round behind the chair and very gently lifted the stained towel. Asia's fine, light brown hair was matted around the wound with drying blood, but even so, Gemma could see the gash in the scalp. It was below the crown, and just a bit to the right of center. The wound was still seeping and its edges were ragged.

"Ouch," she said, folding the clean towel into a pad and placing it carefully over the injury. "You've got quite a cut there. Do you remember feeling faint? Hitting your head on something as you fell?"

"No. I rang you, though, didn't I? I remember taking the phone with me out to the greenhouse, in case you rang me back. I must have dropped it, mustn't I?"

"We'll have a look. I'm sure we'll find it," Gemma reassured her.

"Was that you? At the door?" Asia still sounded muzzy. "I heard the bell but I couldn't quite manage to get up . . ." Asia wrinkled her brow in puzzlement. "I don't understand. How did you get in the house if I didn't let you in?"

"Mrs. Armitage brought us through the garden. Miss Ford, you're going to need some stitches in that cut, I'm afraid. And the medics will want to give you a good going-over." She glanced at Kerry, who already had her mobile out and was speaking quietly into it.

"But I'm fine, really. I—" Asia made as if to stand, but fell back into the wicker chair with a thump.

Kerry was giving the ambulance service the house number.

"I'll go with you to hospital, dear," said Mrs. Armitage, sitting down beside Asia and patting her free hand.

Gemma took the opportunity to slip out onto the patio. The smell of the wisteria eddied round her as a breeze blew through the garden, and pale purple petals drifted down from the canopy like confetti. It took a moment for her eyes to adjust to the dim light after the brightness of the kitchen.

She stood in the doorway, studying the scene, wishing they'd not tramped through the space like a herd of cattle. The only way she could visualize Asia having inflicted that injury on herself was if she had fallen backwards, catching her head a glancing blow on something as she fell. But Asia said she'd come to with her face on the bricks. She'd fallen forward.

Popping her head back in the kitchen, she asked, "Asia— Miss Ford—can you tell me exactly where you were when you fell? No, don't get up," she added, seeing Asia's muscles tense. "Just tell us."

"I was half in the greenhouse and half out. I must have looked a sight." Asia's color was returning, Gemma saw with relief.

"But it was your head in the greenhouse, and you're quite certain you were facedown?"

"Yes, but—I don't see how—I wish I could remember what happened. I feel so stupid." Asia touched her cheek, and for the first time, Gemma noticed a small graze. "Did you find my phone?" Asia asked, a little fretfully.

"Not just yet. But I promise we will."

Turning, Gemma walked carefully a few steps forward into the patio.

It was easy enough to spot, she thought, once you knew what

you were looking for. It was a brick, a few feet from the stack Asia had been using to pave the greenhouse floor. Taking the little pocket torch from her bag, she took a step closer and squatted, playing the light over the brick. Bright flecks of blood winked back at her.

She stood and went back to the door. "Kerry," she said softly, "we're going to need the uniforms here as well."

Kincaid climbed back into the car, still thinking about the end of his conversation with Doug. Angus and Edie Craig were dead, as were Ryan Marsh and Michael Stanton. But someone else had seen the Craigs—or at least Angus—that night. Denis Childs.

What time had Denis gone to the house? Had he seen anyone, or anything? What had he said to Angus Craig, and vice versa?

Denis had not contradicted the murder/suicide assumption the next morning, when they'd stood gazing at the ruins, but he had been quietly furious—and something more. Now, Kincaid wondered if he'd been frightened.

He needed more than ever to talk to Denis, damn him. As soon as he was back in London, he'd ring Diane Childs. At least he could check on Denis's progress without going through channels.

Having made that small decision, he started the car. His mobile immediately pinged with a text message. Swearing, he took his mobile out of his pocket once more.

The text was from Simon Gikas, and read, "Found Stanton flat. Requesting warrant." He had added an address in Hackney that was, Kincaid thought, in the same estate as the false address on Stanton's driving license.

"Meet you there in an hour," he texted back.

He'd actually managed to get the car in reverse when the damned mobile rang. "Bloody hell," he said aloud. He was tempted not to answer, but then he saw that the caller was Ronnie Babcock.

"Duncan," Ronnie said when he picked up. "Bad news, I'm afraid. You know that retired copper I told you about? Frank Fletcher? He's dead. That's why I hadn't seen him in the pub."

"Dead, how? Was it suicide?"

"Um, not exactly. Accident cleaning his gun. Blood alcohol sky high, which doesn't surprise me, the way he drank in the pub. I had a look at the postmortem report. It seemed pretty straightforward."

Bugger straightforward, Kincaid thought. "At the moment, I'm not inclined to trust a postmortem report as far as I could throw it," he said through clenched teeth.

"I could talk to the investigating officer," suggested Ronnie.

"No, don't," Kincaid said sharply. He didn't believe in gun cleaning accidents, and he didn't want Ronnie going round asking questions of the wrong people. "Keep your nose clean, mate. But is there anything else you can tell me about Fletcher? Did he ever hint about working undercover, for instance?"

Kincaid heard the sound of a door closing, shutting off the muted voices he'd been hearing in the background. "Sorry," said Ronnie. "Can't think with all that racket. So you still think there might be some connection with your undercover cop? Small world."

"Too small for comfort," Kincaid said. "And I don't know. I'm pulling at threads. Anything would help."

"Well, I've been trying to remember. It's too bad, really. I liked Frank. I'd hate to think— Well, neither option is pretty, is it?"

"Ronnie—"

"Hold your horses," Ronnie said, in his strongest Cheshire drawl. "I'm thinking. I told you Frank did lots of muttering about people not believing the things the Met got up to. I thought it was conspiracy bunk. But maybe that's what he was getting at."

"And he never said exactly who he worked for?"

"No. I did ask one time, I remember, and that shut him up completely. He even left an unfinished drink."

Kincaid was about to thank him when Ronnie added, "Oh, and I could never make any sense of it, but sometimes, when he was completely pissed, he'd mumble something like, 'Follow the money. You always have to follow the money.'" Kincaid could almost see Ronnie shrug over the phone. "I thought he was going on about *The Wizard of Oz*. Bonkers, if you ask me."

OCTOBER 1994

He knew he wasn't going to be able to avoid the group meetings in the Earl's Court flat forever. So when he had a particularly nasty message from Red Craig telling him that he was failing to bond with his fellow officers, he pulled himself together and started for Earl's Court. At least now he had a purpose.

It was a crisp autumn evening and he got off the bus at Kensington High Street.

But the closer he got to Earl's Court station, the queasier he felt. Psychosomatic, he told himself. Get a grip, Den. He'd never seen the purpose of these little get-togethers, except to remind them of who they were and where their loyalties lay. And to make certain that they knew there was always somebody watching.

Reaching the flat, he fought a wave of dizziness as he climbed the stairs. It was the smell, he thought, stale smoke and stale alcohol, and urine where someone had pissed in the landing. He hated this shithole.

The queasiness grew worse as he entered the flat. They were all there, the usual suspects, except Lynn, whom he'd come to think of as his only ally among them.

He avoided meeting Mickey's eyes. He knew Mickey would take it for cowardice, but he was afraid that if he looked at the vicious little bastard, he'd kill him. Every time he closed his eyes he saw the look on Mickey's face as he'd thrown the bottle at the man in Westbourne Park Road.

Sheila gave him a big smile and tottered over with an open bottle of wine. "Long time, no see, big fella." She kissed his cheek and the smell of the wine on her breath made his stomach turn over. "Come on, join the party," she urged, grabbing a dirty china cup off a nearby table. He knew she'd been drinking more and more over the summer, but tonight she was downright blotto.

"I'll pass," he said, as easily as he could, giving her arm a squeeze.

It was Mickey who started the jeering. "What's the matter, big fella, can't handle the booze? Pansy," he added, as if that were the height of insults. "Or are you just missing your girlfriend?" Watching Denis's face, he laughed. "Oh, I know all about the girlfriend. No secrets here, brother." He emphasized the last word, his little private joke.

"Well, you can't have it both ways, can you?" Denis replied, trying to make a joke of the childish insults.

Sheila had lurched back into Mickey's orbit. Reaching out, he yanked her to him and cupped her short-skirted buttock in his hand. She twitched away from him, looking annoyed, but he pulled her back, this time throwing an arm round her so that his hand rested on her breast.

"Bugger off, Mick." Sheila jabbed him with her elbow, hard enough to make him drop his arm and swear, and Denis wondered *if she was really as drunk as she seemed.* "I can do better than you in my sleep. Keep your hands off or it'll be your goolies next."

Dylan West laughed, smirking at Mickey's discomfort. Jim Evans looked uneasy. And on Mickey's face was a flash of the rage Denis had seen at Carnival.

"Leave her alone, Mickey," he managed to croak.

"What are you going to do about it, Mr. Goody-Goody?" Mickey gave a high-pitched giggle and Denis realized he was drunk as well.

Someone had lit the cheap electric fire and the room was stifling. Denis's nausea grew so intense that he could feel himself beginning to drool. Then, his bowels cramped, almost doubling him over.

Jesus, he thought. What was this? Some kind of monster bug? He had to get out before he was sick all over himself. Humiliating himself in front of Mickey was more than he could bear, and he wasn't going into that hellhole of a toilet where everyone in the room could hear him puke. He turned and clattered back down the stairs, out where he could take gulps of fresh air.

He managed to walk, then, back towards the lights of the main road. He must have looked a fright because passersby detoured around him, but he didn't care. The first pub he came to on Earl's Court Road looked like salvation, and he made it all the way to the gents' without disgracing himself.

A half hour later, he emerged from the toilet, feeling weak and empty, but a little steadier and more clearheaded.

He had to go back. He had to confront Mickey, or he would never live it down. Not with the others, and not with himself. He'd washed his face and washed out his mouth, slicking his hair back with his wet hands. When he stepped out into the chill night, he *began to shiver. By the time he'd walked back to the flat, he was shaking all over. But there was nothing for it but to go on.*

He let himself in the downstairs door and began to climb. There was no sound from above, and the stairs seemed to be moving beneath his feet. He wondered if he was delirious. Blinking back the sweat that had begun trickling from his brow, he reached the landing and walked in the door to the flat.

Sheila was lying on the floor. Why, he wondered, dazed, was she lying on the floor? Lynn was crouched beside her, smoothing down her friend's tiny skirt.

Then, Lynn looked up at him, and he saw that she was sobbing.

And then he realized that Sheila was dead.

CHAPTER TWENTY-TWO

Taking Jean Armitage's chair, Gemma explained to Asia that she thought she had been attacked.

Asia looked almost as stunned as she had from the blow to her head. "No," she protested. "How could—why would anyone want to hurt me?"

"Did you see or hear anyone before your fall?" Gemma asked.

"No. I was in here. But, I remember now, I was worrying about the alcohol, wondering if I could possibly have made a mistake. I had two full bottles of grain alcohol, for the next batch of limon-cello, and one is missing. I suppose I shouldn't have kept it in the greenhouse, but I never thought . . ."

"Was it visible from outside the greenhouse?" Gemma asked.

"No, there's a closed cupboard under the potting bench. The alcohol and lemon zest have to infuse in a cool, dark place for about six weeks before you add the sugar and water. There's not much room in the kitchen cupboards, so I just keep it all out there together." Asia was beginning to sound exhausted, although she'd put down the cloth and her head no longer seemed to be bleeding.

Kerry had gone up to the door with Mrs. Armitage, and Gemma could hear sirens in the distance. Her time to get answers was running out.

"Asia, when you rang me, you said you were worried about 'the boy.' What did you mean?"

Asia looked reluctant. "I don't think I should have mentioned it. It wasn't fair of me . . ."

"Why don't you let me worry about that. I'll sort it out, I promise. Did you mean Jess Cusick?"

Asia nodded. "I saw him in the garden this morning. When he should have been at school. And, then, when I saw the bottle was missing . . ."

"But why would you think Jess would do something like that?"

"Because he knew where it was, and what it was. He was here when his mother helped me mix the finished batch for the garden party. And, because, well, you know what kids are like . . ." Asia sighed. "Or at least that's the sort of trouble we got into when I was at school. I was worried about him, you know, after what happened to poor Reagan." Her eyes filled with tears.

Gemma patted her hand. The sirens had stopped and she could hear voices from upstairs. "I'm sure he's fine," she said, although she felt a jolt of worry. "Asia, did you tell anyone else about the missing alcohol? Or about seeing Jess?"

"Well, I told his mother, of course."

Like Ryan Marsh's, Michael Stanton's flat was on the ground floor of an ordinary estate. Kincaid thought that for someone maintaining a false identity, the ability to come and go without alerting all the neighbors would have been important. It was the neighbors, however, that had led Sidana's team to the flat. Although the flat number on Stanton's driving license had not corresponded with an existing address, Sidana had organized a house to house, starting at one end of the estate and systematically working across it. Eventually, a resident had identified Stanton's photo as, "That unfriendly bloke two doors down."

Other neighbors and the property records had confirmed it. Sidana had got her warrant and a locksmith, and she and Sweeney had just got the door open when Kincaid arrived.

It was an unremarkable flat in an unremarkable estate—not too posh, not too poor, fairly well kept, some of the renovated flats obviously bought from the council, the parked cars relatively new models.

"Sir," said Sidana, giving him that look of grave concern he'd come to expect in the last few days. He wanted to reassure her that he was fine, but he couldn't.

The locksmith, packing up his kit, said, "Nice lock for a council flat. What's this bloke got in here? Gold?"

It seemed, however, that Michael Stanton—or Michael Stanley as he once was—hadn't much at all. The flat had a sitting room, bedroom, bathroom, and kitchen. It might have been a hotel. The furniture was anonymous and, although not cheap, looked as if it been bought en masse. There was a very large new flat-screen television on one wall, with a gaming system. Most of the games, from Kincaid's quick perusal, were of the latest and most realistic first-person-shooter type. Sweeney examined the system with a covetous expression.

There were no pictures on the walls, and no reading material on the tables or chairs—not even a newspaper.

Sidana did a quick look through the kitchen. "Looks like the guy lived on baked beans and frozen ready meals," she said. "There's nothing fresh at all." She wrinkled her nose, her disapproval evident.

"There's no computer," Sweeney called from the bedroom. "Nothing but a phone charger on the bedside table."

Kincaid joined him. There was a depression in the duvet, and the pillows were bunched together on one side of the bed—so far the only sign of actual human presence in this place. He checked the drawers in the single chest—socks, Y-fronts, sweaters, and T-shirts—then the wardrobe. One decent suit, not cheap, but not expensive. Shirts, casual wear, a few ties.

Then, he stood in the middle of the room, looking around, thinking. He didn't believe that any person lived without a few possessions that expressed their identity and history. Even the homeless carried about odds and ends of things that mattered to them in their trolleys. He thought of Ryan's cache. If Stanton had been undercover, rogue or not, he must have had something similar.

"Look everywhere," he told Sweeney and Sidana. "Under things, behind things, inside things. We're missing it."

It was Sidana who found the cache. "I think there should be cabinet doors here," she said a few moments later, rapping on a flat panel beside the cupboard that held the tins of baked beans. "And feel it." She ran her fingers over the surface of the panel. "It's a good match, but I think the paint is slightly different, and it sounds like a hollow space."

Carefully, she removed the tins of beans and tomato sauce and soup from the neighboring cupboard, then felt inside the space. "Solid. Or at least, there's a partition, but I can't—" Her severe face split in a sudden smile. "Blimey." For Sidana, this was serious swearing. "There's a little catch on one side."

It took her five minutes to maneuver a black duffel bag into the bean cupboard, then out onto the kitchen floor. It was carry-on size, perhaps one foot by one by two, and it had been squeezed tightly into its hiding place.

Glancing at Kincaid, who nodded and said, "Your find," she slipped on latex gloves and unzipped the bag. As she removed each item, she laid it on the large trash bag they'd spread on the floor.

The top of the bag was stuffed with utility clothing—black combat trousers, black shirts, a black heavy cotton jacket. Clothes for night work. Beneath the folded items, there was a pistol. A Glock, Kincaid thought. Sweeney, who did not have Sidana's distaste for swearing, breathed, "Holy shit."

Frowning again, Sidana put it carefully on the cloth. There were also two boxes of ammunition, and something wrapped in black cloth—a T-shirt, Kincaid saw as Sidana carefully unfolded the fabric.

In the T-shirt was an expandable baton, similar to those every officer carried on his or her duty belt. Collapsed, the short cylinder didn't look all that threatening, but deployed they were vicious. And looking at it, Kincaid thought about the wound on Denis Childs's head.

"Bag that separately, and very carefully," he said, but he didn't explain why.

Sidana did as he asked, then went on with her methodical unpacking. There were expensive binoculars, odds and ends of camping equipment, and, in a leather wallet, two passports and several thousand pounds in banknotes. Neither passport was in the name of Michael Stanton nor Michael Stanley, but carried the same photo as Stanton's driving license. "Nice job," Sidana commented.

"They look like real government issue." Kincaid didn't comment on that, either.

Near the bottom of the bag, something made a crinkling sound. Sidana felt round the edges, then pulled out a manila envelope. She'd started to open it when Kincaid said, "Mind if I have a look?"

He pulled on gloves, then carried the envelope to the kitchen table. It was light, and from the feel of it, contained paper. Gently, he slid the contents onto the table.

There were photos, many yellowing with age. Some were obviously of Stanton as a child—one a family portrait with a man who looked much like him and a tired-looking woman, one as a small boy at the seaside, holding a bucket and trowel and smiling. In the photo, the boy was about Toby's age, and it filled Kincaid with dismay to think that child had grown into the man they knew as Michael Stanton.

Something slightly thicker was stuck to the back of one of the photos. He grasped it by one corner and very carefully peeled it free. It was a Polaroid, its color faded, its surface slightly tacky. It showed half a dozen people crowded together in what looked like a cheap sitting room.

Kincaid peered at the photo, trying to make out the faces captured in the disintegrating emulsion. The two women were in the front of the group, one blond, rather serious, one brunette, startlingly pretty. Behind them stood the men. He immediately recognized Stanton—Stanton a good twenty years younger, his head buzzed and a small tattoo plainly visible on his neck. And the tall, gaunt man, with the shaggy, dark, collar-length hair and the stubble—dear God, that was Denis Childs. Kincaid wasn't sure he'd have recognized him if not for the familiar almond shape of his dark eyes.

He was so gobsmacked by the sight of Denis that it took him a moment to place the man standing slightly to one side. Short hair, neatly brushed, although the photo was too faded for the color to be distinguishable. A little military bristle of a mustache. A supercilious expression, the same expression that had been leveled at him just a few months ago when Kincaid had interviewed him in his study. It was, without a doubt, Angus Craig.

"What have you got, boss?" asked Sidana.

Kincaid's back was to the room. "Just some old photos," he said, and, almost without thinking, slipped the Polaroid into his breast pocket.

Leaving Kerry to deal with transferring Asia to the ambulance, and with instructing the uniformed officers to secure the patio and greenhouse, Gemma hurried to the Cusicks'.

Nita answered the door on the first ring, looking startled and not particularly pleased to see Gemma. "I'm sorry," she said. "This isn't a good time. I was just going out." She wore, not business attire, but yoga bottoms and trainers.

"I'm afraid it won't wait." Gemma stepped inside, uninvited, and with a shrug, Nita led her into the sitting room. The white roses, Gemma saw, were still in their bowl, but wilted, and the room had a stale, unpleasant smell.

Nita turned to face Gemma, her arms crossed over her breasts, small under the thin T-shirt. "If this is about Edward Miller, I'm sure you know you've harassed my client for no reason. I don't appre—"

"Mrs. Cusick, your neighbor Asia Ford was attacked in her greenhouse a few minutes ago. Have you seen anyone in the garden?"

"What? What are you talking about?" Nita stared at her, her face blanching beneath her makeup. "How— That's impossible. Is she—is she all right?"

"She's going to be fine. She needs a few stitches."

Nita sat on the nearest sofa as if her legs had been knocked from under her. "Thank God. But who . . ."

"I was hoping you might tell us that. Were you home all morning?"

"I had my yoga class, early. Then I ran into the office to do some paperwork. And then, Asia rang me . . ."

"You went to see her?"

"I stopped in, yes. She was very upset. She was going on about people stealing things from her. I thought she might be confused."

"About the alcohol being missing?"

"Ye-es. I suppose."

"Has Asia been confused about things before?" Gemma asked, sitting down opposite Nita.

"Well, no, but—I couldn't imagine that someone would—"

"Nita." Gemma was losing patience. "Asia rang you this morning because she was worried about Jess. She said she saw him in the garden, after school starting time. Where is he?"

Nita's face crumpled and she put a hand to her mouth. "I don't know. The school rang. He didn't sign the register this morning. Now that Reagan's gone he makes his own way to school on the mornings I have yoga class. He was gone when I got home, so I just assumed . . ."

"Of course you did," Gemma said. "But it was hours ago that Asia said she saw him in the garden—"

"I don't believe for one minute that my son got into her alcohol," Nita broke in, sniffing. "I told her. Jess would nev—"

"That may be true. But someone has been hurt, and your son is missing. We need to find him," Gemma insisted. "Do you have any idea where he might have gone?"

Slumping, Nita shook her head. "He only goes to school and to dance. He's not at school, and there are no dance classes until after school hours." She looked up at Gemma, tears in her eyes again. "He's only ten."

"Almost eleven," corrected Gemma, coming to sit beside her and giving her shoulder a pat. If, as Chris Cusick had guessed, Jess had made his way to Finsbury Park and back on his own last Saturday, he was a pretty savvy kid. "We'll find him," she told Nita. "In the meantime, you stay here, so that you can let us know if he calls or comes home. Okay?"

"Okay." Nita gave her a tentative smile. "But what if—"

Gemma was already shaking her head. "No. Don't worry. You've checked Jess's room?" Nita nodded. "Did he take anything unusual?"

Nita thought for a moment. "His dance bag was gone. He usually picks it up after school."

After making certain that Nita had her mobile number, Gemma left her and went back to Asia Ford's house. The paramedics were still checking Asia, so Gemma called Kerry into the front hall and filled her in.

"Can you have a look for him in the garden?" she asked.

"I can, but, look, Gemma. If this kid stole Ford's high-proof alcohol, he could have given it to Reagan, then smothered her. He's a strong kid, with physical training. He could have done it. Then, maybe he was worried that Asia would connect him to the missing booze, so he hung around this morning waiting for an opportunity to get rid of her."

"I don't believe it," said Gemma. "There's no actual evidence that he took the alcohol. And even if he had, I don't believe that Reagan would have agreed to a midnight tryst in the garden, with drinks, with her ten-year-old charge."

"Okay, okay." Kerry rolled her eyes at Gemma's vehemence. "I agree it's pretty unlikely. But, then who took Asia Ford's alcohol? What was the boy doing in the garden this morning? And where the hell is he now?"

"I don't know, but I'm worried about him. We know he's been angry and uncommunicative since Reagan died. He and Reagan were close. What if he's not just grieving? What if he knows some-thing? Or saw something? We have no idea what he was doing the night Reagan was killed. In my experience, ten-year-old boys don't normally go to bed when they say they will, and if his mother took a sleeping pill, she couldn't check on him."

"Oh, hell." Kerry blew out a breath. "Don't tell me we've got an endangered child on our hands. Before we call out the cavalry, let's look in all the obvious—"

Gemma's mobile rang. Thinking it might be Nita with news, she waved a hand at Kerry to excuse herself.

It wasn't Nita, however, but Thea Osho, the young woman they'd met at Bill's. "Detective," she said, a little hesitantly, "you wanted me to ring you."

Gemma stepped outside. "Thea, why was Reagan arguing with Sidney at the piano bar on Friday night?"

"Sidney?"

"Yes, Sidney. None of you told us that."

There was silence on the phone. Finally, Thea said, "They're my friends, wankers that they are. I didn't want to get them into trouble. Reagan found out that Hugo used one of Sidney's papers on a major degree project. She was furious with them both. She couldn't bear people being dishonest."

"She was going to break up with Hugo over that?" asked Gemma.

"She said if he cheated on one thing, she could never be sure he wasn't cheating on something else. And, well, I think meeting Edward Miller put Hugo in a new light."

"Smart girl," Gemma murmured after she'd thanked Thea and hung up. It would have been a good decision—if Reagan had lived to see it through.

But what had any of this to do with Jess having gone missing?

Gemma stood, staring blankly into Blenheim Crescent, shivering a little in the breeze that had come up with the scudding clouds. Where would you go if you were a ten-year-old boy, and you were angry, and maybe frightened? She didn't believe he was hiding in the garden. He hadn't gone to his father—they'd just seen Chris Cusick and she'd no reason to think he had been untruthful with them.

She thought about the things Chris had said, and what Nita had told her just a bit ago.

And suddenly she knew where to look.

"Bugger the chain of evidence," Kincaid said aloud as he drove from the Hackney flat to Holborn Police Station. But the Polaroid felt like a weight in his pocket. As soon as he'd got in the car, he'd transferred the photo to an evidence bag, but he hadn't logged it in, so it would be useless as proof of anything.

But he couldn't get the image out of his mind. They'd guessed that Stanton had worked undercover. They'd guessed that Denis had worked undercover. But they'd had no reason to think that the two had been connected. And what the hell had Angus Craig to

do with them? From his appearance in the photo, it was highly unlikely he'd been working an undercover assignment. And he was
older than either of the other men, so had probably been senior in
ranking.

"Bloody hell," he said as the thought struck him, then braked
hard to avoid bumping the car in front of him.

Angus Craig had been their handler. Everything he'd ever
learned about Craig told him that Craig would have reveled in the
control that came with the job. Control, manipulation, opportunity.

It also meant that Denis Childs had had a long, and by necessity,
fairly intimate relationship with Craig. And that Denis Childs and
Michael Stanton had known each other, and probably well.

He was still mulling over the implications when he got to his
office. Checking messages and reports, he saw there was no further progress in the investigation into the death of Michael Stanton, other than the discovery of the flat and its contents.

Its contents . . . Angus and Edie Craig had been shot with a
semiautomatic pistol, but the gun had been left at the scene. Ryan
Marsh had been shot with a semiautomatic pistol, which had also
been left at the scene. So there was no connection between the gun
in Stanton's flat and either of the weapons used in the murders—
assuming he was right and they were murders. No connection
except for Stanton himself. He'd known Angus Craig. He'd been
seen near the Craigs' on the night of their deaths.

And, he had known Ryan Marsh.

Had Stanton killed the Craigs?

Had Stanton killed Ryan, using a different gun but the same
method?

And if either of those things were true, how would he ever
prove it?

He saw again the baton they'd found in Stanton's things, and he thought of the description of the wound to Denis Childs's head. There were no crime scene photos of Denis's injury to use for a comparison, but he'd be willing to bet that the depression in Denis's skull would match the thin, flexible end of a deployed baton.

But he couldn't suggest a comparison to his team, or to the team investigating Childs's assault, without revealing why he had made the connection. And that took him back to the purloined photo.

He needed to talk to Doug. And King's Cross was nagging at him. Why, if Michael Stanton lived in Hackney, had his body been found in the Regent's Canal, a few hundred yards from King's Cross station and St. Pancras station? St. Pancras, where the white phosphorous grenade had gone off in the great train shed. And the spot on the canal was just a short distance from the Caledonian Road, where Ryan had lived with Matthew Quinn's protest group. Coincidence? Probably. But he didn't like it.

Glancing at his watch, he texted Doug. "Meet me in an hour. The Driver."

Doug replied, "Why the hell there?"

"Will explain," Kincaid sent back, although he wasn't at all sure he could.

Leaving his office, he murmured an excuse to Sidana.

He strolled out of the building, trying not to hurry, trying not to feel the Polaroid burning a hole in his pocket, and a few minutes later exited the tube at St. Pancras/King's Cross. The sky was now completely overcast, and a chill little breeze had come up from the north, welcome after the morning's heat.

He walked into the wind, due north up York Way, thinking he'd circle round to the Driver via the canal towpath, and have a look at the spot where Stanton had been fished out of the water. Passing the sparkling new complex that housed the *Guardian*, he remembered when one wouldn't have chosen to walk along the canal in the daytime, much less at night, but with all the development in the King's Cross area the canal had become a desirable attraction. And desirable real estate.

Pausing, he looked down at the towpath from the York Way bridge. The canal looked serene, the left side lined with cheerful moored narrow boats, the right, with the sheer walls of offices and flats. He knew, however, that farther east, nearer to the Caledonian Road, there were sections where the moorings were vacant, where foliage blocked the towpath from sight on the left, and where the buildings on the right had small windows like blind eyes. It was in one such section that Michael Stanton's body had floated to the surface.

He found himself thinking of Ryan again. Ryan, who must have known this area intimately, having lived for months in the flat on the Caledonian Road. Had he photographed it, Kincaid wondered, the way he'd photographed Hambleden? Many of the shots in and around the village had been very good, almost professionally composed.

What, he wondered, had happened to Ryan's camera? It had not been among the things stashed on the island. Had it been with him the night he died, perhaps in the open backpack in the sitting room of the Hackney flat?

The wind picked up with a gust that blew dust in his eyes and rattled rubbish along in the gutters. He turned and, instead of taking the stairs down to the towpath, walked back the way he'd come.

When he reached King's Cross again, he rounded the corner and walked up the Caledonian Road. He wondered if Matthew

Quinn was still there, and if Matthew might recognize the photo of Stanton. Matthew, he realized, would not know Ryan was dead. Ryan Marsh had disappeared, as far as the group was concerned, on the day of the St. Pancras explosion.

The flat, he saw, had not yet succumbed to the inexorable march of gentrification. The Georgian building looked grubbier and more run down than ever, and when he rang the bell, there was no answer. He'd almost turned away when he recognized the friendly face of the proprietor of the halal chicken shop next door.

"Medhi," he said, going in. "Medhi Atias."

Atias, a middle-aged, dark-eyed man with a small paunch, looked up with a surprised smile. "Mr. Kincaid. How nice to see you."

Kincaid had become acquainted with Atias during the investigation of Matthew Quinn's little protest group. He'd liked him, and Ryan, he remembered, had liked him, too. "How are you, Mr. Atias?" Kincaid shook his hand across the counter. "How's business?" The shop, unlike the rest of the building, was clean and bright. Atias had told him that the development of the area had been a good thing for him, because tenants of the new office complexes needed decent, reasonably priced food.

"Better than ever," Atias said. "I deliver lunches now to some of the buildings. And you?"

The smell of frying chicken and chips, and hot coffee, made Kincaid's mouth water. He realized that he'd completely missed lunch.

"Can I get you something, Mr. Kincaid?" Atias asked.

Kincaid was tempted, but a look at the clock above the counter told him that he'd be late to his meeting with Doug. "Thanks, but I'd better not. Mr. Atias, is Matthew Quinn still in the flat upstairs?"

"Alas, no, they are all gone. And the students below them. I think the developers are now waiting for all the leases to finish. Mine will be up the end of the year."

"I'm sorry to hear that," said Kincaid, genuinely.

Atias shrugged. "I'll find another place. Near Brighton, my wife says."

It occurred to Kincaid that, like Matthew Quinn, Medhi Atias would have no reason to know that Ryan was dead. The women in Matthew Quinn's group had liked Ryan, but, Kincaid knew now, to Ryan they'd been a part of his job. Medhi Atias might have been the closest thing Ryan had to a friend.

"Mr. Atias, I thought you should know. Ryan Marsh is dead."

"Ah." To Kincaid's surprise, Atias merely nodded, his dark eyes unreadable. "I assumed so," he said. "Thank you for telling me."

"Do you mind if I ask why you assumed it?"

"It is more than two months now and he has not collected his pack. He said it was very important and that I should look after it for him." Atias shrugged. "He would have come if he had been able."

Kincaid just stared at him. "His pack?"

Wiping his hands on his apron, Atias ducked into the shop's back room, returning with a small day pack. "I would not have given this to any of them," he said, nodding towards the now-vacant flat. "Or the police if they'd come asking. But you, I think, are also an honorable man."

Kincaid took the pack. It was dark blue nylon, nondescript, about the size of a lady's handbag. Whatever was inside felt hard and lumpy. "Do you know what this is?" he asked.

"His camera, of course," said Atias. "Usually, he carried it with him everywhere. But on that day, the day the boy died, he did not."

OCTOBER 1994

He tried to touch Sheila, to find a pulse, hoping against hope that he was wrong, but Lynn pushed him aside. "Don't touch her," she snapped. "There's nothing you can do. I've rung Red from the call box on the corner."

"But we've got to ring for an ambulance—"

"No. He said not to move, not to call. He's coming."

Denis sat down hard on the nearest chair. His teeth were chattering and his legs wouldn't seem to hold him up. "But she was fine. A little drunk. She—"

"You have no idea how much shit Sheila took." Lynn scrubbed the back of her hand across her face. "This time, she took too much and it killed her."

"But—" He thought of Sheila's little skirt, bunched up until Lynn smoothed it. And was that bruising on her throat? His vision was blurring. He tried to get up for a better look, but sank back helplessly into the chair.

"Mickey," he croaked. "Mickey was touching her. Should never have left her alone with him. He must have—"

"There was nobody here, Denny, I'm telling you." Lynn peered at him, and when she spoke again, her voice seemed very far away. "What's the matter with you, Den? Are you ill?"

There was a clatter of footsteps on the stairs and Red burst into the room. "Jesus Christ," he said, staring at Sheila. His sharp gaze swiveled to Denis. "Did he do this?" he barked at Lynn.

"God, no. I think she took an overdose."

"We should call—" began Denis, but it came out a whisper.

"Shut up," said Craig. "You, listen. Both of you. We are not calling anyone. There's nothing we can do for her, and the force

can't afford to have any awkward questions right now. Do you understand?"

After a moment, Lynn said quietly, "Yes, sir."

When Denis didn't answer, Craig said to Lynn, "What's the matter with him? Is he drunk?"

"No, I think he's ill."

"Jesus Christ," Craig said again, this time in disgust rather than shock.

Denis watched him as he stood for a moment, thinking, but he couldn't summon the strength to protest.

"We'll get him into a taxi," said Craig. "No ambulance. Come on. Help me get him down the stairs."

Denis didn't protest as they hoisted him from the chair, one on each side, and manhandled him down the stairs, Craig cursing under his breath the whole way. Craig held him up while Lynn walked to the corner and flagged a cab in Earl's Court Road. When the cab pulled up, Craig opened the door and shoved him unceremoniously into the backseat.

"A bit too much to drink," Denis heard Craig tell the driver, passing over a wad of notes. "Just dump him out on his doorstep and ring the bell. His wife won't be best pleased, I can tell you."

"Not drunk," Denis tried to say, but no words came out. As the cab began to move, the last thing he heard was Red Craig calling out his own address in Sekforde Street.

CHAPTER TWENTY-THREE

It was the odd hour of the afternoon—too late for lunch, too early for tea—and the café at the Tabernacle was empty except for the young woman working the service counter.

"Have you seen a boy about this high?" Gemma asked, raising her hand to shoulder level. "Blondish. Dances here on Saturdays."

The young woman shook her head. "Sorry. I've been in the back making hummus."

Thanking her, Gemma wandered slowly through the dining area, then climbed the stairs. When she reached the first-floor landing, she checked the doors to the theater. Locked. She went into the vestibule of the dance studio, where she'd first seen Jess, but it was empty. The doors to the studio and the office were also locked.

She sagged a little with disappointment. She'd been so sure that she was right, that this was the place Jess felt safest, most at home.

Now where? Did she go to the ballet school in Finsbury Park? Did Jess intend to show up for his regular class? And then what? Go home, hoping his mother wouldn't know he'd been absent from school? She didn't think so.

She was now seriously worried, and that carried over into anxiety about Duncan, too. She hadn't heard a word from him since he'd left that morning, saying he was going to Hambleden to see a man about a dog. What the hell was he doing?

Giving her head a sharp shake, she went into the ladies' loo to splash water on her face and check her messages. She had to find Jess before she tackled anything else.

God, how she hated her freckles, she thought as she gazed at her face in the mirror. The last few days of hot, sunny weather had brought them out in full force. It was quiet in the bathroom, and cool, and the water felt soothing to her hot cheeks. She dried her hands slowly, reluctant to go back out into the world.

Then it occurred to her.

As quietly as she could, she went back out into the vestibule and stood for a moment, listening. There was a tiny squeak, perhaps from a door hinge.

She walked to the men's toilet and swung open the door. "Anybody in here?" she called.

There was no answer, but she heard a little gasp of breath. The stall doors were closed and no feet showed underneath when she bent to look. But he hadn't managed to pick up the dance bag when he tucked himself up on top of the toilet lid.

Gemma leaned against the sink. "Jess, come on out. It's Gemma James. I know you're in there."

There was no response.

After a moment, she said, "Jess, you have to come out sometime. I'm not going away. Look, I promise I won't tell your mum where you are."

After another long moment, there was a shuffling noise and the boy's feet dropped into view. "You're not supposed to be in here," he said, but he didn't unlatch the stall door. He sounded as if he'd been crying.

"There's no one up here. And if someone comes in, I'll tell them it's out of order."

More shuffling, but the door stayed closed.

"You must be hungry," said Gemma. "I've got a PowerBar in my bag."

"I could have it?"

"Absolutely. Chocolate and peanut butter."

Slowly, the stall door creaked open and Jess Cusick came out, clutching his bag. He ducked his head, but not before Gemma saw that his eyes were red and swollen.

She was shocked at the sight of him. The skin was stretched across his cheekbones, with hollows beneath. He looked as if he'd lost pounds since she'd seen him a few days ago. "We could go into the vestibule," she said, to cover her dismay.

He shook his head violently, his ash brown hair flying, and half-retreated into the stall. "No. I don't want anyone to see me."

"Okay," Gemma said quickly. She glanced round the small space. "Look. We could sit over there." With the PowerBar in her hand, she gestured to the few feet of wall at the back of the room. His eyes followed the motion. She might have been enticing a stray dog.

Gemma slipped past him, careful not to touch him, and sat down against the wall. When she started to unwrap the bar, Jess sat down beside her and said, "I can do it." He was wearing a

T-shirt and jeans, rather than his school uniform, and had that particular boy-sweat smell she recognized from her own sons. His trainer-clad feet stuck out in front of him, too big in proportion to the rest of his body.

She handed the PowerBar over, politely looking away as he tore the rest of the wrapper away and wolfed the bar down.

When he'd finished and balled up the paper, he said, hesitantly, "Thank you."

"It's hard to think when you're hungry."

Jess nodded, glancing warily at her. "Are you going to tell my mum where I am?"

"Not if you don't want me to. But maybe you should tell me why you skived off school this morning."

Jess worked at the paper wrapper, balling it more and more tightly. Finally, he said, "I had to do . . . something." When Gemma didn't speak, he went on after a bit. "In the garden. I wanted to see where she . . ." His voice trembled. A sideways glance showed Gemma that his jaw muscles were clenched tight. "Died," he managed. "I couldn't look before. But I had to see."

"Why did you have to see, Jess?"

"Because . . . because it was all my fault." He was fighting back tears in earnest now.

"How could it be your fault?" Gemma asked. It occurred to her that if this boy had done what Kerry suggested, she was alone with him in a deserted place, but she didn't feel the least bit frightened.

"Because of Henry."

"Henry Su? The boy who died?"

Jess nodded, gulping. "His dad, Mr. Su, came up to Re-Reagan and me at the garden party. He said horrible things. That it was my fault that Henry died and that I was going to pay for it. Reagan told him to shut up, that it wasn't true and that he couldn't say things like that. I thought he was going to hit her. He said she'd be sorry, too. He was . . . I think he was drunk."

"Then what happened?" Gemma said, but she was thinking frantically that they had checked Ben Su's alibi and his colleagues had confirmed it. Had they lied for him?

"Reagan took me away. She said he was a bully and she wasn't going to put up with it. But I didn't want him to hurt her, so I told her . . . I told her it was true."

"You what?" Gemma scooted back on the cold tiles so that she could look Jess in the eyes.

He looked determined now, and the tears had stopped. "I told her it was true. It was my fault Henry died."

"But—"

"He was always teasing me. He was . . . rotten. You know? Mean. He did . . . things . . . to Arthur, until Arthur's parents sent him away. Then he started on me, but he said I couldn't tell because I'd get into trouble for lying. I couldn't—I couldn't make him leave me alone." The words were pouring out now. "The only thing that bothered him was if he couldn't find his inhaler. He was always going on about his bloody inhaler.

"That day, it fell out of his pocket and he didn't notice. I picked it up. I thought I'd let him sweat a bit when he noticed it was gone. I didn't know he was going to shut himself in the stupid shed. I just went home. And then . . . and then he was"—Jess took a gulping breath—"he was dead. And I couldn't tell anyone what I'd done."

"Oh, Jess," Gemma breathed. "How awful."

"I worried all week. And then I told her," Jess said. "I told Reagan. I told her I still had the inhaler."

"What did she say?"

Jess swallowed. "She said I had to tell Henry's parents. She said that it was a dreadful accident, but that if I didn't tell, I would carry it round with me my whole life." He looked earnestly at Gemma. "She didn't mean the inhaler, you know."

Gemma nodded. "I know."

"But she said that first my mum had to know."

"Of course she did," said Gemma, and felt a chill that had nothing to do with the cold tile.

"So I—I told her. I told Mum. She said they would have me arrested—Henry's parents—and that I could go to jail. That I'd never dance again. She said Reagan was going to ruin my life, giving me ideas like that."

Gemma sat for a moment, trying to formulate a question. "Jess, when was this? When did you tell your mum?"

"On Friday. Reagan came into my room after. Mum must have talked to her. She said she was very sorry, but she wasn't sure she could stay with us any longer." He was crying again, the tears slipping down his cheeks. "I was mad. I went to bed. She came in to talk to me again before she went out, but I pretended I was asleep."

"And on Saturday?"

"When I woke up, my mum was gone, and Reagan was gone. At first, I thought maybe she'd gone away, but her things were still there. So I—"

When he halted, Gemma gave his arm a pat. "So you got on the bus and went to the tryouts at the London Boys Ballet School."

Jess stared at her. "How did you know?"

"I spoke to your dad. He guessed."

"But— Was he—"

"He understood." When Jess relaxed a little, she said, "Jess, what were you really doing in the garden this morning?"

Jess glanced at her, then away. "I couldn't find it," he whispered. "The inhaler. It was in my room, in my drawer. I wondered if . . . if Reagan had taken it . . . Maybe if she knew she was going to meet Mr. Su. And . . . So I had to look."

"You didn't find it."

"No," he said.

"Jess," Gemma said slowly, "what do you think happened to Reagan on Friday night?"

He was quiet for a long time, rolling the paper wrapper into an ever-tighter ball. "I think—I think she must have talked to Mr. Su. He—he said he would hurt her."

"Do you think Reagan would have talked to Mr. Su without your permission?"

Jess didn't answer.

"Jess, do you know what happened to Reagan's phone?"

He shook his head. "No. But I—I took her laptop. When my mum said she was dead, that she'd killed herself—I thought maybe it wasn't true. Or maybe she'd left me a message . . ."

"And did she?"

"No," he said, his face bleak. "There wasn't anything for me."

Gemma tried to marshal her whirling thoughts, tried to stay calm. Nothing mattered more now than this child's safety. "Jess," she said. "I think we need to call your dad."

If carrying the Polaroid had made him anxious, carrying the bag containing Ryan's camera had Kincaid looking over his shoulder every few minutes.

Kincaid guessed that Ryan had left his camera with Medhi Atias that day, perhaps as a last-minute thought on the way to St. Pancras. Although he hadn't been in the group with the other demonstrators, Ryan couldn't have guaranteed he wouldn't be arrested if things went pear shaped.

So, what was on the camera that had prompted Ryan to take such precautions? Kincaid held the nylon bag more firmly under his jacket. There was nowhere he could look at the memory card until he got to the pub.

Finally, he saw the plant-bedecked building ahead. The vertical garden covering the walls was in full bloom, but he didn't stop to admire it. He entered the bar and blinked as his eyes adjusted to the dim light. The pub wasn't yet crowded and he had no trouble picking out Doug at a table in the back corner—and with him, Melody. They both stood up to greet him, and he kissed Melody lightly on the cheek.

He saw she'd cut her hair, and the boyish style made her look, if anything, more feminine. She seemed fragile to him, taut with tension.

"I know you probably don't want me here," she said. "But I've been left out of enough things, and Ryan was important to me, too."

Shaking his head, Kincaid took a seat across from them. "No, I do want you here. I should have asked. But I thought you were taking over for Gemma temporarily."

"I'm sure I'll get a right bollocking from the super for skiving off this afternoon, but I don't care."

After checking to see if either of them wanted another round—Doug was drinking a half-pint, and Melody what looked like club soda—Kincaid went to the bar and ordered a half-pint of bitter.

When he came back to the table, Doug said, "I told her about . . . Hambleden. About Ryan."

"I don't believe it." Melody clutched her glass, her knuckles white. "I don't believe he could have done those things—he wouldn't—"

Kincaid leaned forward, keeping his voice down even with the buzz of the pub to cover it. "We don't know that he did. All we know is that he had a connection with the village, and with the Craigs, because of his photos. And that he was in the village with Michael Stanton on the evening of the night of the fire. And, if Mr. Wilson is correct, he was arguing with Stanton. What I'd like to know is whether Ryan or Stanton was still working for the force."

"But we've assumed they were both—at least at one time— working undercover for Special Branch," Doug said. "Or in Ryan's case, one of the newer groups keeping an eye on domestic extremists, under SO15."

"You know that the 'domestic extremism' designation has always been bollocks," Melody said hotly. "Basically, it means any protest group that might potentially do something to disrupt public order. And the definition of 'public order' is anything that might be inconvenient to the police or to the government. Anyone who's ever shown up for a protest can be labeled a 'domestic extremist.'"

"You've been reading your father's newspaper again." Doug grinned at her. She shot him a dagger look, but relaxed a little. "Not that I don't agree that going round spying on protesters is out of line," Doug went on after sipping his beer. "But we're talking about spying on Angus Craig here. He had nothing to do with protest groups."

"That's where you're wrong." Kincaid slipped the Polaroid from his pocket and passed it across, careful to touch only the edges.

Doug stared at it, then took his glasses off and peered more closely. Frowning, Melody slid it away from him. "What is this?" she asked.

"I found it in Michael Stanton's flat this afternoon."

"Stanton?" said Doug. "What are you talking about? I thought you said his address was false."

"It was. But Jasmine Sidana found the flat and got a warrant. It was Undercover Anonymous, I can tell you. But he had a cache, just like Ryan. Same sort of stuff—cash, passports, gun—with the addition of tactical clothes. The only really personal thing was an envelope with what looked like old family photos. This was stuck to the back of one of them."

Melody looked horrified. "But that's evi—"

"I didn't enter it into evidence. I didn't show Sidana or Sweeney, either. Look again."

Doug moved the photo back. "That's Stanton," he said. "I get that. I recognize him from the ID photo, even with the skinhead look. Suits him, by the way. But— Bloody hell." His eyes widened. "That's bloody Denis. What's he doing with the hair and beard getup? And they're a good twenty years younger, both of them."

Sliding the Polaroid back, Melody gave him full sarcastic payback for the newspaper dig. "You think? Although I hear Polaroids are making a comeback. No leaks, no naked pictures on the Internet. And it's not that far-fetched that they knew each other. We guessed that Denis and Stanton both worked undercover ops for Special Branch," she added, studying the photo again, "although not togeth— Shit." She looked up at Kincaid. "That's Craig. That's Angus Craig with them. What the—"

"My guess is that he was the handler," Kincaid said, having had time to think about it. "Which means he and Denis knew each other very well. So when Denis went to talk to Craig in Hambleden that night, it wasn't just one senior officer doing another the courtesy of letting him know the sky was about to fall in. That's what I thought, afterwards, you know, and I was furious with Denis." He paused for a moment, trying to work it out. "But I think Denis either knew or suspected the sorts of things Craig had done, and that's why he assigned me to the Meredith case. I also think it was personal. He despised Craig. But that wouldn't have kept him from using the situation—Craig's impending arrest—to get what he wanted."

"I don't understand," said Melody. "What could he have wanted from Craig?"

"Information," Doug answered. "Maybe he thought he could find out who'd kept Craig's nose clean all these years."

"What if," Kincaid said slowly, "what if he got that information? Something big changed that night. After that, Denis started moving pieces on the board. Gemma's transfer. My transfer. Then he organized his liver transplant. And when he came back, well enough to deal with things, he set something in motion."

"Something that almost got him killed." And might yet, Doug didn't add, but Kincaid knew they were all thinking it.

"We found something else in Stanton's cache," Kincaid said. "A baton."

Melody and Doug stared at him. "You mean an ordinary police-issue baton?" Melody asked.

"Denis was hit on the back of the head with something hard, something designed to convey a lot of force. An expanded baton also has reach, so the attacker could have been shorter than Denis and still had the ability to do serious damage."

Doug halted his beer halfway to his mouth. "You think Stanton attacked Denis?"

Kincaid nodded. "I also think that if the Craigs were murdered that night, that Michael Stanton had something to do with it. He had a personal connection with Craig"—he tapped the photo—"and with Denis. But I can't imagine he did either of those things on his own. So who was he working for?

"And who was Ryan Marsh working for? Someone must have told him to take photos of the Craigs. Someone put him in Matthew Quinn's protest group." He felt for the small bag he'd put on the seat beside him, and was suddenly hesitant. Did he want to know what Ryan had thought worth safekeeping? But he'd crossed that Rubicon already, and he knew there was no going back.

"What is it?" said Melody. "What aren't you telling us?"

Kincaid put the bag on the table. "Ryan left this with a friend." He wasn't going to bring Medhi Atias into it. "On the day of the protest at St. Pancras. I just happened upon it this afternoon." When they both looked at him dubiously, he said, "It's his camera. I haven't opened it."

"Can I have a look?" asked Doug.

After a quick glance to make certain no one was paying them any attention, Kincaid pushed the bag across.

Unzipping the blue nylon case, Doug eased out the camera, and smiled. "Nice. It's a Canon SLR. Big enough to take good-quality photos, small enough to slip in a pocket if you want to be unobtrusive." He pushed the Power button. "Let's hope it still has some battery life." The camera made a small whirring noise and the lens extended. "Bingo." Doug sounded relieved.

"The memory card," Kincaid said. "Is there anything on it?"

Melody looked on as Doug began scrolling through images. "Lots of shots in and around King's Cross/St. Pancras," Doug said. "Ordinary, touristy stuff. The canal. Granary Square. Gasholders—

isn't that what that new development behind St. Pancras is called? It's the old Pancras Gasworks."

Frowning, Melody tapped Doug's hand. "Scroll back." Impatiently, she took the camera from him and rotated the scroll wheel herself. "That's"—she looked up at Kincaid—"that's the cop who was on the scene at St. Pancras, after the grenade." Moving the wheel again, she added, "There's half a dozen shots of him. Looks like he's coming out of the Gasholders building. I remember him, because of the silver hair and silver suit. SO15, wasn't he?"

Kincaid reached across for the camera, almost knocking over his beer. He stared at the screen in disbelief. "That's Nick Callery, the detective from SO15. Why the hell was Ryan taking pictures of Nick Callery?"

Gemma had finally convinced Jess to go downstairs for a sandwich and a cold drink. Then, she'd phoned his dad, keeping a firm eye on Jess sitting in the dining area while she talked to Chris Cusick. Chris was surprised that Nita hadn't let him know that Jess was missing, but it occurred to Gemma that Nita hadn't let him know Jess was missing the previous Saturday, either.

"How did you find him?" Chris asked.

"I'd met him at the Tabernacle last Saturday, while I was waiting for my son to finish his class. Jess seemed—I don't know— very happy and relaxed here. So I thought I'd give it a try. Look, Mr. Cusick, of course you'll need to let your wife know where Jess is, but if you could keep him with you for a day or two? I think it's very difficult for him to be there just now, with everything that's happened. I would hate for him to run away again."

"I'll make sure that he doesn't," Cusick said. "Parminder's off the next few days, so there will be two of us to keep an eye on him.

And if Nita wants to gripe about the custody arrangement, that's too bad."

"Um, could you just say Jess rang you? I'd hate to get in Nita's bad books, since she didn't think to look here."

"Oh. Right." Chris Cusick's tone made it clear that he understood exactly what she meant.

Gemma waited with Jess just inside the building's main doors until they saw his father's car pull up in the front. As she walked him out, Jess suddenly tugged at her hand. "I don't want to go home."

While Jess had been finishing his sandwich, Gemma had told him that he must tell his dad everything he'd told her, about Henry, about the inhaler, and about his mother's reaction.

"Your dad understands that," she said now. "He says you don't have to go to your mum's."

Jess nodded, reassured.

Gemma felt reassured, too, when she saw Chris Cusick give his son a hug, and Jess bury his head for a moment against his father's shoulder.

Waving them off, Gemma rang Kerry to check in. But Kerry had been called to another case and couldn't talk.

With a sigh of relief for decisions temporarily delayed, Gemma picked her own children up from school and tried to make the most of what seemed the only normal day since this whole business had begun.

She had, she saw, missed calls from MacKenzie Williams and from Chief Superintendent Marc Lamb, both wanting an update on the case. MacKenzie apologized profusely for having got her into the mess and then buggered off, as she put it, but they'd had a hell of a time rescheduling the catalog shoot.

Gemma didn't return either call. She made the children omelets and salad, which they ate with oven chips that Kit had made from scratch. Kit had come into the kitchen with Captain Jack draped over his shoulders like a fur collar.

How had the kittens got so big, so fast? Gemma wondered. With his piratical swagger and lightning reflexes, the black-and-white kitten was living up to his name. "Watch out, he'll scratch you," she said.

"No, he won't— Ow." Laughing, Kit detached the kitten, put him down, and watched him shoot out of the kitchen, tail in the air.

"Where's Dad?" he'd asked after a bit, cutting potatoes.

Gemma had had a text from Kincaid that said only, "Still at station. Home ASAP." That left a lot of leeway, she thought. "Working," she said to Kit.

"Poor Dad," Kit said, surprising her. "Is he all right? Is he just worried about Granddad?"

The question caught Gemma completely unprepared. "I—I'm sure he's fine, Kit. Just juggling too many things at once, I think."

"I wish we could spend more time with them, Granddad and Nana Rosemary," Kit said. Kit, who had lost so much, adored the grandparents discovered so late in his childhood.

"We will. We'll plan a visit when school's out, what do you say?" She realized as she spoke just how much she would like to do that. "Although you three will have to promise not to wear Hugh out."

Kit went on slicing potatoes with precision. "He is all right, isn't he?"

"He's fine, sweetie. Lots of people have stents in. He just needs to rest up for a bit."

It only occurred to her afterwards, when she was doing the

washing up, that she wasn't sure if Kit had been referring to his granddad, or to his dad.

When she'd given Charlotte her bath and tucked her into bed, then instructed Toby to hop in the tub and wash *everything*, she went back downstairs and poured herself a glass of wine. She desperately needed to talk to someone.

It was Duncan who had always been her sounding board, who might be able to help her decide what to do. He would tell her if she was daft for even thinking she knew what had happened. But he wasn't there. Hadn't been there for a good while, in fact.

So she sat alone at the kitchen table, sipping her wine, and marshaling her argument. Then she picked up her phone and rang Kerry Boatman.

Kincaid thought back to the day of the grenade in St. Pancras. By the time he and his team arrived from Holborn, Nick Callery was already on the scene, representing SO15. He'd told Kincaid he'd happened to be nearby when the call came in. He explained this to Doug and Melody, then said, "But what if he was already in the station? What if Callery knew there was going to be a demonstration, and that they meant to set off a smoke bomb?"

"You think SO15 was running Ryan? And Callery was Ryan's handler?" Doug asked.

"I suppose it's possible." Kincaid lifted his half-pint absently and found it empty. "But, surely, Matthew Quinn's little group can't have been perceived as that much of a threat."

Without a word, Doug scooped up all three of their glasses and dodged his way to the bar. The pub was filling up.

"How's your dad?" Melody asked Kincaid. "I was sorry to hear he was ill. I didn't have a chance to say, before."

With dismay, Kincaid realized he'd gone another day without checking on his parents. "He's doing fine, thanks," he said, making a mental note to ring as soon as he had a bit of quiet. "Melody," he went on, "could you possibly find out who had financial interests in the properties involved in Matthew Quinn's antidevelopment protests? We know, obviously, that his father did, but Lindsay Quinn is not the only shareholder in King's Cross Development. And I'd still like to know why your father was hinting about Denis's 'checkered past.'"

Doug returned with two carefully balanced half-pints and a glass of white wine for Melody. He took up where'd he left the conversation. "If Callery was Ryan's handler, he must have been pissing himself when he thought Ryan had died in that blast."

"Even if Ryan was working for the counterterror spooks," put in Melody, "it doesn't explain why he had photos of Callery, instead of the other way round."

"No," Kincaid agreed. He didn't say that neither did it explain why Ryan had been so afraid that the grenade was meant for him that he'd gone into hiding. Or what any of the St. Pancras debacle had to do with Angus Craig. Or why Ryan was dead.

What was Ryan Marsh's connection with Michael Stanton? And if Stanton had attacked Denis, had it been personal—an old grudge acted on, perhaps—or had someone told him to do it? And who the hell had knifed Stanton and thrown him in the Regent's Canal?

He remembered suddenly the phone call that afternoon from Ronnie Babcock. "Frank Fletcher," he said to Doug and Melody. "Does that ring any bells?" When they shook their heads, he relayed what Ronnie had told him about the former Met officer who'd mumbled about wild police conspiracies when he was in his cups.

"Another convenient suicide?" asked Doug.

Kincaid shrugged. "Ronnie said he was drinking a lot—out of control, from Ronnie's description. Could have been an accident, I suppose, in that case. Or a genuine suicide if the chap thought he was losing it. I didn't ask Ronnie to look further. Just in case someone reported him nosing around."

Doug and Melody exchanged a look and he wondered if they thought he'd gone completely round the bend. "Well, I might as well have a look," said Doug. "Seeing as how I've already been poking wasps' nests."

"Just do it carefully, then." The light slanting in through the pub's slatted shades was softening. Kincaid realized it was getting late. "Speaking of drinking—" he lifted his beer and finished it. "Thanks. My shout next time. I've got to dash."

He left Ryan's camera and the memory card with Doug, who said he'd go through the photos on his laptop and see if he could come up with anything more useful. It wasn't until Kincaid walked out of the pub that he realized he'd done just what Ryan had done the day he'd left the camera with Medhi Atias. He told himself not to be stupid. He wasn't walking into a demonstration that could very likely go wrong.

Perhaps because he was irritated with himself, or because the beer had made him a bit reckless, instead of walking back the way he'd come, he kept going north. When he reached the Regent's Canal, he took the steps down to the towpath and turned back towards King's Cross, just opposite the way he'd meant to walk earlier in the evening.

Most of the canal was now in deep shadow. Lights blinked on in the occasional flat or building, and he passed a few joggers. Coming to the section where Stanton's body had been brought out of the water, he found a fragment of police tape fluttering from the iron fence atop the stone wall on the north side of the towpath. The SOCOs wouldn't have shut the towpath down for long. Just a bit farther along, a few metal-doored lockups fronted the towpath. A bit odd, he thought, wondering if they served as storage for the flats above, but the area would be unlit and not much overlooked at night.

He trusted Sidana to be thorough, but still he wanted to make absolutely certain that no one in the buildings on either side of the canal had seen a suspicious encounter.

When he came to York Way, he took the stairs up, then continued until he reached the rear of the great train shed at St. Pancras. He could see the dark iron silhouettes of the Gasholders buildings, the old gasworks, rising beyond the curving path of the canal.

There was no connection that he knew of between Michael Stanton, dead in the canal a few hundred yards back, and Nick Callery, other than the fact that they had both known Ryan Marsh—and that was basing Ryan's acquaintance with Callery on the slim evidence of a few of Ryan's photos.

But, Kincaid thought, what if Callery had shown up so quickly at the scene in St. Pancras, not because he was shadowing Ryan, but because he lived nearby, in the Gasholders flats.

They'd known no reason why Stanton, who'd lived in Hackney, should have been killed in King's Cross. But what if it was Callery that connected Stanton to King's Cross?

That was not only tenuous, but likely downright bonkers, he thought.

Shaking his head, he entered the terminal, glad of the warmth, and headed towards the front of the shed and the entrance to the tube station. As he passed the site of the grenade's detonation, he couldn't help thinking about Matthew Quinn's protest group again. Well-meaning, most of them, but their silly stunt with what they'd thought was a smoke bomb had turned deadly. He remembered that Matthew's father, the property developer, had admitted he told some acquaintances about Matthew's little campaign to save historic London from the bulldozers. Lindsay Quinn hadn't taken his son seriously, but someone—Kincaid now felt certain—had.

He'd spoken to Lindsay Quinn once before, but he hadn't pressed the point. He needed to talk to Quinn again.

NOVEMBER 1994

He'd ended up in hospital. Severe gastroenteritis, they'd called it. They'd kept him for a few days, making certain he was rehydrated, then had sent him home with instructions for at least a week of bed rest. The doctor, looking at his chart, had frowned, but when Denis had asked what was wrong, the doctor had merely shaken his head and told him not to worry.

At home, he'd fidgeted, but he was too weak to do anything other than complain. Diane was more patient with him than he deserved—his illness had frightened her badly.

By the end of the week, he'd graduated from the bed to the sofa in the sitting room, and clothes instead of pajamas and dressing gown. He was glad of it when the bell rang and Diane ushered in Angus Craig.

"Sir," Denis managed to croak, sitting up.

"I see you're getting on," Craig said heartily. "Good, good. I checked with the hospital. They said you were in a bad way."

Diane was hovering, giving him anxious glances. "Can I get you something to drink, Mr.——" Craig had apparently not introduced himself.

"No. This won't take long," Craig told her. "If you could give us a few minutes, darling." He smiled at her in a way that made Denis's blood rise.

Pinching her lips together, Diane said merely, "Right. I've some shopping to do."

She left the room and a moment later, Denis heard the front door slam.

Craig sat, uninvited, in the best armchair and pulled a letter from his breast pocket. "I thought you'd prefer this in person." He handed the envelope to Denis.

Denis tried to stop his hand shaking as he took it. Slitting the envelope with his thumb, he unfolded the paper inside. It was an official letter of transfer, informing him that he would report in two weeks' time to a major crimes team in Charing Cross. They were putting him back in CID.

"You'll keep your rank, of course," said Craig. "I should think you'd be glad to get back to some real policing."

"But"—Denis stared at him—"what about my campaigners? What about my exit strategy? I can't just disap—"

"All taken care of." Craig waved a dismissive hand. "Your 'cousin' has been to visit your landlady. Your old dad was taken very ill and you've gone to Norwich to look after him. Indefinitely. I'm sure the word will get passed along. Some postcards will be sent, eventually, with the news that your father has died and you've decided to travel."

"But what about Sheila?" Denis pushed himself to the edge of the sofa. His head spun from the effort. "What about Mickey? He killed her. I'm sure of it. You can't just—"

"Sheila died from a combination of drugs and alcohol. I've had the postmortem report. Unfortunate, but there you are. Mickey

Stanton had nothing to do with it. He was at the pub with the rest of the lads."

"But he—"

"I like what you've done with the place," Craig broke in, standing and walking round the sitting room, examining the plasterwork. "Georgian, isn't it, the house? And your wife— such a pretty woman. I'm quite sure she appreciates your prospects and your dedication to your career. It would be a shame to disappoint her, now, wouldn't it?" Craig paused, his hands behind his back in parade-ground manner, and stared him straight in the eye. "Do we understand each other, Detective Inspector?"

Denis, the letter still clutched in his hand, could only nod.

DECEMBER 1994

It was the week before Christmas before he managed to find Lynn. He'd known her cover job because she'd confided in him early on, a breach of rules. But between his new assignment and his still-precarious health, only a few times had he managed to watch the building when she was likely to be arriving or leaving. He'd begun to think she hadn't told him the truth about the job—or that she, like him, had been pulled—when he saw her come through the doors of the office building amid the five o'clock exodus. The weather was cold and damp and she was tugging a bobble hat over her blond hair.

He fell in behind her for two blocks, checking frequently to see if she was being followed. When she stopped at the next intersection, waiting for the light to change, he moved up beside her. "Lynn," he said softly.

She turned, frowning, and he could see that for a moment she *didn't recognize him. His hair was short, his face clean shaven, and he was so thin that his suit and overcoat hung like shrouds.*

Then, the color drained from her face. "Denis. My God, what happened to you?"

"Can we talk?" he said. "There's a pub just along the road."

She looked suddenly frightened. "I can't be seen talking to you. You know that."

"Give me five minutes." He gestured to the swinging pub sign. "I'll drop back behind you. We can meet at the bar."

She hesitated, but the light had changed and the waiting pedestrians were moving forward. "Okay. Five minutes. But that's all."

The pub was busy enough that they could talk at the bar without being overheard, he thought, pleased with his choice. When he edged himself in beside her, he saw that she was already drinking a gin and tonic. "I'm off wine," she murmured without looking at him. He knew why. It had been Sheila's drink.

When he ordered an orange juice, she gave him a quick glance of surprise. "Teetotal, Den? From the look of you, you could use a few beers."

Now that he finally had the opportunity, he found himself at a loss for what to say. Handing his coins to the barman gave him a moment to collect himself. "You look well," he said at last.

Lynn shrugged. "I'll be out of this soon. Bloody boring job it is, too. New boyfriend, see? Wants me to move to Germany to live in a vegetarian commune, can you believe it?" She shook her head. "Where do they come up with this crap?" She didn't ask where he'd been reassigned, and he didn't offer the information. She looked older, he thought, studying her, and the tension never quite left her face.

"Lynn," he said carefully. "About that night. Sheila. We can't let Mickey get away with it."

She shot him a horrified glance, then looked away. "Are you out of your sodding mind?" she hissed. "And Mickey didn't touch her."

"What? But—"

"I'm telling you, Mickey went to the pub with the others. When I got there, I saw Angus Craig walking away from the flat."

He just stared.

"Drink your damned juice and stop looking at me."

Obeying, he wet his dry mouth with a sip of juice, then said, "But— You said you rang him. You rang Angus when you found her."

"I dialed his pager from the call box down the road. He rang me back there. He can't have been far. Maybe he was even watching the flat."

"But why didn't you—"

"What? Say something to him?" Lynn took a gulp of her gin. "I wasn't sure until I came back from the call box and really looked at her that she'd been— Her throat was bruised, and her knickers were torn—" She stopped, her eyes filling. "Jesus," she whispered. "Poor Sheila."

"But he— If he—" Denis tried to take it in. "That bastard. We can't let him get away with it."

Lynn scrubbed at her cheeks with the back of her hand and gave him a disgusted look. "Don't be so bloody naive, Den. Just exactly who would I take that bit of information to? And what do you think would happen to me if I did? Just think about that, clever boy.

"We have nothing. Zilch. And I am not risking my career—or

my life—on a lost cause." Lynn finished her gin, setting her glass down with a little thump exactly in the center of the cardboard beer mat. "You listen to me. If you ever report this, or say anything about it to anybody, I'll deny everything. Don't contact me again. You got that?" She gave him a crooked smile. "Have a nice life, Denis."

She turned and elbowed her way through the crowded pub, letting in a gust of cold air as she pulled open the door and disappeared into the street.

He stood for a long time at the bar, thinking. She was right. He had nothing. If he spoke up, he would put Lynn in danger. He would lose his job, his house, perhaps his wife. And still no one would believe him.

But, he was a good policeman. And he was a patient man. One day, Angus Craig would slip up, and he would be waiting.

CHAPTER TWENTY-FOUR

By the time he reached Notting Hill, Kincaid had once again missed telling the younger children goodnight. Finding Gemma in the kitchen, folding laundry, he'd given her a tentative smile and said, "Hi, love."

She'd looked up from folding one of Charlotte's tiny school uniform blouses, and he could see that she was exhausted.

"I'm sor—" he began but she'd cut him off.

"I don't want to know. Not tonight. Your mum rang, by the way. Your dad's doing fine." Rose, the tortie and white kitten, kept jumping into the basket of clean clothes. Gemma picked her up with obvious irritation and shooed her until she scampered out of the kitchen. "Monsters," Gemma muttered.

He hadn't known where to go from there that wouldn't put him in a minefield. In silence, he'd helped her with the clothes, until she gave him a smile that barely budged the corners of her mouth. "You okay?" he ventured at last.

Sighing, Gemma held the pile of folded things to her chest. He could smell the faint scent of the drier sheet. "I don't know. I'm afraid I may have made a horrible mistake. But I don't want to talk about it. I'll tell you tomorrow."

With that, he'd had to be content.

He'd rung Lindsay Quinn as soon as he deemed it remotely acceptable, at eight o'clock on the dot on Thursday morning. He left a message, not having expected Quinn to answer. To his surprise, Quinn rang him back within fifteen minutes, arranging for Kincaid to meet him, as he had before, in the Booking Office restaurant at St. Pancras.

Kincaid had just time to leave his car at Holborn Police Station and grab the tube to St. Pancras for the nine-thirty appointment. The company of which Quinn was a major shareholder, King's Cross Development, had offices in one of the new complexes north of King's Cross, but Quinn had told Kincaid that he preferred to hold private meetings at the bar in the restored Renaissance Hotel, and Kincaid couldn't say he blamed him.

The hotel was grand Victorian Gothic, stunningly renovated, and the bar, which had been St. Pancras's original booking office, was its gem. It opened onto the ground floor of the hotel on the west, and onto the first floor of the terminal on the east. Kincaid entered through the terminal doors. When his eyes adjusted to the lower light, he picked out Lindsay Quinn at the corner table in the very back, where Kincaid had met him before. This time, he didn't need to ask the hostess for direction, and threaded his own way to the back.

Quinn, a tall, lanky man in his fifties, his curly hair just going gray, closed his laptop and stood to greet him. "Superintendent Kincaid. Tea?" He gestured at the tea service already set up on the table. "It's Assam this morning. I order it from an estate in Ceylon. Please, sit."

"Thank you for seeing me on such short notice," Kincaid said as he took the offered chair. He waited while Quinn filled his teacup, having learned in their previous interview that for all the fact that Quinn did business in this casual environment, he liked observing his courtesies. He added a little milk to the steaming, deep orange tea, smelling the distinctive malt in the brew.

Quinn rotated his cup, a little nervous movement that was the first thing to betray any tension in his manner. "I hope this visit isn't about my son," he said with a smile that didn't make it to his eyes.

"Only in a roundabout way," Kincaid reassured him. "How is Matthew doing?" He didn't add that he knew Matthew had left the Caledonian Road flat.

"I've cut off his allowance. He's no longer living in the flat, so I can't consider it a caretaker's fee. I've told him that if he returns to university to finish his degree, I'll pay his expenses, but so far he hasn't made that decision."

"He's living at home, then?"

Quinn made a face. "I've given him another month to choose university or find a job."

Kincaid thought Quinn was entirely too generous, and that being forced to find a job by lack of funds and shelter might be Matthew Quinn's saving grace. He also knew, however, that it was much easier to make such judgments about other people's dealings with their children. And that unless Matthew broke the law, it was none of his business. "I wish him well, whatever he decides."

"Very generous of you, considering he's been a royal pain in the arse." This time Quinn's smile was genuine.

Kincaid sipped the tea. It was as rich and complex as fine wine on his tongue. There were benefits, he supposed, to having boatloads of money. "I have sons, too," he volunteered, wanting to make a connection with Quinn. "The oldest is about to turn fifteen. Kids can be difficult." He hoped to God Kit never did anything as hare-brained as Matthew Quinn, but he knew there were no guarantees.

"Obviously," Quinn said with a touch of irony. "Since you didn't come about my son, how can I help you, Mr. Kincaid?"

"It does have to do with Matthew's campaigners, in a way," Kincaid said. "Do you remember, Mr. Quinn, telling me that you thought you mentioned Matthew's group and their concerns to a few people? I was wondering if you could tell me exactly who those people were."

Quinn went through the ritual of pouring more tea, his face un-readable. "Can you tell me why you need to know?" he asked at last.

"No, I'm afraid not. Except that it does not in any way concern your son."

Quinn added infinitesimal amounts of milk and sugar to his cup, then met Kincaid's gaze and shrugged. "I don't see why not. It was an informal get-together to discuss the state of the King's Cross revitalization initiative. As you probably are aware, many of the projects here took much longer to get off the ground than was initially expected, but things are now moving apace."

Kincaid nodded, trying to contain his impatience, and Quinn frowned, as if searching his memory. "Do you mind if I make notes?" Kincaid asked, taking a small notebook from his pocket.

"I don't see why not," Quinn answered. "There was nothing secret about it." He went on to give Kincaid a list of perhaps a dozen names. Some, Kincaid recognized as having been involved with high-profile redevelopment projects, others didn't ring a bell. He wrote them down, figuring he would research them when he got back to Holborn. Slipping the notebook back into his pocket, he was about to thank Quinn when Quinn added, "Oh, and your Deputy Assistant Commissioner Trent. She likes to stay up with things, since we have an international terminus here."

Kincaid stared at him. "DAC Trent?" Evelyn Trent had been one of the first people to visit Denis in hospital, expressing concern on behalf of the top brass to Diane Childs. Something niggled at him, something familiar about Trent. Neat, blond, well-groomed, always in command—all those things creating an impression that made it difficult to visualize her features . . .

Then, he had it.

Evelyn Trent had been one of the two women in the Polaroid.

"I've put my not-diminutive arse on the line for you," Kerry said as she picked Gemma up in front of her house. "Nice place you've got here."

"Thank you." Gemma nodded at the house, accustomed now to people wondering how two cops could afford this part of Notting Hill. "Long story," she said. Glancing down, she saw the papers protruding from the briefcase that Kerry had tucked next to the console. "And thanks for that. I thought you'd tell me I was daft."

"I think you are daft. But . . ." Kerry shook her head. "I can't take the risk that you're *not*. And I managed to convince a magistrate using your argument, so that's a point in your favor."

In another moment, she'd pulled up in Blenheim Crescent. "You haven't changed your mind, have you?" Kerry gave Gemma a searching look as she turned off the engine.

"No. It's just . . . if I'm right, the consequences are dreadful."

"Consequences are not our job, thank God." Kerry glanced in her rearview mirror as a panda car pulled up behind them, then a crime scene van. "Let's get the show on the road."

By the time they reached the door, the uniformed officer had joined them, and the SOCOs were getting their gear from the van. Kerry punched the bell. When the door opened, she said, "Mrs. Cusick, may we come in? We have a warrant to search the premises."

"What?" Nita Cusick stared at them. "What are you talking about? You said you needed to speak to me, and I've already delayed my business appointment . . ." She seemed to take in the uniformed constable, and then the two SOCOs carrying their evidence cases. "What the hell do you think you're doing?" Her voice was shrill. "If my bloody husband has put you up to this—"

"Mrs. Cusick." Kerry held up the warrant. "If you can just confirm that you've seen this document."

Nita Cusick peered at the sheet of paper, then looked back at Kerry. "No. You can't just come in my house. You can't persecute my child."

"Is your son here, Mrs. Cusick?" Kerry said with a glance at Gemma, as she knew very well that he wasn't. "Because, if so, we can have a family liaison officer come sit with him."

"No. No, he's—he's not here."

"Then, I suggest we go inside." When Kerry and Gemma and the constable, who was very large and very dark skinned, moved forward, Nita Cusick stepped back. The officers shifted direction to the right, into the sitting room, so that Nita had no choice but to step that way. "Why don't we have a seat?" Kerry suggested.

The constable, who Gemma had learned was named Jacobs, took his place by the door, relaxed in parade-rest stance. They could see the two SOCOs come through with their kits, one going upstairs, one going down. They had instructions to look for specific items, as well as anything else they thought might be germane to Reagan Keating's death or the attack on Asia Ford.

Nita had backed up to one of the sofas and sat down as if unaware of her actions. She was dressed, not in the yoga gear she'd worn the previous day, but in a fitted gray linen dress. The color did nothing for her sallow complexion, and as she sat, the dress rode up unflatteringly on her thighs.

The spoiled roses were gone, Gemma noticed, although the room still seemed stuffy even with yesterday's drop in temperature. Once again she had to fight the urge to open a window.

"You can't just go through my things," Nita said, starting to rise again, then subsiding as she glanced at the constable. "What are they looking for?"

"Mrs. Cusick, it's routine to search the domicile of a person who has been murdered," Kerry told her. "It should have been done much sooner, but the circumstances of Reagan Keating's death were a bit unusual. Why don't I go make us some tea while we wait?" she added, as she and Gemma had prearranged. "I'm sure this won't take long."

"But I don't—" began Nita, but Kerry had already left the room.

"I'm so sorry we have to put you through this, Nita," said Gemma. "I'm sure it's unnecessary." She rolled her eyes in the direction Kerry had taken. "Regulations can be such a pain."

Nita visibly relaxed, but the look she gave Gemma was still wary. "How did you know Jess wasn't here?"

"Oh, we contacted his father. Routine with a missing child. He told us Jess was safe and sound and that he might be less upset away from reminders of Reagan for a few days."

"He would say that." Nita's mouth tightened. "That—that

nurse probably egged him on. I told him he was violating his custody agreement and that I'd be calling my solicitor."

"I'm sure you want what's best for your son," Gemma said, going for soothing if noncommittal.

"Well, yes, of course. But his audition for the Royal Ballet is coming up, and his father has given him some silly idea that he should stay where he is."

"That's the London Boys Ballet School, isn't it? Where Jess takes classes during the week? I thought it was quite good."

"*Quite* good sums it up, I would say. It's merely a stepping-stone to training with a world-famous company."

"Oh? I'd thought of looking into it for my son."

"Your boy is, what, seven?" Nita gave Toby and his future dance career a dismissive shrug. "I doubt it will matter much where you send him."

Gemma forced a smile. "Jess has his heart set on the Royal Ballet, then?"

"Of course he does," Nita said, frowning, as if Gemma had just uttered a blasphemy.

"Then it would be a terrible shame if anything—or anyone—was to stand in the way of Jess succeeding at the audition."

"That's what I told her—" Nita clamped her mouth shut, the wariness returning in full force.

"Do you mean Reagan?" Gemma asked. "Surely she agreed with you?"

"Of course she did. She understood how important this is for Jess."

Gemma made an effort to keep her tone light, as if the question was of no importance. "So she would never have suggested that Jess do anything that might jeopardize his future in dance?"

"Of course not."

"And you wouldn't have minded her encouraging Jess to tell Henry Su's parents that he'd taken Henry's asthma inhaler on the day Henry died?"

For an instant, Nita Cusick's face went completely blank, as if Gemma had spoken suddenly in a foreign tongue. Then her eyes opened wide with shock and the color drained from her face. "I don't know what you're talking about," she whispered.

"I think you do," Gemma said quietly. "Jess told Reagan that he'd picked up Henry's inhaler on the day Henry died. Jess was fed up with Henry's bullying, and decided it would serve Henry right if he got in trouble for losing the inhaler. He put it in his pocket and went home. He didn't know that Henry would get himself stuck in the shed and panic.

"Jess wanted to tell the Sus. Reagan supported him, but told him he had to discuss it with you first. You, however, told him that telling his secret would ruin his life *and* his dance career, and that you'd take any steps to see that didn't happen."

"But you can't know—that's absurd. Jess would never—"

Gemma had no intention of admitting that Jess had told her. "We've recovered Reagan's computer," she said, as if that explained everything. They had, in fact, as it had been in Jess's backpack and his father had brought it into the station that morning. Whether there was anything useful on it remained to be seen. It was password protected and Jess had not known the password.

"Reagan told Jess on Friday evening that she might be leaving your employ—she thought that forcing Jess to keep his secret would haunt him for the rest of his life. Quite an annoying stickler for honesty, that girl." Gemma shook her head in mock dismay.

"Honesty?" Nita said with sudden venom. "She was a bloody

self-righteous prig. How could she possibly know what was best for Jess? I'm his mother."

Gemma nodded. "Of course you are. And I can understand that. I wouldn't want someone else telling me what to do with my kids. Or someone telling me where my son should dance, after all my hard work and sacrifice to give him the best opportunity."

"Jess has to dance for the Royal Ballet." Tears trembled on Nita's lower eyelids. "Otherwise it will have all been for nothing. All these years, all the things I've given up . . ."

It didn't look to Gemma as if Nita had given up much at all, but she nodded and leaned forward, inviting more confidence. "You must have spoken to Reagan. Tried to talk her into staying. And to dropping any silly idea about Jess going to the Sus."

"I—she went out. I never saw her again."

"But you texted her, when she was out with her friends on Friday night. They told us you did. They also said she was very upset and didn't want to talk to you." Gemma had no problem with her invention.

"No, I didn't text her. I'm sure I didn't." Nita's body seemed to be curving in on itself, knees up, shoulders forward, in almost a fetal position. "I can't think why she'd have said that. It's not true."

"But Reagan always told the truth. She was breaking up with her boyfriend because he was dishonest."

"She didn't tell me about Edward Miller," Nita said in a flash of spite that drew back her lips. "That wasn't honest."

"She meant to," Gemma said, soothing again. "I think she would have told you sooner, but when Jess told her about the inhaler it threw a spanner in the works. And she wanted to finalize breaking it off with Hugo Gold before she entered into any kind of relationship with Edward."

"She was living in my house. Eating my food. Poisoning my child with her ideas." Nita wiped at her mouth. "And then she— she seduced my client. Edward."

For the first time it occurred to Gemma that Nita might have had designs on Edward Miller, had perhaps mistaken his friendly demeanor for something more.

"Behind your back," she agreed. "Even more reason to be angry with her."

Nita nodded, her head bobbing with the ferocity of it. "She had no right. Just like she had no right to tell Jess what to do."

"So, of course you wanted to talk to her," said Gemma, moving past Nita's denial of the texting. "You had to know what she meant to do about Jess. If she meant to tell the Sus about the inhaler. I know," she added confidingly, "I wouldn't have been able to stand not knowing. But maybe she wouldn't want to tell you. Or maybe she wouldn't tell you the truth." She realized now that it would never have occurred to Nita that Reagan wouldn't lie.

Gemma had been aware for some time of the hum of activity in the house—soft voices, footsteps, the creaks of the treads on the stairs. She only hoped Kerry would give her a few minutes more. Jacobs the constable stood unmoving as a statue, out of Nita's line of vision, and Gemma didn't dare glance in his direction.

"You thought if Reagan was tipsy, she might tell you, didn't you, Nita? The only problem was that Reagan wasn't much of a drinker. But what if she drank something really tasty—a gin punch, maybe? You must have had a good supply of Red Fox. Then, she wouldn't notice if the alcohol was a lot stronger than she was used to."

Nita stared at her, her eyes dilated, her thin chest rising and falling rapidly. Gemma thought of a rabbit caught in the glare of oncoming headlamps.

Swallowing, Gemma went on. "It was such a lovely night. Warm. Unusual for May. A perfect night for a chat in the garden. With a candle, a pitcher of punch, two pretty glasses. And Reagan in her white dress. She might have walked out of a fairy tale.

"And it worked a charm, didn't it? Just the two of you, on the soft cool grass, with nothing but the stars and the flicker of the candle. She drank the punch and she giggled. When her head started spinning, she flopped back onto the grass, the white dress spread all around her like foam."

"You can't know," Nita whispered. "You can't possibly know that."

Gemma clasped her hands together to stop them trembling. "But when you asked her what she meant to do about Jess—surely, you said, she must understand how essential it was that nothing interrupt his progress—she said that nothing was more important than Jess doing the right thing. That she'd help him in any way she could. And you couldn't have that, could you, Nita?"

Nita blinked, once, but there was no flicker of emotion in her eyes. Thinking of Asia Ford's bleeding head, Gemma was suddenly very glad of the constable's presence in the room.

"*Just shut her up*," Gemma murmured, a thread of sound. "*Shut her up*, you thought. Stuff her mouth with that soft white skirt. And she must have felt soft, too, with her girl's skin, almost like a child's. She struggled a bit. The candle tipped and went out, the wax spilling on the grass. Poof. And then she was gone, just like the candle.

"But you couldn't leave her," she went on, swallowing against the nausea. "Rumpled like a rag doll. So you straightened her dress. You laid her out as if she'd just fallen asleep, didn't you, Nita?"

Another blink, and the slightest shake of the head, not quite a negation.

Gemma took a breath. "Where did Reagan leave her phone, Nita? In the kitchen? In her room? It must have been a shock when you'd tidied everything away, then the text came through. From Edward. Surely, not *your* Edward, you thought. Did you recognize the number? What if he came here? You must have panicked. So you texted back, just in case.

"Where's the phone, now, Nita? Did you keep it? You had to read the texts and the e-mails, had to see if she'd told anyone. It must have been an even bigger shock the next day when you found her computer gone. Had she given it to someone? Had someone been in the house?

"But nothing happened except that Jess stopped talking to you. He wouldn't tell you where he'd been on Saturday morning. Did he know something? Guess something?" Gemma was relentless now. "Had he loved her more than you? Then, when Asia rang and said she'd seen him in the garden when he should have been in school, you panicked. Real panic, this time. Asia told you she thought he might have taken her alcohol, but you didn't want anyone connecting you, or Jess, to the missing bottle.

"Asia told you something else, too, didn't she, Nita? Roland Peacock saw you that night, coming back across the garden. He was coming to tell Asia their tryst for that night was off. His wife had come home unexpectedly, and his son was ill. He didn't dare use the phone to ring her. Neither of them wanted to speak up, for obvious reasons." It was Roland who'd rung Gemma that morning and haltingly said that since the attack on Asia, he'd decided he couldn't keep anything from the police, even if it meant coming clean to his wife. The affair, he'd admitted, had been going on for some time, and more than once Clive Glenn had glimpsed him leaving Asia's house at daybreak.

Nita's eyes had widened, but she didn't speak. Gemma took a breath and went on. "So you took your chances, Nita. You had to shut Asia up, too.

"But it didn't work, and Asia told us Jess never touched the bottles. Only you, Nita."

"You can't know," she whispered, running her tongue around her lips. "You can't know any of it. I won't tell you."

"Would Roland Peacock have been next? Where would it have stopped, Nita?"

The spasm in Nita's hand told Gemma more than enough. When the hall door opened, she looked up with relief. She couldn't bear another moment in the room with Nita Cusick.

It was Kerry, beckoning her. When Gemma stood, she found she was soaked with sweat.

Jacobs, his face still impassive, but his eyes warm with understanding, nodded at her as she went out. When the door closed behind her, she leaned against the hallway wall for a moment.

"Gemma?" said Kerry. "Are you okay?"

"Yeah. Fine." Gemma straightened up. "What have you got?"

Kerry held up two evidence bags. One held a mobile phone, the other an asthma rescue inhaler. "Found both of them in her bedroom drawer, buried under her frilly knickers. People, honestly." She rolled her eyes. "The phone is not password protected. It's Reagan Keating's. And Nita can't claim the inhaler. It has Henry Su's name on the label."

"Christ." Gemma sagged against the wall again, her knees weak.

"Not to mention," Kerry continued, "the bottle of grain alcohol in the back of her liquor cabinet. The fingerprint techs will have a field day with it. And," she added, not to be interrupted, "they found the shoes you described her wearing yesterday. The

UV light brought out what looks like blood spatter on the toes. Did you get anything from her?"

"An admission? No. Confirmation?" Gemma nodded. "Yes."

"Then let's get her down to the station," said Kerry, "and we'll cross our own frilly knickers that the prosecutor will run with it."

It took effort on Kincaid's part to extricate himself quickly from the meeting with Lindsay Quinn, and without showing anything other than mild interest in what Quinn had told him. He thanked Quinn for the tea, shook his hand, and left the man looking mildly puzzled.

When he came out of the bar into the upper concourse, someone was pounding on the nearer of the two pianos in the lower concourse. Rachmaninoff, he thought, one of the piano concertos, well played. It was the music his mother had listened to when cleaning house, or when working out a knotty problem, but at that moment it made Kincaid feel like his head would explode. He headed quickly for the nearest exit, but as soon as he came out into Euston Road, his mobile rang.

It was Doug. "You won't believe what I dug up," Doug said when Kincaid answered. "Your bloke in Cheshire who topped himself? Retired Chief Inspector Fletcher?"

"What about him?" Kincaid asked, ducking his head and covering his other ear to shut out the traffic noise.

"He worked for Deputy Assistant Commissioner Trent. SO15."

Kincaid felt like he'd been kicked in the gut a second time. "Shit." He took a breath, trying to patch things together. "We need to talk. Not on the phone. Where are you?"

"Home," said Doug. "Skived off work, didn't I? Melody, too. She's at the paper. We'll probably both lose our jobs."

"I only hope that's the worst of it," Kincaid muttered, thinking furiously. He didn't dare meet them at King's Cross, or anywhere near Holborn. "Look. Meet me where we met the other day, okay?" Maybe he was being ridiculously paranoid, but he didn't care. "And ask Melody if she can check whether our DAC has roundabout financial interests in King's Cross Development or its subsidiaries. Then meet her in Kensington and come together. Take a taxi."

Doug laughed. "You're taking the piss."

"No, I'm bloody well not," Kincaid snapped. "Just do it."

He walked. It would take Doug and Melody some time to get to Hatton Garden, and he needed time to think. Taking Gray's Inn Road south, he passed Wren Street and Roger Street and the Duke, the pub where Denis had felt safe meeting him on Saturday night. He hoped he was not as naive as Denis had been, in thinking he wouldn't be traced to the Scotch Malt Whisky Society.

It wasn't until he reached Greville Street that he remembered the whisky society didn't open until twelve. Feeling a prize idiot, he settled in the pub downstairs, texting Doug accordingly and nursing a coffee. The pub had begun to fill for lunch and a sudden shower had drenched the streets, then vanished as quickly as it had appeared. By the time Doug and Melody spilled out of a taxi in Greville Street, it was straight up noon.

He met them outside and together they went upstairs to the society rooms above the pub. Kincaid ordered them all sandwiches and more coffee, then told them what he'd learned from Lindsay Quinn. Taking the Polaroid from his pocket, he passed it to them.

"Bloody sodding hell," Doug said succinctly, staring at it.

"That's her, without a doubt," agreed Melody, "but who's the other woman, the pretty brunette?"

"Not germane at the moment," Doug told her. "You do realize Evelyn Trent's Nick Callery's boss, too? I found his home address, by the way. It is in the Gasholders complex. So, did Callery set up the meeting with Stanton, or did Stanton arrange it on Callery's patch, thinking he could get the upper hand?"

"If he did, he certainly failed." Kincaid had a thought. "Although, when Nick Callery showed up for no apparent reason at Holborn on Monday, he had a cut on his right hand. He said it was a kitchen-knife accident."

"Maybe Stanton attacked him," Doug said, "and it went pear shaped."

"I'd call 'dead in the canal' pear shaped, all right." Kincaid flashed a smile at the barmaid as she delivered their coffee. When she'd moved out of hearing distance, he continued. "Now, I'm wondering if Callery turned up at Holborn because he knew how close Tom Faith is to Denis, and he was fishing for information."

"Well, it gets worse," said Doug, and glanced at Melody.

"I didn't have time to do much." She shrugged apologetically. "There's nothing as obvious as her name listed as a shareholder in KCD. But when I followed the links into some of the subsidiary corporations, I found an Evelyn Jaynes-Trent. I don't think it would be a stretch to think they were one and the same."

The three looked at each other in silence, their coffee cooling. Then, Kincaid summed it up. "So, is it reasonable to assume that she's been using her position to protect her financial interests?"

"Rogue ops?" said Doug, but it wasn't really a question. "Okay. I can run with that. Murdering people who are inconvenient? Sure. But what are we going to do about it? I don't want to end up like

Ryan. Or like Stanton, evil bastard that he was. Or like your sad bloke in Cheshire. Who would we take this to that would believe us? And that we could be certain wasn't on her payroll? It seems not even Denis Childs had the answer to that." He sat back while the barmaid set down their sandwiches, then, when she'd gone, leaned forward again, his eyes earnest behind his glasses. "Putting Ryan into Matthew Quinn's protest group might have passed as legit. But everything since is completely bonkers. And who's going to question her, for God's sake? She's counterterrorism!"

"I know who," said Melody.

She might have dropped a bomb in the center of the table. Kincaid and Doug swiveled to stare at her, Doug already with a mouthful of roast beef, fear not having dampened his appetite.

"What are you talking about?" Doug mumbled around his sandwich, frowning.

But Kincaid suddenly understood. "Your father. He knew about Denis being attacked before anyone else did. And his hints about Denis's past —maybe he knew about the undercover ops."

"My dad's never liked the idea of the police putting spies among ordinary citizens who aren't committing a crime. It was one of the reasons he didn't want me joining the police."

Kincaid knew Melody had never wanted to trade on her father's power and influence—or to be seen by her colleagues as an untrustworthy source of leaks.

He also hoped that he'd so far managed to keep Melody and Doug off Trent and Callery's radar. If Melody took what they knew to her father, and Ivan used it, it wouldn't take long for Trent to work out Ivan Talbot's "undisclosed source." "Melody, you'd be putting yourself right in the line of fire," Kincaid said.

"Every second we wait puts us all at risk," she answered. "You, me, Doug, Gemma. Your kids. You can't think she won't make those connections."

Kincaid knew she was right. Doug did, too, as he gave her a reluctant nod.

"What about putting your father in danger?" Kincaid asked.

"He's broken bigger cases than this. And the paper has the resources to do a lot of digging that we can't do. I barely skimmed the surface."

"You're sure?" Kincaid asked.

Melody pushed aside her untouched plate. "Yes. And I'll go now." An unexpected smile lit her face. She added, "Before I lose my nerve."

They watched her go. Doug said, with a mixture of irritation and pride, "Bloody stubborn woman."

But Kincaid had gone back to worrying over Evelyn Trent. "Why Craig?" he asked. "The others make sense, I suppose, in a demented sort of way. But if she had Angus and Edie Craig killed, why take such an enormous risk?"

"They go way back, obviously." Doug tapped the Polaroid, which still lay on the table. "Who knows how many pies she's had her fingers in over the years? Maybe he had something on her, and he threatened to use it if she allowed charges to be brought against him."

Kincaid stared at the Polaroid. "You can't discount Denis. How much did he know? And what did he do when he came back from Singapore that made her set her dogs on him so quickly?" He picked up a crisp, put it down again. Like Melody, he'd lost his appetite.

"It's too bad we can't ask him," Doug said. "Otherwise, I don't know where we go—"

Kincaid waved a hand to cut him off. "I'm an idiot," he said. "A blinking idiot. There is one person who would know what Denis did. I just never thought to ask."

Diane Childs had told Kincaid she was just leaving the London, but would wait for him in the hospital café if he could come soon.

Kincaid felt more uncomfortable now than ever, visiting the hospital, but he didn't want to put Diane off by asking her to meet somewhere else. He walked from Whitechapel tube towards the hospital complex, his jacket collar turned up against the wind, but the cold chill he felt had nothing to do with the weather. Twice, he looked back, the hair standing up on the back of his neck. The second time, he thought he glimpsed a man in a silvery gray suit, slipping through the crowd. But when he looked again, there were only some Asian teenagers in tracksuits, and a group of sari-clad women carrying shopping baskets.

He found Diane Childs waiting as she'd promised, at a table in the corner of the hospital café. Her blouse, today a deep magenta, looked startlingly vivid against the room's institutional colors. She stood, greeting him with a smile and an unexpected hug.

"Are you all right?" she asked when he'd sat across from her. "You sounded worried on the phone."

"I'm so sorry to bother you with this," Kincaid said. "You have enough on your plate as it is." He was feeling his way into it, not sure how to put things. "But something has come up that I thought you might be able to help me with. It might have to do with the reason Denis was attacked."

Diane's fine, dark brows lifted in startled inquiry. "Go on."

Taking a breath, Kincaid plunged on. "I don't know how much Denis confided in you, but some years ago, I believe he worked with a man named Angus Craig."

Diane looked more puzzled. "If you're asking me if Denis was in Special Branch, yes, he was."

"An undercover assignment?"

"Yes. Although I'm not sure I'm supposed to say that. And he did work with Craig. I only know because Craig came to the house once back when Denis fell ill." She grimaced. "Horrible man."

Kincaid couldn't argue that point. "Denis was ill?" he asked.

"Yes. We didn't know at first what it was. It ended his Special Branch assignment. The first time, they said it was a severe virus, but the same symptoms kept recurring. It was years before they diagnosed it as hep C. Still, it got him out of that job." She shook her head. "But something happened at the end of that posting, just as he was taken ill. I don't know what it was—he would never tell me. But it . . . I'm not sure I can explain. He was never quite the same after that." Sighing, she added, "I'm being fanciful, aren't I? I should be thankful that whatever happened, it kept him at a desk."

"Did Denis ever mention having worked with DAC Trent in those days?"

"Evelyn?" Diane looked surprised. "No, he didn't. I always assumed Special Branch was very much a boys' club." She frowned. "Honestly, I never got the impression he liked her much. I was surprised when she came to the hospital to see him. Policy, I suppose." The look she gave him was sharp now, curious and wary. "But what does this have to do with some mugger hitting Denis over the head?"

"I'm not certain," Kincaid temporized. "But can you tell me one more thing? When Denis came back to work after his liver transplant, did he do anything unusual?"

Diane considered a long moment, pushing her empty coffee cup an inch in either direction. Then she met his eyes. "I suppose it's all right to tell you. It was Angus Craig and his wife. I met her once or twice at police functions. Lovely woman. I could never see—well, never mind that. They died, in the autumn. Craig shot her, Denis said, then set their house on fire and shot himself. At least that's what the investigation ruled."

"But Denis didn't believe that."

"No. He was quite ill at the time. He was so upset, I was afraid for him. We'd already made the arrangements to go to Singapore, thank God, and he agreed to go ahead with the surgery. Afterwards, I thought he'd dropped the matter. Then, when we came home, he told me he meant to pull the case files as soon as he was back at the Yard. Stubborn bastard." She smiled at Kincaid. "But you can ask him yourself."

Kincaid gaped at her. "What?"

"He's been conscious for two days. I was just going to ring you when you called. He told me I could tell you and Tommy, but no one else."

CHAPTER TWENTY-FIVE

There was no way she was going to talk to her dad at the paper, or in a public place. Knowing that her mother had gone early to the country house for the weekend, she rang Ivan and asked if he would meet her at the town house.

"Lunch?" he'd asked.

"No, no, I'm all right," Melody assured him. But when she arrived at the town house in Kensington Square, Ivan was already there and in the kitchen. He'd taken off his jacket and tie and thrown his old apron over his bespoke shirt and trousers. The door to the patio stood open, framing the shifting shadows thrown by fast-moving clouds.

Her father wrapped her in a hug, then held her at arm's length, which as usual made her feel like a six-year-old. Ivan didn't wear cologne, but he always smelled slightly of shaving soap, a clean scent that made her feel comforted. "No coffee," he said, frowning as he released her. "You look peaky. And you're even thinner than you were on Sunday. Here, I've made you a sandwich." As he moved aside, she saw a plate holding a granary-bread sandwich and a sliced green apple. And, beside it, a glass of milk. Definitely, six years old.

She sighed and sat. There was no help for it. Unlike her mother, who'd grown up expecting to be fed and cared for by other people, her father had a deep-seated need to look after people in a concrete way. Conversation was impossible without acquiescence.

The sandwich, she saw, was thick ham, with cheddar and pickle, and once she took a bite she realized she was ravenous. The milk was perfect, smooth, cold, and creamy, and by the time she'd finished both, she thought she could speak without shaking. While she ate, Ivan had made a pot of tea. He sat down across from her and poured for them both. "Now, what's all this about?" he said.

In the taxi, she'd thought of all sorts of beginnings, but now she simply said, "Dad, how do you know Denis Childs?"

"Ah." He studied her over the top of his cup, assessing. It suddenly occurred to Melody that her father and Denis were much alike, two big men who moved with unexpected grace. Two men, near the same age, who handled power and position with intelligence and moral integrity. "I wondered if you might ask," said Ivan, settling back to tell a story, cradling his delicate china cup in his large hands. "I'd moved up to a desk at the paper, you see, but I couldn't resist getting out in the street with a camera when things were going on. It was Notting Hill Carnival in, let's see, it would have been 1994. Things turned ugly. Some white thugs taunted a group protesting Stephen Lawrence's murder. One of the protesters stood up to them, then went to the aid of an injured bystander. I got a great shot—front-page worthy—but I never published it."

He shook his head, his gaze abstracted by the memory. "I couldn't have said why. Something wasn't right. The guy didn't feel like a protester to me. Too decisive, too much in command under pressure.

"I didn't think much more about it until a few years later. I recognized him as the DCI handling the press conference for a high-profile murder case. I made a point to have a chat, afterwards." Ivan shrugged his big shoulders. "We've kept up over the years, Denis and I. Never publicly, you understand."

No, of course not, thought Melody. Ivan had always avoided public alliances. He said they kept him from saying what needed to be said. "How did you know, when Denis was attacked?" she asked.

"Tom Faith called me."

Melody nodded. She should have known that, too.

"I thought it was an unlikely mugging," Ivan went on. "And that perhaps your lot should look into it." His Geordie accent came out strong and deliberate.

"Why didn't you just say so?"

Ivan grinned. "The paper can't be involved."

Melody couldn't help smiling back. "You're Machiavellian, you know that?"

Ivan sobered. "Maybe so. As is our chief superintendent, but maybe this time he was a bit too Machiavellian for his own good. What's happened? I've heard nothing from hospital."

Melody told him, starting, haltingly, with Ryan Marsh's part in the St. Pancras protest, with his disappearance and their discovery of his hideout, and of how he'd given them information that had led them to the killer in that case. The tremor came back to her hands as she told him about Ryan's death, and how for the past months she'd lived with thinking he'd shot himself, that they'd all somehow failed him.

Ivan Talbot was a good listener. He let her start and stop, not interrupting, watching her with no sign of impatience. She struggled to put the events of the last week—less than a week—into a linear form. There had been Kincaid's meeting with Denis and Denis's subsequent attack, Kincaid's growing certainty, confirmed by Rashid, that Ryan's death had been murder and that Denis had been deliberately targeted. Then, the discovery that Ryan Marsh was somehow linked with Angus Craig. Ivan's eyebrows rose at that, but still he didn't interrupt.

"Doug and I figured out what you could have told us," she said with no small annoyance. "That Denis was undercover, probably for Special Branch." When Ivan merely nodded, she went on. "Then a body turned up in the Regent's Canal, but the guy's fingerprints didn't match his ID and his prints said he was a cop. Not a very good one, either. He had the records gap that indicated undercover work, but he also had a history of violent behavior and had disappeared altogether in the last few years."

"Do you have a photo?" Ivan asked, surprising her.

Melody took out her mobile, pulled up the photo of Michael Stanton, and handed it across.

Ivan studied it with a frown. "It was years ago, but I'd swear this is the man who threw the bottle that day at Carnival, the one who injured the bystander. He was convincing, I can tell you. I'd no idea *he* was a cop. Special Branch must have put spies into both camps. The tension over the Lawrence murder was explosive."

"We think Angus Craig was their handler. They were all connected. Then, Duncan found—" Melody stopped, pulling the edges of her cardigan tight across her chest. She'd managed to talk about Ryan's death—his murder, even—but this, she wasn't sure she could say. Her dad waited. She sipped her cooling tea, swallowed, managed to go on. "Duncan found a witness who saw Ryan Marsh with Stanton—this guy"—she tapped her mobile— "in Angus Craig's village on the night the Craigs died. I don't think—I can't think—that Ryan was responsible. But we believe that the Craigs were murdered, too. We started to wonder who didn't want Angus Craig to go to trial, and what Denis knew, or might have learned that last night, from Angus Craig."

"I would back up," Ivan said thoughtfully, "and ask who put your undercover cop into the protest group that was causing trouble for development in King's Cross."

Spoken, Melody thought, like a true journalist. "We got there, in the end." She looked her father in the eyes. She could quit here. She could walk away. If she told him, what would she be getting him into? What damage might it do to both her parents? And to the paper? Was it worth the risk?

But she knew, from the expression on his face, that she'd already gone too far. Ivan Talbot wouldn't stop now. Here was a story to rival the biggest of his career. And the safety of a man he considered a friend was at stake.

"We think," said Melody, "that it was Deputy Assistant Commissioner Trent." And then she told him why.

He slept, uneasily. They had cut off his sedation, but he still felt fragmented, unanchored. His head ached, and his dreams left him sweating. When he woke, he fretted over the things he couldn't remember. He knew he'd met Duncan at the pub. He remembered walking to Roger Street. He remembered talking at the table. He remembered leaving. And after that, a blank.

They'd told him where and how he'd been found. Had he been watched and followed? he wondered now. Or had someone known his route and lain in wait? Had he compromised Duncan? His wife kept assuring him that Duncan was fine, but he couldn't shake the feeling that he'd unleashed havoc on more than himself.

He slept again, this time dreaming of fire, and fear, and faces from the past. When he woke, she stood at the foot of his bed. "Why did you walk out?" he asked.

Then, he realized that had been the past, and that he knew now why she'd walked away from him that night in the pub more than twenty years before. His head was suddenly clear and a frisson of fear made the hairs rise on his arms. He groped for the bed control, raising the head until he could look her straight in the eye. But then he fumbled the keypad and it tumbled away, dangling out of reach at the end of its cord.

"But I just got here," she said, and smiled.

"How did you know I was awake?" he asked with a slight frown, conveying—he hoped—only a mild curiosity. He saw that she'd pulled the privacy curtain separating the bed and the main part of the room from the door.

"A little bird in your friend Tommy's office." She shook her head, made a *tsk* of disapproval. "Den, did you think I wouldn't notice you'd pulled the Craig files? I thought you had more sense. Why, after all this time, would you care what happened to Angus Craig? I'd say he got his just desserts."

"No one deserves to be murdered, not even Angus. And what about Edie, Lynn?" The photos in the case file were still sharp in his mind. A surge of rage made him clench his fists in the flimsy blanket, but he kept his voice calm. "Was she just collateral damage?"

"Angus Craig had every reason to commit suicide. And it's unfortunate that angry, desperate people often take those closest to them." Evelyn Trent shrugged, and he could have sworn he heard the silk of her very expensive suit rustle against itself. "We both know that, Denis." She might have been correcting a slow child.

He looked at this woman, wondering how he could ever have thought her a friend. When he first began to suspect her hand in the seeping corruption within the force, he'd told himself she hadn't been bad in the beginning. But now he knew that the rot had been there from the first, and that the failure to see it had been his.

"I know," he said, "that Angus Craig, whatever else he may have done, did not murder his wife. And he did not commit suicide."

Lynn looked amused. "Not even you could tell that from the investigation file."

"He told me himself."

"What?" For the first time, she looked startled. And irritated. "Don't be daft. He couldn't have."

"But he did. I went to see him that night. I wanted him to admit what he'd done to Sheila. I wanted to know if she was the first. He laughed at me and told me I was a fool.

"It was you who killed Sheila, he said. When you paged him that night, he'd just left Mickey and the others in the pub. He knew it wasn't Mickey who'd throttled her. He knew it wasn't me. I could barely stand, much less strangle someone."

"Denis." She shook her head, as if exasperated, but she moved a step closer, her hand resting lightly on the foot of the bed. "You really are ill. What utter nonsense. Are you going to suggest I raped her, too?"

"She wasn't raped. There were no signs of sexual assault. All that business of straightening her skirt, that was for my benefit. Window dressing."

"Really?" Lynn said, frowning, cocking her head a little as she looked at him. It was a mannerism he remembered. He'd once found it fetching. "Assuming for a moment that the blow on your head didn't knock you completely senseless," she went on, "why on earth would I do such a thing?"

"Because she was a spy." He licked his lips. "A spy among the spies, a cat among the pigeons. Ironic, don't you think? And put there by Angus Craig himself—irony of ironies—because he didn't trust us not to go native. If you were feeling too much sympathy for your antidiscrimination protesters or your animal rights activists, who would you confide in but party girl Sheila?

"But Sheila found something completely unexpected. You were playing both sides of the coin, taking payoffs from your protest group in return for information on police activities. You were always seen together, you and Sheila. Someone approached her, thinking she was in on the deal. Sheila must have tried to talk to you about it, because you were friends.

"What you didn't know when you decided to shut her up was that she'd already told Angus." His throat was going dry. Very deliberately, he reached for his water cup and took a sip from the straw, wondering if he could throw the water in her face. And what good it would do if he did. His hand shook.

"Assuming any of this rubbish was true," Lynn said slowly "why didn't he stop me?" Her voice was still controlled, but he could see the rapid rise and fall of her chest.

"And blow open his whole Special Branch operation, the operation he'd spent years putting together?" He managed a croak of laughter. "But he had an even better reason than that. Leverage over you. It served him well for more than twenty years as you rose in the ranks. Complaints against him were ignored or dismissed. But he asked too much the last time, didn't he, Lynn? He was blown, facing assault allegations and a manslaughter charge at the least. He wanted you to make it all go away. Threatened you, in fact, if it didn't. Angus Craig had been as useful to you as you were to him, but you'd had enough, and you couldn't be certain he didn't have something that could hurt you.

"He was cocky that night," he continued. "Certain you'd come through for him and all his troubles would vanish in a puff of smoke. Which they did, just not in the way he expected." Denis looked at her with revulsion. "Who did you get to do such a job, Lynn?"

"Stop calling me that," she snapped, and it was instantly clear that she'd dropped all pretense. "I'm Evelyn. I was always Evelyn. As for Angus, your old friend Mickey came in very handy. He never liked Angus much, especially after Angus deemed him unfit to continue in the job.

"Mickey didn't succeed as well with you, unfortunately for both of you. But he, at least, is no longer a problem."

"Dead?"

"Mmm. He thought he could take out his handler. Stupid of him. But when you kept breathing, he was afraid—rightfully so—that his usefulness had come to an end, so he tried to extricate himself. It's too bad he didn't hit you harder." She quirked an eyebrow. "I'm surprised, because he liked you even less than Angus." Sighing, she shook her head. "I'm sorry you woke up, Denis, really I am. It was very inconvenient of you."

Forcing a smile, he said, "What are you going to do, Lynn? Smother me with a pillow?"

"Don't be so dramatic, Denis," she said, but her voice was hard, the malice palpable. She stepped closer, leaning towards him. "You know I don't need to do that. You do love your wife, you know.

That's always been your weakness. I don't think you could live with yourself if anything happened to her."

He shook his head. A mistake. The room rocked and it was a moment before he could gather himself for a denial. "That won't work with me twice, Lynn." But even as he said it, his dream came back to him, the fire and the terrible fear, and he wasn't sure he could hold firm.

Kincaid reached the lift corridor and hesitated. Diane had told him she'd already rung Faith. If Denis trusted the detective chief superintendent that much, was he a fool not to?

He paced, moving back so as not to block the lift, and keeping a watchful eye on the visitors going up or coming down. Then, his decision made, he found a secluded corner and called Tom Faith's mobile number. He might be a fool, but not fool enough to go through the station's phone system.

When Faith answered, he identified himself, then said, "Diane told me that Denis is awake. I'm at the London. Look, sir, you may think I'm daft, but I think he needs protection. I'll explain, but in the meantime, could you—"

"I'm on my way now," Faith told him. "I'll have a couple of uniforms meet me there. Then you can tell me what the hell is going on." The phone went dead in Kincaid's ear.

Going up in the lift, Kincaid checked for messages from Doug or Melody, but there was nothing. Not that he'd have expected to hear from either of them this soon, but he felt even more alone. Switching his phone to Silent, according to hospital visiting regulations, he slipped it into his pocket.

What, he wondered as the lift doors opened, was he going to say to Denis? Where would he even start?

It was the quiet of the afternoon, the lull in hospital routine, and the corridor was empty. When he reached the room, the door was closed. He debated knocking, then decided that if Denis was napping, he wouldn't wake him. Easing the door open, he stepped inside as quietly as he could manage.

He saw immediately that the privacy curtain between the door and the bed area had been pulled. When he heard the murmur of voices, his first thought was to back out and wait in the corridor until the nurse or aide had finished. But, then he heard Denis say, "Angus Craig, whatever else he may have done, did not murder his wife. And he did not commit suicide."

Then, a woman's voice murmured something Kincaid didn't recognize, but he caught the words "case files." His heart leapt into his throat as realization dawned.

Christ. It was Trent. It had to be. She hadn't sent Nick Callery— she'd come herself. He stood for a moment, paralyzed.

The voices grew louder. He could make out what she was saying now and suddenly he knew what to do. Taking a careful step nearer the curtain, he slipped the mobile from his pocket and found the voice recorder app, hoping to God it would capture the conversation on the other side of the curtain. Then, he stood, hardly daring to breathe, holding the mobile up as he listened in growing horror. Trent's heels clicked on the tile floor as if she'd stepped nearer the bed.

She said, clearly, "You do love your wife, you know, Denny. That's always been your weakness."

Kincaid couldn't make out Denis's muffled response. Panicked, he yanked the curtain aside and charged into the room.

"That's enough," he barked. "Don't touch him."

Evelyn Trent stood a foot from the head of Denis's bed. She whirled round, her face contorted with surprise. It seemed to take her a moment to recognize Kincaid. Then, she spat, "You. What are you doing here? Get out."

"Step away from the bed," Kincaid said levelly.

She must have seen something in his face, because she backed away from Denis in a movement that seemed almost involuntary.

"I heard everything," Kincaid told her. "You're not touching him. Or Diane."

But he saw her control returning, and with it, her contempt. "Really, Superintendent?" she said. "Or is it Inspector, now? I understand you've had a demotion recently. Something to do with your unprofessional conduct. I don't know what you think you've heard, but I'll have no trouble seeing you get a medical discharge."

"Like Frank Fletcher?" Kincaid asked. When her mouth tightened, he knew he'd hit the target. "Oh, yes, we know about Fletcher. We know about a lot of things." Kincaid pulled the mobile from his pocket and held it up. "And I got every word just now. Oh, and what do you know." He bared his teeth in a smile. "It's still recording."

Denis, who looked gray with exhaustion, managed a thumbs-up. "Good lad."

Trent's eyes went wide with shock. "You little shit." She glanced from the phone to his face and back again, calculating. Then she launched herself at Kincaid just as Chief Superintendent Faith came bursting through the door.

Kincaid managed to catch Trent's wrists as she scrabbled for his phone. Panting, he'd pinned her hands behind her back when Denis said, "You'd better give Mr. Kincaid a hand, Tom. I think the deputy assistant commissioner has done quite enough damage for one day."

CHAPTER TWENTY-SIX

"The only thing we haven't worked out," Kincaid told Gemma on Saturday morning as they nursed second cups of coffee at the kitchen table, "is why Kate Ling falsified Ryan Marsh's postmortem." It had taken him two days to catch Gemma up, and they were still talking over the details of the case.

"It's the pathologist's call on that type of injury," Gemma objected. "You said so yourself."

"Still, her judgment will come into question. You know that."

The gentleness of his tone made her bristle. "Let me talk to her. Off the record. I can't believe she was part of Trent's network."

"You don't want to believe it." Before she could argue, he added, "Neither do I. I suppose it can't hurt for you to have a word. She'll have read about Trent in the papers."

That morning, the *Chronicle* had published a front-page spread on Trent's arrest, promising a full investigation into the DAC's two decades of allegedly corrupt and illegal activities.

So it was that just after lunch, Kincaid having promised to drop Toby off at ballet and take Charlotte to the park, that Gemma found a parking spot on the Fulham Road, not too far from the Chelsea and Westminster Hospital. She'd left a message for Kate, asking if she could see her for a few minutes.

She found Kate Ling in her office, in jeans and a T-shirt, packing things into cardboard boxes. Gemma realized she'd never seen Kate out of scrubs. The pathologist's shoulders looked bird thin under the light fabric of the cotton T-shirt, and her jeans hung loosely on her hips.

"Gemma." Turning, Kate gave Gemma a smile, then crossed the room and gave her a most unprofessional hug.

"Kate." Gemma, taking in the open drawers and toppling stacks of books and papers, was shocked at the disarray. "What on earth are you doing?"

"Leaving." Kate shrugged. "I'm retiring from the service."

"What? Why?"

Kate pushed back the broomstick-straight hair Gemma had always envied from her forehead and blew out a sigh. "Maybe we'd better sit." Looking round, she moved a filled box from a chair and gestured Gemma into it, then perched against the only uncluttered corner of her desk. "I think I told you my mother was ill?" She touched a few silver-framed photographs which were, unlike the rest of the room's contents, stacked tidily, facedown on the desk. "She died on Thursday."

"Oh," said Gemma, feeling totally at a loss. "I'm so sorry."

"She had cancer. It wasn't unexpected. And she was very peaceful at the end."

"But—" Gemma gestured at the desk, then tried to start again. "I mean, I understand you must be reeling, but why this?"

"I'm in charge of her affairs, which are quite . . . complicated. And I need a rest."

It was true, Gemma saw. As soon as Kate relaxed, the exhaustion was clearly visible, her dark eyes smudged with weariness.

"What did you want to see me about?" Kate asked. "Is it the girl in the garden? I'm afraid I still don't have the DNA results."

"That's not why I'm here." Gemma hesitated, then made herself go on, as much as she hated now to do it. "It's about another post-mortem you did. Back in February. A man called Ryan Marsh."

"Oh, God," Kate whispered. She seemed to sink into herself, her cheekbones suddenly sharp against her pale skin. She looked so faint that Gemma quickly urged her into her own chair, moving books from another so that she could sit beside her.

She patted Kate's hand. "I'm sorry to upset you. But can you tell me about that postmortem?"

"The body came to me," Kate said slowly. "It looked like a routine suicide, except I thought it odd that I hadn't been called to the scene. And odd that I was getting a death from Hackney, but sometimes that happens when the other pathologists on the rota are overloaded. Then, a man showed up—he said he was a detective but he never showed me his identification. He was very charming at first and I didn't think anything out of the ordinary. We chatted a bit. Then, he smiled at me and said he was sure I would find the case a suicide.

"Do you know something I don't?" I asked him, puzzled. Then, he smiled again and said that if I didn't find it a suicide, my mother would learn what my father had been up to—" Kate took a breath and pressed her fingertips hard into the hollow of her cheeks.

"You have to understand," she went on, after a moment, "that my mother came from China when she was eight years old. Hers was a very strict Chinese family. My father—my father is third generation. The old values don't matter to him. But to my mother, there is nothing worse than dishonor to the family."

Gemma nodded. "I understand, I think. And your father had done something that would tarnish the family?"

Kate nodded. "Gambling debts. And he'd made bad investments in property. This man, this detective, said that if I didn't do as he asked, all of those debts would be called in. My father would be bankrupt. The family honor would be ruined."

From what Kincaid had told her, Gemma thought, it was classic Evelyn Trent manipulation, using for another purpose information she must have garnered through her property dealings. And Trent had, as usual, used a surrogate. She said, "Kate, this detective. He never told you his name?"

Kate shook her head. "No. You understand that none of this was said so baldly. He was—at least I thought at first—so reasonable about it all. And he was so good looking that I—I thought he—." She shook her head, coloring at the admission. "But when I realized what he was asking, I was mortified. And furious. I told him I'd make whatever determination I saw fit. He smiled and said he wished me the best.

"I meant to try to find out who he was. But then, when I'd done the postmortem, and I was sure it wasn't suicide, I was . . . afraid. The more I thought about him, the detective, the more I believed he would do what he said. There was something so cold beneath the charm, and I just hadn't the courage to risk my mother's peace of mind." She brushed at tears. "Who was he really, Gemma? The dead man? I've dreamed about him."

Gemma hesitated, but decided that if anyone had a right to know, it was Kate. "He was a cop who refused to do what the same people asked of him. I can't tell you if you made the wrong or the right decision, Kate. But I can be pretty certain they'd have carried out their threat if you hadn't. And your refusal wouldn't have helped their victim."

"Thank you," Kate said quietly. Then she sighed. "But it still doesn't make what I did right. I destroyed my honor, too. I knew I couldn't go on with the job after that, but I also knew if I quit, my mum would think I'd given up my job because of her illness. But now . . ."

"Can you describe the man who threatened you?" asked Gemma.

Kate grimaced. "I don't like to think about it. But, yes." She closed her eyes for a moment, as if concentrating on the memory. "Forties. Well built." Again, the flush of embarrassment. "Good looking, but the most striking thing was his hair. He was prematurely gray. And his eyes were gray, too. Gives me the creeps now, thinking about it."

"Bloody hell," said Gemma as it sunk in. "That was Nick Callery." She'd heard him described often enough that she had no doubt. Kincaid had called him "the gray ghost." Callery was the elusive piece in the puzzle. Other than the fact that he worked directly for Evelyn Trent, they had nothing concrete on him.

"You know him?" asked Kate.

"Not personally, no. But he works for DAC Trent."

"Bloody hell," Kate whispered as the implications sunk in.

"Kate, do you think you could identify him from a photo?"

She nodded, slowly. "I'm certain of it. He's not someone you'd forget."

Gemma took a breath. "I know it's a lot to ask, but would you testify about what he asked you to do? If you've read today's *Chronicle*, you'll have an idea what you're getting yourself into."

Kate was silent for a long moment. Then, she stood and went back to the box she'd been packing when Gemma came in, and shoved in another stack of books. "I love my job," she said at last, her voice rough. "And I'm bloody good at it. Whatever else that bastard did, he cost me my integrity. Yes, I bloody well will testify."

The heavy sitting-room curtains came down in a billow of dust. Melody stood back, surveying her handiwork with satisfaction. The dark brocade hangings had come with the flat and she'd always hated them. She'd kept them for the practical reasons—of which her mother never failed to remind her—of keeping the morning sun from fading the furniture, and of blocking the noise from Portobello Road.

"To hell with the noise," Melody said aloud, then sneezed from the dust. *And* she liked the morning sun. Cranking open the casements, she let fresh air stream into the flat, and went out to shop.

Two hours later, she came back loaded with carrier bags. She'd bought bright cushions for the sofa from a stall under the Westway, and two original photo prints of Portobello Road that she thought were perfect for the window wall.

Then, olives and fresh bread, some cheese, fresh fish, vegetables, and a riotous armful of tulips.

She busied herself, putting away groceries, hammering and hanging, finding a vase for the flowers, and lastly, setting her small dining table with the china and crystal her mother had given her. Why, she wondered, had she never done this before? Even when Andy had stayed with her, they'd eaten pizza or fish and chips at the coffee table.

As a reward for her labors, she made herself a cup of tea and sat down to work on the garden-center list she was making for tomorrow morning's shopping expedition with Doug. Although last weekend's unseasonably hot weather hadn't returned, it was clear and fine, and promised to continue so through the morrow. It would be perfect gardening weather.

When the flat bell buzzed, she started, nearly spilling her tea. She wasn't expecting anyone and her heart thumped with the old panic. But when she went to the intercom, the fuzzy voice she heard was Duncan's. Buzzing him up, she looked around a little wildly. He'd never been to her flat. No one, except Andy and her parents, had been to her flat, not even Doug.

When Kincaid pressed the flat bell a moment later, she unlatched the door and invited him in.

He stood just inside the sitting room, looking round with interest. "Nice place," he said. "It suits you. And a great view." He wore jeans and a cotton shirt, and looked a bit rumpled. Following her gaze, he picked a dried leaf from his hair. "Kids," he said in explanation. "Charlotte and I went to the park. Look, Melody, I'm sorry to intrude like this. But I have a few minutes before I have to pick Toby up from dance, and I'd been wanting a chance to talk."

"No, it's fine. Please, sit down," she blurted out, embarrassed at her lack of manners.

He took the single armchair, but sat on the edge, looking tall, and for Duncan, unusually awkward.

"Can I get you something?" Melody asked. "Tea? Some lemonade?"

"No, really, I won't keep you but a minute. I just wanted to say thank you. For speaking to your father."

Melody knew that Deputy Assistant Commissioner Trent was

being questioned on multiple counts, although it looked as though the prosecution might focus at least their initial charges on the crime with the most likelihood of direct physical evidence—the murder of Detective Constable Sheila Hawkins in 1994.

Tissue had been collected from under Hawkins's fingernails, but investigators had not tested Evelyn Trent for a match at that time. Trent's DNA had now been sampled, and considering the things Trent had said to Denis in the hospital room, a positive result was likely.

"You gave us insurance," Kincaid said. "It will be months, perhaps years, before we know who else was under her influence, what strings she might have pulled. Without the paper's involvement . . . I hate to think what might have happened, to all of us."

Melody nodded, unsure what to say. She could imagine all too well, but she still wasn't ready to talk about it.

"How's Andy?" Kincaid asked, gesturing at the dining table. "Somehow I thought he was still on tour."

"Oh. He is. In Norway at the moment, I think."

Andy had rung her, finally, on Thursday night. He'd had his phone stolen in Hanover, he said, and with the tour schedule, it had been a bitch to get a new one. And, he'd said, sounding nervous, the tour had been extended for at least a few more weeks, maybe more.

"It's all right," Melody had told him. And it was. She'd realized she needed time. Time to work things out for herself, to see who she might be when she wasn't worrying about anyone else's expectations—or rebelling against them.

Now, seeing Kincaid's confused glance at the dining table, she laughed. "I do have a dinner date, if that's what you're wondering. Hazel Cavendish said we should get together, so I invited her."

"Oh, good," he said, and she could tell he was relieved that he hadn't stumbled into a secret affair. "Give her our love. We should get together with her soon, ourselves." He stood. "Well, I won't keep you."

But when she walked him to the door, he hesitated, then said, "Melody, I'm not sure if this is the right thing to do. But when I went to Ryan's island, I found this." Reaching into his jeans pocket, he pulled out a neatly folded square of blue cloth. "I thought," he added as he handed it to her, "that you might like to have it."

Melody took it. Even before she unfolded the cloth, she knew what it was. She smoothed Ryan's blue bandanna with her fingers.

"Yes," she whispered. "I would. And thank you."

Kate Ling had done a wrong thing for a right reason, Gemma thought as she drove back through Kensington. Would she make peace with herself, eventually? Gemma wondered. She hoped so.

But thinking about Kate brought her no closer to knowing whether she, too, had done a wrong thing for a right reason.

MacKenzie Williams had rung her as she was leaving the hospital. MacKenzie had been devastated by the outcome of the investigation into Reagan Keating's death. She'd felt responsible for getting Gemma involved, and betrayed and disgusted by the fact that the woman she'd considered a friend could have done such a terrible thing. And, like Gemma, she was worried about Jess.

"Let me keep the kids tonight," MacKenzie offered. "To make up. You and Duncan go out somewhere nice. You need a break, just the two of you."

Gemma had to agree. She and Duncan had talked, but they'd either been interrupted by domestic crises, or were too exhausted to do more than brush the surface. She understood now why he'd kept things from her, understood why he'd turned to Doug and Melody for help rather than to her, but that understanding had not dissolved the barrier that had grown up between them. She could feel it, just like she could feel her resentment, a hard knot in her chest.

As she reached Notting Hill Gate, she glanced at the car clock. Toby's ballet class was finished and Duncan would have picked him up. The children would be home. There were chores to be done, and then the shopping. And the small matter of deciding what she would wear to dinner.

But there was something more important she had to do first.

Leaving the car in Powis Square, Gemma walked through the leafy front garden of the Tabernacle. It might have been last Saturday, with families eating and children playing, and what she would have sworn was the same dog tied to a table.

She went in the redbrick building, up the stairs and into the quiet of the upstairs landing. For a long moment, she stood outside the doors to the dance studio vestibule, not sure she could face disappointment. But having come this far, it would, she told herself, be silly to turn back. She pushed open the doors. The vestibule was empty, but the thump of the piano came from inside the studio. Through the glass panel in the studio door, she caught a glimpse of bodies moving to music. Children, the girls in leotards, the few boys in the familiar white T-shirts and black tights. It might have been Toby's class, fast-forwarded a few years. The dancers were taller, their bodies more developed, their movements precise and graceful.

And, there, in the center of the whirl of bodies, she saw him, his light brown hair flying out as he spun, his face joyously intent.

Quickly, she turned away before he could catch a glimpse of her.

But all the way down the stairs and out to the car, and for a long time afterwards, the image stayed imprinted in her memory.

Jess was going to be all right.

Gemma had chosen Carluccio's, the branch of the Italian café just off Kensington High Street. It was still warm enough to sit at one of the outside tables. "You could have picked something more posh," Kincaid had teased, but she said it was fancy enough for her, and she'd been wanting to come here when the weather turned fine.

They ate chicken liver pâté with red onion relish, then spinach ravioli, and sipped glasses of chilled prosecco. Kincaid sat back as the waiter cleared their plates, watching Gemma in the softening light. She wore a sundress in bright spring teals and corals, with a white cardigan thrown over her shoulders. The freckles from last weekend's sunshine were fading, and he missed them.

He'd missed her, too, more than he'd realized, but he didn't know how to tell her.

When the waiter returned for their dessert orders, he offered them a complimentary limoncello. Gemma gave a quick, emphatic shake of her head, and Kincaid ordered coffee for them both instead.

"Denis is home," he said, when they were stirring cream into their cups. "I talked to him this afternoon."

"We should take them something," Gemma said. "Maybe tomorrow, if he feels up to it."

"As long as it's *not bloody flowers*," Kincaid said, imitating Denis at his most irritable. "He said," he went on, carefully, "that dominoes would undoubtedly fall in the Met. That there would be a need, at the Yard, for good police officers."

Gemma looked at him across the table, her gaze unreadable. "He's offering you your job back?"

"Or a pick of jobs, I think." They were close enough that he could easily touch her hand where it rested on her cup, but he didn't.

"Will you take it?" she asked, but he still couldn't tell what she was thinking.

He looked away, trying to formulate what he felt. After a moment, he said, slowly, "No. I don't think so. I like where I am. I like the people I work with. Well, except for that ass Sweeney." Tom Faith had told them that Sweeney had come into his office with a memo while he'd been speaking to Denis on the phone from the hospital. DC Sweeney was now suspended from duty pending an investigation into his activities and connections. "But I always thought he was a rotten apple," he added, stirring his coffee again. "Anyway, the thing is, I don't want to be seen as having profited from the damage. And I've had enough of internal politics to last me a lifetime."

Gemma's smile, when it came, lit her eyes. "I'm glad. It would be going backwards, I think. But what about Doug? Will you leave him slaving away doing data entry at the Yard? He's too good a detective to waste."

Kincaid shrugged. "Maybe the brass's good feeling will extend to finding him a place at Holborn."

"Oh, dear. I can just see Doug butting heads with Jasmine Sidana." Gemma was laughing now, and he couldn't remember how long it had been since he'd heard her sound happy.

"I'm sorry," he said in a rush. "I'm sorry I kept secrets from you." This time, he reached across the table and rubbed his fingers across the tender flesh at the base of her thumb, then clasped her hand. When she didn't pull away, he said, "It won't happen again."

"Promise?" Looking up, she held his gaze.

"I promise. But there is one thing you should know." Feeling her tense, he squeezed her hand and grinned. "I had a good talk with my mum before I left Nantwich. She thinks we should consider buying the bookshop from them."

"What?" Gemma gaped at him. "No way. You're taking the piss."

"I'm not. Can you see us, living the quiet life in the country?"

"Get off," said Gemma, shaking her head, but she still didn't remove her hand from his. "Just don't tell Kit."

"Why not?"

Gemma picked up her spoon with her free hand and needlessly stirred her own coffee, now undoubtedly cold. "I've, um, sort of promised him we'd go for a holiday. When school is finished. He wants to see your mum and dad."

"Well, fine. We can do that. I'd like to see them, too. And I won't give Kit any ideas about staying." He slid his fingers to the inside of her wrist, where he could feel the beat of her pulse. "But in the meantime," he said, softly, "I think I'd like to go home."

AUTHOR'S NOTE

While all other characters in this novel are entirely the product of my imagination, Stephen Lawrence was very much a real person. The young black man was murdered in south London in a racially motivated attack while waiting for a bus on the evening of April 22, 1993. The case became one of the highest profile racial killings in UK history, its fallout including profound cultural changes to attitudes on racism and the police, to the law and police practice, and the partial revocation of English double jeopardy laws. Two of the perpetrators were convicted almost twenty years later in 2012, but as of this writing, the investigation into Lawrence's murder continues.

ABOUT THE AUTHOR

Deborah Crombie is a native Texan who has lived in both England and Scotland. She lives in McKinney, Texas, sharing an historic house with her husband, three cats, and two very demanding German shepherd dogs.